THE HARBINGER

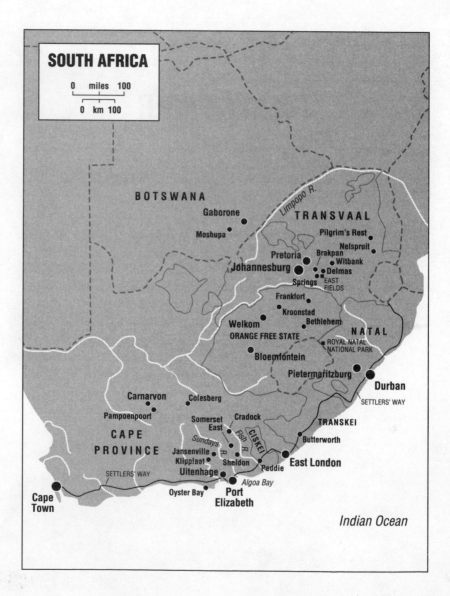

SOUTH AFRICA

0   miles   100

0   km   100

BOTSWANA

Gaborone

Moshupa

TRANSVAAL

Limpopo R.

Pilgrim's Rest

Nelspruit

Pretoria   Brakpan

Johannesburg   Witbank

Delmas

Springs   EAST
FIELDS

Frankfort

Kroonstad

Welkom   Bethlehem

ORANGE FREE STATE

NATAL

ROYAL NATAL
NATIONAL PARK

Bloemfontein

Pietermaritzburg

Durban

SETTLERS' WAY

Carnarvon   Colesberg

Pampoenpoort

Cradock

TRANSKEI

Somerset
East   CISKEI

Butterworth

CAPE   Sundays   FISH R.

PROVINCE   Jansenville

Klipplaat   Sheldon   East London

SETTLERS' WAY   Uitenhage   Peddie

Oyster Bay   Algoa Bay

Cape   Port
Town   Elizabeth

Indian Ocean

THE
HARBINGER

Mark Graham

A Donald Hutter Book

Henry Holt and Company
New York

Copyright © 1988 by Mark Graham
All rights reserved, including the right to reproduce this
book or portions thereof in any form.
Published by Henry Holt and Company, Inc.,
115 West 18th Street, New York, New York 10011.
Published in Canada by Fitzhenry & Whiteside Limited,
195 Allstate Parkway, Markham, Ontario L3R 4T8.
Library of Congress Cataloging in Publication Data
Graham, Mark, 1950–
The harbinger.
"A Donald Hutter book."
I. Title.
PS3557.R2158H37   1988   813'.54   87-32304
ISBN 0-8050-0725-3

First Edition

Designed by Susan Hood
Printed in the United States of America
10 9 8 7 6 5 4 3 2 1

ISBN 0-8050-0725-3

For Brooke,
family, and friends

My thanks to Susan Manchester for help generously given, to Arnold Goodman for setting me on the right track, and to Judith Shafran, whose editorial advice and good humor have proved invaluable.

THE HARBINGER

PROLOGUE

THE EXILED BLACK MAN STOOD, ERECT and somber, at the river's edge and stared back at his homeland to the south. Luminescent black water snaked beneath the ancient pier, lapped and curled at the feet of rotting timbers. Here, the Limpopo River cut a ragged border between South Africa and its northern neighbor, the landlocked Botswana.

For three years he had prepared for this night. There, to the south, beyond the solitary acacia of the bushland, caught in the shroud of this moonless night, lay his redemption: the richest gold fields in the world, the Achilles' heel of his accusers.

On the far shore, the South African border patrol watched the man's every move through high-powered binoculars. Christopher Zuma was an unimposing sight in his ill-fitting, tattered suit, but the choice of clothes, he realized, served both purpose and memory; he had worn the same suit on the day of his expatriation. But it was a memory, Zuma told himself, too strong for this occasion, and the good fortune of rain broke through the reverie.

He turned his attention instead to the woman at his side, his steady companion on these "visits" to Gaborone. Nonchalant and sultry beneath their umbrella, she laid her head upon his shoulder. It was a calculated scene played many times over for the benefit of their audiences on both sides of the river. They were silent now. There were no more words to be spoken.

A small dory drew up to the pier. The oarsman arose, and a steady hand escorted the couple on board. A canopy had been erected at the rear of the craft, protection, ostensibly, against the intensifying storm. The couple was not to be deterred; the rain was their ally tonight.

Together they settled back beneath the canopy's flimsy walls. The oarsman launched the craft into the middle of the river's lazy current. In his excitement, he felt the wasted energy of adrenaline, and knowing better, calmed himself in the melody of the rain.

The border patrol on the distant shore was accompanied this night by a member of South Africa's National Intelligence Service, the

1

NIS; Christopher Zuma was their special charge. The officer followed the course of the dory with stark blue eyes and a condescending grin. Zuma's predictable behavior left him amused, disappointed. For two years, the black leader had been elusive, active, a challenge to his keepers. But since then, they'd watched the steady erosion of his involvement. He was left with this, his romps in Gaborone. They joked about his woman. Always the same. Painted, overdressed, cheap.

Thunder cracked, rumbled like wild horses stampeding from the east. Shafts of lightning ripped away at the delicate skin of the horizon, illuminating ebony thunderheads. The river swelled beneath the onslaught of their harvest.

The riverboat was unnecessary tonight, the NIS officer told the border guards. There would be no romance on the Limpopo in this weather. The guards found amusement in this proclamation, and a gust of wind drove them, laughing, back to the shelter of their guardhouse.

On the water, the oarsman fought the wind and the current with powerful, exhausting strokes. He surveyed banks both north and south, and when the river narrowed, he broke away from the main channel.

The dory swept around a wooded bend. The dim lights of Gaborone were consumed by heavy branches. Here the river took them momentarily from the preying eyes of the South Africans, now a half kilometer downriver. This was the moment.

On the north shore, soldiers laden with automatic weapons and binoculars moved deliberately from the protection of their own guardhouse. Swearing and grumbling, they trudged the length of a narrow jetty to the river.

Thirty seconds later, they caught sight of the boat, a vacillating intrusion on the Limpopo's impervious concourse. The canopy flapped violently in the breeze as the oarsman allowed the dory to drift toward the bank. The expression on his female passenger's face sent waves of remorse through his tired limbs; what she faced once they reached shore, he would not wish on anyone.

The senior officer, a sergeant in rank, half drunk on sweet-potato rum, raised his binoculars. Lightning flashed, closer now. The river fluoresced, rising and falling in the blinding glare. He pressed forward suddenly, cleared his eyes of rain, and focused again. It couldn't be, he thought, frantic at what he knew to be impossible. Zuma. He was gone. The binoculars dropped to his side. He gripped his rifle.

The oarsman steered the dory into the shallows along the jetty. He tied his boat off. Then, silently, he took the woman's hand and she stepped, very much alone, ashore.

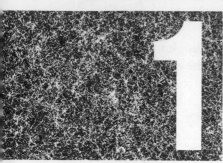

IAN ELGIN TREADED THROUGH FOG TO-
ward the brooding arches of Port Elizabeth's
King George train station.

At this late hour, the archaic building was
bathed in a sullen glow, oozing melancholy
and loneliness. Elgin hunched his shoulders and buried his hands
into the deep pockets of his silk suit; the last thing he wanted to do
now was draw attention to himself.

Behind him, he heard the car door slam, the kind of resentful
explosion that says far more than angry words ever can. But he
didn't look back. Delaney would still be watching, and it was best,
he told himself, to ignore her when she was in this state. So maybe
it was his own fault, but admitting it wouldn't change a thing.

Off to his left, the clash of steel wheels resounded from the train
yard. A foghorn split the night, a rush of sound so stark and full it
sent a chill down Elgin's spine. With an effort, he picked up his
pace—sluggish steps that belied his anticipation of the rendezvous
which lay ahead.

The meeting with Delaney hadn't gone well. The restaurant and
the wine had only provided a public forum for arguing. Delaney
knew something was wrong, but even drunk he couldn't bring himself
to tell her. Who would believe it?

Darkness opened a gateway to the past, and Elgin realized he
could hardly recall the beginning himself anymore. . . .

It was seven years now since he had gotten himself into this goddamn mess with Cecil Leistner, the minister of justice, and those
bloody gold mines. Seven years that had passed in a flurry of illegal
arms shipments and surreptitious labor deals. Seven years. Elgin
shook his head as if the passing of those years was more fantasy
than fact.

He couldn't help but wonder how the whole thing had gotten
this far. It had seemed incredible at the time, still did, but not
impossible, not the way the third member of their triad, Jan Koster,
had explained it.

Even now, Elgin wasn't certain whether to call Koster a bloody
genius or a raving lunatic. The Deputy Minister of Mineral Resources

4

and Energy Affairs; it was an absurd title. Yet, between the three of them, they were on the verge of sending the country into a tail-spin. . . .

Purposely, Elgin trudged past the concourse that led to the main terminal. A sudden gust swept fallen leaves across the pavement. He glanced over his shoulder. Delaney's car was still in the lot, but swirls of fog blocked his view of her. *No, lady, I'm not that smashed.* He never used the main entrance. Instead, he turned south on a narrow walk that fronted the depot. At the side entrance, he paused, found himself hesitating.

An image assaulted him, the object of this late-night tryst, and it left him weak and excited. He could imagine the sight of her, the fragrance and the taste, hear her cries. It was all so foreign to the lovemaking he and his wife shared, or had shared way back when, that he found himself craving it like an addict craves his next fix.

Moreover, he was honest enough to admit that the shoddiness of the station itself and the vulgarity of its transients lent an earthy element to their rendezvous, an element that was now essential for him. It's this thing with the mines, he told himself. As the day drew nearer, their escapades grew more lurid. The motel room in Summerstrand had given way to the restricted beaches up north. Then it was the balcony overlooking the speakeasy and its drunken crowd. And for the past three months now, here at the station. . . .

The sound of approaching footsteps, growing louder in the fog and closing in on him, pushed Elgin inside.

The shoeshine stand outside the Men's Club was deserted, and he was grateful. He heard laughter coming from the information booth along the west wall. As usual, the creep from the ticket counter watched his every move.

Hesitation surrendered fully now to the burden of discretion, and he moved on. The lady at the newsstand smiled hopefully, but he would forgo the paper this time. He had cigars enough, and idle chitchat did not appeal to him tonight.

At last, the one-dimensional cutout of a black female stared down at him from above the lounge door. NET SWARTES. BLACKS ONLY. He paused at the water fountain, buying time and watching for the perfect moment. This was always the hardest part, the most uncomfortable part. But it was always the picture of her legs spread wide across the mattress that spurred him past this temporal barrier, and tonight the image was especially vivid. He pushed aside the curtain.

The sitting room beyond was dim and deserted, and he pressed against the wall like a common criminal catching his breath. He saw the chiffon scarf hanging on the coatrack, limp and forlorn, and a surge of unexpected wrath swept over him. She'd left it. How could she leave it in this place, for God's sake? Here, among the riffraff and rabble. Why it hadn't been stolen was beyond him.

Then he glanced at his watch and found to his dismay that he was late. Damn late. Had she come and gone already? That would explain the scarf.

He hurried past the door into the locker room.

"Sylvia." There was no answer. He felt a draft, chilly and damp, and noticed the broken window above the last bank of lockers. He paused, conscious of the tapping of his own heart and the warning shout of the foghorn as it rode the wind into the corners of the room and deeper yet into the recesses of his own brain. "Sylvia?"

Why was he sweating? He struggled out of his suit coat and walked unsteadily into the sleep room behind the last lockers. He didn't bother with the light; he knew the room now like his own bedroom. Perfume hung in the air, a thin veil that caused him to inhale greedily. It wasn't her perfume, but the stirring he felt didn't bother with distinction.

Suddenly, he paused again, alert to a sound that he couldn't identify. The muffled *clang* of a locker closing? Or the muted *screak* of a shower-stall door? He wasn't certain, wasn't certain his dulled faculties weren't playing tricks on him. Slowly, as a hunter might stalk a buck at the edge of a clearing, he hung his coat across a chair and crept back to the doorway.

"Sylvia?" He nudged into the faint light, wiping a bead of moisture from his forehead. "Hey, lady, quit screwing around, will you?"

He heard the rustle of the wind outside, a branch slapping at a wall nearby. But there was another sound, one closer, and he peered through the gloom toward the showers. He stepped back out of the light, straining to hear. Then the water pipes overhead rumbled, and air filled his lungs with relief.

He hastened back into the sitting room.

There he bought a can of pop from the Coke machine and absently flipped through the pages of a yellowing magazine. Finally, he returned, almost unwilling, to the lockers. Then, pacing, drinking in the air, and sipping the pop, Elgin started to best the effects of alcohol. With near sobriety came a distorted renewal of confidence. Laughter. She'd never leave, he told himself. She would wait all damn night if she had to. He was her ticket out of the shantytown jungle that waited, like a bad dream, outside these dingy walls. No, something must have delayed her. There could be no other explanation.

Meandering led to the washbasins and showers adjacent to the lockers. Elgin flipped the light switch. Fluorescent tubes sputtered and buzzed. And then he heard it again, the same tinny noise as before. He stared down the long line of shower stalls. Opaque glass doors hid all but one stall.

"Is that you, kiddo?"

The pop can collapsed in Elgin's clammy grip.

He forced himself to move; halting steps led him reluctantly toward the showers. With quick stabs, he opened each door one at a time. Each stall was empty. Relieved, he moved quickly back to the washbasins. He splashed cold water on his face, ran his fingers roughly through his hair. Discarding the pop can, he returned to the main room and checked his watch again.

His nerve ends tingled. He swiped aggressively at an opened locker door.

Pacing, he crossed behind the second bank of lockers. And there, in the grimy reflection of a broken mirror, he saw the man, a stocking cap covering his head and tan gloves hiding his hands, standing less than a meter behind him.

The first blow caught Elgin just below the neck, a fierce strike that spun him around in a daze. In that moment, a singular thought flashed through his mind. *The letter. I should never have sent that bloody letter.*

The second blow sent Elgin sprawling across the floor. Stunned, he watched helplessly as his attacker lunged toward him, curious that the man now held an umbrella in his hands, like a sword.

There was an instant of pain, and the last thing Ian Elgin heard was the bellow of the foghorn, a faint cry in the distance.

At the intersection of Castle Hill and Main, Chief Homicide Inspector Nigel Mansell brought his unmarked GM sedan to a halt. Along the eastern horizon, a translucent wedge of light crept between the shoulders of low-lying hills. The fog was lifting now, though its dissipating veil still clung to the roofs of the sleeping city.

Before Mansell, a fleet of minibuses rumbled down the deserted thoroughfare on their way to outlying black townships. There, he knew, the city's proletarian work force would be awaiting their arrival; like the ball of fire inching its way into the sky, another certainty of dawn.

The light changed. The convoy, along with its indictment, disappeared in a wake of dust and dried leaves, and Mansell returned his attention to the road. He eased the car beneath a six-lane overpass known, anachronistically, as Settler's Way—a tribute to the ambitious English immigrants who first landed on the shores of Algoa Bay a century and a half ago.

An access road led past the towering, red brick Campanile, a town crier of sorts, and the clock below the belfry read 5:17. Mansell filled his lungs with the smoke of his second cigarette.

The waterfront lay before him now. The railroad station stretched out along the face of the bay to his left, and kilometer after kilometer of steel rail traversed the shore here. Mansell circled the depot to the terminal parking lot. He found an empty space up front labeled FOR WHITES ONLY, and the telling assemblage of police vans and patrol cars stirred the reluctant well of nervous energy.

Mansell unfolded from the front seat, a tall, lean figure, whose thirty-seven years he was certain could be counted in full this morning. Long fingers pushed lank golden hair off his forehead. He faced the ocean for a moment. Pale eyes focused on a lone sailboat. He massaged the outcropping of a day-old beard. The bay sparkled in the dawn, turquoise swells and purple caps.

Normally an instantaneous elixir, the sea itself seemed to share his dilatory mood.

The telephone on Mansell's nightstand had rung at 4:58. The body of a white male, presumed dead, had been discovered at the train station jammed inside a locker in the ladies' lounge. The Blacks Only ladies' lounge. The dispatcher had, Mansell remembered, emphasized the difference in pigmentation with a certain vigor, but there was something else. Something in his voice. The tone or perhaps the visual image portrayed by the tone. Mansell wasn't certain, but it, whatever it was, had left him with a sense of urgency. And yet he had delayed, actually debated over which tie to wear. And then procrastinated over whether to shave or not. It was only a matter of seconds, this he knew, but it was enough nonetheless. *Dread* was not the right word, he told himself that, and yet . . .

Another cigarette materialized in ritualistic preparation.

Long strides carried him toward the terminal entrance. The main building was four stories of granite, marble, and wood, flanked to the north by 150 meters of warehousing and backed by loading platforms and storage sheds. Overlooking the arched entryway was a circular marble-faced clock. Embossed lettering above the face read "King George Station—1905."

Barricades and solemn-faced policemen formed a cordon across revolving doors, and Mansell was met inside by Detective Joshua Brungle. It never failed, Mansell thought, hopeless in his attempt to suppress a grin. Joshua's suit was, as always, immaculately pressed. His tanned face was shaved and alert, and waves of curly black hair somehow managed to appear both styled and windblown at the same time.

Mansell took him by the arm as they entered the terminal. He said, "Do you think, Detective Brungle, it would be possible for you to look a little less presentable at this hour of the morning?"

Joshua glanced at Mansell's unshaven face. "And come to work looking like you? Do me a favor."

Mansell tipped his head forward just slightly. "On the theory that the youthful upstart is doing whatever it takes to impress his aging mentor, I'll let the matter lie."

"Aging mentor?" Joshua remarked. "An inspiring lesson in diplomacy. Thank you."

"All in the line of duty." Mansell produced a leather-bound note pad from his sports jacket. Business supplanted jocularity. He asked, "So how does it stand?"

"The call was taken by a night patrol at four forty-two. Our victim is a male Caucasian, discovered, curiously, in the ladies' bathroom. That much you know. But get this. The body was found by a railroad employee, right? A male railroad employee."

The inferences, Mansell realized, were blatantly obvious; the maggots from Security Branch would have a field day. But the unease he had felt before returned now with renewed vigor, and he knew there was no way he could explain this to Joshua.

"Identification?"

Joshua shook his head. "The victim's face is turned inside the locker. Messy."

The passenger terminal resembled a cavernous pavilion, a single hall that opened onto an atrium with a vaulted ceiling of glass and timber. Mansell gazed upward at four brass-and-glass chandeliers that hung in a cluster from huge beams.

"The Transport people won't like it much, Joshua, but we'll have to reroute all incoming trains, until noon at least. Outbounds, the same treatment."

"We dragged the stationmaster out of a toasty bed, speaking of diplomacy, and as you can imagine, he's elated at the prospect. Our main concern for the moment is a Blue Train from Cape Town due in at five twenty-five."

Mansell nodded and then turned his attention to the rows of head-high wooden pew benches that dominated the main floor of the terminal. Three families huddled around a sunken bar in the White Race Group Only section, and a handful of college students watched the proceedings with growing interest. The businessmen seemed a molded lot: matching fedoras, opened newspapers, and a wonderful aloofness that Mansell found improbable but amusing.

Further on, a broken candy machine stood vigil over migrant laborers as they slept head-to-toe on the same benches. A colorfully robed mother fed her baby on an exposed breast, while her oldest ran from aisle to aisle and her husband snored.

The smell of cheese sandwiches grilling caught Mansell's attention, and he saw smoke rising from behind the counter of the soda fountain. As they passed the doorway to a restaurant called The Depot, he heard two waitresses complaining about the bloody barricades and the goddamn cops and "isn't it amazing how they think they own the whole blessed world and . . ."

Directly ahead, wooden barricades and rope formed a half circle across the face of the south terminal wall. At the hub of the circle stood the entrance to the ladies' lounge, and like a magnet, it reached out to Mansell.

The black detective who stepped forward to meet the chief inspector was built like a misplaced athlete. A trimmed beard lent a note of distinction to Merriman Gosani's persona, but the effect was at once victimized by a rumpled, knee-length trench coat. He removed a toothpick from the side of his mouth and said, "I've talked to the stationmaster. He'll reroute passenger traffic to the Summerstrand station. They'll use shuttles for the passengers, and something equally as exciting for the luggage."

"And the five twenty-five Blue Train?"

"Same scenario." Merry used his toothpick to gesture toward a glass-enclosed office on the west wall. "I've set up shop in the station-master's office. We've got the guy who made the initial find there. A baggage worker named Anthony Mabasu."

"All right. Merry, you'll handle the center, then." Mansell set his shoulders and peered intently in Joshua's direction. "Joshua, I think Mr. Mabasu deserves your personal attention first thing."

At last, the chief inspector broke the plane between the barricades and the lounge. Steenkamp, the team pathologist of sour demeanor and superior skills, his *in situ* photographer and sketch artist, Anna Goodell, and Chas du Toits, the chief of forensic science, observed the signal, and together they stepped past the floral curtain that stood watch over the entrance. Beyond was the sitting room.

The floor was cheap linoleum with a worn footpath leading inside. The walls were a crusty tan, water-stained from exposed overhead pipes. Head-high windows, painted shut, looked out to the south.

Cracked vinyl chairs, red with chrome arms, lined one wall. There was a pop machine, a broken candy dispenser, full ashtrays, and an empty magazine rack. A single chiffon neck scarf, expensive, and very out of place, Mansell thought, hung from a wooden coatrack.

They skirted the beaten path, past a solemn policeman, through a hinged door into the locker room. The scent was more disinfectant than death, but Mansell could feel its presence.

The locker room was even drabber, if that was possible, than its antecedent. Cracked and flaking paint was pee-colored at the edges. Rust-colored tile lay unevenly on the floor. Fluorescent bulbs emitted an annoying buzz and stained the olive green lockers with the dull patina of neglected bronze. The third bank stood flush against the back wall, and latched windows ran the length of the room above it. Mansell was drawn immediately to the shattered glass in the middle window.

Steenkamp followed the chief inspector's feline gait to this third row. A dozen locker doors stood ajar, but a shoulder and arm protruded from one near the center of the bank. Mansell sucked air into his lungs.

The body had been jammed sideways into the locker, the face peering across the inside shoulder hiding unsuccessfully from death. A ligature of nylon rope was tied fast about the neck. The rope extended to a coat hook inside the locker, thereby holding the body upright. Two of the victim's fingers were still caught between the cord and his neck. Swelling about the neck was a ghastly black and blue. Blood, now brown as it dried, had smeared along the inside of the locker and on the door.

Steenkamp stepped forward gingerly. At the foot of the locker lay three coins, and these he straddled. "He's definitely dead," he muttered after a time. "Body's still warm. Rigor hasn't set in yet. Perhaps two to four hours."

"All right, then," said Mansell, glimpsing on the faces of his confederates the inertia that death inevitably brings to the living. "Let's get some photos first. Anna, start here with this room. Follow up with a baseline sketch. Do the same in the sitting room."

The echo of footsteps interrupted them. An abrasive voice clashed unharmoniously as the staccato claps grew in volume. Mansell wheeled around. Wolffe, he thought coldly.

"So what have we today?" A thundering voice exuded an air of bravado and spurious good humor.

Two men appeared in the aisle. The first, a squat, bloated man stuffed like a sausage into the gray-blue uniform of the Security Branch, was, indeed, Major Hymie Wolffe. Good humor took its true place when he saw the inspector. "Mansell!"

The chief inspector tipped his head. "This must be your lucky day, Wolffe."

Security Branch was the appointed handler of all matters, subtle and high-minded, concerning the "Security of the Republic." There was no love lost between Security's "elite" circle, as Wolffe fancied it, and Mansell's lowly Criminal Investigation Branch, the CIB.

"Luck, Inspector, has not one thing to do with it." Wolffe removed his gloves, sniffing the air. He stepped over the wooden bench that faced the locker. A blue-and-white rag, once surely recognizable as a bandana, lay on the floor a meter from the victim. Stubby fingers swept it up. Rheumy eyes pondered it without effect, and he held it to his nose. Then, as if shaken from a brief slumber, Wolffe peered at the locker. "And who is our victim today?"

He reached for the locker, but Mansell brushed the hand aside. "Identity," he said, "hasn't been determined yet, Major. Shall we do it according to the law this time? Just for fun?"

Major Wolffe glared at Mansell through thick wire-rimmed glasses.

"My law," he hissed, and with a quickness belied by his bulk, plunged both hands into the locker. He grasped the victim's head and brutally twisted it about. The face was caked with blood and losing color rapidly. Still, recognition was instantaneous.

Steenkamp paled. "Superb police work, Major. And a fair catch at that. The thorn in Pretoria's side."

"Elgin!" exclaimed Wolffe. "God almighty. Ian Elgin."

"Yes, a curious ossuary for the vice-chairman of our fair nation's most notorious mining union, wouldn't you say?" Steenkamp's sardonic wit lay in wait for moments such as these, and he added, "Ah, but that hardly does the man justice. Doesn't he also own some oblique title with the dockers, and the stevedores, and all those other hardworking chaps at the harbor, as well? But then dead is dead, isn't it, Major?"

Mansell was still grappling with the foreboding he'd felt before, though now at least, he told himself, there was some substance to its being. Substance, however, did not wash away the feeling, and he saw that Wolffe, too, could not keep his eyes off the distorted, pain-struck face. Mansell had to rid himself of Wolffe's presence somehow, and he decided to use the death mask to this end.

"This looks like something right up your alley, Major," he said. He glanced over his shoulder at Wolffe's companion, a slight man with a manicured moustache and the insignia of a lieutenant. "Maybe we should leave it with you and your investigative wizards, then."

This seemed to shake the major from his momentary lapse. He struggled into his gloves and dabbed beads of sweat from his upper lip. "Very amusing, Inspector. But you will continue with your investigation. As will Security. Lieutenant Rhoodie here will handle liaison between our investigations, and he will have free reign to observe your actions and to carry out his own tasks without interference from you. Do I make myself clear?"

The slightest hint of a smile touched Mansell's lips, and he stepped forward. He extended an arm around Wolffe's shoulder. As they approached Lieutenant Rhoodie, he removed the bandana from the major's grasp. "We wouldn't have it any other way, Major."

"As I said."

The words fell on deaf ears; the chief inspector had already returned his attention to the body. Wolffe departed less the ceremony of his arrival. Chas du Toits held out a white paper bag, and Mansell set the bandana inside. Anna Goodell proceeded with her rendering of the scene.

"As if the major had never been here, Anna," said Mansell.

A forensic team entered the room carrying trays of black and silver fingerprint powders, camel-hair and fiberglass brushes, and spray atomizers for silver nitrate and ninhydrin solutions. Carefully, they set up floodlights and lampstands with ultraviolet and infrared lights. Last came an array of photographic equipment. Mansell, in his early years, had loved the process: dust, spray, photograph, lift, and photograph again. Methodical, graceful, precise.

Forensic set to work in the immediate area of the body the moment the sketch artist finished.

Mansell pushed a wooden bench over in front of the third bank of lockers. He stepped lightly up. Cool sea air rushed in through the broken window. "Chas," he said, calling out to the forensic chief. "Have a look at this, will you?"

Chas du Toits lumbered up next to the inspector. The top of the lockers reeked of neglect. Shards of broken glass lay over a thick layer of dust, telltale signs of damage recently done, but the window latch was still in its locked position.

Mansell gestured to an oval impression at the edge of the locker. "By chance?"

"If you're suggesting a footprint, I would say yes," du Toits replied, his eyebrows raised in delight. A kid in a technological play-house was Chas du Toits—gas chromatography, photomicrography, neutron-activation sampling. "I'll send one of my chaps round back for a look-see. This becomes interesting at last, Inspector."

Pathologist Steenkamp returned to the body after forensic had made its mark, and Mansell pointed a finger at SB Lieutenant Rhoodie. He motioned toward a closed door at the rear of the room. A Do Not Disturb sign hung from the doorknob.

"Make yourself useful, Lieutenant. Check out that back room over there. Carefully."

"Yes, sir," answered Rhoodie. He used a handkerchief on the doorknob and the tip of a nail file to flip the light switch.

Mansell watched him. So be it, he thought. A murdered union official bounced between departments like a Ping-Pong ball. Fuck it. Security would soon take over the whole affair anyway.

Methodically, Mansell toured the attached washroom area. Toilets, shower stalls, basins, trash cans. He emerged carrying an empty Sprite can, a used toothbrush, a box of disposable douche, and three magazines. The pathologist called him over.

"The victim was almost certainly dead before he was hung in this locker, but other than that, there's no sign that he's been moved," Steenkamp said. "I do so love a tidy killer."

"The confrontation occurred here then, in this room?"

"More than likely, on this very spot." The pathologist used his little finger in describing the damage to Ian Elgin's face. "Lividity of the mucous membranes, quite obvious. Petechial hemorrhages of the conjunctival sacs, here and here. Contusions and abrasions around the neck and jaw. Note the discoloration of the lips, the frothing about the mouth, and the groove in the neck, a lovely thing which runs beneath the larynx in front to this point just below the base of the occipital—"

"Asphyxia from strangulation," said Mansell.

"For a preliminary, yes. By the way, there's some discoloration at the wrist and on the ring finger, you might note."

"His watch and wedding band. Both gone." Mansell felt gently about the victim's shirt and pants pockets. "Empty."

Lieutenant Rhoodie had returned with similar findings, adding, "And there's a sports jacket draped over the back of a chair in the other room. No wallet. No papers. It's a sleep room. Two mattresses. One's been slept in."

"Chas."

"I heard, I heard," du Toits replied, rubbing his hands together as his team carefully packaged laboratory samples.

A uniformed policeman appeared at the locker entryway. "Excuse me, Inspector. The district prosecutor is here, sir. And Detective Gosani says he'd like you to have a look outside that broken window."

Mansell nodded, an absent gesture accented by fixed eyes and the remoteness of deep thought. How does a man like Ian Elgin, he asked himself, end up in a place like this? He set a hand on Steenkamp's shoulder and stared at the rope slicing into the victim's neck. He said, "Let's get this body out of here as soon as you're ready, Joe. I'd like the autopsy done today."

The union headquarters of the United Dock Workers was located a stone's throw from the King George terminal on Charl Malan Quay. Plagued by the prospect of her own empty house, Delaney Blackford had come straight here following her confrontation with Ian Elgin the night before.

The lingering effects of that confrontation had made work impossible. Sirens at dawn had driven her from the restlessness of her office cot.

At 8:05, the telephone rang. It was the union's general secretary. His call informed her that Ian's body had been discovered at the station, a victim of foul play. Details were sketchy, he said, and . . . Delaney replaced the receiver without a word. She blamed this shortfall in etiquette on fatigue, and brewed tea on the office hot plate.

Then she took her cup and a day-old pastry to the tiny porch out front. But she wasn't surprised when the tea tasted bitter, less so that she had no appetite. Her ankle throbbed, and she leaned heavily on her walking stick, her constant companion. "A memorial," as she called it in those frequent bouts with cynicism, "to the black holes in an otherwise lukewarm past."

Delaney set the cup down, discarded the pastry. Blooming in planter boxes along the porch railing were Hilton daisies, and her hand idly sought out their fragile petals. A protea, uncanny in its resemblance to a pincushion, took her eye momentarily. On most occasions, the flowers were a priceless source of escape; this morning they were of no interest.

Three hundred meters away, beyond the laden cars of a slow-moving freight train, police vehicles and uniformed officers swarmed over the same parking lot on which she had stood hours before. She watched an ambulance plunging down Military Avenue, lights ablaze. It swept past the barricades and the policemen and came to an abrupt halt at the station's main entrance. When the wail of its siren had spent its last breath, Delaney set out across the quay without knowing exactly why. This morning, Ian Elgin was a victim of foul play. Last night, he had talked like a man struggling to keep his head above water. . . .

"Pretoria has taken it upon itself to see to it that the unions toe the line." At twelve o'clock at night, the restaurant was dimly lit and nearly deserted, and Elgin's voice reflected his somber mood. "They know damn well I can't be thinking of toeing any bloody line. The unions wouldn't stand for it. They've had their taste of power. They've had their taste of the penthouse and the champagne cocktails and the expensive cigars." Elgin gazed forlornly across the table in search of sympathy, a gift he himself never bothered to offer. "Pretoria doesn't like sharing the penthouse with anyone, Delaney."

"This is news?" Delaney made no attempt at concealing her sarcasm.

"And Jo'burg's nearly as bad. I swear I can't make a move without some asinine gold-mining official complaining about the price of their precious metal. The masters of gold. To be sure. It's their last and greatest illusion. If they only knew the truth. . . ." Elgin consumed his wine with a vengeance, avoiding her gaze. "But it's not just that. It's the foul weather, the ill-tempers, the . . . blank stares."

16

"Meaning things are lousy at home, as usual." But Delaney could see that it was more than just politics, and business, and an empty family life.

"There's something about Port Elizabeth, though, kiddo. It's like a cocoon. They can't get to me here. They can't." Delaney searched his words and found an almost indistinguishable thread of panic.

Over coffee, which Elgin refused, Delaney brought up the matter of the additional responsibilities she had been seeking with the Affiliated Union.

"The recommendation has been with your board for over a month now. Is there a problem?" Her rising voice caught the attention of their waitress, but Delaney pressed on. "It's in your hands. A simple 'yes' is all it will take. I've earned it."

"Things are working well just the way they are, Delaney. Opening up another vice-presidency? I don't know if it's warranted at the moment, kiddo."

"Let's be candid, Ian. You see me emerging as a threat to your position and you don't like it."

He concealed the truth with a display of anger. "I'm the only one who makes threats where the Affiliated Union is concerned, Mrs. Blackford, and don't you forget it. . . ."

The ripples of a coal train's shrill whistle rode a brisk wind up the coast and chased this last thought from Delaney's head. She crossed the tracks to the station.

Front and center, it was a production, she admitted, worthy of the South African police. Barricades the length of the terminal sealed the premises from defacing intruders. Police lamps revolved over empty patrol cars, red on blue raking the scene with the ominous regularity of prison spotlights. Policemen paced. Their raptorial gazes studied each onlooker with individualized suspicion, generally by race. Ignoring this was easy, Delaney realized, disregarding it was not.

Last night, the fog had obscured the station's hulking mass, shrouding it in mystery. The coming of day transformed it again into a grounded beast void of secrets. The rear doors to the ambulance swung open in tandem with those at the station entrance. A gurney emerged, propelled by beefy attendants and escorted by a graying physician. Taut sheets rendered a protuberant corpse a prisoner without escape. The crowd stirred. Craning necks vied for a better view.

Delaney pressed between bodies to the guardrail. She was awe-struck. Though not, she realized, by this ghoulish display of death on wheels, but rather by the sterility of the doctor, the brutal formality of the attendants, the craving and boredom of insensitive spectators. But then, Ian was dead. What did he care?

She tried to picture his face. She glanced at the stretcher again as it was hoisted into the ambulance. Ian had indeed, she thought, found his cocoon in Port Elizabeth, after all. She searched herself for evidence of remorse. The discovery eluded her. Emotion, she told herself, would emerge in time.

Delaney followed the course of the departing ambulance until it was out of sight. Her footsteps took her to the side entrance that had provided Ian Elgin access to his fateful climax.

In the alleyway beyond the door, policemen and technicians were gathered in a surrealistic diorama beneath a broken window, the opaque glass of a rest room. One man commanded the attention of the others. He stood tall and erect, his head tipped forward slightly. In his hand, he cradled a cigarette. Smoke spiraled above his head. When he moved, his gestures were liquid, choreographed with intent. Delaney tried imagining the sound of his voice; their meeting, she knew, was a foregone conclusion. Then, the blue and gray of Security Branch muscled its way into the picture, and she turned away.

Pacing in the sand along Algoa Bay's golden shore, Delaney realized there was nothing she could do about Security's inevitable inquiries. But to their poisonous questions, the answers, she told herself, would be of her own choosing.

Along the south side of the terminal, rectangular plots of turned soil lay beneath each window group. The tread impression of a single car tire cut through the plot directly below the broken window in the ladies' lounge. The matter of smoking was Mansell's way of getting his bearings and harnessing snap judgments. Then he bent down. The semicircular impression was nearly unbroken. Pieces of cloudy glass were scattered among the dirt. Mansell discovered evidence of torn masking tape nearer the wall. Using steel tweezers, a forensic specialist placed the tape in druggist's paper and samples of the glass between layers of cotton.

A scattering of shoe prints was less distinguished. The soles were distorted, as if made by worn tennis shoes or desert boots. One set faced the wall. The wearer, it appeared, had been standing on the balls of his feet, testing the limits of his reach. The height of the window above ground level, a good two meters, and the positioning of the car, Mansell determined, gave credence to the theory that the would-be intruder had used the hood of the vehicle as a boost.

It was this image that Mansell carried with him as he drove the two blocks back from the waterfront to the three-story brick edifice on Military Avenue and Main Street that served as the Port Elizabeth Police Station.

He parked in a tow-away zone out front. Overhead, a stark yellow sun shone among estranged feather clouds, and Mansell dismissed any romantic notions of rain.

He mounted the stairs to the main floor, a distortion in terms more appropriately dubbed "The Pit." As he wove his way among the standard-bearers of this overcrowded arena, the duty officer caught him by the shoulder.

"Terreblanche's got a burr up his ass," he said. "Very testy. Up on three. Joshua and Merry are on their way."

Mansell took the stairs to the third-floor communications center. Air-conditioning sent chills down his spine. Egg-white computers lined three walls. The fourth wall was an enormous map of the district: west to Oyster Bay, north to Somerset-East, and east to Alexandria. Green lights denoted nine other stations within the district. Blue lights denoted misdemeanor infractions committed within the last seventy-two-hour period; red lights denoted felonies. And like a festive occasion, Mansell thought, glancing at the wall, the Port Elizabeth map was always forthright in its display of color.

Noting the arrival of his chief inspector, Captain Oliver Terreblanche, a bearish man with thinning silver hair, reduced the length of his pacing by half but did not look up.

"This is just lovely, Inspector." Terreblanche punched a meaty paw at a copy of the Elgin preliminary report. "It's not enough that we have a township ready to go up in flames, now some lunatic decides to squash the vice-chairman of the country's largest union inside a clothes locker."

"Yes, most inconsiderate," Mansell replied ripely. He nodded as detectives Joshua Brungle and Merriman Gosani came through the door. "When we find the guy, I'll have a talk with him about his timing."

"I don't like it, Inspector. We've got a mining union facing contract negotiations, and the dockers wrapped up in arbitration. Some people might call it a coincidence. I don't. And in the Kaffirs' lounge? There's a bloody message in there someplace, don't you think?"

Kaffir. Terreblanche had used the aspersion without blinking an eye, as if Merry were a fence post. Mansell felt the hair rise on the back of his neck.

"It was the Blacks Only lounge, actually," he said, "and if there is a bloody message to be had, Captain, then it's Security's case, isn't it? And it won't matter what I think one way or the other."

"I keep asking myself," Joshua interjected, "why the ladies' lounge? I mean, Elgin's coat was hung as neat as a pin over the back of a chair in the sleep room. Would a killer do that?"

"Elgin was at the train station for a reason. Let's find that reason," answered Mansell. He consulted the nearly indecipherable scribbling in his notebook. "Elgin didn't live in P.E., did he?"

"He kept an apartment," Merry answered. "Home's Jo'burg."

"Okay. Merry, let's find out who benefits by Mr. Elgin's sudden demise, shall we? Start with his family."

"It could be a long list," Joshua said. "If our victim's blood-and-guts reputation is even half accurate, then you can bet he's made at least as many enemies as he has friends."

"He spent most of his time in the Transvaal," Terreblanche told them. "It was one of those love-hate relationships. The money in Jo'burg thought the guy walked on water. Pretoria, on the other hand, wasn't quite so fond."

"The thorn in Pretoria's side," Mansell uttered. "Steenkamp's words."

"A sobriquet Mr. Elgin no doubt found amusing."

Mansell glanced up from a single-page summary of the victim. "What do we know about the miners? Any word on their negotiations?"

"I think they were more concerned about the rumor that Elgin was considering a position in our esteemed prime minister's cabinet," Terreblanche answered. "The vacancy in Industry and Finance, I believe it was."

The very sound of his own words seemed to disturb the CIB captain, and he broadened the range of his pacing. The report clenched in his fist, Mansell noticed, looked more like crepe paper now.

"There's been some trouble on the docks," the chief inspector said. "We know that. Is that related to arbitration?"

20

"From what I've heard," Joshua replied, "the dockers weren't too thrilled with Elgin's last proposal to the Harbour Association. Some of the locals stepped out of line."

"Elgin didn't like it," Terreblanche added. "It was . . . a personal thing, you might say."

"Meaning he wrapped a few knuckles, right?"

"Elgin's charm was that he could turn your life upside down and not give it a second thought."

"Nice guy," Mansell said distractedly. "Merry, we're going to need some help on this thing, I think. Jo'burg, Durban, Cape Town for starters. And let's dig out anyone who's made waves in the union recently and have them brought in. Who knows?"

"For what it's worth," Joshua interjected, "Anthony Mabasu worked on the docks for a while."

Mansell's eyes widened. "He was in the union, then."

"He got the boot two years ago. He appealed, right? They denied. And guess whose name appears on the rejection? Anyway, I found that interesting enough to leave the follow-up for you. Mabasu's downstairs. The file's on your desk."

A computer operator handed the chief inspector printouts from the Bureau of Records, the Labor Bureau, and Printmatix. He and the two detectives started out.

"Inspector!" Oliver Terreblanche held the ruffled preliminary out like a communal offering.

"Captain?"

"This needs a solution. Yes?"

Mansell tipped his head forward. "The right solution, yes."

Terreblanche's narrowed eyes returned to the district map, and after a moment, Mansell backpedaled to the door.

The gold mines that occupied Ian Elgin's thoughts in the hour before his death were of equal concern to a man now seated in the cramped, stuffy passenger compartment of a Westland-TL helicopter.

The Westland-TL, a seven-rotor job equipped with a Rolls-Royce turboshaft engine, was on permanent call to the minister of justice. The private terminal in Pretoria was located on Church Street adjacent to Strijdom Square and a field of bronze horses.

Outside, the stark yellow sun that preyed upon the shores of Port

Elizabeth, eleven hundred kilometers to the south, was, this day in the Transvaal, trapped behind a wall of bone-black clouds.

Jan Koster, the Deputy Minister of Mineral Resources and Energy Affairs, tightened his seat harness.

Next to him, Minister of Justice Cecil Andrew Leistner dozed, his eyes closed, his breathing deep and irregular. Left to the discomfort of his own thoughts, Koster's blue eyes gazed down at the implant scar on Leistner's right cheek. Not for the first time, no. Indeed, for the last seven years he had made a study of Leistner's few weaknesses and built defenses against his considerable array of strengths.

It had taken all of those seven years to fully test the limits of Koster's survival instincts; seven years to learn that he would do anything to stay alive, even . . . Yes, Koster thought, even that.

He would never forget that gusty, restless morning, those seven years past, that day when he discovered the sealed envelope locked inside the top drawer of his desk; and it took all of his strength now not to dwell on the sixteen prosperous, glorious years that had come before that day. How had they expected him to react? Like a well-trained robot, that's how. Exactly as he had. . . . Well, not exactly. Leistner must have received a similar message, but they had never talked about it.

The undertaking had been "suggested." Resistance, Koster had determined then, would have been unacceptable. Oddly, he had also determined that resistance might well serve as his one chance for survival.

Koster watched now as the pilot ran a final check on his instrument panel. The engine turned over. Rotor blades whipped stagnant air into a lather of dust and dried leaves, and a moment later, the chopper leapt into the air.

He and Leistner had taken this same flight once before; it was five years ago, and Koster could recall every word they had spoken, every crazy notion they had discussed, and every knot that had eaten, like a starving tapeworm, into his stomach. Knots that had seemed a permanent part of life ever since. But he wouldn't think about that now. Instead, he thought about another day, and another conversation concerning South Africa's most inviolate treasure, and the moment he knew their plan was actually possible . . .

"The whole bloody thing started back about a hundred years ago, Mr. Koster, when some half-drunk prospector, name of George Harrison, stumbled on this gold-bearing outcrop of rock. Was on a farm they called Langlaagte." The old miner spoke through a huge gap in his teeth, and his tongue worked its way between the space when he was thinking. The conversation took place in a shack that rested upon the bank of a played-out stream twenty kilometers east of Johannesburg. "The miners took to calling it the Witwatersrand, the White Waters Ridge. Back then, after a good rain, when the sun came out, the hills round here shimmered with a brilliance the sun itself would've been proud of. The shimmering was gold."

"The birth of fair Johannesburg," Koster said.

"Yes, sir," the old miner replied, smiling without provocation. "The city was born that same day, near that same farm. Hell, you didn't need much back then. A pickax, a muzzle-loader, maybe a strong stomach for deceit and death. Skill didn't have one damn thing to do with it. Gold lay on the surface like moss, and prospecting spread like an out-of-control brush fire. Soon enough that shimmering was nothing more than a memory."

"And that's when they went underground?"

"No choice. The fever and greed of gold are strong, Mr. Koster. By then, the gold lay trapped hundreds of meters below the surface. The prospector, the donkey, the pickax? Disappeared. Gave way to pneumatic drills and dynamite. Nowdays it's ultrasound and computers. Yes, sir. Left an old sourdough like me out in the cold."

"Times have changed, haven't they?" Koster remarked.

"You take a look out over the Witwatersrand these days and it's like a huge pegboard. Access shafts and boreholes everywhere you look. Two-thirds of the world's gold spews from those shafts, son. Two-thirds."

"Yes, I've been told," Koster replied, fully aware that the lion's share of what remained lay beneath the frozen tundra of the Soviet Union, equally aware of the power and leverage that could spring from the confluence of those two sources.

"For every access shaft you can count a hundred tunnels, Mr. Koster, a thousand in some cases. How many tunnels from one end of the Wit to the other? No one knows. It's like a gigantic honeycomb carved in solid rock down there. Good God, a man could roam those tunnels for a lifetime and never meet another living soul. . . ."

"And an entire army," Koster whispered, as the helicopter hit an air pocket and dropped like a yo-yo, "an entire army could hide itself in those same tunnels for months."

Next to him now, the minister of justice arched his back and grunted. A fierce yawn escaped, and his eyes popped open.

Leistner's first instinct was to reach for the pipe in the inside pocket of his suit coat. He filled the bowl and torched it. Dark eyes examined the spent match for the longest time. His voice, when he spoke, sounded raw and jagged, the tone more coarse than husky.

"You were reminiscing, yes, Mr. Koster?"

Surprise must have registered, at least briefly, on Koster's face, and Leistner chuckled. But there was scant humor in the laugh; they weren't close, Koster and he. Had they met under different circumstances, at a cocktail party on the diplomatic circuit, they would have been leery of one another, opposites to be avoided.

Peering out the window, Leistner settled his gaze upon a dim spot among the rolling hills and evergreens of the East Rand. "How much further, Mr. Koster?"

"Not far, Minister. Ten minutes."

Yielding to his aversion toward postmortem examination, Nigel Mansell decided on the witness before the autopsy.

His office was thirty square meters on the second floor—vintage oak furniture, walls lined with geographical maps, and a barber's chair. The Mabasu file was waiting for him on a desk strewn with textbooks.

Realizing he hadn't eaten, Mansell stopped at the station cafeteria. He poured hot water over tea bags in two paper cups, stashed a half dozen creams and sugars in his pocket, and started for the door. On impulse, he bought two candy bars.

Anthony Mabasu sat on a narrow couch in a holding cell reading yesterday's newspaper. The cell was four meters square, clammy gray concrete lit by fluorescent tubes. Mansell introduced himself. He motioned to a circular table in the middle of the room. He set a cup of tea and a candy bar in front of Mabasu and emptied cream and sugar from his pockets. Making an issue of the witness's file, Mansell fumbled purposely for a cigarette.

"So what did you think when you first saw the body?"

"You kiddin' me? I think, man, you got a shitload of trouble on your hands. That's what I think."

Mansell offered the pack. "His face was pretty beat up, wasn't it?"

"I didn't need to see no face to know he was dead, boss."

"You work in the baggage department. Your shift starts at two o'clock. And you found the body at four-thirty. Now, that wouldn't be your lunch break, would it? More like a shift break." Mansell stroked his chin. "So what did you do first?"

Mabasu stared down into a cup of untouched tea. "Do? I'm here, ain't I? You know what I did, man. What I shoulda done was got the hell out of there. I'm an easy target, and you bastards sure as shit know it."

Mansell smiled thinly. "Eat your candy bar, Anthony, and listen. This isn't target practice. This is the real thing. The ladies' bathroom is off limits, and you know it. There are questions that need answering. Now, I'm not Security. Understand? So I suggest you talk to me now, because they'll be talking to you later. Hear?"

"You and Security. There's a difference?"

Spent ash fell from Mabasu's cigarette onto the table. Glazed eyes stared at it momentarily, and then, with the flick of his wrist, he swept the remains onto the floor.

"The baggage department," Mansell said, "is on the opposite side of the depot from the ladies' lounge and down in the basement. That's a long way to go for a ten- or fifteen-minute break, pal, and most of the men I know don't normally hang out in the ladies' locker room. Why you?"

Mabasu's eyes drifted. Callused fingers strummed the tabletop. "Sylvia. My lady. See, it's her privilege to clean that filthy pigsty they call a bathroom. Great job, huh?" His fingers stopped. He buried his hands in his lap. "Trouble is . . . ."

Mansell leaned across the table. "The trouble is what?"

"Trouble is, she ain't got a goddamn . . . work permit."

Mansell sat back, arms extended, disappointed. But as he stared across at Anthony Mabasu's leathery face—his sheet gave his age as twenty-nine, but he could have easily passed for forty—disappointment gave way to embarrassment and a new thought occurred to him.

"Your wife. Sylvia. She wasn't at work last night, was she?"

Mabasu drew fitfully on his cigarette, like a child sucking on a straw. "See, we ain't been doin' too well lately. Know what I mean?

Anyway, she split yesterday. Tells me she plans spendin' some time with her sister."

"And you were going to try and cover for her."

"That's right."

"By cleaning the ladies' lounge during your breaks."

"Yeah, that's right."

"Yeah," said Mansell calmly.

Silence, the policeman's ally, charged into the room. Fluorescent bulbs hissed. The walls seemed to close in. Mabasu chewed nervously on a candy bar, and Mansell pushed strands of tawny hair off his forehead, watching.

"Tell me about your sister-in-law."

"Her name's Flora. Flora Amadi. She lives in Butterworth, in the Transkei. You need more, ask her."

"What route did you take from the baggage department to the lounge? Through the terminal?"

Mabasu shook his head. "I walked along the freight platforms back of the terminal. It's quicker, less law."

"Then you would have walked down the drive that passes along the rear of the ladies' lounge. Did you see anything out of the ordinary? Did you see anyone? Or hear anything?"

"I didn't see nothin', okay?" Their eyes clashed. Silence again. Mansell touched cold tea to his lips. Mabasu slouched down in his chair, sighing. "All right. There was a guy, in a ticket agent's uniform. Catching some air or something."

"Where?"

"Just walking, man. Just walking."

"Why didn't you say so before?"

"Because the guy was white, that's why."

"Bullshit." Mansell slapped the table and stood up.

"All right, all right. He was smoking a number. Pot, you know? He could lose his job, man. Hell, I could lose my job just saying so."

"I asked you what you did when you saw the body."

"I ran, God damn it. I ran to the information center. The phone's free there if you ask. I called you bastards. I didn't think I was gonna get hauled in for being a good citizen."

The phone's free there if you ask. Mansell dissected the phrase, played the tone of it back in his head, watched Mabasu's hands as they gripped the teacup.

"We found a blue-and-white handkerchief in the locker room. A blue-and-white bandana. You know the kind I mean. Yours?"

"No, man, not mine. Blue and white ain't my colors."

The chief inspector excused himself to refill their empty cups. Anthony Mabasu was escorted to the lavatory.

Mansell took the stairs two at a time to his office. A note from SB Lieutenant Rhoodie was propped up against the desk lamp, requesting a briefing later that day. The initials at the bottom belonged to Major Hymie Wolffe. Mansell wadded the paper into a tiny ball and propelled it haphazardly toward the wastebasket.

He reached for the in-house telephone and punched two numbers. When Merry Gosani came on the line, Mansell explained about Mabasu's wife.

"She left on a sour note. And on top of that, she should have been the one cleaning that locker room last night."

"Does that give Mabasu an alibi or a motive?"

"Probably a coincidence, all in all."

"Except you don't believe in coincidence."

"Exactly. So I want you to track down the wife in the Transkei. Don't make an issue out of the work permit. Just follow up on Mabasu's story. Try and spend a minute talking to the sister. She should have an inside ear on their marriage. All sisters do."

His second call caught Joshua in the middle of his own question-and-answer session with the sales clerk at the depot's newsstand.

"It's beginning to look like our victim spent more time at the train station than your ordinary man in the street," Joshua told him.

"Excellent."

"No one seems to know why, though."

"Did you get a statement from the ticket agent? A white guy. . . ?"

"Horwood. Thomas Horwood," answered Joshua quickly. "His shift ended at seven this morning, but he left early. Around five, according to the other agent. A matter of the flu or something. Somehow he managed to slip past our cordon. I sent Piet Richter to his house. Shall we bring him in?"

"No. Not yet. Let's hear what he has to say." Finally, Mansell mentioned the Mabasu interview and said, "I'm curious to know what Mabasu's co-workers down in the baggage department think about our witness. It could be important."

"I'm on it."

"Good. We'll conference at six unless something breaks before."

Mansell called the elementary school where his wife, Jennifer, was the assistant administrator. He was relieved when they told him she wasn't available; disturbed, however, by the very potency of that feeling. He left a message saying that he would probably have to spend the night at the station.

At the door to the holding cell Mansell loosened his tie, unbuttoned the top button, and mussed his hair slightly. Appearances, he thought. Always stay in line with your witness.

The Westland-TL swooped down over the city of Springs. Gold mines the envy of every nation in the world appeared on the horizon. Huge mountains of discarded ore formed an artificial range for as far as the human eye could see.

From his briefcase, Jan Koster produced a gridded geological map of the East Rand. Blue squares pinpointed the locations of twenty-two active mines covering 225 square kilometers. Near the center of the map he'd drawn a red circle, and within the circle lay four blue squares and a black X. Koster opened the panel between the passenger compartment and the cockpit, tapped the pilot on the shoulder, and motioned to the circle. The pilot nodded. He cut power in half and altitude to 400 meters.

Koster alerted the minister to the facility ahead. "Target One," he said. "Highland Vaal."

Leistner placed a hand on Koster's shoulder. Tension and excitement colored his face. He thrust a square jaw forward and absently passed his other hand through the silver streaks that now touched what had once been coal-black hair.

Highland Vaal Mining Corporation was the world's deepest mining operation, tunnels and shafts creating a maze of stone five kilometers below the earth's delicate skin. The chopper swept over an industrial complex seething with energy and enormity. Blue flames licked at the sky from the roofs of the refinery. Cloudlike plumes of smoke gushed from the exhaust portals of the reduction plant. Acre after acre, it stretched out before them: concrete and steel storage tanks, conveying systems, trains and trucks and tractors, drilling components, warehouse space, office facilities, and living quarters. The site, as always, left Koster's stomach filled with butterflies.

"We can't be serious about this," he whispered, to himself as much as to the minister. "It's impossible."

"But we are," Leistner replied. "And it is possible, Mr. Koster. It is."

Koster raised a hand, pointing to an ore dump five kilometers to the east. "The tunnels from Highland Vaal run that far in every direction, Minister. Those same tunnels . . . They overlap and intrude upon all but one of the other mining operations within this circle."

The irony, the irony that made their entire operation possible, was not lost on the minister of justice; his head bobbed in response.

The helicopter banked in a lazy arc over the area. Ore dumps twenty-five stories high surrounded Target Two, the White Ridge Mines, the jewel of the industry. And over the next ridge lay South Africa's most productive mine. This, Homestake Mining Incorporated, was Target Three on Koster's telltale map.

The circle closed. Five kilometers to the southeast was Brakpan Holdings. Target Four. An older mine than her three illustrious neighbors, the shining star over Brakpan's head had not dimmed much with age.

"They sucked forty-two thousand kilograms of gold out of that hole last year, Minister. Not a dozen other mines in the free world can boast of that kind of production, and yet, it's hardly worth mentioning compared to the other three. The miners call her the 'Ragged Bitch.'"

"And we have our own private back door."

Koster nearly smiled. "Yes. An apropos analogy."

All four targets were under union contract. All but six of the major mines in the country were now unionized, and Koster had to credit Leistner. It represented a show of remarkable political maneuvering, and not a dozen people realized the extent of the minister's hand in the matter.

Koster signaled to the pilot again: the black X. They drifted lower. The mine taking shape below them was miniature in comparison to its four neighbors—ninety acres helplessly under siege from below. Its name, East Fields Mining Corporation.

"That's our baby, Mr. Koster," Leistner said.

Koster nodded, remembering the old miner's story. . . .

Originally, the land had been owned by an Afrikaner farmer from Germany named Ira Mueller. This was back at the turn of the century, when Johannesburg was in its embryonic stage and gold was mined only to the west of the city. When Mueller's wife died of tuberculosis in 1899, he lost his interest in farming in favor of a new pastime: drinking. One year later, trapped by the hands of alcoholism and penury, Mueller lost his plot of land in a poker game.

The land's new owner was Alfred Jurgen. A man already wealthy because of his holdings in two prosperous mines along the west basin and two brothels located in the heart of the city's red-light district, Jurgen had no need for ninety acres of farmland. Still, he hung on to it.

Even when the big mining corporations began snapping up huge chunks of the East Rand for outlandish prices, Jurgen held out. He passed the land on to his second son, who in turn deeded it to his son, Cyprian Jurgen.

Unlike father and grandfather, however, Cyprian Jurgen was a temerarious fool. Despite inherited wealth, a seat on the Transvaal Provincial Council, and a membership in the ultrasecret Broeder-bond, Jurgen decided, rather abruptly, that he needed his own private gold mine. The year was 1955.

East Fields died a premature death three years later. The reason: simple arithmetic. Even in those bygone days, when gold could still be found a few hundred meters below ground, the cost of bringing a mine on-stream was a hundred million in dollars. Jurgen's wealth was not that great, nor was his influence. He submitted a public offering. Few investors responded. He submitted second and third offerings with the same result. In 1958, the project ceased. Cutting his losses while the cutting was good was how Jurgen described it. Facilities half built were abandoned. Four boreholes, four hundred meters deep, were sealed but never filled. Tunnels outfitted with electric cables and wench ropes were vacated on a day's notice.

There were no buyers. The four potentials—Highland Vaal, Brakpan, White Ridge, and Homestake—were unsympathetic. They didn't need Jurgen's ninety acres. The ground beneath the mine became fair game. The four giants extended their own systems beneath East Fields, gobbling up every ounce of gold-bearing reef, and in turn, leaving empty tunnels by the hundreds.

Came that day, seven years ago, when Jan Koster found his life forever altered, Cyprian Jurgen had lost much of his wealth. An aberration with sudden purpose, Leistner had called him.

It had taken Koster, Deputy Minister of Mineral Resources and Energy Affairs, six months to discover East Fields. It had taken Cecil Leistner, Minister of Justice and fellow Broederbonder, ten minutes to convince Jurgen to accept their proposition—a twenty-year lease for R20,000 a year, and one very critical stipulation: complete confidentiality. It was a stipulation Jurgen gladly accepted.

Alterations began six weeks later.

The first step was to acquire skilled, safe labor, so Koster recruited mining engineers from East Germany. Laborers were hired from Malawi—experienced miners and hard workers.

Living quarters were modified and replenished to meet the needs of a swollen population. Rusted train cars and idle shaft elevators were rebuilt. Pneumatic drills, ultrasound equipment, and computers were brought on site.

Access shafts leading from the surface were reconstructed. A pumping system capable of pushing a million cubic meters of refrigerated air through sweltering tunnels every day was installed. A second pumping system was required to clear tunnels of underground water, an ongoing task.

In time, existing tunnels beneath East Fields were connected with existing ones from beneath each target, and reconstruction of the primary tunnels initiated phase two. Lighting was restored. Debris was laboriously cleared. Electric cable systems, winch ropes, and tunnel tracking were all replaced.

The first breakthrough, into the Homestake system, occurred a month before the first snow, two years ago.

Over the course of the next eighteen months, connections were made with each target, and the last hookup, one leading to a "dead" access shaft directly below Highland Vaal, had been completed and duly celebrated on New Year's Day, seven months ago.

The minister of justice remembered the event without emotion. There had been no emotion then either, and he wondered what his reaction would be come the twenty-second.

Craving a drink, Leistner busied himself instead with his pipe and asked, "So our status, as of this moment, is what exactly?"

"We still have about seven, maybe eight hundred men working underground. Say two hundred others on the facility," answered Koster.

"That's cutting it damn close, Mr. Koster."

"Close, yes, but the contracts on all but a handful expire on

Sunday, the sixth. We'll be fine, I assure you." Koster passed Leistner the file containing their operational plans. He felt a sudden vacancy in the pit of his stomach. "Beyond that, we're on schedule. The tunnels are all fully stocked, and we have immediate access to all four targets. As you already know, we're waiting on one last shipment of arms. The freighter ARVA II is due in New York tomorrow morning for pickup. We'll distribute our current arms stock as soon as the labor force is gone, a week from today latest. And, as for our friends in Mozambique, a day's notice is all they'll need."

"I wouldn't call twenty thousand gun-toting Kaffirs our friends, Mr. Koster, but I assume you'll leave for Maputo tomorrow anyway."

Koster nodded. "Figure two weeks to move the whole lot."

"Very well. And the detonators, beneath each of the target mines, have they been—"

At that moment, the spit and crackle of the chopper's radio filled the cockpit, and the words stuck in Leistner's throat. He watched as the pilot answered the call, his head as it turned, and his hand as it opened the panel.

"For you, Minister. Urgent, he says."

Leistner hesitated for an instant before accepting the headphones and his eyes flashed unreadable clues in response to the message. Then he returned the phones and absently closed the panel.

Koster recognized the signs. "What is it?"

"That was my press secretary, Oliver Neff."

So, Koster thought, the little weasel who likes his . . . No, this wasn't the time. Neff was surely Leistner's loyal servant, but he was also his Achilles' heel. "And?"

"Elgin. He's been murdered. In Port Elizabeth."

"Murdered? My God. How?"

"How? Is it important how? He's dead. . . ."

"And we have a problem."

Leistner faced him. "I don't know what astounds me more, Mr. Koster. Your equanimity or your gift for the rhetorical."

"Nonetheless. Do we abort or do we postpone?"

"Neither," growled Leistner. "We proceed as scheduled. Is that clear? We don't need Elgin now. I'm not sure we ever did."

After a moment, the minister opened the cockpit panel. "Church Street," he ordered the pilot. "With speed, please."

The Westland-TL sprang forward, and the browning hills of the East Rand were soon behind them. Pretoria loomed in the foreground.

The remainder of the excursion passed in silence, two passengers lost in thoughts as different as night and day.

Thirty-five minutes into their second session, Mansell was pacing, smoking, and reading the last page of Anthony Mabasu's now obsolete passbook. Still, for police purposes, a useful guide into past indiscretions. The binding showed years of use, cracked and shedding leather; bleached pages curled at the edges. Mansell tossed it back on the table. He dropped into a chair.

"Nasty things, aren't they?" he said. Like an embarrassed urchin, Mabasu stowed the book in his hip pocket. "Why were you fired from the docks?"

"You read the book, boss. You know the answer."

"You missed three months' worth of dues payments and took a swing at your foreman. A class act."

"It wasn't worth my job."

"No? You petitioned the union. They turned you down. Elgin's name's on the rejection."

"I made twice the goddamn money there. Still, a measly fourth what the whitey doing the same job made. You hear that? A measly fourth. . . ."

"So fucking what? You don't like it here, move. Move to Nigeria. You'll do twice the work and make half as much. Better yet, move to England. You won't work at all." Mansell crushed out his cigarette. "All right. Tell me what kind of trouble you and your wife were having."

"It's private, man. You hear? Private. How's your marriage? Perfect?"

Touché, thought Mansell. He felt the muscles in his throat constricting and the invisible hands picking away at his stomach. In self-defense, another cigarette materialized. He told himself the question hadn't mattered and changed direction. "You knew Ian Elgin came to the railroad station on a regular basis."

"How would I know that? I work at the other end of the terminal and down in the basement. You said that yourself."

"And you knew Elgin had a hand in the situation you're in now—a baggage handler scraping to make ends meet. You didn't go to the ladies' lounge to clean up after your wife. You know it, and so do I. Elgin had money. He didn't care who he stepped on, and last night he was on your turf."

It didn't happen—the quick change of expression, the slight twitch of the hand, the shortness of breath. It was as if Mabasu hadn't heard the accusation at all; his answer, Mansell thought, was equally confounding.

"What do you want me to say, man? Say I fixed the guy and then stuffed his body in a locker just for looks? He's some high-and-mighty and I ain't nothing, right? So maybe the high and mighty had it coming his way."

Mansell found himself thinking about the three coins that lay at the foot of the locker. Here was a killer who was thorough, painstakingly so. He'd stripped Elgin's watch and ring and emptied his pockets. He'd made a point of taking Elgin's wallet, papers, and keys. Yet the coins remained. Why? It didn't make any sense, and maybe . . . that was the whole point.

Mansell pushed away from the table and gestured toward the door. "I think we're finished for now, Anthony. I'll get you a ride. It's been a long day. Get some sleep before you go back to work."

Mansell ordered a car. He also arranged to have Mabasu's house in New Brighton watched.

It was 3:35 in the afternoon, and the dread of formaldehyde filled his nostrils.

EIGHT THOUSAND MILES TO THE NORTHWEST, WHERE THE ASTERS and rose of Sharon of summer were blooming and the muskrats and fox had long forgotten winter, another man paced in a warehouse outside of Wethersfield, Connecticut. His anxiety was the result of a taxing, yet lucrative business venture. A venture that dated back to an equally balmy September, seven years ago.

The entrepreneur's name was Karl Simon Brinker. Brinker was an arms dealer, a seller of lethal weapons in a trade that, next to narcotics, was the most lucrative in the world.

Brinker's office was a partitioned corner in an otherwise open warehouse. The walls were cluttered with army memorabilia and framed paintings of such champions as Secretariat, Man O' War, and Citation. A pull-string lamp hung over a small wooden desk, and a half pint of brandy sat on the desk top.

Brinker poured three fingers' worth into a paper cup. The roar of a forklift echoed in the background. He heard his foreman shouting directions. Not long now, Brinker thought, pacing again.

In time, he paused before an eleven-by-fourteen-inch color photo of two army officers with their arms draped around one another. Father and son dressed in their formal army blues. A lieutenant colonel's silver cluster glistened on Brinker's lapel. The two stars on the general's chest seemed dull in comparison. The father retired with three stars some years after the photo was taken; Karl Brinker left for Korea the next day. The Twenty-fifth Infantry Division landed on Korean soil in July, and Lieutenant Colonel Brinker caught a bullet in the hip in August.

The Purple Heart, still in its case, was tacked on the wall next to the photo. Brinker stared at the emblem, a gold heart with a raised profile of George Washington in the center. Cracked fingers stroked the purple-and-white ribbon. A hundred years ago, he thought. The drinking started soon after. The pain, he reminded himself, had been unbearable. He was transferred home. An interest in horses led to the track, which led to the gambling.

The discharge, fifteen months later, was honorable, true, but no one knew better than Brinker himself that the "early retirement" was the army's way of ridding itself of a bad apple.

But the contacts were still there. Papa Brinker's old comrade, General Armstrong, opened the doors for the business. It was his recommendation to the armament director that secured Brinker's franchise. Family money provided the backing.

Now Brinker was franchised by the United States government to sell small arms at a profit and to keep stock on his premises. He dealt with wholesalers and retailers, gun clubs, police forces, and militia units, most national but some foreign. He dealt in odd lots, irregular orders, and flexible prices.

But money was still Brinker's elusive companion, his nemesis still the same: the wager and the bottle.

Initial contact with Liberian Defense Minister Mustafa Okoya occurred seven years ago. It had been a cool, vibrant day filled with the rusts and golds and yellows of the ash and the oak and the hickory. It felt wrong from the beginning.

Brinker knew Okoya's reputation: the mistress in Monrovia, his growing addiction to coca paste, the "service" contracts with several Eastern-bloc countries. But in the end, it was pure finances that sucked the arms dealer in. Thirteen million dollars' worth of small arms over a six-year period. A fee plus a percentage. It was an offer too good to pass up. The order, for his own convenience, Okoya had said, was broken up into five shipments. It consisted of assault rifles, handguns, light mortars, machine guns, grenade and rocket launchers, and ammunition—nothing Brinker would have to order out of normal channels.

After the first shipment, Brinker's delirium gave way to reality and nagging questions. The orders were too big for a dealer of his stature. The prices were too extravagant. Brinker also knew that the Liberian State Police, proposed recipient of the goods, consisted of two thousand men, not twenty thousand. But by the time Okoya let on about the "peculiarities" in the paperwork, Brinker was a lock.

The paper cup was empty.

Brinker took a pull off the bottle and walked to the office door. He watched the forklift hoist the last crate into the rear of the tractor trailer.

His dock foreman entered the warehouse with a clipboard in one hand and a leather pouch under his arm. The State Department inspector followed him toward the office. Brinker capped the brandy and stowed the bottle out of sight.

They gathered around the small wooden desk. Brinker initialed the shipping manifest. He passed it to the government man, who checked each item against his own list. Finally, he initialed the document, retained two copies, and passed the original back.

"A tidy bundle," he said with a grin. "Someone over there must be plannin' an awful big safari, eh?"

Shut your face, Brinker thought, as the agent leafed through the leather pouch. When he came to the End-User Certificate, the document that guaranteed the identity of the rightful buyer of the goods and thus their rightful "user," he took a light meter from his belt and ran it over and under the parchment paper on which the document was printed.

Sweat formed on Brinker's brow. "What the hell is that?"

"Infrared. It's new. It picks up the tracers we're puttin' in the End-User paper now." Brinker leaned forward, but the agent withdrew the meter, chuckling again. "Well, I can't show it to you right now, but I can tell you it's been damn effective."

"I'm thrilled," Brinker replied.

The agent replaced the End-User. He inspected the sales agreement, the export and import licenses, and finally the export permit. Halfway down the page, he paused, and his brow furrowed. He pulled on his ear. Brinker lit a cigarette. In time, the inspector made a brief note on his own ledger, initialed all four documents, and filed them back in the pouch. He passed the lot back to Brinker.

"Looks okay," he said absently. "We'll see you next time around, eh?"

The foreman escorted the State Department man outside. Brinker watched the agent get into his car. Then, turning a blind eye to the trembling of his own hands, he filed the leather pouch in the side pocket of his jacket. In the other pocket, he filed a second half pint of brandy.

The forensic laboratory occupied the entire basement floor of the police station.

Autopsy had its own private cell in the southeast corner. As it should be, Mansell thought. He bolstered himself for the session ahead by lighting a fresh cigarette at the entrance. He coughed from the pit of his lungs. Then, as if expecting to interrupt an embarrassed corpse, Mansell knocked.

Joseph Steenkamp was hunched over a long table occupied by the remains of the victim.

"Ah, to be certain. My favorite infrequent visitor, the chief inspector. Of Homicide of all things. Where have you been? Nearly done here." Steenkamp spoke Afrikaans, the Dutch-German confluence that first appeared in South Africa three centuries ago, and, as Afrikaners loved to claim, the only indigenous language of the country. "There are paper bags on the counter if you insist upon being sick."

"You're a gentleman."

"A gentleman being one who insists his guests have adequate facilities to deal with their phobias."

"Exactly." Mansell picked up a copy of the preliminary report at the foot of the table. Steenkamp added side comments as he read.

"The victim was only fifty-six years old, poor chap. Hope I've got more than a year left, old boy."

"You'll outlive us all."

"I have high hopes." Steenkamp pointed to the report. "Postmortem lividity, the onset of rigor mortis, body temperature, and digestive tract contents all put the time of death between three-fifteen and three forty-five this morning. Cause of death is still asphyxia due to strangulation."

Mansell made a quiet note of Ian Elgin's physique. He was not a tall man, but his chest was broad, and his forearms and shoulders suggested a man who exercised with both regularity and vigor.

"Occlusion of the greater vessels of the neck obstructed the flow of oxygen to the brain. Inhibition of the heart muscle was caused by extreme pressure on the vagus. An unpleasant way to die, I assure you." The pathologist reached for a rotary saw as he spoke, and Mansell held up a hand. Steenkamp grinned. "Squeamish fellow for a man in your particular trade, aren't you?"

Mansell propped up against an empty examination table. He stared down at the paper in his hands. Some event, he thought, compelled two men to enter the same women's locker room within an hour of one another, and within that common denominator, he told himself, lay the solution. Sylvia Mabasu?

Unconvinced, he laid the paper aside and asked, "Any surface prints, Joe?"

"None."

"Fingernails?"

"Clean and unbroken. Not very considerate. The fingers on the right hand are bruised, but not the left. Resistance was minimal," answered Steenkamp.

"What can we tell from the groove in his neck?" asked Mansell, moving back to the body.

"Narrow, but very deep. The cord, as you know, was nylon." Abrasions and contusions covered the neck and the skin beneath the cheekbone. Tiny hemorrhages had occurred around the eye sockets, but not on the forehead or cheeks, Mansell noted. Bile filled his mouth. It was the taste of anger he always felt looking down at a murder victim; the anger of being an imperfect, cruel animal in a world filled with imperfect, cruel animals. "The groove runs from the upper end of the trachea in front, high around the neck, to a point just below the base of the skull."

"So the killer was above the victim," Mansell suggested. "Or the victim was slumped down."

"We found dirt stains and scrapes on the victim's hands and on his knees, indicating he'd slumped forward on the floor. My opinion is that his assailant was standing next to him, on his right side."

Mansell bent his head forward. He tapped the paper with his index finger. "The victim was either unconscious or in a state of severe disorientation, then. From the blow to the nose?"

"There were two blows," corrected Steenkamp. "One to the back of the neck. One to the nose, which was broken."

"The one to the back of the neck would have been first."

"The blow was delivered with power, but it wasn't clean. Too low on the collarbone to cause unconsciousness. The second blow, the one to the nose, was square."

The chief inspector asked himself why, if the victim was unconscious after the second blow and if the motive was robbery, the thief had thought it necessary to kill the man. Had they known each other? Did he panic? Or was robbery simply a smokescreen?

Mansell studied the victim's hands. Two fingers on the right hand had been hooked beneath the rope as the victim hung in the locker, his last futile attempt at salvation, but this did not support the theory that the victim was unconscious. Yet the thumb and finger showed only minor bruising and the fingernails looked as if they had just come from a manicurist. Mansell expelled a sharp breath. He pushed strands of hair off his face.

"So was he conscious or not?" he muttered.

"What was that, old boy?"

"Nothing. Just the meanderings of an illucid mind."

Steenkamp grunted. "So be it."

Mansell started for the door. He called out over his shoulder, "I look forward to your final report, tonight I hope."

"Look for it in the morning," snorted the pathologist in reply. "Oh, Nigel. Would you like to know what the man had for dinner?"

When Mansell turned, his expression conveyed restrained exasperation. He was always in too big of a hurry to leave this room. "A late dinner," he said. "Yes, please."

Steenkamp's surliness dissolved into an avuncular grin. "Pasta."

"Pasta? With fish or meat?"

"Ah, smart boy. There were traces of pork and beef. Italian sausage and meatballs would be my astute conjecture."

"Beretta's. That's Elgin's style, I imagine. Or maybe that place on the west side, The Factory." Mansell didn't claim to be a connoisseur of Italian cooking.

"Or Dardano's," added Steenkamp. He picked up the rotary saw again, pulling the trigger for just a second. "It's out in Sunridge Park."

"Never heard of it."

"Try it sometime. The linguine would be my personal recommendation."

The door was already closing. Mansell heard the whine of the saw, and he hastened his exit with lengthening strides.

At the Church Street heliport, Cecil Leistner's press secretary stood slight and pale with hands clasped behind his back, his eyes turned skyward.

Oliver Neff's few friends described him good-naturedly as a wisp of smoke on a winter's eve. There was little more to the man than that. His face, from a distance, was as delicate as a child's. Age had done little to tarnish his pristine manner, but the sparkle behind his gray-blue eyes had dimmed in recent months.

Fifty meters away, the helicopter landed in the center of a square pad lined with concentric circles. Neff watched as Leistner and another man deplaned and trotted in his direction. He groaned inwardly.

Absently, Leistner introduced Jan Koster by name and title. Then he took Neff by the elbow and spoke directly to the subject. "We'll want this matter handled by Security Branch, Oliver. We don't want things to get out of control."

Neff answered, saying, "I've been informed that an investigation is well under way, Minister."

"Of course. And who's in charge?"

"Major Hymie Wolffe."

Leistner knew the name, but not the face. They crossed the concourse to a circular drive, where Leistner's personal car awaited them. "All right," Leistner said. "Let's inform our CIB people down there. . . . Who would that be?"

"Terreblanche. Captain Oliver Terreblanche."

"Terreblanche. Yes." Both a face and a name Leistner recognized. "We'll inform the captain that the matter is now under Security Branch jurisdiction."

Neff scratched the bridge of his nose nervously. "That might be touchy, Minister. CIB has already instigated a full-fledged investigation. Their initial report has it listed as murder subsequent to robbery. That's not a clear Security matter."

"The victim was white. His body was found in a Blacks Only. I deem that a Security matter. Case closed."

A black chauffeur ushered them into the rear of a long limousine with cross-facing seats. The inside reeked of well-tended leather and pipe tobacco. Koster sat opposite the minister.

"If you'll excuse me, Minister," Koster said, disturbed by the direction of the conversation and covertly raising an eyebrow at Leistner. "Why draw undue attention to the situation? Two investigations certainly can't hurt, and Security Branch would normally have precedence, if it came down to that. Correct? Consider this. Why not invoke the Police Act? Keep the press out of it. Publicity can't help. I'm assuming that's within your jurisdiction, of course?"

Koster had a habit of delivering his suggestions, Leistner thought, like a mother hen chastising her baby chicks. It was a habit that would make his removal that much less painful. Still, he considered the idea.

"It's a thought," he heard Oliver Neff saying. "The Police Act would give the local police the authority to forbid publication or disclosure of any information concerning the arrest or the investigation, if you're willing to deem the matter security-related or—"

"Related in any way to the prevention of terrorism. Thank you, I know the law," Leistner snapped. "That's the easy part."

The act also prohibited the identification of any person connected with said investigation or arrest. Which meant, Leistner thought, the media didn't touch it. Unauthorized disclosure of information under the Police Act carried an automatic ten-year jail sentence, and a dozen journalists wasting away behind the bars of Modder Bee Prison could testify to the authenticity of the act.

Leistner sucked air into his lungs, suppressing a grimace; it wasn't a decision without complications. Koster watched him. The red telephone hidden in the armrest in the middle of the backseat provided a direct line to the commissioner's office in the Palace of Justice, and when Leistner lifted the receiver from the cradle, Koster looked away.

It was not the chief homicide inspector's favorite duty. Had it been within his power, he would have dispensed with it altogether. But, though the press hounds in Port Elizabeth were patient, they were also persistent.

Therefore, at 5:01, Mansell relented. Five minutes, he told them.

Ian Elgin, in death, warranted a larger gathering than the average homicide victim. Besides Port Elizabeth's two locals, the *Cape Province Bulletin* and the *Port Elizabeth Daily Mail*, there were reporters from *Die Vaderland* in Jo'burg, *The Argus* in Cape Town, the *Rand Daily Mail*, a black-oriented magazine called *The Press*, and Reuters.

Mansell gave them a brief synopsis of the crime and the current status of the investigation. He answered a half dozen questions as elusively as possible and then referred them all to the front desk.

And while the reporters from Reuters, *The Press*, *Die Vaderland*, the *Rand*, and the *Bulletin* all took Mansell's advice, the baby-faced stringer from *The Argus* had a 5:20 deadline to meet, and he was on the phone sixty seconds later. Likewise, the journalist from the *Port Elizabeth Daily Mail*, a newspaperwoman with twenty-two years' experience, went directly to the phone booth next to the front desk. Her rewrite man was standing by, and the story went to press on the front page ten minutes later.

The person-to-person call from the commissioner's office in Pretoria caught Captain Oliver Terreblanche completely off guard.

The Police Act, bloody Christ. It was the last thing he expected or needed, and what made it worse, the order had been issued directly from Leistner himself. Christ damn.

Terreblanche jumped up from behind his desk, raced out of his third-floor office, and down the corridor to the stairwell. He took the stairs at a run, nearly colliding with a policewoman carrying two cups of tea, to the first floor.

He stopped on the last step, stretching on the tips of his toes. He stared out over the tops of innumerable busy heads. The conference room was empty, and he couldn't spot Mansell anywhere. Terreblanche recognized the *Daily Mail* reporter as she left by the front door. He saw the junior reporter from *The Argus* step out of the phone booth, smiling. He was replaced by another man who Terreblanche recognized by face only, a nervous type in a fedora and tan trench coat: the reporter from Reuters International wire service.

Waiting on Mansell's desk were two sweet rolls and a half liter of milk. Waiting behind the desk was Joshua Brungle.

"Don't get up," Mansell said to the detective. Then he noticed the food. "That for me?"

"My guess is you haven't eaten a thing all day," answered Joshua. "And man does not live by caffeine and nicotine alone."

"Scholarly. Socrates or Lovejoy?"

"Nietzsche, I believe."

"Of course." Mansell shed his sports jacket. He dropped into an office chair, stretching long legs over the oak desk top. He needed a shave and a shower, but the pit in his stomach took precedence. He finished off the first roll and washed it down with milk. "Thank you, sir. You're a better mother to me than my own wife."

"Does that come under the definition of a compliment?"

"Good question." Laughter filled the room for a time, and then, when the second roll had been eaten and he was sipping on the last of the milk, Mansell asked, "So what have we found out so far? Anything earthshaking?"

Joshua opened a notebook. "The clerk at the newsstand knew Elgin, not by name, but by sight. She says she would see him two, sometimes three times a week whenever he was in town. Always after midnight. Always very dapper. A nice guy. Sometimes he'd buy a paper. So she figures he goes to the Men's Club for a short workout or a steambath, right? But the club attendant says he saw

Elgin maybe once a month, if that. The shoeshine boy at the club confirms—"

They were interrupted by a knock at the door, and SB Lieutenant Rhoodie stepped past the threshold.

"The little bird who sings in the ear of the beast," snapped Joshua. "The songfest has been canceled, pal. Shove off."

"I left a note earlier, Inspector," Rhoodie said. "I was hoping for a conference. May I—"

"The note said 'Wolffe.' "

"By his authority. I suppose that was my thinking."

"The major has no authority in this office, Lieutenant." Mansell finished his milk and returned to the rush of nicotine. He gestured to a chair. "Come in and sit down."

Joshua repeated his summary for Rhoodie's benefit, and then continued. "Neither the attendant at the club nor the shine boy knew Anthony Mabasu, but the boy knew his wife by sight. 'A nice piece,' he called her. And he thinks he saw her and Elgin talking together sometime last week."

"Do we suspect either of them or the newsstand clerk?" asked Rhoodie energetically.

Joshua regarded him with disgust. Then he passed Mansell one of the files. "The lady at the newsstand is sixty-six years old. The shine boy has a club foot and a bad limp. But the attendant's a different story. He's a weight lifter and a bit too subdued for my liking. Anyway, I've got Piet Richter doing a follow-up."

Joshua waited while Mansell scanned the file. The attendant's name was Martin Engels. A law-school dropout with a business degree from Cape Town University, he'd been employed at six different jobs over the last two years. His police record showed two petty-theft charges, both dropped, and a harassment conviction, again all within the last two years.

"Our weight lifter has a chip on his shoulder," Mansell said, closing the file. "Let's wait and see if Richter can add anything to the rise and fall of Mr. Engels. Who's next?"

"The lady at the information center had a little dirt on everyone. Who smokes pot, who snorts coke, who's doing it with who. And she claims that our victim was dipping his wick into a couple of the female *swartes* who work the night shift."

"Names?"

"No names. And so far I haven't heard even a whisper of confirmation. We're still looking."

Remembering the chiffon scarf hanging in the sitting area outside the locker room, Mansell scribbled a note to himself. Then he asked, "What have we heard from our ticket-agent friend, Thomas Horwood? Recovered from the flu yet?"

"I think Mr. Horwood's covering something," Joshua replied. "I think both ticket agents are. I can feel it. Piet Richter talked to Horwood this afternoon. He's white. Big enough and surly. Says he had an attack of the runs or some mysterious affliction this morning. He's made a remarkable recovery according to Piet. Horwood says he left by the front entrance around five-fifteen, but the officer on the barricade says no way. Horwood claims he doesn't know Mabasu or his wife, and he says he's never laid eyes on Ian Elgin. Oh, and he says he won't talk anymore without a lawyer present. I talked to the other agent myself, and the best she could do was confirm my suspicions. She's black, not pretty but shapely, and she flaunts it. Said of course she knows Sylvia Mabasu, right? But she chokes up the minute I show her a picture of the victim and claims she doesn't recognize him. I don't know. Bad vibes, Nigel."

"Horwood's a pot smoker, we know that much," said Mansell. He told them about Mabasu's encounter with the ticket agent outside the depot.

"Chapter two," Joshua replied, on his feet now and rummaging through his notebook. "The same habit cost him a job at the harbor a few years back. Horwood was a pilot trainee at the time. Good record. Good advancement. But he was nailed smoking a joint on the docks one night, in the cab of a forty-ton boom crane. The union expelled him the next day. He appealed the dismissal. They all do, right? It was denied. Rumor has it that he threatened the local president over the issue, but nothing ever came of it."

"Let's bring Mr. Horwood in for a private chat, Joshua."

"The man's guilty of a misdemeanor offense," snapped Lieutenant Rhoodie. "And he's withholding information. There's no excuse for that. He should be—"

"We know his weakness now," Mansell cut in. "He'll cooperate."

That left Mansell's interview with Anthony Mabasu. The contents, the chief inspector deemed, were not yet meant for the SB lieutenant's ears, so he explained about the food contents found in Ian Elgin's digestive system.

"Lieutenant," he said. "It's your task to find out where Mr. Elgin dined last night. Who did he dine with? Did anyone notice anything out of the ordinary? How many bottles of wine did they drink? Which wine? You know all the questions."

"You mean now, sir?" Rhoodie wore a hurt expression.

"Now would be fine. Yes, I think now." Mansell's smile was ever so brief.

The door closed, leaving them alone. Mansell saw the worry lines on Joshua's face. "He'll have to wait in line," he said. "I sent Merry on the same job an hour ago."

"Was I worried?"

Joshua found a dozen holes in Anthony Mabasu's story, and one adjunct. "The clerk at the soda fountain told me that Mabasu stopped at her counter for a Coke sometime between one-thirty and two this morning. Before his shift started. He was jittery, she thought. Nervous. He kept wiping his forehead with a rag."

"The bandana."

"Maybe. When I asked her about the color she told me I was making her dizzy."

"Meaning Mabasu could have been in that locker room before he checked in for work."

"My thought exactly," said Joshua. "My other thought is, should he be out on the street?"

Mansell shook his head. "He's not going anywhere. Let's see what Forensic has for us in the morning."

"If it's still our case."

Joshua left twenty minutes later, at 6:35. The three men who worked with Anthony Mabasu in the baggage department would be waking up about now.

Nigel Mansell dialed his home phone number, but there was no answer. He wasn't surprised. Still, he let it ring another thirty seconds on the slim chance that Jennifer might be in her darkroom.

Craving drove him to dial the cafeteria. He ordered a cheese sandwich and a pot of English tea.

He pushed an office chair across the room to a long narrow workbench and switched on the IBM office computer. The mutation, Mansell called it. He punched into Crime Research Bureau's main data banks and asked for the personal file on Ian Elgin. Two error messages brought on a string of expletives. A third attempt proved, Mansell told himself, that even a dumb cop can run a computer, given time.

Ian Elgin was born in 1934 in Durban to English-speaking parents.

His father worked on the docks, a crane operator. His mother kept the books for a coal-mining firm. Elgin was educated in the public schools. He was raised in the Presbyterian faith, which he abandoned when he was twenty-one in favor of the Dutch Reformed Church. Admirable, thought Mansell, his first political maneuver.

In 1952, Elgin left Durban to attend the University of Natal in Pietermaritzburg, Mansell's own alma mater. He earned a four-year degree in pre-law, attended law school at the University of Pretoria, and graduated ninth out of a class of 112. His specialty was industrial relations, an unusual field at the time, which led to employment with Ford South Africa in Port Elizabeth.

Departing Ford in 1968, Elgin joined the legal department of Anglovaal, a coal- and gold-mining company. The file offered no explanation for the move and no information on his new position.

Just three years later, he hooked up with the Chamber of Mines, the largest employers' group in South Africa. Nearly all mining-related companies of any size belonged to the Chamber. Its functions were multifarious—anything from mining research to safety regulation to wage standardization.

Ian Elgin's job description with the Chamber read "staff association liaison." Staff associations, Mansell recalled, were self-contained black organizations meant to placate any drives toward unionization. But a staff association held no bargaining power. Its leadership was government-sanctioned, and thus white. It handled complaints and suggestions by offering sympathy and excuses, in truth functioning as nothing more than an ineffectual social apparatus.

But next to Elgin's job description, the computer flashed an "SB EXTRACT," or Security Branch footnote. The extract explained that Elgin had taken a special interest in the Durban harbor staff associations, and, in 1975, managed to unite the railroad workers, the dock workers, and the stevedores together in what the extract termed "clandestine organizational meetings."

A year later, under Elgin's presumed guidance, three simultaneous strikes occurred. The effect was unprecedented; South Africa's foremost harbor was paralyzed. The government refused to negotiate. The armed forces were called up. During the ensuing four days, 632 arrests were made. Finally, the strike was broken, and on the fifth day, the docks resumed functioning.

Ian Elgin was suspected, but never implicated.

It appeared, in fact, to Nigel Mansell, that Elgin's stature redoubled. Shortly thereafter, he was transferred to Johannesburg, given a salary hike, and assigned by the Chamber to the task of upgrading the security methods used by individual mining operations. Two months later, Elgin was added to the staff of the government's own Agency of Policy and Security Development, again for the purpose of evaluating plant security in the mines. Interim coordinator of the PSD at the time was Deputy Minister of Defense Cecil A. Leistner. Mansell half expected an SB EXTRACT to follow up, but none was forthcoming. He wondered why. While he was making a note to himself, an employee from the cafeteria brought in a tray with a sandwich and tea. Halfway through the sandwich, Mansell returned to the file.

Elgin's star continued to rise. In 1979, four months after the installation of the current prime minister, Elgin received a nomination to a government-appointed commission of inquiry: the Wiehahn Commission. His nominator was again Cecil Leistner, the new minister of justice. An extract informed Mansell that, until 1979, the Wiehahn Commission was strictly a research and lobbyist tool. That year, the commission strongly recommended that labor laws be loosened. Ian Elgin voted in favor of the recommendation. The government capitulated, and black unions became legal.

Eighteen months later, Ian Elgin resigned from the commission and accepted the positions of vice-chairman and chief negotiating officer for the black Federation of Mineworkers Union, the FMU.

In June of 1985, backed by a recruited membership of 72,000, Elgin negotiated the union's first wage agreement with, ironically, Mansell thought, the Chamber of Mines.

In May of 1986 the Affiliated Union of Dockers, Stevedores, and Rail Workers hired Elgin to handle its contract negotiations with the Harbour Association, and Elgin accepted the oblique title of board consultant. A position he held until his death.

That year, with 430,000 new FMU members, Elgin again took the Chamber and several independent mines to task over housing, safety, retirement benefits, and wages. The Chamber decided to flex its muscle. Contract talks were severed. Elgin responded by calling wildcat strikes at six gold mines and a walkout by the United Dock Workers locals in Port Elizabeth and Durban. Negotiations resumed a week hence.

A last SB EXTRACT appeared for March of this year. At that time, the Nationalist party offered Elgin an unchallenged seat on the Transvaal Provincial Executive Committee. Very prestigious,

Mansell thought, noting that the position would have required Elgin to forsake his union positions and take on formal party membership. The offer had been refused.

Remembering the cabinet position Elgin was reportedly considering at the time of his death, Mansell pushed aside his cafeteria tray. Elgin, he thought, had meddled in enough hotbeds over his career, and stepped on enough toes, to acquire a healthy list of enemies. Unionization had seen plenty of careers catapult and plenty of others tumble. Pretoria distrusted Elgin to the point of resorting to bribery. Professional vendetta, Mansell found himself thinking, was disturbing enough. But political vendetta. . . .

He was copying the Elgin file on the printer when Captain Oliver Terreblanche knocked on his door. He entered cradling a bottle of Glenlivet Scotch and two glasses.

"I do so love a hard worker," he said, spilling into an office chair. He set his CARE package on the desk and filled both glasses, neat.

Mansell joined him. "Where's the ice?"

"Never scar quality Scotch whiskey with mere ice, Inspector." Terreblanche had just gotten off the phone with the Afrikaner in Johannesburg, a man who knew the exact buttons to push, and like a black hole there seemed no end to his "requests." Terreblanche tipped his glass in Mansell's direction, selecting his words with care. "I was a little hasty this morning, Nigel. Pressing for a quick solution to this Elgin thing. How baroque. As if you would do anything less. I apologize."

Terreblanche's voice was still strained, Mansell thought, watching the captain over the rim of his glass. Mansell remembered the rumors about Terreblanche's "leanings," and the rumors about the native boy that he "kept" in an apartment in Uitenhage. But that was two years ago, and like a bad joke, the rumors had fallen into memory. Terreblanche had emerged from the gossip with a wounded reputation, but his career had weathered it thus far.

"Elgin was an important man," Mansell replied. "The economy can't afford any major upheavals right now. Matters are tense enough. We have a jailhouse full of rioters, a funeral march tomorrow, and a township set to ignite like a tinderbox. A strike is the last thing we need."

Captain Terreblanche finished off his drink aggressively and poured a refill. "And to add melodrama to an already boorish plot," he announced, "the case has been put in a straitjacket."

"The Police Act. When?" Mansell bent his head forward. He sipped Scotch calmly. "I've already given it to the press."

"Oh, my, really? Procrastination will be the death of me. I heard the news, oh, fivish or so I'd say. And now I suppose they've already gone to press. Pity."

An impervious smile creased Mansell's face. He took up his glass. "You, Captain, are a beautiful man."

"Well, I suppose." They both drank. "But you were so busy at the time, and . . . Shall we have another?"

Small victories, Mansell thought sourly. "So the commissioner and our exalted police minister couldn't keep their hands off of it," he uttered.

"No, not the commissioner this time. This one came straight from the boys at Justice."

"Leistner? Really? So it's Security's case, then."

"That's what you wanted, isn't it? Wolffe and his gang?"

"Hatchet men, termites, and leeches." Mansell expelled a sharp breath.

"Yes," said the captain, draining his glass. "Therefore, I think we shall continue with this one, Inspector."

Mansell nodded. Scotch stung the back of his throat pleasantly. He was lighting a cigarette when the phone rang. He raised the receiver deliberately, listened for thirty seconds, then said, "Thank you, see you in the morning," and hung up. Terreblanche's eyebrows arched in anticipation.

"Detective Gosani."

"Another late worker. And?"

"And it seems that Ian Elgin dined quite late last night at a restaurant called Dardano's. And it seems that he didn't dine alone. We have a name."

"So." Oliver Terreblanche capped his bottle, preparing to leave. "Oh, yes. Major Wolffe has an appointment with our forensic people tomorrow morning at nine-thirty. I told Chas du Toits that you would be in his lab by seven-thirty. Can you make it?"

It was a rhetorical question. The captain had already turned away. "Thanks for the drink," said Mansell.

"Get some sleep, Inspector."

The sandstone clock behind his desk read 11:05. Nigel Mansell decided on a shave and a shower before driving the kilometer back to his own bed.

While a waxing moon hovered over the dormant city of Port Elizabeth, an evening sunset broadened across the eastern seaboard of the United States. Rush hour.

Traffic, the like of which the inhabitants of Port Elizabeth could not have fathomed, consumed the Long Island Expressway and the two semitractor trailers that were its captives.

Karl Brinker opened the window on the passenger side of the lead truck. A cool wind embraced his clammy skin. He was half drunk by this time. Tension infested the cab.

Twenty minutes and ten miles later, they swung south onto the Brooklyn Queens Expressway, the last leg of their journey.

Brinker double-checked his papers. He stared at the End-User's Certificate. Pros and cons. The document itself was genuine. Fine, terrific. Yeah, and so was Defense Minister Okoya's signature, but Foreign Minister Tseka's was a forgery, pure and simple. Masterful, sure, a work of pure genius, but still a forgery.

Brinker took a pull off his bottle, studying the export license. State Department–issued and –authorized. He stared at the paper, drawing strength from it, knowing that the next document, the sales agreement, had as many holes in it as the courage he was now stoking. The forged signature of the undersecretary of arms disbursement, Edward Murphy, bothered him more than anything.

Yet the State Department inspector had been more concerned with the export permit than anything. Why? It was perfect, thought Brinker, as he stowed the papers. He stared out the window. A mile away, rising like misplaced monoliths from the tip of Manhattan Island, were the towers of the World Trade Center. But the trucks didn't cross the Brooklyn Bridge.

For this operation Karl Brinker had chosen a small private terminal in Brooklyn at the foot of Fifty-ninth Avenue and Bay Ridge Drive. Brinker believed in the private entrepreneur; fewer rules, fewer scruples. The Bay Ridge Terminal was owned and operated by a Portuguese immigrant named Dom Andrada. Brinker had cultivated his relationship with Andrada for eighteen years with prompt payments and numerous cases of Portuguese wine. Andrada reciprocated by discouraging undue customs interference and by arranging all towing and pilotage for Brinker's carriers.

The trucks swung right off the expressway onto Shore Parkway. Another right on Bay Ridge Drive led down a narrow concourse five hundred yards to the waterfront. A twelve-foot-high chain link fence formed a cincture around the terminal. Inside the gate, a matchbox-sized building hugged the ground. The sign out front read, UNITED STATES CUSTOMS DEPARTMENT.

The drivers parked inside the gate, and Brinker climbed down. He entered the office without knocking. Two uniformed men and a woman glanced up from telephones and typewriters.

Brinker bestowed a congenial smile. "Good evening. Karl Brinker with Brinker Inc. We have a cargo scheduled for shipment tomorrow, the fifth. ARVA II is the carrier of record, I believe."

The older of the two men wore a wrinkled tan uniform and a basset-hound pout. He lumbered over toward the counter and shoved a knobby hand out. "Papers."

Brinker passed over the pouch. "Export and import licenses. Export permit. End-User's. Sales agreement. Shipping manifest. The whole works."

The customs agent waved at the door.

"Pull 'em down to the inspection station. Somebody will be with you in a bit."

After the trucks were secured, the drivers strolled down to the piers. Karl Brinker went straight to the ramshackle building that served as the terminal's office and found it deserted. He stacked two cases of wine neatly on a secretary's desk, slumped into a tattered recliner, and finished off the last of his brandy. Minutes later, Dom Andrada clambered through the door. A litany of cursing and back-slapping culminated in two tall mugs of wine. As they neared the bottom of the first bottle, there was a knock on the door. It was the customs agent.

"Mr. Brinker," he said. "There appears to be a question or two about your papers. The export permit and the End-User's Certificate have been sent over to the customs house on the island."

"A problem?" rumbled Dom Andrada.

"Time will tell."

"What kind of questions?" asked Brinker.

"Your export permit is dated May thirtieth. The End-User's, too."

"That's right. Yeah," Brinker said, trying to control the muscles in his face. He felt the involuntary shaking of his wineglass and forced his hand back down on the table. "So?"

"So both documents denote Monrovia as the port of entry," the agent answered. "The port of Monrovia has been closed for the past nine weeks. You didn't know? The Liberian Foreign Ministry didn't inform you of that? Strange. Trouble of some sort. The stupid maniacs. No ships are being allowed in or out, I'm afraid. You really should have been notified."

A single dead bolt protected the door to Nigel Mansell's brick bungalow. He turned the key and stepped inside quietly. A silk lampshade, illuminated by a yellow bulb, cast soft light over cream walls. A coatrack lounged in a dark corner. An overstuffed chair cradled discarded magazines.

He stood with hands buried in his pockets, conscious of a half life. A silk jacket draped over the back of an oak dining chair. Home, he thought. A brass centerpiece sheltered neglected candles on a matching oak table. An empty coffee cup. A half-gnawed English muffin. An empty carton of peach yogurt. Home? Why doesn't it feel like home? Why doesn't it reach out to me with open arms and warm sheets?

He stepped lightly into the hallway. Hardwood floors and cold echoes. He stared at the closed door that hid her darkroom.

He didn't knock. Couldn't. It had been months since he last knocked.

But the image of her; the image appeared to him, momentarily radiant. Why? Slender, sleek like a snow leopard, stealthy. *But without the strength,* a voice from within told him. Pale firm breasts, ivory skin cut by the patient hands of a sculptor. *But cold to the touch, like marble,* the voice argued. The muscle tone of a gymnast, controlled, capable of wide thunder; a caldron of mystery. *But the lightning has run dry,* he heard, refusing to listen. Blond, waves after waves of blond, and the power in her hips, the liquid fire; magic claws and violent incantations.

Then he saw the scarlet mass of Ian Elgin's chest cavity; swollen utricles of black and blue around his neck. He heard the shriek of the rotary saw. The door to the darkroom opened. The man had silver hair, razor cut; a silver moustache, manicured; and a gold chain around his neck. He was fifty, Mansell calculated without understanding. A Mediterranean tan of constant care. Money. They stared at one another.

Jennifer stepped out into the hall, laughing. The sight of her husband destroyed this jovial display. "Nigel. What are you doing here? I thought you were staying. . . ."

"I live here." His voice was acutely low. His pale eyes that much paler. "Remember? And he doesn't. Get him out of here."

"I don't—"

"Now." Cold. His head tipped downward, eyes forever upon her.

The man fidgeted with his glossy hair. He touched his chain, and then her shoulder. "Jen. I must go, at any rate. I'll see you in class."

She escorted him to the door. Mansell retreated into the kitchen. At the sink, he turned on cold water. He searched his pockets for a cigarette. When he was dizzy from the smoke, he leaned over the basin and watched the water disappearing in swirls across endless fields of white porcelain.

IN THE CORNER OF THE FORENSIC LABORATORY, PARTITIONED OFF by plastic curtains, was an area reserved for the science of moulage, the casting and molding of impressions. The molds were made from plaster or paraffin, Plasticine or liquid latex, organics or dental materials, silicone rubber or molten sulfurs.

Chas du Toits pushed aside one curtain, and Mansell followed him into the cubicle. Upon a wooden table, highlighted by white floods, were four castings. Photos of the original impressions, taken outside the ladies' lounge at King George Station, were presented on easels behind the castings. A sketch of the drive and the plots of ground outside the lounge dangled from one of the chief inspector's hands, a cigarette cupped in the other.

Mansell ordered himself back into the present; last night was a dull ache trying desperately to capture his thoughts. Hurt was not an emotion he cared to acknowledge. He would push it aside and then, like an obsessive thief, it would sneak back again and the battle would begin anew.

"We were able to secure four complete shoe prints and an exceptional impression of the front left tire," du Toits was saying, steam rising from the cup in his hand. "Also a  complete set of fluorescent tire marks from the sidewalk. The drive was obscured by overlapping from other vehicles, but we still managed an exact wheelbase measurement. Not bad, if I do say so."

The molds were cast at the scene from white silicone rubber tinged with aluminum dust, a silver fingerprint powder. The aluminum dust brought out remarkable highlights on the surface of the impressions. The fluorescent tire marks taken from the concrete were produced by using ultraviolet light. The invisible prints absorbed the ultraviolet rays, thus transmitting fluorescent traces, which, if correctly photographed, produce remarkable details. Mansell was pleased with the results.

"The tire circumference is two hundred and five centimeters," du Toits continued. He handed Mansell a statistical printout. "One of those beleaguered compacts, I'm afraid. Wheelbase dimensions confirm this. The tire shows less than seven thousand kilometers of wear on it." He gestured at the casting. "There's a nail mark here, and two significant defects here and here."

Mansell ran a hand over the churned-up mound along the side of the cast. "We'll run it through the tread guide in the computer. With luck it was manufactured here in P.E.," he said. "All right. The maintenance man at the station reported that the garden plots under the windows were turned over on Wednesday afternoon, thirty-six hours before the murder. Can you improve on that?"

"Inspector, please." Du Toits feigned disappointment. "The westerly wind peaked at forty k.p.h. Thursday evening at five-ten. The impression shows no sign of drifting or eroding. True, the area is enclosed to a point, but there almost assuredly would have been indications of wind damage. Further, we had an hour's worth of light rain at six-thirty that evening. No evidence of rain damage either. Age of the impression, nine hours maximum."

"Very good, but it doesn't narrow it down enough." Mansell took notes as smoke rose from the nub of his cigarette, burning his eyes.

Du Toits raised a hand, saying, "But I can tell you that the fluorescent exhibits indicate to us that the vehicle was parked outside that window less than thirty minutes. The driver made a U-turn in the drive and returned the same way he'd arrived, from the west."

"You're an artist. And the shoe prints?"

"Ah, yes. The shoes." The forensic scientist offered two other castings, also silicone rubber with aluminum dust. "The impressions were made from patterned crepe soles. Luck, fickle creature that it is, Inspector, does at times ally itself with science. You see, crepe soles are like fingerprints. No two are exactly alike, even if they come from the same die. Shoe size, 10½-D."

"That has to eliminate Anthony Mabasu. His size can't—"

"Size 9-C." Du Toits sniffed unctuously. He cleared his throat. "We checked his file. I hope you don't mind."

"I'll control my irritation," replied Mansell. "There was also a partial on top of the locker. Salvageable?"

"If you please." Du Toits removed three photos from their respective easels. Photographs of dusty prints required oblique lighting, and the pattern in the crepe registered, Mansell thought, with remarkable clarity. Du Toits said, "We lifted the impression later using a rubber lifter, but I'm not pleased. The shoe is the same, however.

An exact match of the right print found outside. All well and good, except for one small problem."

"Explain."

"We couldn't find one other print from these same shoes inside the locker room itself. We checked the floors, the wooden benches, the tops of the other lockers, everywhere."

Does a killer remove his shoes before entering his arena? Mansell wondered as they left the cubicle, or does a thief have second thoughts?

"I'll take some of that tea, with your permission," he said. The pot was across the room, and he called over his shoulder. "Tell me about the rope."

"It's a pure nylon with traces of blue rayon running through it. A fine mesh, tightly woven. Extremely resistant and lightweight. Probably expensive. You wouldn't tie luggage onto the roof of your car with this stuff. Mountain climbing, more likely. The killer wore vinyl gloves, almost assuredly, but there's also trace evidence of human flesh other than the victim's."

"Any idea on the age of the rope, or prior use?"

"As far as prior use, I'd say none. As far as the age, I can't say about the manufacturing, but I can say that the rope hadn't been out of its wrapping more than a couple of days before the killing."

"Good. With luck, a recent purchase."

They stopped in front of a long narrow bench covered with sterile white paper. Evidence lined the table. Each item was appropriately packaged, string-tagged, and labeled. Du Toits picked up a paper bag sealed with tape.

"We found hair from three different people on the victim's sweater. One being the victim himself. We ran an SEM on the others," said du Toits. He raised an eyebrow dourly, and saw Mansell smiling. "A scanning electron microscopic, for the less learned."

"The toys of aging children."

Du Toits ignored the remark. "Two of the hairs were thirty-five centimeters long. Blood type A-positive, female. Black, coarse, and wavy. A minute degree of sun bleach. Protein analysis showed the hair belonged to a Europoid/Bantu."

"A coloured." In South Africa, individuals of mixed race, white and black primarily, were termed "coloured." "That narrows it down. And the other?"

"Short, twenty-five millimeters. Light brown, very fine. Four good samples with sheath cells bearing. Europoid. Male. Blood type O. A very dry scalp but no sun bleach at all. Curious."

In a climate where the sun shone nine out of every ten days, a trace of sun bleach was almost inevitable. "Curious indeed," said Mansell.

Du Toits gestured next to a transparent plastic bag. The fibers inside reminded Mansell of pubic hairs. "These were found on the victim's sweater, as well," said the forensic scientist. "The fibers are one hundred percent wool. Woven and dyed, a bit unevenly. It's a black-and-gray blend, and almost certainly from another sweater. Probably from his own closet."

"We're opening up Elgin's apartment today," Mansell interjected. "Have a team ready and we'll find out."

Mansell studied a sketch indicating the exact locations on the victim's sweater where the fibers and hairs were found. Then he studied the fiber again, but his mind wandered. His feet took him back to the teapot.

"Anything confirming on the victim's suit coat? The one from the sleeping room?"

"Fragments of his own sweater on the inside and traces of his own hair on the outside. A single hair, long and black, matching the ones found on his sweater. The coloured woman's."

"Good. And the used cot?"

"It seems that *used* is an appropriate word," chortled du Toits. "We found identifiable traces of semen, human hair, sweat, and other—how should I put it—other body fluids."

"Ian Elgin's?" asked Mansell.

"I'm afraid not." Du Toits shrugged. "But we do have a rare bird. A male with AB-negative blood. And I place the time of use at between midnight and one-thirty A.M. Friday morning."

"A very telling item, come."

Du Toits grimaced at the remark, and they moved on to a soft paper bag containing the blue-and-white bandana.

"We found traces of Elgin's blood on the bandana, true," said du Toits. "But not stains. Dried blood."

"Obtained when Wolffe used it to turn the victim's face."

"Perhaps. That, by the way, will be in my report."

"They'll probably give the bastard a citation," Mansell replied. "Anything else of note on the bandana?"

"Old bloodstains, a month or more. Blood type, A-negative. Male. Bantu. Any guesses?"

"The same as yours, I suspect." Mansell picked up a small pillbox.

58

It was tagged with blood type, securing date, officer's name, and the case number. He asked, "Anything of consequence from the bloodstains inside the locker, Chas?"

"Not much. Proved conclusively to be that of the victim. Also, that he'd been drinking heavily. Blood alcohol level measured two and a half times the legal definition of intoxication."

"Any indication that Elgin had had sex over the last twelve hours of his life?" Mansell was extemporizing—the chiffon scarf and a dinner companion with long black hair.

Du Toits shook his head. "He went out with a whimper, I'm afraid."

The scarf itself lay toward the end of the table wrapped loosely in white tissue paper. It was a rose-colored chiffon with delicate embroidery.

"Elegant, isn't it," said the chief inspector. "Traces?"

"Only hair," answered du Toits. "A black woman. A black woman with taste and money, I daresay."

Mansell stroked the sheer material. "Or," he said softly, "a companion with both."

The three coins found at the base of the locker were now inside a soft paper folder buffeted with cotton swabs.

"This will interest you, Inspector," remarked du Toits humbly. "Two identifiable fingerprints were lifted from these. One being the victim's. And a second set, the thumb and middle finger, belonging to one Anthony Mabasu. We cross-checked with Printmatrix in Research and the Bureau of Labor. Mabasu's prints were also lifted from the locker door itself and the wooden bench."

The bleak expression that swept across the chief inspector's face said far more than any words he might have used, and Chas du Toits took this as a sign.

He pressed on, saying, "There were no prints to be found around the broken window nor any on the top of the locker, but we did find adhesive tape around the outside of the glass. A match for the tape which you found in the dirt below the window. We found smudge marks on the sticky side of the tape that indicate the intruder wore gloves, vinyl or rubber."

"Could they be the same gloves as on the nylon rope?"

"Certainly, but it's impossible to say. Sorry. As for the rest of the print search, we lifted dozens of perfect ones from the scene, and we checked them all with Printmatrix." Du Toits handed Mansell a thick folder containing the slide negatives of all the prints seized that day. "And, with the exception of three, they would all appear to be accountable."

"Three? Elgin, Mabasu, and. . . ?"

"Does the name Thomas Horwood mean anything to you?"

"Our pot-smoking ticket agent."

Mansell dispatched two detectives with samples of the nylon rope and photos and a description of the chiffon scarf. Then he went upstairs to his own office to type out a daily report, yesterday's daily report.

Directly north of the police station on Main Street stood the Port Elizabeth City Hall. The 123-year-old structure was a masterpiece of colonial architecture. On September 11, 1977, three hours before dawn, an arsonist poured turpentine and gasoline through every office window on the first floor, and the ensuing conflagration proceeded to gut the city's most time-honored relic in less than ninety minutes.

The colonial front, the Victorian belfry, and marble-faced clocks were all wiped out. Only the Japanese bells, themselves forged of solid bronze, survived.

The citizens of Port Elizabeth hardly flinched. The arsonist was captured and quickly sentenced to thirty years in prison. Two weeks after the blaze, plans were laid to rebuild the landmark. The original plans were located in the city archives. International businesses contributed half the necessary funds. Reconstruction began. The English firm that first constructed the clock tower still possessed the original drawings, and they were again retained. Three years and R16 million later, the restoration was completed.

The courtyard fronting City Hall was a large mosaic of marble tiles and cut stone in the design of a mandala. Planter boxes, park benches, and antique gas lamps dotted the square in pleasant symmetry.

Nigel Mansell left the police station without finishing his report. He used the side entrance, took a left along Main, and strolled one block to the courtyard. Around the periphery of the street, native peddlers were setting up carts filled with handwoven baskets, fresh vegetables and fruit, hand-spun cloth, and carved figurines. A Xhosa boy played the flute on a park bench, his hat on the ground before him. Appreciating his fortitude as much as his talent, Mansell tossed a rand note in the hat.

At the far end of the square, Merriman Gosani and Joshua Brungle lounged on a bench beneath a small acacia.

"Nice place for a rendezvous," Joshua called out. "What's the occasion?"

"He's buying us breakfast," Merry interjected.

Mansell looked in Merry's direction and a grimace gave way to something akin to a smile. There was a saying in South Africa: "Keep the Kaffir in his place and the coolie out of the country." Years back, Mansell had made a mockery of the adage by promoting Merry from a uniformed beat cop to detective. In official circles, the elevation had been hailed as far-reaching. Two commendations, for extraordinary conduct, were received with less enthusiasm. In a private memo, Captain Terreblanche had referred to them as "perhaps a gilding of the lily." Mansell remembered the pleasure he had taken from putting a match to that memo.

"Wolffe's making his presence felt around the office. You'll have to see him about breakfast," he said, taking a seat. He closed his eyes to the heat of the morning sun. "What did Mabasu's work mates have for us, Joshua? Anything spicy?"

"He's having marital problems. His wife's been screwing around. At least Mabasu's convinced she's been screwing around. And he went so far as to stake out the sleep room in the ladies' lounge a couple of times."

"An amusing way to spend your lunch hour," quipped Merry.

"He's been driving his buddies up the wall about it. They also said that Mabasu has a short fuse, but that he's never mentioned being laid off at the docks. He's a hard worker. In general, a nice guy. Not the killer type according to these guys. He did mention to one of them that his lady had gone off to visit her sister. Her idea, not his, and he wasn't pleased about it. And they all said that Mabasu owns a blue-and-white scarf."

"It's his bandana," Mansell said. He handed out copies of the forensic report. They spent thirty minutes reviewing. Then he said, "Merry, anything significant yet from Research?"

"Elgin knew a lot of people in Johannesburg and Durban. A lot of them didn't think much of him. Both districts have started full-blown backup investigations. Cape Town, as well."

"Good."

"We've collared sixteen possibles here in town: eight convicted

61

felons with union ties, six agitators that Security's been watching, and two recent parolees with union-related offenses. It's not much. We're checking their stories now. I'm expecting reports from Jo'burg, Durban, and the Cape this afternoon. I'll follow up then."

"Something's bothering you." A bag of donuts next to the big detective lay undisturbed. "What?"

"Sylvia Mabasu. We haven't been able to locate her."

Mansell cocked his head. "Anthony Mabasu's wife?"

"She boarded a Sea Lanes bus at six-twenty, Thursday, the morning of the third. Her sister lives in Butterworth, in the Transkei. It's four hundred and ten kilometers one way. The bus arrived in Butterworth at seven-ten that night. Sylvia Mabasu wasn't on it."

"Settler's Way runs right through Butterworth. How many stops does the bus make along the way?"

"Nine," answered Merry. "And the bus route never leaves the highway. Her sister was waiting at the bus station. I checked an hour ago. Still no sign of her."

"Did you inform the Transkei police?"

"I had to, Nigel. They're working at it from their end."

"All right. Check with the bus driver—"

"I talked to him myself. Asshole. Said it's not his responsibility to keep track. Said he didn't notice that her goddamn luggage was still on board."

Joshua stood up, pacing suddenly. "Passengers?" he asked.

"There's not a passenger list. But I've got fifteen names."

It felt disturbingly ominous. Still, Mansell found himself theorizing. "We know she and Mabasu were in the middle of it. It's possible she needed time alone, and—"

"What? Without her luggage?" Merry cut in. "Her sister has a goddamn telephone. She wouldn't call?"

"We'll find her. Merry, if you have to take a car up to the Transkei, go ahead and do so," said the chief inspector. "Joshua, see what you can find out about that tire tread, will you? And let's bring in our uncooperative ticket agent first thing. Maybe a suspected murder charge will cool his obstinate mood a bit. I'll talk to him myself."

When the two detectives had gone, Mansell absorbed a full minute of sunshine. A purple-and-white bunting landed in the tree above him. He listened to a brief chorus, and then the bird set off again. Jennifer's face intruded behind closed eyelids, and Mansell stood up. His stomach ached. He plucked a chocolate donut from the forgotten bag, hoping the pain was hunger.

His footsteps led him across the railroad tracks in the direction of the waterfront and, conceivably, the last person to see Ian Elgin alive.

At 5:56 in the morning, as the cargo ship *ARVA II* approached the great port of New York and New Jersey, Captain Amil Aidoo ordered his machinist to cut power to a single aft engine. Near the Ambrose Light, at the tip of the Ambrose Channel, Aidoo relinquished command of his vessel to the harbor pilot.

Thirty-five minutes later, the 620-ton freighter, her bow raking and her bridge caked with rust, slipped through the passive waters of the Upper Bay into the calm of the Bay Ridge Channel. At the Bay Ridge Terminal a half mile further on, ARVA docked behind a 1,000-ton vessel called the *Falcon Express*.

Colonel Karl Brinker waited alongside. Hung over, he cradled hot coffee in two hands. Sunglasses shielded bloodshot eyes from the harsh glare of sunrise. Behind him, two loaded semis remained in quarantine at the inspection station.

Following the harbor pilot's departure, Dom Andrada and a female customs agent climbed the gangplank to *ARVA II*'s cluttered main deck. Over the protests of Captain Aidoo, the freighter's papers, though indisputably in order, were confiscated. Dom Andrada explained the nature of the delay to Aidoo, and the sailor's face dropped.

This was not the kind of news Aidoo had expected. Indeed, he knew the entire picture. And yes, he was even willing to make the dangerous rendezvous at sea, later. He was paid to know, well paid, but enough to face the quarantine of his ship? That was not part of the bargain.

"Yeah, yeah, I know what you're thinkin', mate," Dom Andrada said, seeing a look of insurrection overtaking the sailor's coal-black face. "Forget it. Leave port now, my friend, and you might as well hang a sign out that says 'Guilty as Charged.' Yeah? Listen. Do this instead. Give your crew a half day's leave. Make an issue out of it. We'll know more by noon, I'll guarantee it, okay? I'll even make a call or two. Listen, there's breakfast in the shed. You're welcome to it."

So calls were made, and breakfast was eaten, but still the morning passed begrudgingly. Finally, at 11:45, a federal agent arrived in a beige Chevy with two customs agents at his side. Karl Brinker had succumbed to brandy again, and his hand was nearly steady when the fed passed him a manila envelope containing his papers.

"We checked with the Liberian Foreign Ministry, Mr. Brinker." The agent sounded put out. Blood drained from Brinker's face. "I'd suggest you keep better track of your paperwork. It's going to cost you."

"Yeah, I . . . ."

"And?" urged Dom Andrada.

"And they have authorized transfer of your cargo to Grand Cess," answered the agent. "It's a little pisshead port along the south shore, I guess."

Brinker covered his nausea with a fit of laughter. He tried to speak, but Captain Aidoo intervened, saying, "Aye, a pisshead of a port it is, sir, but with the grace of above and a steady breeze at our backs I think we'll manage. Sorry for your inconvenience. Truly sorry."

Dom Andrada poured wine into plastic cups. He showered the woman customs agent with a smile. "Sorry we are, but as we say in Portugal, a glass of sweet wine mends all."

Outgoing pilotage was scheduled for 3:30 that afternoon. The rusted holds of *ARVA II* lay open and waiting.

At eleven in the morning, on a day better spent beside a warm fire or wrapped in a blanket with a warm female, Jan Koster traveled in his own private plane to the Mozambique capital of Maputo. The port city was the flip side of Johannesburg, sultry and feverish. A battered taxi shuttled Koster the twenty-two kilometers from the airport to the University of Baia de Maputo. The old English campus, abandoned eleven years before in favor of a modernized facility in the city, was now being rented by the East German consulate for fifty thousand dollars a year. At the railroad crossing opposite the old stadium, Koster paid the cabby in American money and walked the last kilometer to the campus.

Housed behind the heavy wrought-iron gates that guarded its sprawling forty-five acres were twenty thousand Cuban-trained black men. How they had settled upon that final figure, Koster was never completely certain. Twenty thousand seemed too many in his opinion, too few for Leistner's tastes.

His reasons for selecting Maputo as their base of operations were less vague. South Africans, being a suspicious people, tolerated their neighbors without the slightest thought of trusting them. Surveillance was a constant. Mozambique was an exception. Its relations with South Africa were governed by an accord of noninterference and cooperation. An uninspired way of saying, Koster thought, that the two hostiles had found it more productive to leave each other alone. This was the overriding reason for the choice. The other was distance; the targets lay to the west a scant four hundred kilometers. The campus, discovered three years before by Colonel Rolf Lamouline, the mercenary in charge of military operations at East Fields, was an unexpected bonus.

Lamouline's office was on the first floor of what had once been the administration building. The building was crafted from thick blocks of granite. The office was an odd mixture of Victorian wallpaper, metal furniture, land maps, and African memorabilia. Koster drew up when he saw the two photos on the wall behind Lamouline's desk.

"Take a look," the colonel said, chuckling. "Gifts from my ANC brothers."

The first was a barroom scene. A toast. Eight black men hoisting tall beer mugs in tribute to a friend. The friend was a bearded man and in his hands was a flimsy document upon which indecipherable writing could be detected. The photo was entitled "The Charter, 1912."

"The bearded one's Dupree, they tell me," Lamouline said. "Solomon Dupree, the founding father of our notorious African National Congress. According to legend, Dupree's brainstorm took root one blustery evening while he and several colleagues, lawyers of considerable optimism, I guess, were drinking rum and beer in the back room of a Cape Town speakeasy called the Blue Shebeen. Dupree, they say, scribbled their charter on the back of a paper napkin and they each signed the thing in black printer's ink.

"I wonder," Lamouline added, "if Mr. Dupree knew his organization would form the backbone of our charming band of desperadoes."

"I imagine there are quite a number of things about his organization that Mr. Dupree would have trouble recognizing in this day and age, Colonel."

"Like the fact that his pet project has become an arm of Soviet political strategy in South Africa? And I don't remember a thing in his charter about sabotaging police stations or government offices or power plants, do you?"

"But then I doubt Mr. Dupree knew much about mass arrests or detentions or bannings either. And if memory serves me, Colonel, in 1912 the Bolsheviks were too busy patronizing Lenin and Kerensky to care much about South Africa, and still a few years away from power," Koster replied, looking now at the other photo. This, a black-and-white print of poor quality, showed a round, dour face peering from behind the bars of a prison cell. "Mandela?"

"Yes. I'm supposed to be inspired."

"But you're not, right? This is all just for the money?"

"Don't be putting words into my mouth, now," answered the colonel, gesturing to one of the maps. "Why don't we talk business? Politics and patriotism make me nervous."

A plan for mobilization was finalized within the hour. It would be set in motion the following evening at ten o'clock when fifteen hundred men would depart the Baia de Maputo grounds. Each night thereafter, for fourteen nights, like groups would follow. Each man would carry with him official travel documents, passports, and temporary work permits for a site on the East Rand called East Fields Mining Corporation. The documents could not be challenged; Cecil Leistner had seen to that. The migration would not arouse suspicion; one-quarter of South Africa's labor pool came from outside the country, and migrant workers in the Transvaal were as common as cattle in the kraals.

Justice Minister Cecil Leistner sat across from the South African prime minister in a cozy drawing room on the third floor of the Union Building drinking tea and smoking Brazilian tobacco.

Like a loyal servant of his country, Leistner reiterated the worsening conditions: eleven killings in the last fifteen days in the Cape Province alone, a funeral riot in Port Elizabeth this morning, Cape Town in flames, another black policeman stoned in Soweto, the Indian population in Durban shouting for additional police surveillance.

An unrestricted, nationwide state of emergency had been mentioned twice in the last month. Leistner suggested it again. "It's a drastic measure, I'll admit that, but frankly, I'm at a loss for alternatives."

The prime minister frowned. Fingertips formed a steeple in front of pursed lips. "*Drastic* is a particularly accommodating adjective, Cecil. Twice in the last five years, and the results were hardly cause for celebration."

"The localized version has proved ineffective, Minister. Too many loopholes, you know that."

"Our opponents in the House will no doubt call it 'running scared.' It occurs to me that they might just have a point."

At last, the prime minister agreed to reassign a number of commando units in the Johannesburg area and in the Cape Province to more troublesome locales. He would leave the reassignment to his minister of justice. As for a renewed state of emergency, the prime minister reluctantly agreed that a voice vote should be called for at the next cabinet meeting, Tuesday.

Minister Leistner poured tea for them both. Small steps, he told himself. Small steps.

The ocean brought out the kid in Nigel Mansell.

As he ambled toward the waterfront, Algoa Bay shimmered off to his left. The tide ran high, gentle breakers lapping at golden sand. A score of sailboats skimmed over the water. Thousands of meters of colorful canvas wafted in a cool breeze. The weekend embraced the city of Port Elizabeth despite the funeral demonstrations igniting a township eight kilometers away.

Mansell had spent the last ninety minutes at the railroad station. The night shift was in its final hour. He'd spent the time circulating a photograph of Ian Elgin's dinner companion among station employees. The response was negative; therefore, Mansell thought, inconclusive. He left copies of the photo with the temporary command center. The crime scene was due for release later in the day, so Mansell spent another thirty minutes there reconstructing a dozen different vignettes that all ended with a man hanging in a clothes locker.

Now he stepped across the tracks onto the sandy fringe of South Africa's third largest harbor. Opposite the railroad station lay Charl Malan Quay, a man-made, twenty-two-acre wharf jutting straight out into the bay.

Along the south face of the quay were four vessel berths, container and cargo cranes, train dockings, and warehousing. The backup area was a checkerboard of concrete, steel, and sand: ground storage for containers, truck stops and loading bays, low-lying warehouses and cramped offices.

Mansell walked across a truck runway, through the main gate, and past a block of storage sheds until he came to a cluster of office buildings dwarfed by the very size of the quay.

A white picket fence and a small plot of grass fronted a single-story building that looked more like a cottage than an office. A planter box full of Hilton daisies decorated the front of a small porch. Two blushing brides, in full bloom, dangled beneath the soffit. These partially obscured a sign that read, AFFILIATED UNION OF DOCKERS, STEVEDORES, AND RAIL WORKERS—UNITED DOCK WORKERS ASSOCIATION OF SOUTH AFRICA.

Through an opened door, Mansell heard the pugnacious voice of SB Major Hymie Wolffe, and he pulled up short. A deep breath escaped his lungs. Hoping to rid himself of the sudden bad taste, he lit a cigarette. When disappointment and fury were mastered, he knocked.

A flimsy screen door opened into a long, narrow office. A dozen wooden desks filled a single room. The plant scheme continued from outside. A bleeding heart on one desk, African violets and orange aloe on another, a miniature date palm on the floor, and a Norfolk Island pine nearly touching the ceiling.

Waist-high railings partitioned the office by rank. Hardwood floors were accented by cotton throw rugs. Except for Wolffe and a woman who stood behind a desk at the back of the room, the office was empty.

"Excuse me, I'm looking for Delaney Blackford, please."

"She's occupied," reprimanded the Security Branch officer.

"Ah. Then you must be Mrs. Blackford. Excuse Major Wolffe's impropriety. I'm Chief Inspector Nigel Mansell, Criminal Investigation Bureau."

The woman followed his progress as Mansell stepped past a swinging gate. His calculations stopped at the mere glimpse of her face. Her features were a confluence of extremes: wide oval eyes, dark and inquisitive, a small straight nose, full lips that displayed a fixed pout. Her hair flowed in thick, long waves the hue of a moonless midnight. The color of her skin reminded him of a wheat field after a hard rain. Mansell paused, momentarily transfixed. She wore faded jeans and a silk blouse like a page out of a fashion magazine.

"I have almost no use for a single policeman, Inspector," she said. Her voice brushed him aside, and drew him near. Husky, direct, appealing. "Two are definitely intolerable. Forgive me."

"My forgiveness you have," answered Mansell. Her hands rested upon the knob of a walking stick. She was of average height, he thought, but the word could hardly be used to describe anything else about her. "However, as I'm certain the unflappable major has told you, we have a corpse in our basement. And you may have been the last person to see our corpse alive. At least, prior to his fateful excursion inside the train station. Ah, did you accompany Mr. Elgin into the train station, Mrs. Blackford?"

Delaney Blackford sidled from behind the desk. The limp was immediately apparent. Wolffe intervened, taking two steps toward Mansell. "When I have finished. Yes?" he said.

"Certainly an event worth waiting for." Mansell straddled the back of a hardback chair and opened a notebook.

Wolffe paced, saying, "Do sit down, Mrs. Blackford."

"I think better on my feet." She perched on the front edge of her desk, a view of them both at her disposal.

"Yes. Where were we? Your position with the Affiliated Union. You were explaining."

"I act as liaison between the union and the Harbour Association and the Chamber of Mines. I also act as chief legal counsel for the United Dock Workers."

"And that would be since when?"

"Since this is all in my file anyway, Major, should I throw in a white lie here and there to spice things up?"

"When did you meet Ian Elgin?"

"The AU hired Ian to handle negotiations between our union and the Harbour Association in 1986. Board consultant was the official title."

"Board consultant? Was that not a position that you had desired for yourself, Mrs. Blackford?"

"I can't deny that. But it wasn't expected."

"Wasn't it? I wonder. My information says that you were trying to line up support for the position. It must have been a disappointment."

"So I strangled the bastard."

"And aren't you now in line for that very position?"

Delaney fashioned a grin. "Only if the union wants a qualified replacement, Major."

"Yes, this begins to make some sense. And since you handled

all the legal ramifications for the union, you and Mr. Elgin were thrown together from the start, were you not?"

"In a manner of speaking."

Wolffe faced her, hands locked behind him. "And?"

"And?"

"And it worked. A relationship developed. Yes?"

She stared past Wolffe at Mansell. "Ian wasn't an easy person to work with, but I can't deny that we were effective."

"Effective?" Wolffe stepped into her line of vision. "He was a married man. Was it successful? His marriage, I mean?"

Delaney crossed her legs. Her discomfort appeared as a vague thread among steel fibers. Mansell detected the slightest shudder. She covered it, saying, "My field is law, Major Wolffe, not psychoanalysis."

"A guess then," said Wolffe.

"Ian spent less than a week out of every month at home. If he was homesick, he never mentioned it." On the surface, the reply was routinely delivered, with an almost calculated indifference, and it was this reservoir of self-control that fascinated the chief inspector.

"You dined the night before last at Dardano's restaurant," Wolffe continued. "You arrived in your own automobile. At what time was that, Mrs. Blackford?"

Delaney slid off the desk. She turned her back to them, filling a glass from a water pitcher. Her jeans revealed a narrow waist, slender hips. She said, "We've covered the restaurant scene, I believe, Major, and—"

"For the benefit of the inspector, then."

Nigel Mansell admired Delaney's walking stick as she moved toward him, favoring, as she did so, her right leg. The shaft was tooled zebrawood, the handle carved ivory in the shape of a horse's head. Delaney stopped within an arm's length of him.

"We met at the restaurant at eleven-fifteen Thursday night. The restaurant was my idea. I like to eat late. The meeting was Ian's. He was due in Johannesburg on Monday. The FMU is not having much success in its contract talks with the Chamber, as you may know. There's been talk of a strike."

"It's that serious?" asked Mansell curiously.

"Probably not."

"And the dockers were involved?" Wolffe asked.

"Not really. Our own negotiations are near arbitration." Delaney sought out the railing, leaning heavily against it. "No, this was a

70

favor. And he didn't seem particularly anxious to return to the big city."

Why? wondered Mansell.

"And your meeting lasted until closing time. Two A.M.," Wolffe interjected. He was putting hat and gloves on.

Delaney showered Mansell with feigned guilt. "I must have been having a wonderful time."

"For shame."

"The meeting wasn't altogether cordial according to your waitress and the maître d', was it, Mrs. Blackford?" Wolffe buttoned his overcoat. He glanced in Mansell's direction. "But they left together, according to the valet. Elgin's car remained in the parking lot overnight."

"He was drinking."

"Yes. Yes, you mentioned that," mused Wolffe. And then, patting the girth around his waist, he announced, "I have finished with you for now, Mrs. Blackford. I must insist, however, that you remain available. I'm certain we will meet again." Feigning amused satisfaction, he turned to Mansell. "Inspector, any time I can be of service. Good day."

Wolffe returned to his staff car. It was parked in a small lot adjacent to the Affiliated office. He stuffed himself behind the wheel. He reached for the radio microphone, and the patch to Security Branch headquarters was instantaneous.

"Lieutenant Rhoodie. Right away."

A minute passed before a high-pitched voice answered. "This is Rhoodie, sir. Sorry for the delay."

"Perhaps it's time we had a more personal chat with suspect number one, Lieutenant. Will you see to it, please?"

"Charges, sir?"

"For the moment, let's call it further questioning, shall we?" Wolffe chuckled, a nasal wheeze more than a laugh. "And what develops, develops."

"Yes, sir."

Mansell arose. The air felt lighter. He would use Wolffe's presence to his advantage. He gestured toward the copper teapot on the hot plate next to the date palm.

"I couldn't help but notice," he said. "May I be so bold?"

"Why don't you pour two while you're at it. Cream, no sugar."

"A disgusting man, Wolffe," he said over his shoulder. She appeared not to have heard. "I'd apologize except that might indicate responsibility. I'm afraid that Wolffe is his own creation."

"I might give some credit to our fear-and-loathing system." Delaney bent over the clustered bloom of a red lily, inhaling.

Mansell served. "The George lily. They're one of my favorites," he said, watching her face.

But Delaney didn't reply, returning, instead, to her desk. She sat down for the first time. The response satisfied the chief inspector.

"Do you normally work weekends?"

"Yes, sometimes."

Mansell drew up a swivel chair, but he stood behind it, asking, "Had he been drinking heavily? Elgin?"

"Yes and no. Ian was a cowardly drunk, you see. He talked too much. He tried too hard."

"You fought over dinner."

"I wouldn't call it fighting exactly. I'd been recommended for a promotion. Vice-president of the union's legal department. A position with some punch to it. Ian's board was dragging its feet on final approval. I wondered why." She toyed with a strand of magnificent black hair. Mansell watched slender fingers entwine and then smooth. "Ian was an interesting man, Inspector. On the one hand, suave and totally disarming. On the other, well . . . Some people instantly despised him. A reaction he found amusing. He had a child-like disposition. But I put up with it. I could do that for a while. You see, I was as driven as he was, I suppose. Out in front of me I could envision a clear path to where I wanted to go. Ian Elgin was right in the middle of that path. Sometimes we butted heads."

"We're talking careerwise?"

"Of course."

"You said 'was driven.' Past tense."

"Things change. So do people. No further comment."

"And your involvement with Elgin went how far?"

A thin smile creased her face, eyes drifted. "Do you mean was I fucking with him, Inspector? Maybe with his mind, but not his body."

Mansell found himself seated, his teacup empty. "Earlier you said Elgin wasn't anxious to return to Johannesburg. Tell me why."

"I don't know." Their eyes met, dueled, and Delaney broke away. "I didn't ask, Inspector."

72

Mansell watched her closely now across blank sheets of notepaper. "Okay. Where did you drop Elgin after dinner?"

"I dropped him at the railroad station," she answered after a time. "I parked at the near front entrance."

"You walked inside with him."

"No. I offered to, but he said no. So I helped him out."

"That was it? He walked inside."

"He hugged me, twice. I wasn't thrilled with his condition. He knew that." She sounded apologetic. "But he didn't use the main entrance. There's a door at the southwest corner of the building. I watched until he was inside. He seemed . . . sad, or maybe just tired. I don't know. But that is the last I saw of Ian Elgin, Inspector."

The chief inspector backed off. Set on the corner of Delaney's desk was a jade plant, and Mansell touched one of its succulent leaves. "And you went home from there?"

"No," she answered, watching him. "I came here."

"At what, two-thirty in the morning? You came here to work? That's dedication. You received clearance at the front gate, then?"

"It was two-forty. And no, I have my own gate key. I saw the night watchman at three-thirty or so. His name's Charlie Miles."

"I see."

"Not good, huh?"

"Well, it would have been nice if you'd been snuggled up in a warm bed next to your husband."

"Very cozy. Except there's no husband to snuggle up to," she replied. And then, instantly businesslike, added, "I wouldn't have killed Ian Elgin, Chief Inspector of Homicide Mansell. He was still useful to me."

"Then who would have, Mrs. Delaney Blackford, Chief Legal Counsel for the UDW? Who were Ian Elgin's enemies?"

The answers were cloaked in vagueness. In Delaney's words, Port Elizabeth acted as a sanctuary for Elgin. The union people liked the man, for obvious reasons. The mining faction avoided Port Elizabeth in favor of Jo'burg and Durban. The government faction ignored the port city in favor of Pretoria and Cape Town. She offered a few names. Some Mansell recognized, some he didn't.

"I'm curious about the board consultant's job," he said. "Wolffe indicated that you were a candidate. True?"

"I was certainly interested, yes. But I would hardly call myself a candidate. I didn't have much of a chance, really."

"Meaning?"

This was the one question Delaney had hoped to avoid. Too many complications. Still, she threw her head back, and said, "It was a matter of influence, really. When a particular person has the minister of justice writing letters of reference for him, a job in question is no longer a job in question. If you get my meaning."

"I think I do. Yes." A powerful recommendation, thought Mansell. A cigarette found its way from his pocket automatically. On his feet again, he leaned across the desk. "At two-forty Friday morning, after eating linguine and drinking wine with a beautiful woman, one of South Africa's most powerful union officials drops in on King George Station. He enters the terminal through a side entrance. He's not eager to return to his own bed here or to his own home in Johannesburg. He has no intention of meeting a train. He doesn't go to the Men's Club for a sauna. No. Instead, he struts into the black women's bathroom, walks into the sleep room, and hangs his suit jacket as neat as can be over the back of a chair. He drinks a can of soda. He waits. Why? For whom?"

Delaney stared into her teacup silently. Mansell slapped the desk, reared up, and straddled his chair. "Now, the man likes your company. He likes to drink in your company. He's made advances which you've rejected, but he still likes to drink in your company. He talks too much. He tries too hard. Why? To impress you? To hurt you? To secure your loyalty? I don't know. But I do know I need help. Help me. Why would he do that? Why would he be hanging out at the train station at three o'clock in the morning?"

This time she met his gaze with derision and dismissal. He tried one last time.

"I'm trying to find out who killed the man, Delaney."

"He liked making it with black women. Okay? He bragged about his inane conquests when he was drunk. To hurt me? To impress me? I don't know, either. But I think he had one down at the train station, if that's what you wanted to hear."

At the door, Mansell hesitated. He turned around slowly and faced her, but Delaney Blackford was already attending to a stack of papers. When she didn't respond, he opened the screen quietly and walked back to Main Street.

Someone parks a small car, probably a compact, beneath a window in the Port Elizabeth train station the night a murder is committed.

The front left tire implants an impression in a recently turned plot of ground. The impression is duplicated by bright young scientists in a forensic laboratory, and the casting is handed to a bright young detective, who is told to find out what kind of car it was, where the car came from, and who was driving it.

The bright young detective turns out to be Joshua Brungle. And chances are extremely good, Joshua figures, that the tire was manufactured right here in Port Elizabeth, or, failing that, up the road in Uitenhage. Unfortunately, the computer tells him that the tire doesn't fit anything listed in the *Tire Design Guide* or in *Who Built It and Where*. The computer also tells the detective that its file hasn't been updated for seven months.

Joshua began his quest for unanswered questions in the Industrial Park at Firestone of South Africa. Firestone was one of three U.S. rubber manufacturers in the area, and this, Joshua realized, was a tough time for Americans in Port Elizabeth, what with all the talk of disinvestment and sanctions. It was tough because the Americans here were all well fed, complacent folk who had never had it so good in terms of cheap servants, low prices, and good jobs, and giving all that up wasn't too appealing. It was a dilemma: loyalty to the current rage back home or loyalty to the good life here.

The dilemma was, often as not, reconciled at the expense of the police, and Joshua prepared himself for either indifference or rebuke as he entered the engineering department of Firestone that afternoon. He was expected. In short, he explained to a middle-aged technician with thick glasses and bad breath the complications that had arisen in a current murder investigation.

"Either your computer has the tread on file or else it doesn't," the technician answered with a sullen chill. "They're your rules, not ours. It's completely unethical if you ask me, but according to your police department's policy, we are required to share all tread designs with your research department. So be it. You have what we have. Why on earth bother me?"

"Because a man has lost his life at the hands of a murderer, that's why. Strangled until dead." Prepared for the response Joshua was; he nearly delighted in it. "And I'll tell you more, friend. The dead guy was a high-ranking labor official at that. Know what that means? That means we're calling it a matter of national security. That means that every policeman in the bloody country is sweating

75

his balls off trying to find out who strangled our very important labor official. It means that no white-collar flunky with a degree in condescension is going to stand here and say 'Why on earth bother me?' Understand? Now, I want a cross-check on this tread inside your wonderful computer banks within sixty seconds. Either that or I'll have Pretoria filing a noncompliance order against your wonderful firm by day's end. Your factory will be closed by nine tomorrow morning. And guess whose name will be at the top of my report, friend?"

The report proved negative. The technician went so far as to cross-check with Firestone's American and European plants. Same results.

The results proved equally unfulfilling at General Tire and Rubber and at Goodyear's Uitenhage plant. Joshua's earlier enthusiasm diminished.

He bought coffee and donuts at the Brickhouse Bakery. An uninspired drizzle muddied the windshield of his GM sedan, and he plodded into the next tier of inquiry, the car manufacturers.

He began at Volkswagen's Uitenhage plant. The ten-acre site had been the German company's first chance venture following its country's demise at the end of World War II. Its construction had been considered an act of desperation then, but Volkswagen now manufactured and assembled four different models at the plant. The dimensions of the Jetta matched those of the vehicle, but the tire pattern did not.

Joshua drove back to the city and the industrial complex enclosed by the V-shaped boundaries of Harrower Road and Settler's Way. The backbone of the complex, not unlike that of the River Rouge area of Detroit, rested on the shoulders of General Motors South Africa and Ford South Africa.

When Henry Ford invaded Africa sixty-seven years before, Port Elizabeth was a sleepy harbor community entirely dependent on wool. That year, seventy workers assembled fifteen hundred cars. Three years later, GM established an assembly plant that later developed into a full-service engine and auto manufacturing plant. Last year, Ford SA manufactured and assembled ninety-five hundred cars. And, Joshua thought, Port Elizabeth would never again be called "sleepy."

At Ford's Neave plant, Joshua received his first break.

The engineer was black. His accent told Joshua that he was a Xhosa.

"You're surprised," the engineer said as the computer digested a copy of the mysterious tire tread.

"At this point in the day I'm looking for a surprise, but you're not it." Black men in white collars were patently rare in South Africa. A dangerous trend, Joshua thought sarcastically. White-collar jobs called for educational parity. Another dangerous trend. The Americans amused themselves by flaunting dangerous trends. "A company man, are you?"

"Maternally and paternally. Trained and educated." The printout appeared. The engineer shrugged.

"Nothing," said Joshua.

"It's Japanese."

"Show me." Joshua gestured at the reams of paper.

"It's not in here. That was my feeling from the beginning. The treadlines are typically more parallel, a bit shallower, a bit more give." Joshua looked at him as if to say, "So?" The engineer added, "The Japanese market here is in rentals. The age of the tire confirms that. Less than seven thousand kilometers' worth of wear. Rentals are typically sold to the public later, by the rental company at auction."

Joshua approved of the man's thinking. He said, "Guess again."

"A Honda Civic. Maybe a Toyota Tercel."

Joshua worked the list through in his head as he drove. The airport, the harbor, the bus stations, and the train stations all rented cars. In South Africa, gas stations were licensed to deal in rentals as well. And then there were the individual agencies themselves. A long list, he thought.

Four kilometers ahead, the Campanile jabbed at the sky like a needle in the eye of a sleeping tiger. Joshua drove toward it.

"We have a witness who will swear that you were smoking pot outside the station that night. We also have sperm samples that place you at the scene of a murder the same night."

This holding cell contained no chairs, no table, and no day-old newspapers, just bright light and cold concrete. Thomas Horwood, the white ticket agent on duty the night Ian Elgin died, stood in the far corner, legs spread, arms crossed, face recalcitrant.

Nigel Mansell kept a cool distance. In this light, his pale eyes were gimlet lasers. He held up a copy of Anthony Mabasu's statement.

"I'll have your ass behind bars in five minutes, Thomas. I'll have your job in an hour," Mansell said, his voice rising. "I have a warrant to search your apartment, and I have a man standing by with orders to do just that. You've been using the ladies' lounge to hump your girl friend, Connie. You used it Friday morning. And guess what, tough guy? That makes you our number one suspect in the murder of Mr. Ian Elgin."

Mansell strode across the room. He banged on the cell door. Joshua materialized.

"Detective," snapped Mansell. "You'll do me the honor of booking this man on one count first-degree murder, and one count possession of illegal drugs."

Joshua powered through the doorway. He charged headlong at Thomas Horwood. "With pleasure, sir," he hissed.

Horwood broke down. He cowered in the corner, covering himself. "Wait. Please wait," he muttered. "They'll fire me, sure as hell. They'll fire me."

Mansell held Joshua back by the shoulder. "Is it time for a statement, Thomas?"

"Yes, sir. I'm sorry." He was whimpering, near tears. "I'll tell you what you want to know."

"Get on your feet and quit your bloody whining," Joshua spat.

Mansell led the detective out of the room. "Good show," he whispered. "Theatrical sort, aren't you?"

"Missed my calling."

For all that, the results proved inconclusive.

Thomas Horwood admitted being a pothead. He owned up to his nightly excursions outside the station for a joint or two. He confessed to the occasional use of cocaine, even admitted selling coke to station employees once or twice. Yes, he said, he was making it with Connie Hillock, the black ticket agent. And yes, they had used the ladies' sleep room Friday, just after midnight. Connie had worked it all out with Sylvia, the cleaning woman.

"Sylvia wasn't around that night," he said. "But we took our chances."

Horwood's temporary bout with timidity passed quickly. He didn't remember seeing Anthony Mabasu that night. He couldn't recall seeing anything unusual in the alleyway along the south side of the depot, certainly not an automobile parked in the dirt, and certainly no one climbing through the lounge window.

Mansell studied the witness's return to confidence through a haze of cigarette smoke. Horwood paced evenly, using his hands as he talked. "I was stoned, Inspector, sure, but not stupid. That I would've remembered, don't you think? I use the alley because it's usually deserted. If there's someone hanging around, I go someplace else. My own car, the parking lot, the docks. Someplace. I mean, I look around when I go out there."

"Still, you say you missed seeing Anthony Mabasu?"

"I screwed up, didn't I? Hey, it's a boring job. Inspector, you've got to believe me. You've got to."

"You screwed up all right, Thomas." Mansell glanced at the footnote written in red ink at the bottom of Horwood's file. A ticket agent with seven thousand rand in the bank. Hardly. "You really did."

Later, Mansell walked down Main Street thinking about Sylvia Mabasu and a chiffon scarf. It was 2:15 in the afternoon. He heard a radio shouting about increased terrorism in Namibia. A baby-blue sky had thrown off the threat of continued rain. Mansell was disappointed.

The street bustled with people. Peddlers, shoppers, tourists, business people. On the street, Mansell thought, everyone mingled. Walls created the walls. The open fish and vegetable market had no restrictions. A sign outside Holly's Ice Cream Parlor read WHITES ONLY—NET BLANKES. The laundromat offered two entrances: NET BLANKES and NET SWARTES—NET KLEURLINGE. A restaurant called The Dove—lobsters, spirits, and dancing: WHITES RACE GROUP ONLY.

Mansell bought sardines and hard rolls from a Xhosa woman with enormous eyes and a three-month-old baby on her back.

Cecil Leistner had reserved a suite on the tenth floor of the Broadstreet International Hotel in Johannesburg for his conversation with Lucas Ravele, the president of the Federation of Mineworkers Union. The hotel catered to all race groups and was thus free of any prominent government types. Privacy was one consideration, the amenities were another.

The two men sat in a steam room well into their second Boodles and tonic.

They discussed the recent soccer riot in Kimberley and the Conservatives' new hard line on the Group Areas issue. They debated over the recent visit, a week before, by the American secretary of state and further sanctions being considered by half of Europe.

Finally, Leistner broached the subject. "I've been meaning to call you, Lucas. About Ian Elgin. I know you two were close. I'm sorry. What a god-awful way to die."

"For a moment I'd almost forgotten," answered the thirty-six-year-old union potentate. "A waste of a good man. Has there been any progress?"

"Some, yes." Leistner finished his drink and stood up. "Shall we cool off?"

Private shower stalls led, in turn, to a four-man whirlpool on the balcony overlooking the golf course. Leistner submersed himself. Ravele replenished their drinks and sat in a lounge chair with a towel draped over his shoulders.

"Contract talks with the Chamber have reached an impasse, I'm told," Leistner said at last.

"An impasse? Hardly."

"Still, Ian will be difficult to replace, I imagine."

"No one will deny that, Minister," Ravele said uncomfortably, a drink nestled between his legs. "Ian negotiated straight from the hip, and we will continue the posture. We have little choice."

Cecil Leistner pulled his waterlogged frame to the edge of the pool. He filled the bowl of his pipe and carefully put a match to the tobacco.

"I must tell you, Lucas, that Ian's death was far more untimely than you might guess. I must also tell you that Ian had far more aggressive plans in mind for the FMU than he had yet disclosed to you. In less than three weeks, in fact, the FMU's entire membership will be a part of the largest workers' strike this country has ever known."

"Strike? What strike? I don't know what in the name of God you're talking—"

"You will," replied the minister of justice. The oration that followed lasted forty minutes. Throughout it, Leistner employed the tactics of attack and retreat. He would mention the undertaking on the East Rand, stress the magnitude of its scope, but withdraw before naming the mines involved. He would hint at the existence of East Fields without revealing its location. He would concentrate on the necessity of labor's role and its rewards without delving into the pitfalls. Wide-eyed and speechless, Lucas Ravele listened. Had such a notion come from anyone of lesser stature than Leistner, he would have stormed out of the place. That it came from Leistner at all made it more confounding still.

The minister concluded by saying, "And the FMU has been a part of it all along, Lucas."

"My union—"

"It was never your union," said Leistner, closing the circle. "But it can be. It can be."

"You're saying that Ian sanctioned this . . . this . . ."

"He did far more than sanction it, Lucas. His influence and leadership were vital to it. For now, in Jo'burg and Pretoria, your presence will suffice in Ian's stead. But in Port Elizabeth I face certain . . . shall we say 'inconveniences.'" Leistner toweled his forehead. He relit his pipe. "The situation in the Cape Province is festering. You know that, of course. In fact, the prime minister is considering imposing an unrestricted state of emergency quite soon now, nationwide. A bit of information, Lucas, that is just between us, please."

"Of course," Ravele replied. Shock waves swept the union official into a corner of confusion and indefinable intoxication.

"And a state of emergency can only serve to enhance, in the eyes of the world, the validity of the actions I have just proposed to you. Can you see that?"

"I can see that all hell will break loose if it does happen," Ravele answered. Growing understanding eclipsed the shock of a moment ago. "And you want me to replace Elgin down in Port Elizabeth with one of your own, don't you?"

"Temporarily, yes. Someone who can stand in well with both the FMU and the Affiliated Union people."

"That's a tall order, Minister. Though there is someone. She's well known in P.E. already, and particularly loyal, I might add. You may know her. Her name is Delaney Blackford."

The pendulum of surprise swung rapidly in Cecil Leistner's direction. Delaney? My God, he thought. Is it possible Ravele knows about that?

"I'm sure Mrs. Blackford would be ideal," he said evenly. "But I did have a candidate in mind, actually." Leistner set a final screw. "Call it a favor that will come back to you manifold when the situation becomes clearer to you."

"Most enticing, Minister. When and who?"

Contemplating the arrival of ARVA II, Leistner replied, "The first of the week if that's not rushing things too much."

"And for how long would you anticipate?"

"A month, I would think. Six weeks maximum," Leistner answered, knowing the man would be dead within two. "His name is de Villiers. Steven de Villiers. He's a lawyer from my department. I'll have a dossier sent to your office this afternoon."

Inside the Republic of Ciskei, the gentle hills seem blue from a distance. The rain smells of fresh fruit. Palm trees, orchids, grass huts, and emaciated cattle live side by side, an unnegotiated peace. The Ciskeians, Xhosas and Pondos mostly, prefer the bus to cars and their own feet to those of horses. Highway N2, or Settler's Way, passes through the heart of Ciskei on its journey along the coast.

Peddie was a small town, six or seven hundred permanent residents, but a major transportation crossroads for freight trains as well as buses. It was located at a midway point between the South African cities of Grahamstown and King William's Town.

Detective Merriman Gosani placed his phone call from the local police station, a single-story framed structure with tar-paper walls and a canvas roof. A plastic cuckoo clock, a Hong Kong product nailed to an exposed stud, read 4:30. The temperature was ten degrees cooler here than in Port Elizabeth.

Nigel Mansell was halfway out the station-house door when the desk sergeant hailed him. He took the call at the front desk.

"I have a passenger here who swears she saw Sylvia Mabasu get off the bus at the Peddie station," Merry told him. "She's an elderly lady. An invalid on her way to East London. She told me she likes to watch people."

"Ah. One of those."

"I think she's legitimate." Merry always took his superior literally.

"Good," Mansell replied. "Go ahead."

"And she says she's almost positive the Mabasu woman didn't return before the bus departed. Okay. It gets interesting here. The lady thinks she saw Sylvia Mabasu get into the front seat of a car driven by a white male. But the woman's back was turned toward her, she says, and the car was across the bus-station parking lot."

Mansell heard a high-pitched voice. He heard a train whistle, the squeal of brakes, and the rumble of a bus. "Did we get a written statement?" he asked.

"The lady gave me her name and address, but she'll only swear to the part about the Mabasu woman leaving the bus. She did say the car was small, a 'dinky thing' she called it, and yellow in color." Mansell waited in silence. Merry recognized a deep sigh. "I think I better stay up here, Nigel."

"Stay with it," Mansell agreed, and they rang off.

The desk sergeant passed Mansell a note that read "The D.P. wants to see you immediately." Mansell slipped the crumpled paper into his pocket and stepped into the street.

Detective Piet Richter didn't like his latest assignment. Stakeouts gave him too much time to think. Fancying himself a misplaced sociologist, he outlined each task like a social worker with a guilty conscience.

In South Africa, Richter mused over the incessant crackle of the police radio, the study of demographics is more than a statistical science; an enumerative art described it better.

"Yes," Richter whispered. "Yes, of course. An art form. How depraved."

In the modern community, he thought, such as Port Elizabeth, this artistic sleight-of-hand is accomplished through townships.

The white folk live in the town proper adjacent to the harbor and downtown. They live in houses built of stone and brick, on streets lined with eucalyptus, willows, and pine.

Greenbelts, Richter mused, provide a comfortable buffer between the whites and their coloured brethren further north. In Gelvandale, homes are adobe and brick. The streets are paved. Rosebushes flank the sidewalks. In Bethalsdorp, municipal housing and relief units are clumped side by side, and the grass is brown from a lack of city water.

The blacks are further north yet, but their townships are conveniently surrounded on three sides by the industrial park that lies between them and the city proper.

Anthony Mabasu was living proof of this convenience.

He lived in New Brighton, a shantytown eight kilometers from the train station. Paved streets ended outside of New Brighton, and arteries of dirt began. Old women and naked children gathered at communal water pumps to fill cans and buckets for the evening meal. Houses were fashioned of tin with corrugated roofs or of plywood with sheet-metal roofs—shades of gray, brown, and black. Electricity was a luxury, shared privies the rule of thumb. Laundry hung from clothes wires and trash piled roadside provided the only color. Coal smoke hung disconsolately in the air and, with every breath, festered in the lungs.

Detective Richter sat on the passenger side of a beat-up Volkswagen bug parked on a dead patch of tussock forty meters from the shack Mabasu and his wife shared with another family. He nibbled fish-and-chips and drank hot tea with lemon.

Directly ahead, a column of dust shadowed the approach of an onrushing vehicle. The car, a tan-and-white GM sedan, swept around the corner and rolled to a halt in the middle of the road. It was Security. Richter knew that without thinking. He was reaching for the police radio when he heard a shuffling sound outside the car. A shadow fell across the hood, and a fist flew through the opened window and slammed into his temple. Richter slumped into his seat.

Three men clambered out of the sedan. One climbed onto the hood of the car. The other two walked through a broken gate to Anthony Mabasu's front door.

Forty-five minutes later, Chief Inspector Nigel Mansell received a second summons to appear at the district prosecutor's office. Mansell had just finished typing his daily report and was deep in conference with Joshua Brungle. Their discussion centered upon a psychological profile of Martin Engels, the Men's Club attendant at the train station. The profile noted a strong tendency toward schizophrenic behavior, and a car was dispatched to deliver Mr. Engels for questioning.

Ten minutes later, Mansell tapped at the office door of J. Peter Hurst, the Thirty-second District's chief prosecutor, on the third floor of city hall. Inside, the office smelled of cigar smoke and furniture polish. Mansell's feet sank into thick ocher carpet. Armchairs of wood and velvet were strategically positioned around the room, and floor-to-ceiling windows looked out upon the courtyard. Center-stage was a desk of spit-polished mahogany.

Behind the desk sat Hurst, a moustachioed Afrikaner with a brick-red complexion, black-rimmed glasses, and a glowing Don Diego trapped between pursed lips. Captain Oliver Terreblanche occupied a chair to Hurst's left, and Mansell greeted him with a brief nod.

A second chair, at Hurst's right, was laden with Major Hymie Wolffe. Their acknowledgment reeked of two stray dogs meeting amid overflowing trash cans in a back alley. A bow-legged bulldog with folding jowls, and a high-strung setter with loose limbs.

"You're late, Inspector," snapped Hurst.

"Late, sir?"

"I should have heard from you yesterday, Mansell. Instead, I'm leaving messages for you today."

"My reports weren't delivered?" Mansell set a copy of today's daily on the edge of the desk. "I apologize."

"I received your report, such as it was." The air-conditioning tripped. A soft purr infiltrated the room, and smoke swirled uncertainly along the ceiling. "More importantly, Inspector, there's been an arrest. In the Elgin case."

A hand passed through Mansell's hair. Narrowed eyes sought out Captain Terreblanche. "This was done without my knowledge," he said.

"Of course it was done without your knowledge, Mansell." A nasal whistle accompanied the intrusion of Hymie Wolffe. "When the evidence is at hand, Security Branch does not consult with malingerers on its operations. I believe it was you who said it first: cooperation between offices is a mere courtesy. The tables turn, do they not? So while you've been in your office sipping Scotch and munching pastry, we've been occupied with the business of finding a killer."

The severity of the inspector's gaze brought Wolffe up short, and Mansell faced the prosecutor. "May I ask the details?"

"The accused is Anthony Mabasu. He was arrested approximately one hour ago at his home. A warrant issued by Judge-President Lehman of the Provincial Court was served upon arrest. The charge is second-degree murder subsequent to assault and robbery. The accused is being detained at Security headquarters in the Hall of Justice."

"Standard procedures," Mansell said following a deep sigh. He heard children's voices outside the window. A dog barked. "I'm more concerned about evidence, Prosecutor. Our office, for one, doesn't have sufficient evidence to convict Mabasu. Does Security Branch?"

"I believe they might."

"Then charges have been filed?"

The prosecutor relit his cigar. He peered upward. A brief silence ensued, and Captain Terreblanche cleared his throat. He said, "The Justice Ministry is asking that our office file charges, Nigel."

"The minister of justice. Ah. Without the cooperation of the arresting branch. I see. And can we discuss the evidence here, perhaps, before we walk into a court of law and fall flat on our faces?"

"Complete documentation," Wolffe interjected, "will be presented at the preliminary hearing on Monday. You see, this case no longer belongs to CIB, Mansell."

Out of the corner of his eye, Mansell noticed the CIB commander stiffen in his chair.

"I think I've heard enough sparring, gentlemen," Terreblanche said. "If you've got something worth showing, Major Wolffe, I suggest you do so. You're wasting my time, and I don't imagine our cohorts in Pretoria would appreciate your show of animosity."

"If you insist." Wolffe labored to a standing position. "The accused had not one, but two motives. His wife was having an affair. Mabasu knew that. He sent his wife off to see her sister in Transkei the day before the murder. She never made it. Coincidence? Infidelity is a particularly strong motive amongst the Bantu. Even our esteemed chief inspector would admit that."

"Mabasu suspected she was seeing Elgin or just someone?" countered Mansell. "There is a difference."

"It may be that Sylvia Mabasu wasn't seeing Elgin," the prosecutor interjected. "But we know that Mabasu suspected her. The effect is the same."

"Nigel, your report here," said Terreblanche, holding up Mansell's daily, "says that Elgin did have some type of liaison going on at the station. Perhaps with a black woman."

"Suspected, not proved."

"But it still supports the motive," said Wolffe, pacing now with hands clasped behind his back. "Motive number two. Not only does Mabasu suspect that Elgin is screwing his wife, he also blames Elgin for his release from the docks and for the denial of his appeal. The effect is like throwing water on a grease fire."

"Pure conjecture."

"The accused makes two trips to the locker room that night. First, the reconnaissance run before his shift. The lady at the soda fountain sees him, notices that he's agitated, sweating. Then comes the fateful trip during his break. He knows no one is filling in for his wife, that the lounge is empty. He goes inside with the rope beneath his jacket. Elgin is there. Drunk, waiting for his rendezvous. His coat is already in the sleep room. He's pacing, trying to work off some of the booze. The girl, whoever she is, is late. Mabasu probably expects Elgin to be in the sleep room, so he's surprised when he finds him in the aisle between the lockers. Mabasu panics. He strikes Elgin from behind. Elgin staggers and turns. He sees Mabasu's face. This time Mabasu hits him square, and Elgin goes under. The rest we all know." Wolffe circled the office, his hands working as he talked. "Then, the fabrication. Mabasu claims to be the first person on the scene. That's easy. But then he starts to make mistakes. He says that he ran straight for the information booth, that he didn't touch a thing. Now we know that his prints were all over the locker door—"

"An instinctive maneuver considering the circumstances."

"And we know that his prints were on the money at the base of the locker. Money from the victim's pocket."

"He was scared. Also broke. He saw the coins on the floor. He picked them up, realized his mistake, and then set them back down. Those aren't criminal behaviors. Those are human behaviors."

"What I believe happened was this. After he hung Elgin's body in the locker, Mabasu reached frantically into his pockets, scrambling for anything that felt like money. When he pulled his hand out, three coins fell on the floor. Either he didn't notice, or he panicked. But there they remained. He also left his bandana behind. Why? Perhaps panic again. Perhaps the confusion of the moment. Or perhaps he figured the victim's blood was on it, and he left it on purpose. He did, after all, deny even owning such a bandana."

Mansell grunted, a half laugh. "Two official reports," he said, facing the prosecutor, "mine and Forensic Chief du Toits, point out that not only did Major Wolffe disturb and defile state's evidence by handling the bandana before it was documented and tested, and not only did he tamper with the victim before proper procedures were followed, but it was Wolffe who wiped blood onto the bandana. Dried blood, not the stain of fresh blood. Brilliant police work. I'm sure some smart defense counsel will have a field day with that one."

Hurst held up a hand. He blew smoke from the corner of his mouth. Producing a folder from his desk drawer, he said, "And you, Major Wolffe, and your associate, Lieutenant Rhoodie, have offered statements indicating the stains on the bandana were a result of Mabasu's efforts to remove dried blood from his own hands."

"A pack of lies," said Mansell calmly. "Fiction. Cheap fiction. I'll read it when it comes out in paperback."

"The point, Inspector," said Hurst, "is that we cannot go into court until some meeting of minds occurs on the matter. Otherwise, we have a relatively strong case."

"Someone entered the ladies' lounge through a window sometime during that night. We've narrowed down the type of vehicle. We have footprints. We know it wasn't Mabasu. I think before we take Mabasu to court on circumstantial evidence we should attempt to find out who it was. Another coincidence? I doubt it."

"I believe," said Wolffe, "your very own Chas du Toits indicated that the break-in could have happened anywhere between six the previous evening and four that morning."

"Within the time frame of the murder. Exactly my point, thank you," replied Mansell. "We know Elgin collected a lot of enemies over the years. We know a lot of people will benefit from his death, and we're just starting to put names to some of these people. We have two potential suspects from the train station. We know Elgin had contact with several other people that night. There's the woman, Mrs. Blackford. She and Elgin dined together. She drove Elgin to the station. She—"

"But she didn't have these in her possession," Prosecutor Hurst interjected coolly. He unlocked the bottom drawer of his desk. "These were found in a shallow crawl space beneath Anthony Mabasu's house when Major Wolffe's men searched the premises tonight. Both items have been positively identified as belonging to our victim, Ian Elgin."

Hurst held up a plastic bag, tagged but not yet filed, Mansell noticed. Inside was an Accutron wristwatch with a gold stretch band and a gold ring set with a diamond the size of a sweet pea.

At the Bay Ridge Terminal in Brooklyn, New York, a harbor pilot boarded *ARVA II* dockside. He took his station on the bridge deck. A customs agent returned Captain Aidoo's papers, and at 3:05 New York time, the 620-ton freighter received harbor clearance. Lieutenant Colonel Karl Simon Brinker passed Aidoo two bottles of Portuguese wine. Anchors were raised.

Forty minutes later, her holds loaded with 253 crates of near battle-ready weapons valued at two million dollars, the vessel cleared Ambrose Channel. At the Ambrose Light the pilot departed. Left to his own devices, Captain Aidoo steered his ship in an eastwardly direction along the fortieth parallel intent on reaching international waters by midnight.

A summer storm set their time schedule back twenty minutes, but by the time ARVA cleared the international boundaries two hundred miles from New York, stars were peeking through narrow avenues in the clouds. A slice of silver moon revealed itself off the bow. Exactly one hour later, a tiny blip appeared on the radar screen.

The two vessels converged, exchanging coded messages until visual contact was made. ARVA's counterpart proved to be a small frigate flying a Turkish flag but under contract to a Czech exporting firm.

The purpose of the rendezvous was the transfer of a single passenger. Captain Aidoo knew the man as Andrew Van der Merve. According to his passport, which Aidoo had been required to inspect on their first trip together six years past, Van der Merve was born and raised in the Orange Free State in South Africa. His travel papers and passport listed his occupation as chief purchasing agent for the East Fields Mining Corporation; home office, Johannesburg. Tactfully, Captain Aidoo had never questioned the information.

Rendezvous was accomplished at 1:58 in the morning. The transfer was made, the frigate departed, and four powerful diesels and the currents of the Gulf Stream drove the freighter out across the Atlantic. Its only stopover would be a refueling station in Freetown, Sierra Leone, the first leg of a ten-day voyage.

Following the meeting that afternoon in his office, District Prosecutor Peter Hurst placed a long-distance phone call to a man to whom he owed a certain allegiance. In recent months, the man had exerted considerable influence on Hurst's behalf, and, until Ian Elgin's murder, had asked nothing in return. Now he was asking to be kept "abreast" of the investigation's progress. Hurst knew there was more to it than that, but the man had earned his payback, and the prosecutor knew the importance of playing by the rules.

The connection was made, and a voice more like a whisper said, "This is Martin Montana."

"Things, I'm afraid, are moving a bit faster than we anticipated, Mr. Montana." Hurst rendered his report in brief, crisp terms, and then concluded by saying, "With Elgin's watch and ring, the evidence is just too strong not to act upon."

The man named Montana was more than a little disturbed by the district prosecutor's news. Disturbed enough, in fact, to drive eighty-five kilometers to a municipal airport in Witbank on the East Rand where his own Cessna 164 was docked. Within an hour he was airborne, heading south by southwest, and, left to his own imagination, spent the better part of the trip anticipating the actions of a certain chief homicide inspector.

The road was bathed in darkness except for gas lanterns and coal fires. A tractor roamed dirt paths collecting night soil and trash.

Mansell saw the VW bug on the side of the road with a dozen natives huddled around it. The car was awash in a circle of gas light. He toyed with the idea of throwing the portable flasher onto the roof of his car, but thought better of it. There was no reason for theatrics, he told himself.

Mansell held up his badge as he approached. A corridor opened. Relief swept over him when he saw a woman supporting Richter's head against the front seat, while another held a damp cloth over his temple and eyes. He was coming to in stages.

"He's a police officer," Mansell announced.

"No shit," said a tall, muscular black man. His voice was throaty, challenging, curious. "We knew that. What the hell is he doing here?"

"Doing his job." The threat diminished. Had it ever existed? Mansell wondered. Always and never.

"Not too well by the looks of it," the man countered. "Where's Anthony?"

"We fucked up," answered Mansell. "Security's detained him."

"Fucked up is right. Shit."

Detained was a word vile among South Africans, all South Africans; an understatement that led, thought Mansell, in a hundred directions, all bad. A trapdoor. He regretted its use.

Ten minutes later, he dropped Detective Richter at the local hospital's outpatient clinic on La Roche.

90

At his office, other realities intruded: sleep, home, an empty couch. He sat in a state of dread. He cracked the window, fought the urge to smoke. The words *It's over* resounded in his head like a dull bass drum. A heavy hand on the receiver of the telephone; twice he tried dialing his home number. Anger: the pill that cursed weakness, the tonic that cured failure. Anger prevented it both times.

In a filing cabinet, in a bottom drawer behind alphabetized records, was a blue velvet bag. Inside the bag was a bottle of expensive whiskey, a birthday present from an April gone by. Two ounces didn't faze him. Maybe Wolffe was right, he thought. Maybe law and order were only effective if quickly dispensed. Maybe the example set was more important than the truth uncovered. A high union official is killed in a place of disrepute. Could a bathroom be called a place of disrepute? he wondered. Still, an untruth. Television material. Late-night television material, quietly censored, quickly forgotten. Fuck you, Major. That's your game, your rules. I'll make up my own, if you don't mind. And even if you do.

He drank a third shot, and a fourth. He dozed. Slowly, sleep exorcised him. But the face last envisioned belonged not to Jennifer, as he had expected. It belonged, instead, to a mysterious union official with endless waves of black hair, oval eyes, and a walking stick.

Sylvia Mabasu's body was found wrapped in a tarp at the bottom of an overgrown glen a thousand meters from the Peddie bus station. Her eyes were opened wide, expressing surprise and helplessness, but her mouth was contorted with pain.

An Allenfield-FM helicopter transported the Port Elizabeth chief homicide inspector to the scene. The body had already been disturbed slightly, but the crime scene remained intact, barricaded from the top of the mountain down to the floor of the valley.

The nylon rope wrapped tight around the victim's neck looked eerily familiar. Blood vessels, popped purple and blue, glistened like quartzite around dark brown eyes. *Bastard. Animal.* Mansell talked himself into a state of calm.

The Ciskeian Police Department was not staffed with a medical examiner. The nearest hospital was located eighty kilometers away. Mansell did the preliminary examination himself. A local doctor assisted.

The body was past cooling. The initial tinge of decomposition hovered over it. Rigor mortis had come and gone. Time of death, the doctor estimated, was sixty hours before. Mansell made notes. There was bluish lividity of the mucous membranes, and the lips were a pale steely hue. A trace of froth still lingered about the mouth. They stood in a cool valley shaded by evergreens and oak. Ground cover and wild grass sweated away the last drops of morning dew.

The groove in the victim's neck, in depth and width, resembled that in Ian Elgin's. The neck and jaw were scored with abrasions and contusions. Occlusion had occurred about the greater vessels of the neck, cutting off the supply of blood to the brain. She died quickly, thought Mansell with some relief, noting the discoloration. Both Mansell and the doctor fixed the cause of death as asphyxia due to strangulation.

Merry and the local police combed the area from the scene all the way back to the bus station. A single dirt road wound down from the station into the valley, and then followed a stream southward. The body had been discovered thirty meters from the road. Since July third, the day of Sylvia Mabasu's disappearance, two rain showers had passed over the region. One, the night before last, had been a downpour. They found no identifiable footprints or tire tracks.

The tarp, heavily stained with machine oil and grease, was identified as one missing from the bus station's repair shop. The foreman and three mechanics were thoroughly questioned. When the tarp had disappeared could not be determined, though it was obvious. The repair shop was closed and locked on weekends, unless an emergency arose. None had.

Sylvia Mabasu was not known in Peddie nor in Ciskei, as far as the police could determine. She carried R15 and some change in a purse found with the body. The contents of the purse had not, apparently, been disturbed. The money was still inside a leather change pouch. A gold wedding band set with a pink tourmaline, Sylvia Mabasu's most treasured possession and worth considerably more than the R15 in her purse, was still on the third finger of her left hand. Robbery was not considered a motive.

The Ciskeian doctor thoroughly examined the victim to determine if she had been subjected to any type of sexual abuse. Physical evidence was completely absent. Except for the neck and face, the body was void of any signs of bruises, scratches, or wounds. The victim's clothes were damp, though still clean and pressed, considering. The state of the clothes led Mansell to believe that the body had been carried, not dragged, from the road to its resting place. A statement on the size of the killer.

There were limited signs of a struggle.

The tips of the fingers were swollen. Two fingernails on the right hand were broken off. Mansell examined the fingernail scrapings on both hands for traces of blood, hair, or human tissue. What he found instead were traces of a dark blue material, plastic or rubber, beneath the nails of the index and ring fingers on the left hand.

Attendants laid the body on the stretcher, and Mansell gazed down at Sylvia Mabasu. She was a fair-sized woman, 170 centimeters, he estimated. She displayed a muscle development that came with physical labor. A statuesqueness remained even with death.

Blood oozed from the bottoms of Anthony Mabasu's swollen feet. The hard bricks on which he'd been standing for the past sixteen hours were caked now with thick layers of dark brown.

The interrogation chamber was located on the tenth floor of the Hall of Justice. It was bedroom-sized with padded walls, a card table, folding chairs, and bare bulbs.

Three Security men paced about the cell. A fifth session began with old questions newly phrased. Security never expected resilience or strength from their Bantu detainees. They were becoming impatient. Pretoria was clamoring for a confession.

A first officer, a spare, muscular corporal with a heavy beard and a forest of nostril hair, forced Mabasu's jaws open. A second officer, with red armbands and sergeant's stripes, poured a dark liquid into his mouth. Mabasu gagged, swallowed, and coughed. The liquid was chifir, a Finnish creation carried by Dutch explorers on extended sea voyages, and introduced to the African continent three centuries before. Chifir was a tea concentrated twenty times over. A Finnish miner would work fifteen hours straight on four ounces of chifir. A Dutch sailor would stand the watch for an entire night on two.

A Zulu prisoner, standing on shards of fire brick in pools of his own blood, two-hundred-and-fifty-watt lights glaring in his eyes, and kidneys bruised by bamboo staves, would remain conscious if not coherent for thirty hours on a quart.

The session started. Anthony Mabasu's answers remained consistent.

"Was Ian Elgin waiting in the sleep room when you came into the lounge, or was he sitting on one of the locker benches drinking a pop?"

"No, boss, it wasn't like that. His body was chucked inside one of the lockers by then." Mabasu's arms were numb except for his fingertips. "Sorry, boss, he was dead by then."

"Where did you steal the nylon rope from, Kaffir boy? The rope, Anthony, where did it come from?"

Mabasu shook his head, twice, in slow motion. A bamboo baton slashed across his abdominal muscles.

Veins popped from the thick neck of the interrogator. This was Major Hymie Wolffe's forte. "How much money was Mr. Elgin carrying in his pockets, boy?" Wolffe hissed. "How much money was in his wallet? Was it worth a man's life, boy? Was it?"

"No, I—"

"No, it's never enough, is it?" Wolffe brought his baton near the prisoner's groin and jabbed. Mabasu sucked air and groaned.

"We have your neckerchief, Anthony. Your bandana. Do you want it back now? The blood on it belongs to the man you killed."

"No. I'm sorry."

Wolffe drew out a piece of paper from his breast pocket. He held it under Mabasu's nose, shaking it rhythmically. The quaking sound reminded Mabasu of the sheet-metal roof on his house when the wind shook it at night.

The sergeant snickered. "Tell him. Tell him about his wife," he said.

"Yes," said Mabasu. A baton thwacked the veins behind his knees. He coughed red tea out of the corners of his mouth.

"Not yet," whispered the interrogator. "I think not quite yet."

Purposely, the watch and ring had been withheld from the interrogation until this session. Wolffe withdrew the paper, gestured toward the table, and the corporal retrieved a plastic bag.

Wolffe brought the watch into the light. He dangled it in the prisoner's face. "The crawl space was a good hiding place, Kaffir, but not too original." The ring dropped onto Wolffe's stubby little finger. Mabasu's eyes widened. "We found the ring and the watch in your house, Anthony. Under the floor. How do you think a jury will react to that?"

Mabasu shook his head. He opened his mouth. His voice chimed like the sound of glass breaking in the distance. "They're not mine. Believe me. They're not mine."

The guards laughed. Wolffe stripped away his blue uniform shirt, exposing a sleeveless undershirt. His face glistened with sweat. His knee entered Mabasu's groin with enough force to raise him off the bricks. Mabasu's scream caromed off the walls, and his body fell limp against the rope. A diminuendo of soft yelping followed.

Chifir was readministered.

Mabasu shuddered involuntarily. His head snapped back. His eyelids parted a mere fraction. He felt Wolffe's presence behind him.

"Now, that's a good ol' boy," Wolffe said.

Mabasu felt the tip of the baton dance across his shoulder blades. Muscles constricted. He braced for the assault, but the baton withdrew. A piece of paper floated cloudlike before him. It was filled with handwritten words, but Mabasu's vision was too blurred to see them.

"Your dismissal from the union. Remember, Anthony? Mr. Ian Elgin was the one who got your ass fired from your dock job."

Wolffe used lies the way a woodworker uses a lathe. The baton and the paper added italics and boldface. "And the job you had now belongs to a twenty-two-year-old white Afrikaner. Your marriage is on the rocks. Elgin, the lousy bastard, was doing it to your wife. You knew it. We know how you felt, Anthony. We do. Hell, boy, you felt helpless. We'd all feel helpless under those circumstances. We understand."

The Ciskeian police were more than willing to release the body to Mansell's custody. Violent crime in this Bantu republic was normally a product of wrath or robbery. A drunken husband bludgeons a lazy wife because his prize chicken has been used for dinner. A horse thief is hung from a tree with his own belt. A prostitute makes fun of a drunken client's impotency, and he silences her with a pair of nylon stockings. Repentance is almost always forthcoming.

Mansell charged the local police with the task of running down every compact car within a hundred kilometers of the scene, of photographing tire treads, of questioning owners. Yellow cars should be given priority, he told them. It was an arduous task, but not overwhelming. Cars were few in Ciskei. Most were incapacitated and gathering rust.

The employees of the bus station would be questioned again. Other potential witnesses as well, but this was a second task for the local police. They knew their own people better than Mansell did, and he was not optimistic that anything concrete would come of it.

The helicopter dropped them at the Fleming Street landing pad, one block from the Port Elizabeth police house. An ambulance drove the body to the station, where Steenkamp in Pathology and Chas du Toits in Forensic were awaiting it.

Together, Mansell and Merry walked across the pad to the stairwell that took them below the overpass. The air was thick and dry, redolent of exhaust fumes and burning rubber. Two teenagers were tossing coins against a cement pillar. A portable radio shook with heavy metal.

Mansell felt a clamminess beneath his shirt. What, he wondered, had Peddie smelled of? He remembered a calmness in the air, cool, pleasantly humid—a startling contrast to the winds along the coast. He remembered the stiffness of the people, surely the result of their fearful discomfort in his presence and the presence of violent death.

He remembered a bramble of raspberry bushes and the yellowwood trees. But the smell?

Anthony Mabasu had to be told, he thought.

Did Anthony Mabasu know already?

"**T**his is a statement from your wife, Anthony," said Wolffe. Mabasu strained, but it was useless trying to focus. "Shall I read it?"

Mabasu moved his head. "No," he uttered. "No."

The paper fluttered to the floor. Mabasu watched it settle.

"She admits her affair with Ian Elgin," Wolffe announced. "They used the sleep room as their bordello, Anthony. The cots. The floor. She admits craving it. She admits. . . . Do you want to know what she liked best, Anthony?"

"Tell him." The sergeant's voice cracked with pleasure. "Tell us all."

Mabasu's eyes brimmed with tears, tears that spilled down the hollows of his cheeks. The eyes closed. The taste of salt touched parched lips.

Wolffe retrieved a water bottle from the table. He moved close. "I don't blame you," he whispered. "We don't blame you one bit, Anthony. God, I respect you, boy. I cheer you. I would have killed the filthy bastard myself. If a man ever deserved to die. . . . A jury will be on your side, Anthony. A jury will have sympathy. My report will be sympathetic."

Wolffe pressed the bottle to Mabasu's lips. The water spilled, dripping from his chin to his chest, and finally to the floor. The chifir lost its potency. Mabasu's head bobbed against his chest, and he lost consciousness.

Joshua Brungle emerged from the Hertz rent-a-car agency on Heugh Avenue, just north of the airport, at 12:21 in the afternoon. From the south, a blustery wind slashed over acres of willow thickets and gum-tree groves. Feather clouds curled and looped beneath a stoic orange sun.

Disheveled but enthusiastic, Joshua piled into his GM sedan. He rewarded himself with a blast from the heater. His search had, at last, paid dividends.

The tire was a special design of Michelin radials, as of this year standard equipment on all new Honda Civics imported into South Africa. Thus, their absence from the *Tire Design Guide*, Joshua thought. He pulled out of the parking lot and headed east on Heugh. By the time he was on M9 headed for Settler's Way, he'd been patched into Nigel Mansell's office.

"The car can be purchased by consumers on special order," Joshua said. "But according to the general manager at Hertz, seventy-five percent of the Civics in P.E. are rentals, ninety-five percent of those less than a year old. Most of the Civics go on the auction block after thirty-five thousand kilometers."

"We'll assume it's a current model to begin with."

"Agreed," said Joshua. "The manager said he'd send us all the records of Hondas rented from his five agencies in P.E. and Uitenhage over the last three months by five tonight."

"Let's concentrate on the last thirty days," Mansell said. "Do the rest of the rental companies in town carry Hondas as well?"

"Not the big ones, but the independents carry whatever they can get. Honda's a popular model, apparently."

"It's a start." Mansell's voice sounded metallic, fatigued.

"The rest is footwork."

"And some luck. We might be looking for a yellow exterior," Mansell explained.

"We'll find it," Joshua said. "Hey, listen, I'm sorry as hell about Sylvia Mabasu, Nigel."

"She was a fine-looking woman. She deserved better." Christ, Mansell thought. The perfect epitaph; perfectly trite, perfectly meaningless.

"Have you heard anything from Richter?" Joshua asked. "Is he all right?"

"He'll live. They patched him up and sent him home. I didn't think he needed the time off so I sent him out with the team looking for the source of our nylon rope and the chiffon scarf."

"Slave driver."

"We'll congregate here at six," Mansell added. "I'm on my way to the Hall."

The Hall of Justice was located on Chapel Avenue across from the Visitor's Bureau and the public library. It housed the Crime Research Bureau and the judicial chambers of the appellate and provincial courts of the eastern province. The district office of the Security Branch of the South African Police was also headquartered in the Hall.

Nigel Mansell tried imagining the perfect day: the roses blooming, a gentle breeze off Algoa Bay, a warm sun slow-dancing in a cool, blue sky. He tried to imagine walking to Security headquarters on a day like that. On a day when his mood was cheerful and airy. It didn't matter. Today, his mood could best be described as black. Today, the wind was sharp and chilling, and the roses wouldn't bloom again for months. So he drove instead. He parked in a tow-away zone out front.

The Hall of Justice was ten stories of smoked glass and chrome. Rectangularly boring, thought the chief inspector. Security Branch occupied the eighth, ninth, and tenth floors, while the seventh floor was vacant.

Revolving doors led to a cold reception room with gray tiles and tubular fixtures. A private elevator bank serviced the top three floors. A uniformed guard checked his I.D. Outside the elevator on the eighth floor, Mansell passed through mandatory metal detectors.

Again his I.D. was scrutinized, but this time the sergeant at arms looked uncertain. "I'm sorry, Inspector. I ran it through twice, but clearance has been denied. I'll get the duty officer. Excuse me."

Wolffe, Mansell thought as the duty officer scurried over.

"Is there a problem, Lieutenant?" asked Mansell. "Maybe Major Wolffe can straighten things out."

"The major is unavailable, Inspector. Might I help?"

Mansell bent his head forward. He lit a cigarette. He crossed to a telephone on the reception desk and dialed district headquarters. The duty officer's face paled when Mansell asked for the district commander. He waited two minutes. Their conversation lasted half that.

Moments after Mansell hung up, Wolffe entered the reception area. He exuded the brutish air of a man who has just been reprimanded.

"Inspector Mansell, what a pleasure."

"I'll see my witness now, Wolffe. Right now."

"Suspect, Mansell, not witness. Suspect," replied Wolffe. Beads of perspiration formed on his upper lip. "And the suspect is sleeping at the moment."

"You are a second-rate actor, Wolffe. Hardly better than your police work." A sharp breath punctuated Mansell's words. "I'll see Anthony Mabasu in one hour, in private. Have him cleaned up, if you will."

"You have a visitor, Anthony," announced Wolffe energetically. "A detainee under suspicion of murder, in a case ruled by the Police Act, is not by law allowed visitors. But you are a lucky man. We've made an exception in your case. We don't expect gratitude, only cooperation."

Mabasu lay on an examination table in the infirmary. He had heard only half of what the interrogator said, understood even less. But he did understand the word *visitor*, and the word gave him a measure of hope.

Two aides swabbed Mabasu's feet. Salve was applied. The feet were wrapped in gauze bandages. Another aide spread a thin layer of Instant Heat across his rib cage and lower back. Four meters' worth of bandages formed a tight cincture around his chest and abdomen. His wrists were treated with cold packs, a cloverine gel, and were lightly bandaged as well.

Four aides hoisted Mabasu from the table into a wheelchair. The amphetamine sulfate solution injected into his forearm provided an instantaneous boost. A male nurse set a clipboard on Mabasu's knees. The nurse worked a pen into his right hand.

"Sign at the bottom, please." A new voice, thought Mabasu, gazing into a smiling face. Despite parched lips and a swollen tongue, he tried to return the smile. The nurse tapped the clipboard. "It's so you can visit your visitor. You know, always some crazy paperwork. Here now, let's have some water first."

The water contained a high concentration of glucose and sugar, cold and quenching. Mabasu asked for more, but the nurse showed him the pen again. Mabasu signed the forms without reading and drank and drank.

When Mansell entered the holding cell, Anthony Mabasu was seated behind a rectangular table split lengthwise by a partition.

"Stand up," Mansell ordered. Mabasu shook his head, looking more cadaverous than alive. An hour to patch this guy up? Mansell thought. It would have taken a week. "Was it coral rock this time or hard brick? Madmen. Bloody madmen."

Mansell stripped off his jacket. He loosened his tie. Together, they smoked, in silence for a time. Mabasu smoked as if he had been rewarded with a crust of bread in the face of eventual starvation. Mansell smoked to clear his mouth of the bile of Hymie Wolffe and every nightcrawler he represented. He smoked to clear his head of the inevitable, damning question. Had he truly expected to see Anthony Mabasu in any other condition?

Security would know about Sylvia Mabasu's death within the hour. The similarities between the death of Elgin and the woman were ultimately too striking. By chance or design, it didn't matter; Mansell would approach the murders with the assumption that both were committed by the same person.

"The coins on the floor at Elgin's feet. You touched them. You held them in your hand. Why didn't you tell me?"

"It wasn't enough to steal." The words burrowed their way from Mabasu's throat, guttural and broken. "I thought about it. Shit, easy pickings. But it wasn't enough. You don't know. It was stupid. Damn stupid. I shoulda taken 'em."

"That would've made more sense. What about the locker door? Your prints were all over it. Hey, I'm trying to help you."

"I was scared. The guy was white. Shit, you know what that means."

"It means you weren't scared enough."

"I shoulda let it be. I shoulda run. . . . But it was my lady's job. She was supposed to be there. I thought I could protect her. Shit. That's a joke. I can't even protect myself."

They'd gotten close, so Mansell veered away. He passed a water bottle across the partition and lit two more smokes.

"The blue-and-white bandana. The one you said you didn't own. Not your colors, you said. You left it in the locker room. You knew Elgin's blood was on it, didn't you?"

Mabasu grimaced, shaking his head.

"They showed you a watch."

"And a ring. Said they were the dead guy's."

"They were. They found them in your house. In the dugout below the house."

"Never been under there. I know the kids play there sometimes, though. I'm screwed, aren't I?"

Mansell had gained a measure of respect for Anthony Mabasu over the last ten minutes. Not that every answer rang with truth; it was something else. You search for a man's weaknesses, observe his ability to deal with those weaknesses. You judge a man's capacity for evil based on that ability.

Ian Elgin's watch and ring had been wiped clean of any fingerprints. Mansell had spoken with the two Security officers who had searched Mabasu's house; according to them, strict police procedure was followed. The items were found wrapped in an old newspaper, a four-day-old copy of the *Bulletin*. They had handled both items using a penknife. The articles were then bagged and taken straight to Forensic.

Mabasu was innocent, Mansell was convinced of that. No proof; intuition. Intuition with a loose end. Watching Mabasu's hands, he asked, "Why did you go into that locker room that night, Anthony? Not to clean up after your wife, not in fifteen minutes. We both know that. What made you go in there?"

The right hand tensed; fingers curled into a fist and then relaxed. "Don't know, really. Thought maybe she might've changed her mind, about goin'. You know women sometimes. Somethin' told me. . . . Does Sylvia know yet? Does she know I'm here? I shoulda called her before, but we don't have no phone. I was gonna call from work, but . . ."

He'd lost him, and there was no going back. Mabasu needed to know, and now, Mansell thought, because Wolffe would surely use it; another thumbscrew neatly applied.

Mansell leaned across the partition. He looked into Mabasu's eyes. "Anthony. She doesn't know. She'll never know. Listen, there's no humane way of telling you this. I'm sorry. Sylvia's been killed. Three days ago in Ciskei—"

"No, you bastard." Mabasu grasped the arms of the wheelchair. "No. You're lying."

"Her body was found this morning by the Ciskeian police."

"You lousy bastard. This is a goddamn trick."

Mansell shook his head. He cast his eyes downward. A harsh breath escaped his lungs. "No, I wish it were. I wish to God it were a trick. But I have to tell you now, like this, because the Security Police don't know, or didn't until now. And they'll use it against you, Anthony. They'll use it. I'm sorry."

"You're sorry? Shit. You're an animal, just like them."

A door opened behind them, and Mansell held up a hand. He leaned across the partition again. "I'll get you out of here. Just hang on. Hang on."

On his way out, Mansell stopped at Wolffe's office on the eighth floor. He entered without knocking.

102

"Sorry about our little misunderstanding this morning, Inspector," Wolffe said.

"Anthony Mabasu is sorry, too," answered Mansell. "We're taking the suspect off your hands, Major. CIB is filing charges this afternoon."

"Glad you came around." The words were delivered with a smile.

Mansell stared down at Wolffe. The hairs on the back of his neck stood on end. "I'll send a team around first thing in the morning to pick him up."

Jan Koster arrived at East Fields, via helicopter, at 3:30 in the afternoon.

His mood was predictably foul, and he was hard-pressed to contain it. The reasons were clear. Today was his youngest daughter's birthday. Hannah was nine. At dawn, Koster had made love with his wife, Julia, for the first time in three weeks. Later, he'd taken the family for a breakfast cruise aboard their sailboat, *Die Komeet*. The weather on the cape had been balmy and cool: a sky dotted with feathery tufts, a seafaring breeze blowing in from the west. Together, they'd eaten cake and ice cream on the main deck with a perfect view of Table Mountain. At noon, he was bound for Johannesburg.

The last seven years had taken a heavy toll on Koster and his family. A brief separation, one year ago, had left deep scars. Julia had suspected infidelity. Koster concluded that it was better than suspecting treason. Years ago, during instruction, he had been told that sex was a healthy outlet. Its use in the field was encouraged. Therefore, Koster never strayed.

Seven years, he thought wearily. Life would never be the same after the twenty-second. If he was still alive after the twenty-second.

Koster used a room, one reserved for him personally in the workers' living quarters, to stow his luggage. The cot was neatly made, a reading lamp at the head, a water basin and mirror nearby. He changed from his suit into blue jeans, a cotton shirt, and construction boots. He took a short walk from the barracks to a barn-shaped building called Central Access. Here, the main shafts led to work stations and tunnels below. Outside shaft number four he was issued a miner's hat. A ten-man demolition team and two engineers stepped into the shaft elevator next to him. They began their descent. Three other crews were already underground, each with a similar task.

Two hundred and fifty meters below ground the elevator stopped. The team entered the Main, a cavernous work station twelve hundred meters square and three stories high, bored out of solid rock by drill and dynamite.

A dozen tunnels led away from the Main, but two were conspicuous above the rest. Set side by side at the rear of the station, each was outfitted with electric cables and winch-rope systems—essentials for transporting arms and supplies deeper into the network.

They entered the primary tunnel. It was a claustrophobic two and a half meters square. Caged light bulbs hung from each cross-beam. Members of the demolition team loaded full packs, coils of rubber-sheathed cable, and contact wire into tunnel cars. The engineers carried high-beam flashlights, tremor detectors, and pouches full of chewing tobacco.

When they were four hundred meters into the tunnel, a series of ascending stopes rose sharply to a second station. Packs and equipment were hand-carried and reloaded.

The tunnel leveled out for a time, but it meandered, pointlessly, Koster thought, and its size vacillated nervously.

"A tunnel follows the reef," he heard one of the engineers explain. "And a gold-bearing reef is like a woman, fickle and unpredictable."

The demolition crew found this amusing. Koster thought about Julia and her cries of pleasure and reluctance that morning. His depression mounted. He lost track of distance and direction. The chief engineer spat wads of tobacco juice at the base of each support.

Then, without warning, the primary tunnel and its companion tunnel converged. This third station was called Supply Central. Larger than the other two, Supply Central was an oblong cave with sheared sides and a craggy stone ceiling. Foodstuffs and water barrels lined every wall. Work crews with blowtorches tarried over steel supports and track repairs.

Koster threw himself on the ground next to one of the barrels. The water tasted bitter with chemicals. He drank three cups and poured a fourth over the back of his neck. In defiance of all the rules, he lit a cigarette. He thought about that day, four years ago, when they first discovered the tunnels extending from beneath the Homestake Mining claim. It took another sixteen months of drilling, blasting, and digging to link the largest of those tunnels with the primary tunnel and to create this subterranean grotto, where, Koster thought, in two weeks, the assault would begin.

After the gear had been unloaded from the tunnel cars, Koster traded his metal cup for coils of contact wire and cable. The thirteen-man crew climbed permanent scaffolding into the connection tunnel. At the entrance, the demolition chief positioned a rectangular box containing the detonator switch. Koster watched closely as the lead wires were connected, making a mental note. Then they worked their way through the tunnel, securing the cable to each support. Koster felt the sweltering heat of the rock. Sweat burned his eyes and blurred his vision. The ground rose steadily beneath his feet. Three hundred meters further on, they came to the "dead" access shaft that lay below the central mining facility of Target Four.

The shaft measured roughly ten meters across. Four iron ladders hung from the walls. Each rose from the floor of the tunnel to a deserted work station thirty meters below the surface. An elaborate system of pulleys, ropes, and pallets threaded its way down the center of the shaft from top to bottom.

"Let's get some light and air in here," ordered the chief engineer.

A generator housed at the base of the shaft kicked in. Electric light showered vertical stone walls. A secondary air pump circulated cool air throughout the tunnel.

The demolition team set to work. Their packs contained high-grade plastic explosives, electrical blasting caps, plastic leg wires, and metallic trips. They worked in teams of two, setting charges at staggered points the entire length of the shaft. Jan Koster and the engineers served as their ground crew, feeding them five-kilogram packages of explosives and reams of contact wire by means of ropes and pulleys.

They finished the task at dusk. Confirmation from the other three targets arrived within the hour.

At eleven o'clock that night, while most of the camp slept, Koster returned alone to the connection tunnel beneath Homestake. The tunnel was deserted for now, pitch-black and stifling. Using a small flash, Koster located the detonator box ten meters beyond the entrance and quickly dismantled the back. Disconnecting and camouflaging the lead wires was a simple, if delicate, matter, and five minutes later he was retracing his steps. Lining the access shafts with explosives had been Leistner's idea. "Just in case a show of strength is needed," he had said. Koster had other ideas.

By 2:30 in the morning he had rendered the three other detonators as harmless as the first. By three, he was back in his own cot, fast asleep and dreaming about a small seaboard town thousands of kilometers to the north.

Steenkamp's hands were covered in blood. An assistant sat in a glass cubicle poring over a microscope; another studied X rays. Steenkamp's scowl deepened when he saw the chief inspector enter the room.

"Is it different?" asked Mansell.

"Too bloody similar." The room was cool, almost cold. Still, Steenkamp's face glistened. He waved a bloody finger at a white towel near the victim's feet. "Wipe, please."

Averting his gaze from the table, Mansell dabbed the pathologist's forehead and the bridge of his nose.

"Same prognosis?"

"Strangulation. Yes."

"ETD?"

"Thursday afternoon. Sometime between three P.M. and six P.M.," Steenkamp answered. "The tarp retarded the cooling process just enough. Body tissues were slightly bloated. A few blisters. She didn't die in that valley, though. She died in a sitting position. Lividity on the back of the thighs and the buttocks confirms that she probably remained in that position for an hour and a half to two hours."

"He waited until dark to hide the body." Still, a lousy job of concealment, Mansell thought. Why?

"A logical guess," snapped Steenkamp. "So there she sat. He probably drank a beer and listened to the radio."

"Sure. A man who loves his work." Was it laziness? Mansell wondered, or just contempt for the Ciskeian police? No, he thought, the killer wanted the body discovered. Or—his stomach tightened at the thought—Sylvia Mabasu is not his last target.

"You were right about the struggle," Steenkamp said. "The tips of the fingers were traumatized. The nails snapped off clean."

Chas du Toits amplified on this. He gestured to a tiny mass of bluish-black material wrapped in powder paper. "It's a plastic rubber. It came from under the victim's nails on the left hand. Also traces from the ring finger and index finger on the right hand. One of

106

those synthetic gems with a hundred uses. We're trying to pinpoint it now."

"The dashboard of a car," Mansell said bluntly. He glanced at the forensic chief for an opinion. Du Toits raised an eyebrow and shrugged. "Any traces of human tissue or blood around the fingernails?"

"None, I'm afraid."

Mansell paced. He lit a fresh cigarette. Jabbing at the air with the orange ember, he said, "The attack came from the backseat. She reacted to the attack by grabbing for the dash, hoping to pull herself free. Unconsciousness occurred before she could change her defense to the rope."

"An abnormal reaction," grunted du Toits.

"Yes." Beware of the percentages, Mansell thought. "Maybe."

With his free hand Mansell groomed lank hair as he circled the room. Du Toits said, "The rope is an exact duplicate in terms of make and wear, a nylon with rayon fibers. We tried matching ends with the rope used on Ian Elgin, but without success. There were three sets of prints on her purse. Her own, Anthony Mabasu's, and another set we haven't identified yet, but the narrowness suggests a child. The coin purse inside shows two sets, husband and wife."

"All right." Mansell returned to the table. He scanned the print sheet with Sylvia Mabasu's name at the top. "We found hair, native hair, on the chiffon scarf from the lounge at the railroad station."

"Not Sylvia Mabasu's."

"I don't know if that's good or bad," Mansell said. "Did anything show up on the tarp or on the victim's clothes? Any link?"

"The tarp is an utter mess. We've found plenty of fiber samples, and the oil and grease retained dozens of print fragments. We're running it through a GC/MC now. We'll do a ninhydrin test for prints as soon as that's complete."

"When? It's important." Anthony Mabasu lurked over Mansell's shoulder.

"Gas chromatography takes time, Inspector." Du Toits gestured with upturned palms.

"I know, Chas. When?"

"Tomorrow morning," du Toits replied.

Mansell thanked him and headed for the door. But du Toits waved a hand, his memory suddenly jogged. "Oh, Nigel. I nearly forgot. Good Lord. We finished Elgin's apartment. His clothes are all South African—made. Johannesburg confirmed that from his wardrobe there as well. Sweaters, all native wool. But the black-and-gray wool fibers we found attached to his sweater aren't. They're imports. Italian."

It rains seventy centimeters a year in Port Elizabeth. Rain is an occasion for celebration.

Nigel Mansell saw the first drops alight on his office window at 6:15. The last rays of sunset tinged the drops an iridescent orange. He switched off the computer and started for the door. The telephone rang.

No, he thought, turning the door handle. He glanced back. Bloody hell.

"Mansell," he answered.

"Nigel, it's Richter."

"It's raining, Piet."

"Is it?"

A smile creased Mansell's face. "You sentimentalist."

"We found the rope."

"Excellent." Mansell crossed to the window. "Any purchase records?"

"Six hundred thousand people in Port Elizabeth. Every store in the city sells rope of some kind, right? But only two stock a nylon-rayon mix like this one. They're both closed on Sunday, so I had to roust out the managers. Two purchases in the last month."

"Joshua and Merry are on their way here. Six-thirty. Meet us."

"I'm hungry. I'll make a quick stop on my way."

"Eat later, Piet. I know you better than that."

"I'll bring bobotie."

"Will you? All right then, dinner for four." Mansell hung up. Blackmail, he thought rightfully.

Rain graced the coast for several minutes, and then the clouds returned to the ocean. Stars filled the sky in their wake. Still, the olfactory delight lingered, and Mansell met Detective Richter on the sidewalk.

Cape Province bobotie consisted of curried ground beef, sauteed onions, and milk-soaked bread. They used the chief inspector's desk as a dining table.

When Joshua entered the room he made a show of the bandages covering Richter's head. "Impressive, Piet. Are we expecting a decoration for bravery, or were you sleeping when it happened?"

"And a fine, bloody dream I was having at the time, too. Bastards."

Richter delivered his report between bites. "Like I said, it's not that the nylon roping is hard to find. Every johnny with a sign over his door sells something like it. It's the rayon additive. It's stronger, more flexible, but not an essential if you're only bundling branches up for the trash."

"Or strangling a union official," added Joshua.

"Or a cleaning woman." Raised eyebrows turned in Mansell's direction. "I just talked with Chas. It's the same rope. Same manufacture, same component mix."

"Conclusive, then?"

"There's no way of telling absolutely. Two people killed within hours of each other; same M.O., same weapon, same method." Mansell set the half-finished meal aside. He touched his breast pocket, felt the pack, and decided against it. "Tell me about the purchase records."

"The first buy happened at Sea Port Sports, fifteen days ago. A local commodities dealer named John Mason. He used American Express."

"Which commodities?"

"I thought of that. I reached someone in his office. Mason deals in the ag markets. Soybeans, corn, horseshit. You know," said Richter. The door opened. Merry entered carrying four coffees. "I talked to Mason an hour ago. He told me he bought the rope for his yacht, poor bastard. He claims he was in Bloemfontein Wednesday through Friday. Sounds legit, but I'll have a confirmation on Monday. Okay. The second purchase was eight days ago at The Outdoorsman. It's a sporting goods place in Fairview. It was a cash sale, but the manager made the sale himself, and he thinks he remembers the buyer. Why? Because he was wearing a three-piece suit and said something about spelunking in the Transkei?"

"Exploring caves," explained Mansell. Spelunking was an uncommon sport, which, in its purest form, required the skills of mountain climbing, the nerve of free-falling, and a love of dark places and crawling things. During his college days, Mansell and several friends from the University of Natal spent a month one summer exploring caves in Royal Natal National Park. The one outing had satisfied his curiosity. Ian Elgin had also studied at the same university, but nothing in his file suggested an interest in spelunking.

Mansell wasn't aware of cave sites worth exploring in the Transkei, and he glanced over at Merry. "Make a call to the Parks Service people in the Transkei," he said. "Talk to Eli Leavell. He's an old friend. He'll know where any suitable caves are located. Chances are good that a license is required or some type of registration. Maybe our man's still around."

Merry scribbled the name on a note pad.

"And the chiffon scarf?" Mansell directed his question at Detective Richter again.

"Most of the ladies' boutiques are closed on Sundays, but we called on as many owners as we could get ahold of. All for naught, so far. One says Cape Town, one says Johannesburg, one says New York. We also drew a blank at the department stores." Richter tossed an empty cup into the wastebasket and shrugged. "I'm at it again first thing in the morning."

Searching for a prop, Mansell touched cold coffee to his lips. With a grimace, he pulled it away and settled gratefully for a cigarette. He said, "I talked with Anthony Mabasu again this afternoon. Security's made a mess of him."

"And I heard we're filing charges?" Merry said. It sounded more like a question than he'd intended, but Mansell understood.

"If we don't, he stays."

"Then I'll be at the Hall first thing in the morning."

"Good." Mansell reviewed the interview with Hurst and the evidence being prepared by the prosecutor's office.

"They may have a case," said Joshua.

Merry protested. "On a leaky bagful of circumstantial evidence?"

"The motives are there, like it or not."

"Motives? You don't kill someone because a copy of his signature is on your dismissal notice. There were five other names on it, too, and they're all still alive. Mabasu had it coming, and he knows it."

"He appealed the dismissal," countered Joshua. "And with some vigor, according to union sources."

"Everyone appeals their dismissals. Everyone gets turned down."

"I hate to agree with Hymie Wolffe, Merry," Piet Richter said, "but infidelity pushes as many bad buttons as anything."

"Infidelity with who?" asked Merry. "Mabasu suspected infidelity, but lots of men think their wives are screwing around with somebody. He's never mentioned a name to anyone, not his co-workers, not his neighbors, not to anyone we've talked to."

"True," argued Joshua. "But now the third member of the troika is dead. Does Pathology have an ETD yet, Nigel?"

110

"Seventy-two hours ago."

"Then it fits. Mabasu could've easily taken a bus or car, or hell, even hitchhiked to Ciskei on Thursday, offed his wife, and still been back to his job Friday morning in plenty of time to set up Elgin, right? And the watch and ring. How do you refute that? That's not circumstantial, Merry."

"Yeah, and that bothers the hell out of me." Merry massaged his eyes, yawning. "Why would Mabasu leave his prints all over the locker room, make a spectacle of himself by reporting the body, and yet still take the time to wipe the prints off the ring and watch before hiding them in his own house?"

"A plant," said Richter. "Yeah, I like it."

"A plant?" Joshua retorted. "By who?"

"Forensic checked the crawl space," Mansell said. "Besides those of three neighborhood kids, the only fingerprints they discovered belonged to the Security officers who found the goods."

"If Security planted the watch and ring, where in the hell did they get them in the first place? Unless . . . unless they set Elgin up themselves." Joshua stared through a cloud of smoke at Mansell. "Tell me that's not possible."

Mansell cracked a window. A ghetto blaster passed below them on the sidewalk playing a gospel tune by Ladysmith Black Mambazo. "Merry, how about our schizoid from the train station? Martin Engels?"

"A brick wall. But I think he's capable of murder. He's with Spencer in the shrink ward for the moment."

Mansell nodded, glancing at Joshua. "And the rent-a-car?"

"Fifteen different agencies rented a hundred and twelve Hondas over the last thirty days," Joshua told him. "We're concentrating on the last week to begin with. Okay. Of those twenty-eight renters, two are from Port Elizabeth. Both are still on the road. One we contacted in Cape Town; the other is camping in Kruger National. Sixteen of the rentals were made to South Africans living outside the city; nine have been accounted for. The remaining ten were leased to foreign visitors. Three of those have been returned, and we're working on the other seven."

"Were any of the returns paid for in cash?"

Joshua shuffled through his files. "Here it is. Credit cards were used for all twenty-eight deposits. Of the twelve returns, three were paid in cash."

"Concentrate on those first, I think," Mansell said. "A car back on the lot, cleaned and vacuumed, is a lot safer than a car on the road."

At sundown seven flatbed trucks rumbled along a narrow road among the rolling hills of the East Rand. At a midway point between Delmas and Welgedacht, they approached a chain link enclosure brightly illuminated by four spotlights. A sign, hung on the outside of the gate, read, EAST FIELDS MINING CORPORATION. The caravan rolled to a stop outside the fence. An armed guard pushed the gate aside.

Hurriedly, grim passengers dressed as migrant workers disembarked. They gathered at the foot of a circular guardhouse. Papers were scrutinized, faces matched with photos. One by one, the workers trudged past the gate, down a winding road, to a well-lit compound and rebuilt barracks furnished with multiple bedding, enlarged kitchens, and immense food stores.

From atop a platform next to Central Access, Jan Koster and Colonel Rolf Lamouline watched this harried lot, 240 in all, the first of East Fields's new tenants. A thousand others, workers gathering at train and bus stations in Springs, Benori, Brakpan, Witbank, and Kempton Park, were expected before the night was past.

"Independence, Colonel." Koster gestured at the new arrivals. "A commodity often hazardous and short-lived."

"Independence?" Lamouline shrugged. "The Bantu have battled colonialism, tyranny, and tribalism with spear and spilled blood for centuries, young man. In the end, he gains a parcel of land for farming, and after a season the parcel is overgrown with weeds. In battle, he wins a precious stretch of road, and the road is soon pitted and unpassable. His revolt brings him a cement factory in Nigeria, and he underpays his workers. In Kenya, a crane breaks down and rusts out because he doesn't have the spare parts to fix it nor the wherewithal to buy them. A locomotive in Angola, an essential for hauling oranges and wheat to market, sits abandoned at a railroad siding because no one can fix the goddamn hydraulic brakes. A bakery in Zaire, a gift you might say from departing whites, flounders because there's no flour for bread. . . . Independence? I don't know."

Mrs. Delaney Blackford's file indicated that her grandmother, on her father's side, was of Zulu ancestry. Her grandfather was Dutch, her mother English. She, therefore, lived in a coloured community called Gelvandale.

The suburb of Parkside portrayed the elite side of Gelvandale's varied living conditions. The streets were freshly paved, the grass nearly green, the gardens well tended. Installation of streetlamps was planned for the following spring.

The house on Trevenna Avenue was a stuccoed two-story enclosed by yellowwoods, apricot trees, and a lavender hedge. The night was cool and dry, touched by the scent of freshly tilled soil and burning cedar. Mansell noticed two lights burning, one behind the opaque glass of the bathroom and one behind drawn curtains in the front room. He tapped lightly on the door. In one hand he held a bottle of chilled champagne, keys in the other.

The door opened. Delaney wore a cotton shift exposing tan shoulders and slender legs. She held a walking stick out in front of her and the door close.

"Good evening. It's Nigel Mansell," he said. "I know it's late."

She didn't move. "Harassing Parkside tonight, Inspector?"

"Just your side of the street tonight."

"How kind of you. We were feeling left out."

"I should have called first," Mansell said. Delaney's black hair fell in waves upon her shoulders and back, less tended than before, more appealing even so. "This could be considered a social call. I've heard you fancy champagne."

She tossed her head back, laughing. "Is that what my file says? I didn't realize it was so detailed."

"Actually, your secretary was kind enough to pass a subtle hint," he replied. "Do you always make your hired help work on Sundays?"

Delaney leaned against the threshold. A hint of relaxation.

"I don't like policemen," she said.

"I'm only a policeman part of the time."

"Policemen, Chief Homicide Inspector Mansell, are policemen every minute of every day. You have a cot in your office and stale sandwiches on your desk. Your friends are all cops. You all hang out at the same bar on Main Street, and you talk shop until the wee hours of the morning. Right?"

A glib riposte eluded Mansell. He smiled, a bleak smile he realized, knowing she was right, at least in part. But he didn't want to think about the decaying corpse of Sylvia Mabasu, or the battered figure of her incarcerated husband, and he couldn't face the prospect of his own home. He held up the champagne. "Invite me in."

She pushed aside the screen, and Mansell stepped inside. He paused while Delaney engaged the lock. An oval table, oak with a beveled glass top, dominated the front room. A porcelain vase with a crackled glaze and Japanese brushwork adorned the center of the table. There were no flowers in it, and none were needed, Mansell decided. The table rested upon a rug woven of blues and lavenders. Palms grew in matching planters on either end of a long couch.

"So how's your taste in champagne?" she asked, relieving him of the bottle.

"There's an old saying, Armenian I think. 'Champagne is like vodka; never be impressed by the price.'"

Delaney glanced over her shoulder. Mansell followed her into the kitchen. A cut-glass lamp hung over a butcher-block table. African violets crowded inside a bay window behind the counter. The champagne erupted. The cork assaulted the ceiling. Champagne spilled over her hand into the sink, and they both laughed.

"That's half the fun," Delaney said.

They carried glasses and the bottle back to the living room. Mansell shed his sports coat. He chose a rattan chair with flat, broad arms. Delaney sat on the floor, reclining against the couch, her walking stick by her side.

Mansell noticed it. The shaft was oak, the head a polished oval of solid brass. "Nice," he said.

"I'm a collector. Necessity and desire."

"I'd like to see it sometime. The collection, I mean." The champagne was dry and smooth. Mansell disliked it less than he'd expected.

Delaney touched hers with a fingertip and changed the subject. "How's the investigation? I thought for sure I'd be a suspect."

"Are you disappointed? I could arrange something dramatic. A dawn raid. Helicopters. Bullhorns." Mansell hesitated. He noticed a change: reluctance, sorrow.

"The funeral's tomorrow in Johannesburg," she said.

"Yes, I know." Mansell touched his breast pocket, and then retreated. "The Security Branch arrested a suspect. No charges have been filed yet, though."

"Who's the suspect? Would I know him?"

"I can't say. We're under an information blanket. I don't think you'd know him. No."

"Meaning he's black," she replied. "Will it be in the papers?"

"Elgin's position with the union has led someone very high up in Pretoria to deem the situation an internal security matter. Translated, that means someone's playing politics."

Delaney thought of the minister automatically. She glanced in Mansell's direction, but found him gazing, instead, at the stereo set against the opposite wall.

He said, "What kind of music do you listen to?"

Relieved, she followed his eyes. "Classical, jazz, rock. I'm very diversified," she answered. "Are you hinting that this really is a social visit?"

"Surprise me."

Delaney chose a jazz guitarist named Jonathan Butler.

"The most obvious question," she said, curling up on the floor again, "is, why a policeman? But don't tell me. It runs in the family."

Mansell felt the quick release of laughter, and Delaney joined him. He was amazed by the life in her smile. Equally amazed at how instantly it was contained.

"The Major was a cop in East London. Retired," said Mansell. "Now he's a full-time gardener. He says it's only half as exciting, but twice as productive. Secretly, I think he was hoping for a lawyer or a judge. But Mom used to say that lawyers are generally overrated, and judges are lawyers who even bore other lawyers. Please, no offense intended."

Delaney extended an empty glass. Mansell poured. She said, "Mom's right. It's a boorish lot, but that leaves the field wide open. My father was the Oscar Wilde of our family. He'd always tell me that the incompetents of the world breed opportunity for the competent. He and my mother run a hardware store on the Cape. Retail's just the opposite. Everyone thinks it's easy."

"So that explains all the For Rent signs in the shopping centers these days."

"And I don't like to fail. I chose the easy way out." Delaney glanced at his glass, half full and loitering. "I have whiskey and gin. We may as well both enjoy our drinks."

"Whiskey. I'll pour." She directed him into a sitting room that had once been a library. The liquor cabinet was next to a spinet piano. Photos, all of the same dark-haired child with saucer eyes and an unabashed smile, lined the piano. The wall behind the piano was filled with kindergarten artwork: a finger painting of the ocean, a cut-and-paste Halloween pumpkin, a collage of dragons and dinosaurs.

Mansell returned with Canadian Club on the rocks. He said, "She's a beautiful young lady. Yours?"

"My daughter, yes, but she was definitely her own person," Delaney replied. A distant look was quickly controlled. Instead, she concentrated on the last of her champagne.

"Wrong subject. I'm sorry."

"It's okay," she responded. A long silence followed, filled only by the sound of a solo guitar. Finally, she glanced up into his eyes, ingenuous eyes without expectations. "Her name was Amanda. We were driving home from Cape Town one night three years ago. It was raining. One of those September rains. The coast highway was a disaster. You know how it gets. My husband was driving. He was upset about wasting three days visiting my folks. Three bloody days out of a lifetime. I'll never forgive him that. Outside of Sedgefield, where the mountains border the coast, there was a rockslide. It was foggy. We were going too fast, arguing. Arguing! God. And I'll never forgive myself for that. Amanda was sleeping in the backseat when we went off the road. It was forty or fifty meters to the rocks. She never knew. It was too quick. I'm thankful for that; for her ignorance, that there was no pain. That sounds trite, doesn't it."

"Trite? No, not trite. Normal."

The record ended. The room absorbed the silence.

"I severed my Achilles tendon in the accident. I was on crutches for six months. I used to play a helluva game of tennis, Inspector. Now I collect walking sticks." Delaney stared down at the oak stick at her side, grasped the handle, and pushed it aside. "We stopped talking. He started drinking. I looked in all the wrong places for support. Terribly original stuff. We were divorced fifteen months ago."

Delaney's shoulders sagged for an instant, and then she arose. She retreated to the stereo. She traded Jonathan Butler for Juluka. Mansell produced a cigarette from his jacket.

"I don't know why I told you that," she said, leaning heavily against the record stand. "I don't talk about it."

"How old was she?" he asked.

"Six." Delaney held the walking stick before her like a war shield. "She had just started to live, my baby. She would smell every flower and talk to every tree and listen to the sounds of the ocean. Oh, God, and laugh. . . . She had just started to live."

"Some people never do," Mansell offered. "You must have been doing something right."

"My mistake was bringing her into this sick world in the first place."

"I don't think so. Creating a human life? That's no mistake, Mrs. Blackford. Creating love. It's hard to do any better."

"Very philosophical," she countered. Then, regretting it, she asked, "Do you believe that?"

"Sure," he answered. The wall clock behind Delaney read 11:45. Don't be thinking about a second drink, he ordered himself. Had coming here been a mistake? No. "I admit I've been more successful digging out the dead than creating babies. Maybe someday."

Delaney released herself from the comfort of distance. Crossing the floor, she stopped an arm's length away. "It's my turn to pour," she said, snatching the glass away before Mansell could protest, adding, as she breezed out of the room, "I see you wear a wedding band, Inspector."

Mansell elected not to reply while Delaney replenished his whiskey. When she returned, he hid behind his inspector's mask, asking, "Did you know Ian Elgin well enough to know about his hobbies? Did sports interest him?"

"Male avoidance?" asked Delaney. "I tell you my darkest secret, and then you proceed to ignore a simple observation."

In a single motion, Mansell consumed half the whiskey. Heat spread outward from his stomach like ripples on a pond.

"Sometimes," he said, "avoidance says more than self-pity."

"Aren't they the same thing?" Delaney replied. "I've been practicing for three years. I should know."

Mansell felt the quickening of his heartbeat. He blamed the cigarettes. "One hurts more than the other," he said. "My imagination is too damn powerful. It's a nice attribute for a policeman, but it gets tricky when the day is done. Avoidance is a quick fix, but it adds up. Self-pity's always close at hand, just in case."

"I know." Delaney sat on the edge of the sofa, at Mansell's right. She toyed with her empty wine goblet.

Mansell watched her hands, slender, graceful fingers. Finally, he looked aside and said, "When I was in college, some of us spent a month exploring the underground caves in Natal. It was an unusual sport called spelunking."

Delaney set the goblet down in the shadow of the porcelain vase.

Purposely, she rotated the stem between fingertips. When she released it, she sought out Mansell's eyes.

Eventually, she said, "Ian mentioned it a couple of times. Exploring caves in the dark. It didn't make sense to me. That's probably why I remember it. Ian seemed to be fascinated with it. Were you?"

"I haven't done it since that summer." Mansell smiled, shaking his head. "Did Elgin ever mention any names, or any of the places he liked to go?"

She fell silent, lost in a thought that Mansell could see spread across her face. "They worked in two-man teams. Ian said that good partners were hard to find," she said. "Koster was his name. John or James Koster, I think. He's an official in one of the ministries."

Night was a figment of Anthony Mabasu's blank imagination. Time was an illusion; it had failed to exist hours ago. Mabasu only knew that his feet could no longer withstand the pressure of the bricks. His hands had locked onto the rope suspended above him, joints cemented solid. He dangled from the rope like a side of beef in a meat locker. His arms were gratefully numb, but his shoulders burned from the inside out and his chest glowed metallic from the baton. His heart seemed to speak to him, but it spoke so quickly that the message eluded him.

He wasn't thirsty. Why, he thought, did they continue to pour bitter tea down his throat?

The interrogator, the one with the bulldog face, kept reading to him from his own confession. The signature looked familiar, but those weren't his words, were they?

The picture from the city morgue; that he recognized. The picture made him forget about his burning shoulders, his pulverized feet, his scarred chest. How had he done that? they asked. How had he done what? Mabasu heard himself reply. Kill your own wife, they answered. Yes, we were killing each other, he mumbled. We needed some time apart. It happens to everyone, doesn't it? he asked.

The ugly one, the corporal with hair all over his face and a bare chest, raised his baton. Mabasu swore he could feel the air parting as the bamboo thwacked his kidney. The sound of a breaker slapping the shore, he thought. His lower back felt damp. It felt like an injection, one badly inserted into the muscle and forgotten, he

118

thought. And the very idea of them removing the needle left him afraid.

The bulldog told him again about Sylvia's affair with the dead union official. Details bounced off an invisible shield, and Mabasu's one clear thought was that he had already forgiven her.

This he tried to tell them, but they wouldn't hear of it. Now the other investigator, Mabasu thought, he listened better. And he had cigarettes. Sometimes tea. But he wouldn't fit in here very well, anyway.

The bulldog screamed something. Mabasu saw the assault coming, but it was useless to protest, impossible to resist. This time he lost consciousness.

When he came to again, Mabasu found himself in a fetal position in a pool of red. Involuntarily, he cracked an eyelid. To his surprise, the room was dark. The floodlights were sleeping, he thought. Or had he been moved? The thought was short-lived. His toes touched the bricks. He recoiled into a ball. Shivers raced up and down his spine like an out-of-control locomotive.

Was he alone? From the position he was in, Mabasu couldn't see anyone. Nor could he hear anything. No voices. No sounds. Did it matter? But there was light. Yes, he saw it now. A faint luciferous glow from the room's only window. Still, his brain failed to comprehend the first sign of dawn.

Yet it wasn't the light so much, he thought, as the window. Like his heart, the window spoke to him. But again, he couldn't decipher the words. Why? he wondered. But the sound, the sound at least was friendly. Did that mean he was dying? Was he already dead?

No.

Mabasu heard a chair scrape against the floor behind him. God, no, please, not for a while, he thought. Footsteps. Closer. Silence. The toe of a boot nudged his rib cage.

"Come to your feet, Mabasu."

Nausea raced through him. Tears rolled down his face. Anthony Mabasu stared past the window. Now he saw the light, heard it, and knew why. He called out for a last reserve of strength. Gradually, he rolled onto his knees. He struggled to his feet. A hand grabbed his elbow, but Mabasu wrenched free and ran.

The last thing he thought before plunging headfirst through the window was that the light of day had come at the perfect moment that morning, and he gave thanks.

119

AT 6:12, A TAXICAB RESPONDED TO A CALL FROM THE VICTORIA
Hotel on the corner of Chapel Avenue and Victoria Way.

The cab moved leisurely down Chapel in front of the Hall of
Justice. There was no traffic. Two cars were parked at meters along
the street. The cabby, a Xhosa with special permits, saw the body
sprawled facedown on the sidewalk near the back bumper of the
second car. At first, he figured that a drunk had passed out on his
way to the Donkin Reserve park, but a sea of blood two meters in
diameter convinced him otherwise.

The cabby jumped on his brakes. He leapt from the car, but
stopped halfway to the body. He ran toward the Hall, a dozen steps,
and stopped again. His stomach revolted. He raced back to the taxi,
wiped his face with a greasy rag, and radioed his dispatcher. The dispatcher, in turn, called CIB headquarters on Military and Main.

The moment Nigel Mansell spoke to the responding officer, he
 realized the cabby's change of heart had al-
most certainly prevented a cover-up. He
glanced up at the shattered window ten floors
up; an explanation wasn't necessary.

A newspaperwoman from the *Port Elizabeth Daily Mail* arrived in a beat-up Fiat.
Sixty seconds later, a sleepy-eyed reporter
and a cameraman from the *Cape Province
Bulletin* appeared in a staff car. They ap-
proached the chief inspector with pads and pencils and pale faces.

The woman spoke first. "Inspector, is this thing going to be placed
in quarantine under the Police Act?"

Mansell stared across at the broken body of Anthony Mabasu.
He shook his head. "This one's fair game, Louise. Go to it."

A dozen Security Branch officers, armed with riot guns and night-
sticks, patrolled the scene. Barricades were erected. Major Hymie
Wolffe, aroused from a nap ten minutes before, bleary-eyed and
dressed in wrinkled blues and grays, shouted orders.

Mansell stepped between barricades and approached the body.

120

Shards of glass were spread from one end of the walk to the other.

SB Sergeant Venter, the officer present in the interrogation room at the time of the incident, related the specifics to Wolffe. The reporters crowded near. Mansell bent over the victim.

"What would drive a man to such a state of despondency, Major?" asked the *Bulletin* reporter. Mansell examined Mabasu's lower back. Animals with human faccs, he thought.

"Certainly it's a tragedy," answered Wolffe. "Mr. Mabasu had been detained for questioning, nothing more. His wife was reported killed yesterday in Ciskei. An apparent homicide. We were searching for leads."

Two ambulance attendants laid a stretcher at Mabasu's side.

"Not yet," said Mansell. He ran a hand gently over the backside of Mabasu's knees.

"Was Anthony Mabasu a suspect in the death of his wife, Major?" asked the newspaperwoman.

"He was being questioned. Nothing more."

"Then no charges had been brought?"

"That is correct."

She watched as Mansell examined the mutilated soles of the victim's feet, then asked, "How long had Mr. Mabasu been in your custody, Major?"

"Since Saturday, I believe," Wolffe answered uneasily.

"Since Saturday? Then we can assume, since his wife's body was found only yesterday, that Mr. Mabasu was being held with regard to another investigation?"

"As it happens, yes."

"The Ian Elgin case," she said.

"Now wait, wait just a moment. You know the current status of that case," stammered Wolffe. Make the bastard sweat, thought Mansell. "An official statement on this matter will be released later in the day."

"You're calling it a suicide, then?" she asked.

"Preliminarily, yes."

"I see," she said. Mansell detected swelling about the neck and lividity along the spine. The reporter persisted. "How do you explain the condition of the victim's feet, Major? That certainly didn't occur in the fall."

"I can't say at this time," Wolffe replied.

"Bricks," uttered Mansell. He locked eyes with the pudgy Security man, and Wolffe retreated a step.

"I'm sorry, Inspector," said the newspaperwoman. "What was that you said?"

"Try standing on hard bricks for twenty-four hours and see how pretty your feet look."

Wolffe lumbered forward. "I don't imagine the inspector will want to be quoted on that. Now, when the facts are known, a statement will be issued, and until then, any further questions will be construed as a direct violation of the Police Act. Is that all quite clear enough?"

"Meaning the victim's death is related to the Elgin murder," said the *Daily Mail* reporter.

"That was neither implied nor stated, Ms. Jameson. And I would be wary of suggesting such a thing if I were you." Wolffe waved irritably at the attendants. "Get that body out of here."

"I think not," said the chief inspector coolly. Mansell arose, dragging his eyes away from the body. "Witnesses or suspects to major criminal investigations who die while said investigation is still in progress shall be subject to complete autopsy at the hands of a qualified pathologist. Section something, something, something, of the bloody South African criminal code. Shall I be more specific, Major Wolffe?"

Wolffe mopped his forehead with a handkerchief. "If you think any good will come of it, Mansell, by all means conduct your autopsy. But matters of state security remain."

Joseph Steenkamp led Mansell away from the heavy diet of formaldehyde.

"Perhaps," he said, "I'll try one of those lethal weapons which you so rudely call a cigarette, please."

"Difficult not to be moved," Mansell replied.

They smoked as if the clock had paused just for their benefit. At length, the pathologist spoke. "My good friend Nigel. You cannot win this battle, I'm afraid. No more than you can win your war against the likes of Hymie Wolffe. The disease is malignant. Irreversible. We have seen to it. All of us. Everyone in South Africa is afraid of someone, and everyone insulates himself by one trick or another."

"We should have more faith, Doctor. Government statistics freely admit that only fifty-two prisoners have died in detention over the past decade."

"You're an optimist, Inspector. Your very own source of defiant liberalism, *The Cape Town Argus*, suggests that the number may well be closer to ninety, maybe as high as ninety-five."

Steenkamp's chest revolted in a spasm of harsh coughing. Locking eyes betrayed them; both knew the actual number to be closer to eight hundred.

"How will your report read?" Mansell asked.

"How do all official reports on the subject read, Inspector? Uniformly banal, of course. 'J. Manganyi. Poet, teacher. Slipped in the shower causing a severe hemorrhage.' 'L. Tolwana. Defense Attorney. Fell down a flight of stairs while attempting to escape.' 'R. Timon. Photojournalist. Died from malnutrition brought on by a hunger strike.' 'A. Mabasu. Dock Worker. Suicide.'"

"Exposés," Mansell added, "from the ever-growing skeletons lurking in the closet of the SAP."

"Insulation for the masses." Steenkamp crushed the cigarette between his fingers. He said, "There were traces of blood in the victim's spinal column. This is true. Security will claim it was sustained in the fall. His right kidney was punctured. True. Explanation: sustained while trying to escape. Blood clots observed in the left ear as if from a heavy blow, a blow received at least two hours before death. They'll say the prisoner attacked a guard and had to be restrained.

"He may have been dead when he went through that window. If not, he was certainly dying. But I can't prove it, Nigel."

Fatigue, the by-product of three hours of sleep on an office cot, drove Mansell outside.

A brisk breeze proved a stimulating antidote. He bought day-old plums and grapes from a native boy. He bought hot tea at the cafeteria. He used the station-house locker room for a wash and shave and felt nearly human.

Then he took the stairs to the main floor. The Pit seethed with bodies and high-pitched voices. Like reluctant warriors, each prepared for the moment when Anthony Mabasu's death hit the press. Riot squads donned flak jackets and helmets. A nervous supply sergeant issued stun guns and shotguns with rubber bullets. Two floors up, the communications center coordinated police patrols with local commando units.

Mansell ignored it all.

On the second floor, an office in disarray greeted him. Incomplete dailies cluttered his typing center. Files on Ian Elgin from Jo'burg, Durban, and Cape Town, all tagged with reference notes from Merriman Gosani, filled the hanapers on his desk. Computer printouts on the Federation of Mineworkers Union and the Affiliated Union, with an attached memorandum from Piet Richter, lined the desk top. A long day lay ahead.

Three notes were taped to the shade of his desk lamp.

Mansell started with these, slumping into an armchair as he read the one from Jennifer. They'd been invited to spend Friday, Saturday, and Sunday with the Pruitts at their beach house in Oyster Bay. Could he make it? Was he interested in making it? The paper fell from his hand. His first reaction: muted indifference, a heavy sigh, the return of fatigue. He lit a cigarette.

Staring out the window, he wrestled with an image. He and Jennifer strolling over acres of white sand. Ocean breakers rolling across the beach. Sanderlings racing with the tide. The water would be cold this time of year, but they would swim anyway. An afternoon fire. Sharing a beach towel. Running his hands over the long curves of her back to the strap of her bathing suit. The taste of salt on erect nipples. And then . . . And then the inevitable power struggle, with Jarrad and Harriet Pruitt as their unwilling referees. Would it ever change? Conversations baited with trivia; traps set to spring at the slightest indiscretion. They were both guilty; blame was their constant companion.

Jennifer couldn't have children. Mansell longed for kids; they both did. But adoption, Jennifer insisted, was out of the question. The only babies available were coloured or native. Mansell enjoyed Port Elizabeth. He liked his work despite the drawbacks. Jennifer felt stifled in elementary education, and the police work embarrassed her.

Maybe Steenkamp was right, Mansell thought. A futile battle; a winless war. Maybe it wasn't too late for a break. True, active policemen weren't the recipients of a lot of job offers, but Mansell had an open invitation to join Jarrad Pruitt's public relations firm. Better money. Better hours. Maybe a trip to the beach would give them a chance to talk again. All right, so call, he thought.

He broke two matches lighting another smoke. He stared down at the phone, and it rang. "Bloody bastard," he uttered. It was long-distance, the switchboard said, Pretoria. Mansell had forgotten about the call.

While he waited for the connection to be completed, Mansell picked up the second note. "Good morning, Inspector. Your unexpected visit last night was unexpectedly enjoyable. Thanks for the champagne. D.B." He reread the note twice, folded it carefully, and slipped it into his breast pocket. Unexpectedly enjoyable, he mused. Yes, it was.

The connection was made. He heard a voice say, "This is Deputy Minister Koster."

"Yes, Mr. Koster. Thank you for returning my call. Inspector Nigel Mansell here. Port Elizabeth CIB." As he talked, Mansell scanned the Elgin research file from Jo'burg. Jan Koster was not included. "We're investigating the homicide of Ian Elgin."

"Yes. Terrible thing. How can I be of service, Inspector?"

"Were you close?"

"Close, no. Friends, yes. We shared common interests."

"Spelunking. You and Elgin explored together."

"Yes." Koster's voice reflected surprise.

"When did you first meet?"

"It's been eight years now, maybe nine."

"Under what circumstances, please?" Mansell carried the phone over to the computer. He punched into Research Bureau, calling up the personal file on Jan Koster.

"My field is minerals, Inspector. Ian's, as I'm sure you know, was mining. We were introduced at a conference on mineral reserve management, if I recall. In Johannesburg."

"Introduced by a mutual friend, I suppose?"

"Yes. Is it important?"

"Probably not," answered Mansell. The computer indicated that Koster resided in Cape Town, but the Elgin file from that area didn't list Koster's name either. Curious, Mansell scribbled a reminder to himself. "A man dies. A hundred other men try to find out why. A lot of unimportant questions go into finding the answer to that one question, Mr. Koster."

"A very good retort," the deputy minister replied. "I believe it was Minister of Justice Leistner who first introduced us, if it's helpful."

"I see."

"Ian and the minister had been friends for some time. They were climbing partners, in fact, before Ian and I got together."

"Really? And you and Elgin started exploring together soon after your introduction?"

"No, actually, it was a year or so later, I imagine. Ian asked me to tag along on one of his trips. I picked it up reasonably fast, I guess."

"Where? Did you have a favorite site?"

"Royal Natal. There is no other place."

"No? Then you've never explored the cave sites in the Transkei?"

A long pause preceded Koster's answer. "Are we being serious, Inspector?"

"We don't know each other well enough to be anything less than serious, Mr. Koster." Mansell explained about the recent purchase of rope at the local sporting goods store, and the buyer's comments on the Transkei.

"Most interesting. Such rope is acceptable for climbing, that's true, but the buyer was either misunderstood or joking about the Transkei, I'm afraid."

"Yes. Or lying." Mansell stared down at the computer. "Spelunking is a specialized sport, is it not, Mr. Koster? A good partner, I've been told, is hard to come by. Was there any problem with your introduction to Elgin's team? Any conflict?"

"The search for motive. Very good," said Koster. "But I hardly think Cecil was disturbed. It was a mutual interest we all shared. And wasn't it the minister's recommendation that landed Ian his jobs with the Federation of Mineworkers Union? It couldn't have been a year later, but then I'm sure you were aware of that already."

Our esteemed minister peeks around yet another corner, Mansell thought. He massaged tired eyes. "When did you last see Ian Elgin alive, Mr. Koster?"

"It was three months ago," Koster answered. "We spent a week in Royal Natal, near Rugged Glen."

"And was he disturbed or upset in any way? Did he make any unusual statements about his work or his family? Anything that might have caught your attention? Please try to recall."

"He did say something. Something about the changing loyalties in Pretoria. He joked about it then, and it wasn't until later that I realized he was upset about it. Unfortunately, I missed it at the time."

"I see. Pretoria isn't generally a haven for labor-union officials. Was he talking loyalties given or received?"

126

A moment of silence transpired. Finally Koster said, "Isn't loyalty a two-way street, Inspector?"

Mansell studied the third note while climbing the stairs to the district prosecutor's office. It was from Detective Merriman Gosani. That morning Merry had contacted Eli Leavell, the Parks Service manager in the Transkei. Cave sites suitable for spelunking, according to Leavell, did not exist in the Transkei mountains. Following that, Merry had spoken again with the manager at The Outdoorsman. He, on the other hand, was equally certain that the buyer of the nylon-rayon rope had referred specifically to the Transkei.

The participants in this meeting were the same as the last, Captain Oliver Terreblanche, SB Major Hymie Wolffe, and Hurst himself. Air-conditioning cast a chill over the room. The prosecutor drank iced tea from a stemmed goblet. He polished black-rimmed glasses with the wide end of his necktie.

"Did the autopsy on the suspect Mabasu prove enlightening, Inspector?" he asked.

Mansell handed Hurst a copy of Pathology's preliminary report. "In Dr. Steenkamp's words, the victim might well have been dead before going out the window."

"Truly?" said Wolffe, the sarcasm in his voice only partially concealed. "Despite the fact that an eyewitness saw the man throw himself very much on his own power through the glass and to his very unfortunate death?"

"Unfortunate, indeed." Mansell continued to address the prosecutor. "There were signs of blood in his spinal fluid, his kidney was ruptured, his eardrum was broken, and his feet looked like they'd been put through a sausage grinder. Assuming this so-called eyewitness was telling the truth, and—"

"I resent that, Inspector," snapped Wolffe.

"Of course you do, Major. I apologize." Mansell glanced crookedly to his right. "Still, assuming the victim was not already dead, as the head of Pathology put it, he was certainly dying."

"And I am equally assured," Wolffe replied in a calmer voice, "that the doctor mentioned an overwhelming lack of proof of such allegations."

" 'Overwhelming' was hardly his sentiment."

"But these are not," said Terreblanche, "the first complaints about your interrogation methods, Major Wolffe. We all know that."

"However, in this case," announced the prosecutor, "those methods did provide us, perhaps, with a clue to the suspect's successful suicide." Ceremoniously, Hurst raised a sheaf of paper into the air. "This, gentlemen, is a signed confession to the murder of Ian Elgin. The signature belongs to Anthony Mabasu."

Mansell's eyes wandered over the room. He heard a siren on the street below. "The signature," he asked. "Has it been verified?"

"Don't be melodramatic, Mansell," Wolffe said, chuckling.

"It has been verified, yes," replied the prosecutor.

"And has your office accepted this . . . confession? Our investigation, for one, has several loose ends worth tying up before we hang a murder rap around Anthony Mabasu's memory. Another day, another week won't really matter at this point, will it? And we might all be able to sleep a little better if CIB's report and Security's reached a mutual conclusion. Don't you agree?"

The district prosecutor opened a desk drawer. He removed a cedar humidor. Inside were cigars as thick as a man's thumb. He gestured with the box, and Wolffe accepted with a gregarious nod. Spoils for the victor, thought Mansell as smoke spiraled to the ceiling. It's so much easier to close the books and go home.

"I think, gentlemen," said Hurst, "that we've gathered sufficient evidence, with the confession. Enough for a conviction had circumstances been different. Furthermore, I think Minister Leistner and the Justice Ministry will believe it, too, when they see my report. Let's close this case and move on."

Mansell glanced in Oliver Terreblanche's direction. A protest, he thought, was certainly in order, but none was made. Instead, the CIB captain clambered to his feet. He gathered his coat, put a hand on Mansell's elbow, and followed Major Wolffe toward the door.

"Inspector Mansell," the prosecutor called out. "Might we have a last word or two, please?"

"I'll see you back at the station," Terreblanche said, releasing him. The door closed. They were alone.

"You're not convinced that Mabasu murdered Ian Elgin, are you?" Mansell didn't answer. His stomach growled from hunger. He called on the panacea of a cigarette to help squelch the pangs. The district prosecutor came from behind his desk. "I've arranged an agreement with the Ciskeian police for your office to have complete jurisdiction over the Sylvia Mabasu case, assuming you also consider it a case worthy of further investigation. And, since there are considerable, shall we say, similarities between it and the Elgin case, I will make certain that all the information on both investigations is made available to you."

"I see," said Mansell. Their eyes met briefly, and he nodded. "Very well."

"Oh, and since the incident occurred in Ciskei, Security's not really a factor in this case. We'll have to do without their help, I think."

Four hundred people were demonstrating on the steps of City Hall.

Seeing this, Mansell used a rear exit onto Court Street. He walked down Main to the corner, where another two hundred demonstrators assaulted the entrance to the station house. Kids in dirty T-shirts waved handmade banners. Women in cotton wraps and bright head-dresses shouted "*Amandia, amandia.*" Men in worn jeans and base-ball caps extended fists into the air.

On the opposite corner, next to the Wool Exchange, Mansell sat in a deserted shoeshine stand. He watched two dozen riot police-men sidling behind flimsy barricades. A man in a clergyman's cassock mounted the station-house steps. Thrusting a thick book into the air, he exhorted the crowd, and the chant escalated. "Power, power."

Power, thought Mansell. A many-colored beast. Ian Elgin had wielded enough power in his time to have the minister of justice ramrodding his murder investigation, but not the power to fend off his own killer. True, a sharp blow to the neck wasn't enough to fell him, but a second blow breaks his nose and renders him helpless, maybe unconscious. Had he been unable to defend himself, or hadn't he expected the second blow? Could the blow to the nose actually have come first? A frontal assault that took him completely by surprise? Which might indicate that he knew his killer. Which might indicate that his killer was a woman. The chiffon scarf.

Two things bothered Mansell. First, the fingers on Elgin's right hand, those locked beneath the rope, weren't heavily bruised. The skin wasn't shredded. There was scarcely any indication of bleeding. Second, Sylvia Mabasu had fought off her attacker by reaching for-ward, clawing at the dashboard. Normally, a person aware of his imminent strangulation instinctively reaches for the ligature; fights it without regard for fingernails or skin; fights it until there's no more skin left; fights it until . . . until death intervenes.

Cecil Leistner returned from the prime minister's office in good spirits. With a cabinet meeting looming the next day, the P.M. seemed resigned to the fact that an unrestricted state of emergency was their only course of action in countering the rash of violence currently sweeping the country.

Oliver Neff, his press secretary, greeted Leistner with the news of Anthony Mabasu's confession and subsequent suicide.

"Very dramatic," Leistner replied. He led Neff into his office. "Is the story out yet?"

"The early editions. The streets are full already."

The room smelled of ginseng tea. Neff filled two cups.

Leistner watched the manicured hands of his longtime associate as he stirred cream into their cups.

Since his early days in the House of Assembly, Leistner had cultivated two relationships beyond all others. Two men. One now occupied the prime minister's chair in the office above him. The other was Oliver Neff.

Neff was a gnome of a man with a flair for words and two strikes against him. One, he was homosexual, which, in South Africa, meant certain and immediate expulsion from the Nationalist party, dismissal from the Dutch Reformed Church, and exile from the fraternity of Afrikaner brotherhood. Two, he was an addict, his poison being a white powder made from the leaves of the coca plant. Still, after all these years, only a handful of people knew of his "peculiarities."

But Cecil Leistner knew, had known for twenty-four years, ever since that freak meeting in Madagascar at the resort in Toliara. Yet he had, throughout the years, guarded the secret as if it were his own. In return, Oliver Neff, press secretary, had mastered the art of disinformation.

Neff could plant a story with a simple whisper or a major news conference. He could produce the lies to back up any story or the facts to deny it. His sources were too numerous to name: an aide-de-camp on Margaret Thatcher's personal staff, an aging official in the White House, a colonel in the KGB. His direct contacts in the media were likewise as varied: a Pulitzer Prize–winning journalist from Washington's most prestigious newspaper, an anchorman with the BBC in London, a commissioner with the South African Broadcasting Corporation in Johannesburg.

"Then it's finished," Leistner said in time. "Release a statement from your office immediately. Give it some flair, Oliver. You know, something to do with South Africa's black unions having been the victims of a direct assault by a disgruntled ex-member. Something like that."

"Yes, sir."

Leistner watched the door close behind his associate.

A last task remained. He crossed the office to a chrome-framed mirror situated against the outside wall between two bay windows. The mirror was hinged on one side and secured to the wall on the other by a magnetic catch. Behind the mirror was a wall safe constructed of half-inch-thick hardened steel with three locking bolts and a three-wheel combination lock.

The letter was inside the safe.

It had been written three months ago by Ian Elgin, in what must have been, Leistner thought, a fit of recklessness. He glanced through it one last time, shaking his head. The contents, he recalled, had nearly unraveled him then. His reaction now was more dismay. But in time, dismay was replaced by a bitter smile. It was all over now.

From his pocket, Leistner produced a butane lighter. He held the flame beneath a corner of the letter, and the paper ignited. Orange flames devoured the words. Then, mastering an inexplicable trace of reluctance, he returned to his desk and dropped the shrinking ash into the wastebasket.

An hour later, Leistner met Jan Koster in a coffeehouse on Bailey Street. Government workers, college students, and the smell of baking bread and almond croissants filled the room.

"We're close, Minister. Seven years of work."

"More than that," Leistner replied. "A lifetime." And yours, loyal fellow, he thought, eyeing Koster, has such a few short days left to it. A pity. Koster he would miss.

"And now we can put this business of Ian Elgin behind us. The case is closed," Leistner said, elaborating. "I've turned the whole thing over to Oliver Neff. It will be old news very soon."

"Let's hope so," Koster said vaguely. He knew as much already. He had received a message from Neff forty minutes earlier. It had taken nearly a year to discover Neff's "secrets," but the paybacks since, Koster thought, had been well worth the effort. He thought again of their conversation that night in February and wondered why he had never destroyed the recording. Someday, he mused, I'll hold it under Leistner's nose and we'll have a good laugh over it.

Koster didn't mention his telephone interview with the Port Elizabeth chief inspector. Instead, they discussed Leistner's meeting with the prime minister, and his latest round of talks with Lucas Ravele of the Federation of Mineworkers Union. Then they touched on the last stages of preparation at East Fields: the explosives, the progress of the arms, the "workers" from Mozambique, the expected arrival of Christopher Zuma.

"Unfortunately," said Koster, as a waitress freshened their tea, "we do have a problem. A potentially dangerous problem. It seems that two of our men were arrested this morning in Springs. Drunk and armed. Their work permits were confiscated. Worse, they've been accused of raping a sixteen-year-old girl."

"Christ. White or black?"

"The girl was white, naturally," Koster replied.

"You've notified East Fields?"

"They're aware of the situation, yes."

"Stupid Kaffirs." Leistner's agitation was short-lived. He smoothed his tie and stood up. "I'll make the necessary arrangements."

Jan Koster watched the minister of justice cross the street in haste. Then, pleased with the tenor of their meeting, he ordered another pot of tea and a cheese croissant.

The interior of The Camisole reminded Piet Richter of an Oriental music box. "Lingerie and Accessories for the Woman of Distinction" was the tag line below the shop's name.

Silk hung from the walls like pleated waterfalls. Mannequins dressed in sheer nighties and silk stockings posed beneath soft lighting. Racks filled with undergarments, hosiery, negligees, and brassieres enticed female and male buyers alike. A separate cubicle near the counter displayed porcelain jewelry, funky hatwear, and sheer neck scarves.

"The chiffon comes direct from France. The House of Dior," the owner explained. The rose scarf from the train station matched those on the rack exactly. "We have an exclusive here in Port Elizabeth."

The shop was crowded. The owner indulged each potential customer with a sculptured smile. After exhorting her assistant with a matronly glance, she directed Detective Richter to the back room. Together, they searched sales slips and credit-card receipts dating back to January. The results were negative. Richter asked for the previous year's records. After a weary sigh and lengthy pout, the owner capitulated.

Alone, Richter worked backward from December. Twenty-five minutes later, he found a Visa sales slip dated November 30. A Christmas gift, thought the detective. Brilliant. One chiffon scarf, rose, R49.95. Gift wrapping, N/C. The cardholder's name was Ian M. Elgin.

At 11:40, Lucas Ravele informed Delaney Blackford that her office was to expect a temporary liaison to clear up Ian Elgin's mining business in Port Elizabeth. Since Elgin had been allowed the use of the AU/UDW's facilities in the past, Ravele was hoping that the same courtesy might be extended to his replacement. His name was Steven de Villiers. His plane arrived at 12:25, he told her. Could Delaney please have a car waiting for him.

Delaney might have said that Ian Elgin was an employee of the Affiliated Union, and thus office space was provided to him for his FMU activities as well. What she felt like saying was that Mr. de Villiers could damn well take a taxi and work out of a hotel. Instead, she convinced one of her secretaries that a drive to the airport would be a nice change from the office.

The lack of notice was certainly intentional. Delaney knew that. But Mrs. Delaney Blackford's rise from the legal department of Transworld Express to chief legal counsel for the Affiliated Union of Dockers, Stevedores, and Rail Workers was due in part to her compulsion for knowing more about the people she dealt with than they knew about her.

Delaney placed three calls, and by the time de Villiers arrived at 1:05, she had learned enough to be leery. After twenty-five years of government service, de Villiers, according to one confidant, now held an untitled position on the justice minister's personal staff in Pretoria. A jack-of-all-trades was her description: handler of sticky personnel problems, contract disputes, interdepartmental squabbles. A second confidant was more forceful in his appraisal, calling de

Villiers a hatchet man with a much deserved reputation for ruthless-ness. "And if looks," he had said, "were ever deceiving . . ."

Delaney met Steven de Villiers at the door.

He epitomized, in her eyes, the quintessential image of the book-worm. His bearing was stooped, he was thin, and his complexion waxy. A bristle moustache overshadowed thin lips and dominated a hungry face. A dark blue suit was the liveliest dimension of an otherwise lifeless man, except for the eyes. The eyes were like blue fireflies, magnified by Ben Franklin spectacles, and framed by salt-and-pepper eyebrows. Eyes that studied her with an incisiveness that left Delaney disconcerted and ill at ease.

They shook hands. Delaney noted a bony firmness in his grip. His voice had a tinnient ring to it, melodic and feminine.

"How does one get blushing brides to bloom this time of year, Mrs. Blackford?" he said from the doorway. "They're wonderful. And the plants, what a wonderful distraction."

Delaney introduced de Villiers to the staff, and he announced, "I'm not here to interfere with a thing, Mrs. Blackford. I'll be as invisible as possible. Lucas Ravele asked me to baby-sit Mr. Elgin's chair until they hire a new negotiator. Clean up a few papers, make a few calls. Nothing more."

Then why, Delaney wondered, are you here?

A sky could hardly have been bluer, a breeze more stimulating, a sun more penetrating.

Chief Inspector Nigel Mansell paused at the corner of Fleming and Court. He gazed beyond the pillars of the overpass to Charl Malan Quay, but a flat, ugly warehouse obscured his view of Delaney Blackford's office. He settled for an obstructed peek at Algoa Bay. A fleet of sailboats skimmed across turquoise water, a rainbow of spinnakers and mainsails.

He met his car at the entrance to the police garage on Fleming. Merriman Gosani sat behind the wheel, munching an apple. The police radio barked staccato directives and static.

"It's a gas station in Lorraine," Merry explained. "They have a licensed franchise with Budget Master. There's a secondary passenger stop there for the narrow-gauge and a freight depot."

"Take M7. Maybe the scenery will be enlightening." Mansell

switched off the radio. He shed his jacket, loosened a narrow knit tie, and slumped into the seat.

"Too many late nights, pal," said Merry.

"Too many early mornings."

"Yeah. Chalk up another one for our vaunted boys in gray and blue."

Two kilometers west of downtown, Russell Street connected with M7. This four-lane parkway meandered lazily through the communities of Mill Park and Walmer. Here, the wealthy of Port Elizabeth resided, Afrikaners and English-speakers living side by side, tolerant if not friendly, money bridging the gap. Here, Asian gardeners tended the grounds, and servants served tea and toast beside the pool. Here, Old English, Tudor, and colonial homes from the first half of the century were nestled among towering eucalyptus and statuesque junipers.

At the area's heart lay St. George's Park, home of the country's oldest cricket club. Westbourne Oval, just minutes away, featured cycling, soccer, and the richest side-betting in the Cape. The neighborhood exuded age, prestige, and calm.

"My kind of place," Merry deadpanned.

The chief inspector chuckled. "Two problems, pal. One, you're a cop. They like their protection close at hand hereabouts, but they're not too keen on the protection moving in next door."

"All right, so I'll upgrade my wardrobe."

"Problem two, you put on too much lampblack this morning."

"That's a tough one. It's an image thing, you know."

"Making you about as popular as a cat burglar."

"Sounds like the challenge of a lifetime. I'll talk to my estate agent first thing in the morning." The car filled with laughter. A moment later, Merry said, "Speaking of challenges, Richter called in just as I was leaving."

Mansell perked up. "And?"

"The scarf was purchased at a lingerie shop in Newington in November by none other than Mr. Ian Elgin. Piet checked with Jo'burg just to be sure. Elgin's wife didn't recognize it."

"Obviously the man liked to spread his Christmas cheer around."

"A philanthropist. I'm touched."

"But the object of his benevolence hasn't come around. I wonder why."

"Why should she? I mean, who needs it?"

"All right. We know Elgin's been meeting his lady of the latrine since November. Maybe longer. We know she's black. And we know she dresses in style, if the scarf's any indication."

"So someone in the terminal has got to remember a woman like that."

"Exactly. But maybe that someone was Sylvia Mabasu. Maybe she knew too much." They crossed Circular Drive into Lorraine, an increasingly rural township. Mansell reached for the car radio. The patch was made to the station house, and he spoke briefly with Piet Richter. Then he asked Merry about Eli Leavell, from the Parks Service in the Transkei.

"He was surprised. He said the biggest cave he'd ever seen in the Transkei was about the size of a double-car garage. He also said there were no more than five hundred real spelunking enthusiasts in the entire country, as far as he knew. He said the sport lends itself to three common personality traits: a meticulousness that borders on compulsion, a desire for power, and a lack of conscience. And they generally have one weakness. They tend to lack intuition, and they tend to mistrust it in others. Mean anything?"

Merry eased off the gas. Here, M7 paralleled the Baakens River, a slash of cobalt blue meandering its way to the Indian Ocean. He turned left onto M15. Mansell watched rolling hills, woven of wild grass and red-roofed houses, pass before them.

"A nylon-rayon rope," he said, "is used in two murders within thirteen hours. A week before, a man in a three-piece suit buys fifty meters of the same rope. He makes a point of telling the clerk he intends spelunking in an area where no suitable caves exist. An intelligent killer would hardly be so descript, especially a killer with the character traits you just mentioned. It turns out that our victim is one of but five hundred cave explorers in South Africa. It all proves absolutely nothing, but I still can't let it go."

The tiny town of Theescombe lay at the crossroads of M15 and the narrow-gauge railway, situated among farmhouses and plowed fields. They discovered the gas station at the edge of town a kilometer north of the highway.

A paved lot, enclosed by a chain link fence and surrounded by acacias, was set away from the station. Inside the fence were ten compact cars—Hondas, Toyotas, and Nissans. A lemon-colored Honda Civic was parked outside the fence with Joshua Brungle perched on its hood.

Merry parked near the station, and Joshua hurried forward.

"This is the car," he said. "I did a preliminary overlay of the front left tire, full circumference. It's a match."

The gas-station attendant, a spry man of fifty, approached them with a grease-stained hand extended. His name was Bobby Verwaal.

"I don't need any trouble, Inspector," he said in clipped Afrikaans. "Business could hardly get any worse."

"I'm sure," answered Mansell, taking the hand. "What were the transaction dates and mileage?"

Joshua produced the rental papers. He said, "Rented four-fifteen P.M. the afternoon of the second. Returned Friday morning, July fourth at eight-eighteen A.M. Mileage accumulated, three hundred and fifty-six kilometers. It's three hundred and five kilometers from Port Elizabeth to Peddie in Ciskei and back again. As it turns out, the renter was a foreigner. He used a passport and driver's license for identification. His name is John Martyn. From London, England."

Joshua turned the folder over to Mansell, but Bobby Verwaal shook his head. "You can forget that one, gents. If Mr. Martyn's a Brit, then I'm a Kaffir. And that I'd swear to."

Mansell cocked his head like a snow owl watching a wolverine on the riverbank. He fished a pack of cigarettes from his jacket and held it out. After a moment's study, the attendant selected one. Mansell struck a match for them both, asking, "He was South African, then?"

"If I was the gambling sort, I'd wager not."

"Meaning what?" Joshua asked impatiently. "Speak up, man."

"Definitely European. No question. Austrian, on a guess. Austrian or German."

"That's fine," said Mansell. "And I suppose the car's been completely cleaned?"

The attendant massaged a day-old beard, a grimace tugging at the lines around his eyes. "I'm afraid the answer's no, Inspector. I've got to admit to that. What with help being what it is, I've only managed the outside so far. Sure, I know it's required and all, but the inside just wasn't that bad. . . ."

Unable to control his laughter, Joshua slapped Bobby Verwaal fondly on the shoulder. "Let me see if I can convince the inspector here not to report you on that one. Eh?"

Mansell glanced in Merry's direction and said, "We'll want a forensic team flown up here within the hour. And a sketch artist."

Merry scrambled for the car radio, and Mansell focused in on

Bobby Verwaal again. The way to an Afrikaner's heart, Mansell knew, was through history. For them, the arrival of Jan van Riebeeck in 1652, with three ships and orders to make a permanent station on the tip of what is now Cape Town, was the greatest moment in their history. It was a tool well used by one in search of a willing accomplice. "Your instincts are very good, Mr. Verwaal. You must be of Dutch blood."

"No other."

"A long line of Afrikaners in the Port Elizabeth area, then?"

Bobby Verwaal beamed. "An observant lad, you are, Inspector. My forebearers were among the first five hundred. It's true."

Van Riebeeck was employed by the Dutch East India Company. For the Dutch fleet in search of new lands in the Far East, Cape Town became a necessary port for supplies and a necessary reprieve from the sea. In 1662, when van Riebeeck was ordered further east, he left behind a contingent of five hundred whites. The infant town of De Kaap was aborning. The whites spread inland. Owning Bantu slaves became an acceptable custom, interbreeding with Hottentot aborigines an uneasy practice.

"Mr. Verwaal, the man who rented this car may well be a suspect in a double murder. We're bringing up a sketch artist from the city, and I need you to re-create that man's face for us."

"That I can do, Inspector."

"Good. We'll let you know when she arrives."

Bobby Verwaal thanked the inspector for the cigarette and walked back to the station. The woodwind timbre of a train whistle echoed in the distance. The 3:36 on the Theescombe schedule was five minutes late. Merry returned from his call, and Mansell waved them in the direction of a Coke machine near the gas-station rest rooms.

"Logic dictates," Joshua said, "that if John Martyn rented the car here, he must have come by train from Bloemfontein or Cape Town, right? But if he is our killer, then exposing himself to a twelve- or fifteen-hour return train ride doesn't make a damn bit of sense."

"By plane, he's out of the country in four hours," Merry replied.

"Right. So why does someone come all the way from England or Germany or wherever in the hell he came from to kill a union official and a black cleaning woman?"

Merry shrugged. "Revenge or money. Why else?"

138

"Meaning he was hired."

"Meaning, revenge or money, Ian Elgin would have to have been the primary target."

"Which means driving all the way to Ciskei to off Sylvia Mabasu would have to have been a smokescreen. A damn risky smokescreen," Joshua said.

"Not if he wants to frame the black cleaning woman's husband with both murders."

Joshua ran his hands roughly through his hair. "I don't know, Merry. That's a lot of trouble."

"But if Anthony Mabasu is pinned with the murders, our killer's home free and clear."

"True. And so is the bastard that hired him." Joshua was pacing now, woodenly and slowly, as if in a confined space. "Okay, this guy kills Sylvia Mabasu first, on Thursday afternoon, right? So he must know that Anthony Mabasu will be the one to find Ian Elgin's body. How?"

Mansell bought three Cokes from the pop machine and passed them around. He'd been listening to the conversation with one ear, while adding his own private puzzle pieces: a nylon-rayon rope, climbing in caves, victims who should have fought for their lives and didn't.

For a time, they drank in silence. A breeze sent birch leaves quaking. Overhead, a hawk circled.

"Someone or something convinced Mabasu that his wife would be in that locker room that night," Mansell replied, at last. Absently, he squashed the empty pop can between his palms and tossed it toward the trash container. The can caromed noisily off the side and fell undaunted onto the sidewalk. "We have two victims. Both are found with rope around their necks. Everything points to death by strangulation. Lividity of the mucous membranes, pale blue lips, froth around the mouth. Respiration failure is indicated by a lack of oxygen in the tissue and in the red blood cells. Classic symptoms. But the victims don't resist this terrible path toward death in the conventional way. I keep asking myself, Why? Maybe they were unconscious. Or maybe they were already dead."

In the ensuing silence, a quizzical mask painted Mansell's face. He gazed at both detectives, took two steps toward the car, and paused again. "So what else produces the exact same postmortem appearances as asphyxia due to strangulation?"

He strode toward the police car. Merry and Joshua set out in pursuit. Picking up the radio mike, Mansell looked back at Merry. "What time is Elgin's funeral?"

"Eight o'clock tonight at St. Magdalene's Church in Jo'burg. They're flying the casket up there at five twenty-five."

The station dispatcher acknowledged.

"This is Inspector Mansell. Get hold of Dr. Steenkamp. He's to meet me in Pathology in thirty minutes. I want an immediate organ review performed on the remains of Ian Elgin and Sylvia Mabasu. I'm on my way in from Lorraine right now. Do you have that?"

The dispatcher repeated the message, and Mansell signed off.

"Joshua," he said, walking around to the passenger side. "I'd like you to stay here, if you would. Follow up with Forensic and the sketch artist. Check in with me as soon as you're back. Merry, you'll drop me at the station house. Then I want you to see if you can find out how Mr. John Martyn of London, England, came to be in Port Elizabeth."

Steenkamp sat behind a desk filled with specimen jars, slide samples, and two high-powered microscopes. He hunched forward, worn but determined, the picture of an aging Atlas bearing his burden. He applied an eye to one of the microscopes, studying tissue from the heart muscle. He started with the eyepiece at 10X. He rotated the objective lens carefully.

The chief inspector's message, Steenkamp realized, conveyed much more than the written words indicated. Mansell suspected something. A missing link more than a hunch; an oversight as opposed to a mistake. The chief inspector of homicide did not call for an organ review on a body due for burial in four hours based on a hunch.

The staff toxicologist, a thirty-one-year-old Afrikaner with a crew cut and a weak chin, charged into the room. Steenkamp's posture remained fixed. He explained the nature of their inquiry, and they set to work.

Methodically, they finished analyzing the heart. Then they set about tissue-sampling the kidney. A picture is a layered affair, thought the pathologist, with hope as the only clear fixture in the distance. The toxicologist took cuttings from the victim's liver. His excitement swelled as the examination progressed, while Joseph Steenkamp's depression grew exponentially.

He had missed something. He felt deflation, not disappointment. Police pathology called for teamwork. He knew that. The head of the investigation, Mansell, was just another member of the team. His skills, meshed with those of the other team members, led to a discovery. Correct and logical. Yes, Steenkamp thought, but if Anthony Mabasu had died senselessly . . .

Footsteps—staccato, crescendoing—announced the arrival of Nigel Mansell.

"We've narrowed it down," was the extent of Steenkamp's greeting.

"Poisoned?"

"Exactly."

The toxicologist ran tests, first according to classification. Irritants, mineral acids such as hydrochloric and organic acids such as hydrocyanic, were dismissed out of hand; redness or ulceration of the intestinal tracts would have been detected in autopsy. Gases such as phosgene and carbon monoxide produced certain asphyxiation symptoms, but death was time-delayed. This didn't fit the M.O. surrounding Ian Elgin's death.

The most commonly used poisons in cases of murder were found in the metallic group, arsenic and antimony. They started there, spent the better part of an hour at it, and found the results uniformly negative.

Finally, they pinpointed their poison among the organic and vegetable groups at 4:59. The toxicologist, his voice serene, said, "I've never encountered such a mixture."

"Nor I, young man," agreed the pathologist. He hailed the chief inspector, and Mansell turned aside as the remains were hastily removed. "We've found our villain, Nigel. The victims were poisoned by a minute mixture of ricin and atropine. Between a grain and a half and two grains, I imagine. A very rare combination. I don't understand how I missed it. I must be getting old."

The toxicologist intervened; a restoration of face. "Excuse me, Doctor. I must beg to differ. A poison of this nature, Inspector Mansell, in such a small dosage, is undetectable in the first twelve to eighteen hours after death. I believe the first autopsy was performed the day of the murder, and the second, on the woman, three days after death. After sixty hours, absorption is complete, detectable only through chemical analysis. And the poison would be most effective administered in the neck area. Point of entry was disguised by the rope."

A suggestion of a smile crossed Mansell's lips. In time, he said, "Atropine is obtained from the belladonna plant, is it not?"

"It is, yes sir. It's a poisonous crystalline alkaloid."

"Death by respiratory failure," added Steenkamp. "Ricin is an extremely toxic protein. Comes from the castor bean. It has the effect of clumping red corpuscles together."

"Internal strangulation," said Mansell.

"It is initially isolated as a white powder," the toxicologist said. "It can be liquefied by heat treatment, and, under those conditions, I daresay, its potency magnifies."

The toxicologist stored his equipment and packed tissue samples. Mansell stripped off his coat. His appetite had returned for the first time in three days. Across the room, he spied the tea kettle, steam rising from the spout.

"Fine work, gentlemen," he said. "I'll expect a complete report from Toxicology by morning. Possible?"

"Seven o'clock on the dot," were the young man's parting words.

In private, Mansell poured tea. "Mabasu didn't kill anyone," he said.

"Impossible," agreed Steenkamp. "It would take a chemistry lab to concoct that mixture, as lethal as it was and in such minute quantities. Good Lord, I doubt Mabasu ever heard of ricin and atropine."

The pathologist led Mansell into his office. A backgammon board dominated his desk. Mansell scooped up the dice.

"How would it be administered?" he asked.

"Our youthful colleague was right. Injection. The tissues of the neck are particularly susceptible."

"Very professional." Mansell saw the inside of the ladies' lounge. The worn linoleum. The water-stained walls. The drab olive lockers. The smell of disinfectant. The killer lying in wait in a shower stall. Ian Elgin enters, woozy from alcohol. He calls out Sylvia Mabasu's name; no answer. Satisfied, he hangs his jacket in the sleep room. He returns to the lockers, sipping a soda. He hears footsteps. Anticipating his rendezvous, he is startled at the sight of another man. Still, the man's manner placates him. Discovering that this is the ladies' bathroom, the man displays embarrassment. Laughing. Well dressed. He carries a cane, or an umbrella. Perfect. The pellet containing the poison is concealed in the end. The man apologizes. He gestures with the cane, in an instant bringing the point against Elgin's neck. A triggering device releases the pellet. Apologizing again; how clumsy. Elgin stumbles. The blow to the neck. Dazed, feeling the effects of the poison. The blow to the nose; he crumbles. A minute later, he is dead. The man proceeds with his portrayal of strangulation and robbery.

Mansell cupped the dice. Answers, he thought, but even more questions. He shook the dice lazily and tossed them across the board; four on three.

The Honda Civic sat amid spotlights and flood lamps in the gas-station parking lot in Theescombe.

The interior of the car seemed to be layered in huge multicolored moth wings, an effect created by painting every inch of exposed surface with black, silver, dragon's blood, and aluminum powders, using fine camel-hair brushes. The finish on the outside of the car resembled silver peach fuzz, the result of a light spray of ninhydrin. A technician switched on an ultraviolet lamp and the fuzz crystallized, turning purple.

Photographing and lifting proceeded swiftly, the unfortunate result of a lack of evidence.

Another member of the forensic unit inked and mounted each tire. He made an impression of each on special photographic paper. An acetate overlay would serve as a comparative print for enlarged photos. He used silicone rubber to cast the left front tire.

Floor and trunk mats were secured for lab analysis. Beneath the front hood, the oil filter, the distributor, the spark plugs, the car-buretor, the oil cap, and the dipstick were all sprayed and photo-graphed.

Bobby Verwaal, the station attendant, spent ninety minutes with a sketch artist. A face materialized.

Eventually, the car was laid to rest on the back of a tow truck, facing further examination in Port Elizabeth.

An Allenfield-XM helicopter transported Joshua Brungle and a sketch of John Martyn back to the city as the sun set a thousand kilometers to the west.

The funeral procession meandered over manicured hills of grass newly mowed, hedges meticulously sculptured, and jacarandas majestically postured. The narrow road cut a path through fields of chiseled headstones and elaborate mausoleums. At last, the hearse came to a halt at the foot of a neatly fenced plot. A sprawling canopy hovered above pearly arrangements of roses, mums, and proteas. Neat rows of folding chairs flanked an open grave. Above this rectangular tabernacle, a bronze casket hung, an object in temporary suspended animation thanks to a luckless hoist and four aching chains.

The processional caravan doused headlights and parked haphazardly along the shoulder of the road. Delaney had rejected a half dozen offers of transport in favor of her own rental, knowing there was far more to this occasion than simple grief.

As it was, an elegantly dressed man with a pencil-thin moustache approached her the instant she stepped from the car. The general secretary of the United Dock Workers Association. So it begins, she thought. Word had already gotten around, and if rumors were to be believed, Delaney was a cinch for Ian Elgin's position with the Affiliated Union, while the mining union was said to be considering her for the chief negotiating position left vacant by Elgin's sudden demise. Certainly she should have felt honored. So why, she asked herself, didn't she?

"The aborigines," he said, offering her his arm, "leave their honored dead in the outstretched branches of the acacia tree. It makes the task of burial so much easier."

"And of course the scavengers of the bush are always quick to oblige, aren't they?" Delaney replied, glancing at him with raised eyebrows.

"The job is yours, you know," he said as they approached the grave site. "Board consultant? The title fits you well, Mrs. Blackford."

"I'm flattered, I'm sure." Delaney removed her hand from his arm. "Though I was thinking it a trifle obscure. Now, vice-president; that has a ring to it, don't you think?"

The family of the deceased was escorted to seats immediately adjacent to the grave. A wife unveiled, stoic, distant. Children grown, undisturbed, pampered. They'd come as well-planned addenda to Elgin's busy life, articles well managed by a mother with no other interests and thus, he had told Delaney, not to be tampered with.

The minister stepped in front of the casket. A hush worked its way through the gathering.

Prayers were offered. A eulogy spoke to the heart of Ian Elgin's better side. Delaney observed that tears were a rare commodity among the English, and the Afrikaners seemed more embarrassed in their attendance than sorrowful of the occasion. Black mourners, an elite few, observed the ceremony in much the same way as the English who had educated them. But well away from the site, beneath a tall linden, stood a black woman—young, hatless, tastefully dressed. She was lovely, even at this distance. A concourse of tears was readily apparent on each cheek. Delaney watched her dab at the streaks with a crumpled handkerchief. She saw erect shoulders sag, and then, as if suddenly aware of this display of weakness, drawn soldier-taut again, head high.

Delaney knew her face; familiarity without a name. There was recognition in a brief exchange of glances. Delaney nodding, the woman inclining her head quickly and hiding behind the folds of her handkerchief. Yes, she'd seen the face before. The name would come to her.

The minister bowed his head. The Bible closed with the ominous thud of a dead bolt. The hoist lowered its burden into the waiting arms of the earth. Watching the casket as it disappeared, Delaney couldn't help but wonder if anointment oils and a silk shroud were provided for one subjected to the grim ways of a murderer and the rotary saw of a pathologist. For some reason, she doubted it.

The daughter tossed a single rose into the grave, the son a handful of dirt. The wife turned quickly away. A man in a gray overcoat with matching gloves took her arm and whispered eagerly in her ear.

Ian Elgin would have found the charade comical, if not telling, Delaney thought. She watched the exchange and felt an ache deep inside.

"Delaney. A terrible thing, Ian's death. Absolutely shocking." The black man was enormous in all proportions, but his voice was angelic. Daniel Masi Hunter. The president of the Affiliated Union of Dockers, Stevedores, and Rail Workers.

"Daniel, hello." Delaney took his hand. "It seems your opinion would be in the minority here, but I happen to agree."

"Yes." Hunter glanced at the dispersing crowd and then at the grave, chuckling. "Ian once told me that embalming was too good for the bloody Afrikaner and mummification was just short of adequate for the proper Englishman. If I recall, we were drinking ouzo at the time, or something equally lethal."

"That sounds like Ian. I hope he's not too disappointed."

"And I'm hoping," Hunter said, facing her, "that we can make

145

the transition from Ian's death without losing too much ground in our talks with the Harbour Association, or in this contract hassle with International Consolidated. Are you prepared for that?"

"I'm prepared to take the ball and run with it, if that's what you're asking, Daniel. I'm not prepared to tread water, however."

"The reply I was hoping for, thank you."

They shook hands again and the union head lumbered away.

The name came to her. Lea. Lea Goduka. Delaney wheeled around quickly, but there was no one beneath the linden tree now. The woman was gone.

Debris and broken glass littered the streets. Torches lit the air. The demonstration spread from City Hall into Main Street and Court Street and finally joined forces with the throng besieging the police station. The crowd numbered three thousand by now. Police in riot garb, armed with bird shot, rubber bullets, and tear gas, formed a cincture around the buildings. Armored cars and army troops patrolled the streets. Helicopters hovered overhead. Sharpshooters armed with automatic rifles and high-powered scopes kept vigil from surrounding rooftops.

As yet, no arrests had been made.

But the cover of night, thought Mansell as he climbed the back stairs to his office, has a way of drawing sparks from smoldering coals. As he reached for the doorknob, he saw Jennifer standing at the window. Her eyes were fixed on the street below. She wore a cotton blouse, a soft rose color, and a cream knee-length skirt. Shoulder-length blond hair was pulled back and held by acrylic barrettes. By all appearances, she had come straight from school.

Mansell pushed past the door, and Jennifer wheeled around. "Hello," he said. "You've come down to watch the festivities."

"I've been here for an hour and a half. The festivities get boring pretty quick," Jennifer retorted, her narrow face taut with annoyance. "Where have you been?"

"I've been doing the job I get paid to do, remember? Two murders and a suicide equal an extra hour or so. Sorry you had to wait."

"It's too bad you don't get paid for that extra hour or so."

"Dedication. You know." Mansell stepped behind his desk. The carving out of territory, he thought. He loosened his tie. He dug for a cigarette. The timbre of crowd noise seeped through the walls, making the room feel smaller, less private. "But I don't suppose you came down here to talk about departmental wage discrepancies. You could sit down."

Mansell gestured to an office chair, and Jennifer abandoned her station at the window.

"Why don't you do something about the theatrics out there in the street?" she said. "It's disgraceful."

Gazing into blue eyes that were more angry than disgusted, Mansell wanted to tell her how disgraceful Anthony Mabasu looked splattered across the sidewalk in front of the Hall of Justice. Five years ago, he thought, Jennifer would have been out there in the street herself, demanding an explanation for Mabasu's death. But five years ago, on July 29, her youngest sister, Irene, was killed during a riot at a soccer match in Grahamstown. "Trampled to death," was the official ruling. And a part of Jennifer was trampled that day, too. A part of the fire extinguished. She gave up teaching that fall in favor of administration. Now she was the assistant administrator at Donkin Elementary.

"Let's get some dinner," Mansell said enthusiastically. "The cafeteria's got fish-and-chips on Mondays. Real fish, I'm told. Or better still, we could slip downtown to Ivory's for swordfish. What do you say? Shall we do it?"

Jennifer rummaged through her purse. "I can't, Nigel. Not tonight. We have a faculty meeting at school."

"Skip it. Let's be daring."

She found cigarettes and a lighter. Her voice was cold, distracted. "I'm speaking tonight. If you were home once in a while, you'd know that. I came about the weekend. Harriet called. She really wants us to come."

"Still trying to save us, is she?"

"Christ, Nigel. You're an asshole. We could use the time."

"True. We should talk."

"You mean that?"

Joshua Brungle tapped at the door. Jennifer turned away, uttering something under her breath. Mansell held up five fingers, and Joshua nodded.

"I do mean it, Jennifer, but then I'm not the one giving tours of my darkroom to men in gold chains and talcum powder."

"Fuck you, Nigel." Jennifer blew smoke aggressively from her lungs. Standing again, she marched back to the window. "Jason happens to be a colleague and a friend. A damn good friend. And lately, he's been there when I needed someone a helluva lot more often than you."

Mansell raised his arms above his head and drew a deep breath. "Then maybe you should invite friend Jason to Oyster Bay for the weekend."

"Is that what you want?" Her voice was at once calm and suggestive.

"You know, we used to lie in bed for hours together. Remember? With the fan on low. Making love. Talking. Laughing. What the hell did we used to laugh about? We'd take our paddleboards down to the schoolyard, and in ten minutes you'd have a bunch of kids playing with us. We'd plant a vegetable garden every spring, and you'd sprinkle zinnia and marigold seeds everywhere without telling me. How long did it take me to realize all those tiny sprouts weren't weeds? Cucumber-and-tomato salads. Laying out our sleeping bags on the roof, just staring at the stars for hours."

Jennifer stood apart, her back to him.

"Things change, Nigel. People change," she said in a low voice. "They have to. I have to. Change or suffocate. I need to do something more with my life, Nigel. I need, I don't know, something more to hang on to, something more to fortify myself with. Do you understand? And yet these last few years, it seemed like less was better, less painful. Feeling less, thinking less."

"Living less."

"Maybe." She faced him at last. "But sometimes expecting less leaves you stronger, I think. Sometimes opening up too much leaves wounds that never heal. But I'm tired of expecting less."

"Sure."

"I need to move, Nigel. I need another place. Away from Port Elizabeth. Away from street riots and murder investigations. Away from . . . all the memories."

And away from me? Mansell wondered. Yes and no. But he said, "I know. Tell Harriet we'll be down Friday morning sometime."

"Okay. Will you be home tonight?"

"Late."

"Me too."

Recalling a mind game that said creating a diversion would take one's mind off other diversions, Mansell switched on a portable radio in hopes of drowning out the cacophony in the streets. Classical. Someone's been playing with the dial, he thought. Joshua. Mansell recognized Ravel's *Bolero* and upped the volume a fraction.

148

He sat down at the computer. "Daily report. Subject: Homicide Investigation, Sylvia Mabasu." Mansell detailed the discovery of the Honda Civic and the pathology report on the poison. He mentioned the source of the chiffon scarf and the investigative team again combing the train station in search of the scarf's owner.

He dialed the captain's office upstairs and transferred the report via telephone modem. While he was printing copies for himself and the district prosecutor, Joshua entered the office.

Together, they studied the sketch of John Martyn. A face of extreme detail stared back. Transposed by colored pencils, it exuded life and emotion. Or rather, Mansell thought, a lack of emotion. Sunken cheeks and pronounced cheekbones gave the face a cadaverous look that thick, jutting eyebrows and a Grecian nose tended to balance. The hair was fine, short, and light brown. Mansell yearned for the forensic report on the Honda.

"Assuming we're on the right track," Joshua said, watching Mansell's eyes widen, "then the killer wasn't in the country when the rope was purchased from The Outdoorsman. So either we have the wrong rope, or someone else is involved."

"His employer."

"Or the woman with the scarf." Joshua shrugged. He said, "I think it was Holmes who said, 'Assumptions are a risky business.'"

"Holmes? Really? Would that be Sherlock or Oliver Wendell?"

"Mm. Maybe I was thinking of Hesse."

"Maybe we should wait until we hear from Forensic in the morning," answered Mansell, smiling. Ravel gave way to Bach. Mansell passed a copy of his daily report to the detective. "We have a new murder weapon."

"Remarkable." Joshua tugged on his ear. "But why poison?"

"If he was setting Anthony Mabasu up the entire time, then he'd want something that wouldn't show up in autopsy. Obviously, he didn't figure the organ review into his plans. True, Mabasu wouldn't have used poison, but then the killer didn't want to risk strangling Elgin outright. Too much noise on the one hand, and on the other, considering Elgin's size, he might not have gotten the job done."

"That's damn elaborate. Why not a gun with a silencer?"

"You can't hide a silencer from ballistics. The gun Mabasu could acquire, yes, but not the silencer." They pushed it around for another minute, and then Mansell jumped up. "I'm starving. Joshua, take your sketch over to Research Bureau. Send a copy over the wire to Interpol headquarters in Paris, and attach a copy of Martyn's passport and driver's license information. Maybe we'll get lucky. I'll have a word with someone from NIS about the ricin-atropine mixture." NIS was the abbreviated moniker for South Africa's National Intelligence Service. "It sounds like something covert and underhanded, doesn't it? Maybe it's in their files someplace. I'll meet you in the cafeteria in thirty minutes."

The framed houses of Freetown, Sierra Leone, reminiscent of old New England homes, were clothed in darkness by the time ARVA II docked alongside one of the harbor's modernized piers.

Its cargo, ten pallets of precut lumber, baling material, and packing foam, was already dockside. While diesel fuel and fuel oil were pumped from bunkers into the freighter's hungry belly, the pallets were hoisted onto the main deck and covered with tarp.

A review of ARVA's papers took no longer than ten minutes, and by 9:00 P.M., it was under way again.

Mansell ordered fish-and-chips. Joshua settled on pastrami and french fries.

They found a booth, and Mansell said, "If you were a black lady, a pretty black lady who owned an expensive chiffon scarf, would you wear it to work, or around the house, or just for nights on the town? Special nights?"

"Hell with that, I'd wear it everywhere. Why not?"

"And chances are good that, if Elgin gave you a fifty-rand neck scarf, he also gave you other things, other clothes, maybe jewelry."

"And if you're native, that's going to set you apart."

"And people would take notice," said Mansell. "Tomorrow, we'll start over with Elgin's old haunts, where he played, where he worked. She's out there. Maybe she's just a loose end. Maybe."

They saw Merry enter the cafeteria. His normally buoyant face looked haggard. The toothpick was missing.

"You passed up the pastry cart," Joshua needled. "What's wrong with you, man?"

Merry drew up a chair. He stole a french fry from Joshua's plate. "John Martyn bought a round-trip ticket on Air Africa out of Heathrow Airport in London on July first," Merry said. "He paid cash, twelve hundred pounds. The plane landed at Jan Smuts International in Jo'burg at eight-thirty A.M. on the second. He booked a South African Air flight to Verwoerd Airport here in P.E., and arrived at one forty-five P.M. So far so good. His return flight, number 618, was scheduled to leave Verwoerd on the fourth of July at nine thirty-eight in the morning. Martyn never checked in.

"I checked with Johannesburg. Martyn didn't meet his connection at twelve twenty-five that afternoon. He never rebooked. I checked with the railroad. No one using the name John Martyn has purchased a ticket on any outbounds in the last week. That leaves car or boat."

"He could have been out of the country already. Why would he leave town in a car or by boat?" asked Joshua rhetorically.

Merry stabbed another french fry. "He wouldn't."

They both glanced across the table at Mansell, who said, "He's still here."

THE NIGHT PASSED IN RELATIVE PEACE.

Police arrested twenty-three demonstrators. Four others were injured and taken to St. Anne's Hospital. No dead. The news was good, Mansell thought. The crowd dispersed at midnight under its own failing momentum. The funeral in New Brighton on Wednesday, he knew, would be a different story.

Mansell parked his Impala in the police garage and began the trek back to the station. Riot police still patrolled the streets. Maintenance crews used street sweepers, fire hoses, and push brooms to erase the evidence.

Struggling with fatigue, he mounted the station's granite steps, smoking half a cigarette before going inside. Another marathon session had busied Mansell until two this morning, when he had released a nationwide alert for John David Martyn. The circular, he knew, would be on the streets in 84 police  districts, 931 stations, 4 black homelands, and the cooperating states of Lesotho and Swaziland by nine.

Mansell was more concerned about John Martyn's next target. The man had forsaken legitimate passage from the country, and from the chief homicide inspector's perspective, there could be only one reason.

Inside, Mansell proceeded directly to the basement. Chas du Toits was humming something from Verdi's *Don Carlos* and scrutinizing a series of black-and-white photographs.

"So, it's our chief inspector," he said smugly. "I'd expected you earlier."

"Expectations are a dangerous affair at this time in the morning, Chas."

"We labored late into the night for your benefit, my friend. Our little Honda Civic proved an enlightening challenge."

"I'm holding my breath." Forensic reminded Mansell of a futuristic dentist's office. Du Toits's assistants moved with robotic stiffness and smiled lacquered smiles. The lab radiated blue light and gleaming tile.

"Yes, well. Let us start with the dashboard." Du Toits led the way to a long table covered in sterile paper and hosting a row of neatly labeled specimens. Druggist's paper held two fingernail fragments. A plastic bag contained shredded rubber. "You were right. The fingernails here belonged to our second victim, the Mabasu woman. The plastic rubber was gouged from the dashboard on the passenger side. She died quickly, but . . . not without pain, I'm afraid."

Du Toits shook his head. He moved on, saying, "Next, the seat covers. We found eleven hair samples on the headrest, all from the same man, all from a man thinning quite rapidly on top, I'm quite sure."

"Really."

"Hm. Average length, five centimeters. Light brown. Very dry. And an exact match to the ones found on Ian Elgin's sweater. These are the SEM results." Du Toits handed Mansell the printout. Then he held up a transparent bag containing wool fibers. "The black-and-gray fragments found on the first victim's sweater and on the driver's side of the Honda. One and the same."

Mansell felt a pulsing in his veins. "We've got him."

"There's more." The forensic chief passed Mansell an enlarged black-and-white photo. He switched on a fluorescent screen highlighting the corresponding negative. "This shows the carpet in the Honda's backseat. The crusted material is a reddish clay, one not indigenous to this area. Our friend stepped in a puddle of mud and then reached into the backseat. In doing so, he left a single impression from his left shoe. A shoe with a crepe sole, and the impression matches exactly those left outside the ladies' lounge Friday morning."

"We can—"

Du Toits raised a hand. He gestured across the room at one of his assistants and said, "Please note the sleepy lad there toying with the spectrometer. His fatigue, I confess, is due to a bit of a journey we sent him on last night. To Peddie, in Ciskei."

"The red clay."

"Indeed."

The chief inspector nearly smiled. "Careful, Chas, I may be forced to hand out a compliment."

"Do tell," he replied, inserting a specimen sample beneath the lens of a high-powered microscope. "And finally, the trunk. If you look closely, Inspector, you'll see that we detected fibers of nylon and rayon, the exact consistency of the ligature found around both victims' necks."

Mansell pushed strands of gold hair off his forehead. He bent over the microscope. Magnified two hundred times, the fibers looked like eager sperm cells.

"Fingerprints?"

"Sylvia Mabasu's and one other set, still unidentified."

"Probably the gas-station attendant's."

From the presidential stateroom, the Voortrekker Monument was a squat mass set atop the browning hills of the highveld.

Seated in velour armchairs, they gazed out at the scene through beveled windows. They smoked pipes and sipped English tea. It was the prime minister who broke the silence, saying, "I was surprised at the cabinet's support for the idea."

"It is a difficult step, isn't it?"

"You've been lobbying, Cecil."

"Yes, some, I admit it. But I think the time has come, Minister. I think it's that important."

"And dangerous." The prime minister turned in his seat. Eyes the texture and hue of an irreverent shark's locked in on his justice minister. "Dangerous to me."

"Still in all, the situation continues to deteriorate. As your justice—"

"If an unrestricted state of emergency is declared, how do you suppose the opposition will react, I wonder?"

"The opposition is not blind, Minister. And we can weather any—"

"We?" asked the prime minister coolly. " 'We,' you say. And if it blows up in our faces? Will it still be 'we,' Cecil? Who would be in line for my job, I ask myself, if—worst-case scenario—if our Western allies balk at such a pronouncement, if talk of disinvestment and economic sanctions erupts with increased vigor, or if Suzman and Tutu and the rest of the progressives finally get their heads together? Who, I ask myself?"

"Minister, you and I have been aligned for far too long, you know that. Your fate and mine are—"

"Yes. Yes, of course. Be that as it may, we'll give this state-of-emergency idea another week. The turn of the tide will be clearer by then, I would think."

There are times, he thought, when half an hour makes all the difference.

Mansell bounded up the stairs, two at a time, to the main floor. The Pit was a myriad of paper-strewn desks, abject work cubicles, ringing telephones, overworked holding cells, and incessant racket.

Joshua's feet were propped up on his desk top amid a collage of pastry crumbs, Styrofoam cups, paper clips, and pencils. He cradled a telephone between his ear and shoulder while constructing a paper airplane from last week's station-house newsletter. Mansell found an empty chair. He saw steam rising from Joshua's tea and helped himself. He held up a copy of the forensic report on the Honda.

A moment later, Joshua slammed the receiver down. He clapped his hands and said, "John Martyn has a name. Over the telex."

They were on their feet and out the door.

Crime Research Bureau was located on the sixth floor of the Hall of Justice. Air-conditioning hummed at an undisturbed tempo. Eggshell-white and watered-down lavender enhanced the coolness of the room, like vanilla icing on white cake. Proficiency and quiet oozed from every corner.

A tight-lipped woman with straight brown hair pulled off her face and held in a neat bun at the back monitored the international desk. She wore a blue-jeans skirt, midcalf, and a pullover sweater. Her face was scrubbed an ivory white. She wore a trace of red lipstick. Her last fling with rebelliousness, thought Mansell. And yet, despite every effort to the contrary, she was still pretty. Joshua recognized this, and he flirted, openly, but without success.

"Your readout," she announced conclusively, "will be up in sixty seconds."

True to her word, the CRT screen and the printer reacted simultaneously.

INTERPOL—DATA RESPONSE
INQUIRY—IDENTIFICATION ANALYSIS
Port Elizabeth, Cape Province, South Africa
SAP District #32, Police Station #291,
Criminal Investigation Branch
Authorization: N. Mansell CIH, J. Brungle D 1st

155

RESPONSE—Name: Fredrik Willem Steiner
Known alias: Peter Franks, John David Martyn
Date of Birth: 8/3/1948
Nationality: East German
Previous Residence: Dresden
Current Residence: East Berlin [address unknown]
Physical description: Male, Height 1.83 meters, Weight 69 kg,
Hair Brown, Eyes Gray, Blood type A+
Physical I.D. characteristics: tattoo on left tricep—i.e., *Stone Brigade*;
Abdominal scar: vertical, appendectomy

Steiner was arrested in West Berlin on April 25, 1985,
by West German police in connection with the assassination
of West German Defense Minister Adolf Böll. Detained three
days. Released due to insufficient evidence. Deported
May 1, 1985. Current status, unknown. Steiner is reported
to be an active member of the Stone Brigade, an East
German terrorist organization headquartered in Leipzig.
[inconclusive]
Photo and Print File to follow
INTERPOL Paris, France

The officer of the day, a thirty-year man named Sergeant Earlie Chandler, caught Nigel Mansell by the arm as he worked his way through the Pit.

Sergeant Chandler leaned close and said, "You got a call twenty minutes ago. A woman. Nice voice but a little stuffy. You know what I mean? Says her name is Mrs. Blackford. Mean anything? Anyway, I listen. Says she has something about the Elgin case for you."

Mansell shook his head. "The Elgin case is a closed book, Earlie, you know that."

Chandler nodded in return: procedure. "Sure. Why else would I tell you face-to-face?" he said. The chief inspector returned the nod somberly. "Mrs. Blackford says she'll be at the Egg Hatch at ten-thirty if you're interested. So?"

The Egg Hatch occupied a corner at Rodney and Main; no restrictions. An Asian family named Dali owned the restaurant. They specialized in ground coffees from around the world and the best apple strudel Mansell had ever tasted. Checkerboard tablecloths and fresh-cut flowers adorned each table.

Mansell held his enthusiasm in check. A glass of champagne and a thank-you note, he told himself, don't add up to a thing. And when he saw the black girl seated at the table with Delaney, he congratulated himself.

Delaney stood up, extending her hand. "Hello. Thanks for coming." Her handshake was firm and warm, and Mansell held her hand a moment longer than necessary. "This is Lea Goduka. Inspector Nigel Mansell."

"Good morning, Lea," he said. "It is still morning, isn't it? Are we having coffee?"

Mansell ordered Costa Rican for himself and Lea. Delaney chose cappuccino. When they were served, she said, "Lea's employed at the docks by the Harbour Association. She works at the port control tower for the port captain's office. She's also the secretary for the stevedores' local number twenty-one."

Mansell tipped his head. Lea Goduka appeared to be twenty-six or twenty-seven. A bright scarf tied off black hair and highlighted large eyes and a taunting smile. She wore a string of pearls over a cashmere sweater. Her positions at the docks and with the union spoke well for a black, but they didn't explain pearls and cashmere.

"Lea and I have known each other for a couple of years. We ran into each other at Ian's funeral yesterday in Jo'burg."

"A long way to go." Mansell turned pale eyes in Lea Goduka's direction. "You knew Mr. Elgin well, I take it?"

"Yes, sir, I did."

"We sat together on the flight back last night," Delaney explained. "Lea thought it would be wise to speak with you."

"I see. How did you and Mr. Elgin meet?"

Lea's eyes wandered nervously, eventually coming to rest on Delaney. "I think this was a mistake," she said. She pushed her chair back and stood up. "I'd better get back to work."

"Let's say leaving your scarf at the train station was a mistake," said Mansell, wondering at his own feeling of disappointment. "But coming to me wasn't. Please sit down."

Embarrassed, she asked, "You have my scarf?"

"A rose chiffon, nicely embroidered. Very pretty. I'll see to it that you get it back," answered Mansell. "Now about Mr. Elgin. How did you meet?"

"It was about a year ago. Ian—Mr. Elgin, I mean—had come down to the docks. He was meeting a ship. Somebody he knew, I guess. I remember because he kept kidding me about the name.

The ship was called the *ARVA*, you know, and Ian kept saying he thought the *LEA* would have been a more exotic name."

"I certainly agree," said the inspector. Laughter failed to cover Lea Goduka's anxiety.

"Well, Ian bought me a drink later that day, and we . . ." Her eyes met Mansell's briefly. She slipped back in her chair. "I don't want that girl to die with everyone thinking she was the one."

"Her name was Sylvia. Sylvia Mabasu."

"Yes, I know."

"So, then, you and Mr. Elgin became involved."

"Yes. Whenever he was in town. It was crazy, I know, the sleep room at the train station and all. But Ian had a crazy imagination. Something about places like that. I don't know. They turned him on, I guess. It's embarrassing, but we did have a good time. Once we started using the station, Ian would usually bring brandy or wine, and he'd always leave the cleaning lady, I mean Sylvia, five rand."

"Very generous. But you didn't keep your appointment with Mr. Elgin the night he was killed, did you? Or did you?"

"Yes. Well, no. I mean I was on my way, but some guy plowed through a red light and smashed into the front fender of my car. I couldn't believe it. And it wouldn't drive after that."

"What time was that?"

"Around two. We were supposed to meet at two-thirty, and—"

"Where did the accident happen?"

"On Commercial Street. Not far from home. I live in Kwaford near the stadium."

"And the man. Do you remember him?"

"He was nice enough. He said he was sorry, that it was his fault. He asked me not to call the police. He said he'd pay for the damage and gave me five hundred rand."

Mansell ran a hand through his hair. "He gave you five hundred rand for a dented fender? In cash?"

"I was afraid not to take it."

"That's fine. You made a good deal." From the breast pocket of his coat, Mansell produced a copy of the sketch of Fredrik Steiner, a.k.a. John Martyn. "Is this the man?"

As Lea Goduka studied the face, hopefulness dissolved into disappointment. "I really don't think so. I'm sorry. He wore glasses and a hat, a golfer's hat. He just left me standing there in the middle of the night. Finally, the police came, and—"

"What else do you remember about the man?"

Lea Goduka squirmed in her chair. "He was big. Not as tall as you, but bigger. And he wore gloves. I remember that. They were leather gloves. Kid leather, you know? They were a light tan color with a gold buckle across the back."

"Yes. I know the type." Mansell nodded briefly. Gloves and glasses. Hymie Wolffe? The bulldog face crept inside Mansell's brain. Annoyed, he pushed the image aside; wishful thinking. He said, "One more question, Lea. Your scarf. You say you never made it to the station the night Mr. Elgin was killed. Then how is it your scarf ended up in the sitting room?"

Lea hesitated. Avoiding Mansell's eyes, she glanced in Delaney's direction again. "The night before. We were supposed to meet. I waited three hours. Ian never showed up. I guess I was upset when I left."

Mansell nodded slowly. At last, he instructed Lea Goduka to come to the police station later that day to meet with a sketch artist, and the young black woman returned to work.

Alone, Mansell and Delaney lingered over the last of their coffee. He offered details about Fredrik Steiner while she examined the sketch. She mentioned Ian Elgin's new replacement. As they were leaving the restaurant, impulse seized Mansell, and he suggested, "A drink sometime soon? Maybe some music?" Delaney responded with equal impulse, saying, "Why not?"

When Mansell returned to his office, he canceled the search for the owner of the scarf. Instead, he assigned Merry Gosani the task of following up on Lea Goduka's story. He gave the detective details over the phone and then typed out a brief report.

Then he turned to the stack of papers on his desk.

A report from the National Intelligence Service detailed three recorded incidents of ricin and/or atropine poisonings, all within the past six years: a Bulgarian writer whose inflammatory exposé detailed the extremism and domination of the Bulgarian KGB; a former member of the Red Autumn terrorist group who turned state's witness but never got the chance to tell his story; a West German attorney general whose declaration of war against syndicated crime in that country proved extremely unpopular.

A thirty-page report on the Federation of Mineworkers Union mentioned Ian Elgin only once, and then only by name and title.

Piet Richter's personal profile on Deputy Minister Jan Koster indicated a typical Afrikaner official who worked too many hours and spent too many days away from home.

Mansell set the lot aside and went in search of the district prosecutor.

Peter Hurst, with a briefcase in either hand, was hastening from his office when he saw the chief inspector approaching. He hesitated long enough to realize there was no escape, and then continued on.

"What is it, Inspector?" asked Hurst, as they walked toward the elevators on the third floor. "I have twenty-three arrests from last night, a near riot and two deaths at the auto plant in Uitenhage, a hearing on Anthony Mabasu in ten minutes, and an injunction pending against the Wool Exchange this afternoon."

The elevator doors closed around them. They started down.

"You also have a bungled murder investigation on your hands, Prosecutor," said Mansell bluntly. "The results of which, were they to become public, would no doubt see you out of a job come the next election."

The doors parted. Neither man moved. Peter Hurst stared, thin-lipped, at the chief inspector of Homicide. At last, he said, "That case has been closed, Mansell."

Mansell pressed the hold button. He corrected the district prosecutor, saying, "The Elgin case is closed. The Sylvia Mabasu case, on your orders, is still very much open. Peter, our two victims weren't strangled, despite Security's assertions. They were poisoned by a highly sophisticated amalgam of ricin and atropine."

They exited from City Hall by way of the courtyard. The sun stood high in the sky, fluorescent and penetrating. Hurst paused to put on sunglasses.

"Confirmed?" he asked. "Forensic, Pathology, the works?"

"The reports will be on your desk in one hour."

They crossed the Mayor's Garden and stepped into the shadows of the Provincial Courthouse. "This is sticky, Inspector. You realize that."

"Then let's unstick it, shall we?" They stopped at the entrance. The building was a modern heap of smoked glass and chrome. "We've identified the vehicle that Sylvia Mabasu was riding in at the time of her death. It's the same Honda Civic that was parked beneath the lounge windows at King George Station the night Ian Elgin died. And we've identified the driver."

An old Ford cruised down Station Street with the radio blaring. A street sweeper lumbered slowly past, dodging cars along the curb and leaving a thin streak of muddy water in its wake. Mansell held the door open.

Finally, Hurst removed his sunglasses. An exaggerated sigh escaped his lungs. "Mansell, you amaze me. You really do. Meet me in my office at two sharp. I'm on a tight schedule."

Congratulations, thought Mansell, wondering who the district prosecutor would have to consult with between now and two, but resisting speculation.

Fifteen hours out of Freetown, Sierra Leone, ARVA II steamed across the equator into the placid waters of the South Atlantic.

From the freighter's musty hold, a rear derrick crane hoisted eight crates onto the main deck. Then, under the watchful eye of Andrew Van der Merwe, the object of ARVA's rendezvous at sea three days before, the trademarks, superscriptions, and shipping imprints on each crate were methodically obliterated by two crew members armed with power-belt sanders.

When the dust of their labors lay floating upon the blue waters of the sea, other hands set about uncovering the recently acquired pallets of precut lumber, packing supplies, and the baling materials. An assembly line of six men, each equipped with basic carpenter's tools, was formed. Working from a design perfected during five previous voyages, the crew constructed eight new, slightly larger crates.

When the crates were completed, a gas-generated feed pump was brought on deck, and on the bottom of each new crate, the crew sprayed a thin layer of polyurethane foam. When the liquid foam was exposed to the air, it expanded and hardened. A deck boom laid the original crates inside. More foam was added.

Finally, as the last layer of foam solidified, mining implements were carefully arranged upon its surface: a single pneumatic hammer and two pickaxes. The foam swelled, locking the tools in place.

When the foam hardened completely, the crew nailed the lids shut. Baling wire secured the packages further still.

161

A stencil was carefully placed on two sides, and a thin spray of red paint christened the crates with new markings:

EAST FIELDS MINING CORPORATION
EAST RAND—BRAKPAN COUNTY
TRANSVAAL PROVINCE
SOUTH AFRICA, AFRICA

A rubber stamp added the words *Bonded and Secured* on each end.

By noon, all eight crates were safe and snug in ARVA's hold. By 10:15 that night, nails were set on the fiftieth crate. Again, baling wire was secured, and labels were stamped and painted. Finally, as the waxing moon rose ever higher in the sky, the deck was cleared, and the crew was relieved.

Tomorrow they would begin anew.

District Prosecutor Hurst had not been flattered by Cecil Leistner's personal interest in the Ian Elgin murder. Interest, Hurst realized, breeds attention; attention leads to scrutiny.

Equally, Hurst had not welcomed the new evidence presented to him this morning by Inspector Mansell. It meant reopening a case best left closed. It meant exposing himself.

Therefore, Hurst placed a direct-dial call to a certain Mr. Martin Montana in Johannesburg. Montana listened carefully to the new developments. He advised the prosecutor to make a second call, advising him also on what to expect from the call. He also told Hurst it was vital that CIB maintain its investigation into the Elgin-Mabasu murders. Hurst understood what this intimated.

The second connection took ten minutes and three secretaries to complete. Finally, the minister of justice came on the line.

"Prosecutor Hurst, what a pleasant surprise." A voice filled with warmth and acquiescence. Hurst would have preferred cold and suspicious. "How's the weather on the coast?"

"Marvelous, sir. Just beautiful. You should spend a weekend with us sometime, Minister. The sailing is excellent this time of year."

"An invitation I should consider, but, perhaps, not the reason for your call, yes?"

Hurst reviewed the new evidence for the justice minister. If Leistner was irritated or disturbed, he didn't show it.

162

"Intriguing," he said. "My compliments to the inspector. And your opinion on how we might proceed, Prosecutor Hurst?"

The prosecutor loosened his tie against the stuffiness gathering in the room. "The evidence against Anthony Mabasu is hardly concrete at this point, Minister."

"This raises some questions, certainly."

"Yes." There was a knock at the office door. Nigel Mansell entered the room. Hurst waved him to a chair at the rear of the office. He swung his own chair away, facing the windows, and said, "Minister, CIB has already issued a nationwide alert for Fredrik Steiner. It appears he may still be in the country. I think this means questioning the results of the Elgin investigation, perhaps reopening the case, sir."

"Nonsense," Leistner retorted. "It merely means we're following up on new evidence in the death of Sylvia Mabasu. A news conference to that effect might quiet things down in your neck of the woods, Peter. Think about it. Also, remind our ambitious Inspector Mansell that the Elgin affair is still a Police Act matter. And, until something concrete comes of your alert for Fredrik Steiner, it may be that you can find another matter into which the inspector might put his energies. Good day, Prosecutor."

Peter Hurst cut the tip off a Don Diego. He spent a moment savoring the aroma, composing himself. Then he lit the end with a long fireplace match. Eventually, he waved Mansell forward.

"Care for a cigar, Inspector?" Mansell shook his head, and the prosecutor reclined further in his chair. He drew heavily on the cigar, exhaled, and followed the path of ascending smoke as it huddled against the ceiling. At last, he spoke again. "Two blacks, a man and a woman, were knifed yesterday in Uitenhage. You know that, of course, but there does seem to be some confusion in the matter. I'd be grateful if you'd handle it personally. Nip it in the bud. The blacks are accusing the riot police. The police are saying it was an execution of informers by the blacks themselves. Not a unique exposé, true, but nonetheless touchy."

Mansell bent his head forward. "An illegal demonstration at the gates of one of Port Elizabeth's most important taxpayers, the sole purpose of which is to point out wage discrepancies between whites and blacks? An illegal gathering designed solely to create friction between races? By legal definition, flagrant acts against internal security. By law, flagrant acts in violation of . . . of what? The Terrorist

Act? The Suppression of Communism Act? The Gatherings and Demonstration Act? Certainly matters for the Security Branch, Prosecutor, not the lowly CIB."

Hurst sat up, cigar clenched between his teeth. Mansell exuded a quiet indifference. The prosecutor attempted to match it.

"This office and that of the district commander will authorize your investigation, Inspector. Please begin this afternoon. I'll look for a preliminary first thing in the morning."

"And my present investigation? Ancient history, I suppose?"

"No, no. No need to let that die on the vine, is there? Detective Brungle seems competent. Have him coordinate things for a time. Keep an eye on him, of course."

If only humans were blessed with the ability to read minds, Mansell thought. He asked, "You're not closing the Sylvia Mabasu case, then?"

"Absolutely not. Also, if it hasn't been done yet, have the detective expand the alert for Steiner to include NIS," replied Hurst. "Oh, and by the way, the minister of justice commended your diligence on the entire affair."

"I'm flattered. And was it the minister who suggested I be reassigned?"

Hurst glanced in Mansell's direction, eyebrows arched, lips pursed. He reached for the telephone.

"Susan, connect me with Captain Terreblanche's office, please." He covered the mouth of the receiver with his palm. "Will you excuse me now, Inspector?"

SAMUEL CRAWLEY HAD BEEN THE IDEAL INMATE AT JANSENVILLE Provincial Prison. Nothing in his history had suggested that he would be otherwise. Sam possessed the demeanor of a lazy river and the imagination of a child.

But some six years ago, on a cool Saturday in August, the forty-six-year-old African, a quart-and-a-half drunk on grain alcohol and fruit juice, hopped aboard a number seven bulldozer owned by a wheat farmer named Johann and lost control. The cows in Mr. Johann's pasture, Sam told the magistrate at his trial, "looked more like giant robots spittin' fire than they did cows chewin' grass." And the robots, he swore, were marching straight for town. The number seven bulldozer had been Samuel Crawley's idea of civil defense.

As it turned out, it proved an effective weapon. The two-and-a-half-meter blade mutilated and killed nine cows before Johann's son, Isaac, managed to subdue the drunken man. Unfortunately, Isaac Johann was the second person to arrive on the scene. The first was a fellow farmhand named Si Bram-ble. Si was also drunk; not so drunk that he was unaware of Sam's odd behavior, but enough so as to get himself caught beneath the dozer's steel tread, where he was instantly crushed to death.

Samuel Crawley was contrite and repentant. The magistrate was lenient. He received an eight-year sentence, served four, and was released on the condition that he find full-time employment.

The boiler-room job beneath H. F. Verwoerd Airport suited Sam just fine. Mostly he read comic books, "The Dragons of Doom" being his favorite, and worked crossword puzzles, generally without success. And though he hadn't the skills to operate anything so complicated as a pressure valve, Samuel Crawley knew how to stoke a coal fire. So when the airport janitors emptied rest-room trash into a dozen different trash chutes, it all ended up at Sam's basement station. It was his job to dispense of it.

On down days, when Sam remembered how his friend Si Bramble had looked under that bulldozer, he would take his sack lunch to

165

the floor below the boiler room, where sewage and water pipes kept company with concrete and condensation. It was cool and quiet; no one ever disturbed him.

Friday was one of those days.

Sam had carved out a nice spot for himself near the service elevator. There was an old luggage rack for his comic books and his lunch and a folding chair. But today the chair was occupied. Some guy was sitting in *his* chair resting his head and arms against *his* luggage rack. Sam was fit to be tied.

"Som bitch," he hissed, working himself up an ire, truculency being one of Sam's weaker suits. "Mo' fo' can just up and take his goddamn snooze some other place, and thas fo' sure."

Shoulders squared and lunch sack swinging, Sam took long, loud strides across the concrete floor. "Okay, mister," he snapped. "Yeah, you."

But Sam stopped cold. A shiver leapt from his lower back to the hair on the top of his head. It smelled like ol' Jolly Fanon's cell after that stupid guinea pig of his up and died, and ol' Jolly wouldn't take it out of its cage for a week. No, man, Sam thought, this's worse. Guy musta drunk his fill of something awful nasty, an then up an puked right where he passed out.

Sam held his nose. He walked closer. Forty-watt bulbs didn't provide much light, but he saw flies buzzing about the head and something else moving around the face.

"Hey, mo' fo', what the shit you doing down here?" Sam shouted. "Get your ass up, will you? Get on outa here."

Sam grabbed a handful of hair. He pulled the head back, and a black hole jumped out at him from between sunken eyeballs.

Sam screamed first and then threw up.

The telephone rang as Nigel Mansell laid swimming trunks into the bottom of a suitcase. On the third ring, he heard Jennifer answer. He waited thirty seconds before relaxing again.

As he was crossing the floor to his chest of drawers, the full-length mirror next to Jennifer's dressing table caught his eye, and he stood before it. He wore Jockey shorts and slippers. Genetic inheritance having blessed Mansell with a lithe, rangy body, he rarely exercised. Squash and snorkeling when time permitted. Still, he weighed in at eighty kilograms, and most of it was still in the same places it had been ten years ago. But the ivory hue of his skin caused Mansell to sigh. Silently, with shoulders ridged and a smirk on his face, he ordered himself to find time for a few hours of sun this weekend. For the good of your own reflection, he thought.

When Jennifer entered the room, he struck a comic strong-man pose. She didn't notice. "Who was it?" he asked.

"Your office. I told them you'd already gone up to the bay."

"Any message?"

"I didn't ask." Jennifer stripped off nylon stockings. "You're on vacation for seventy-two hours, remember?"

Expelling a sharp breath, Mansell walked to the oak lampstand next to the bed. "I'm not a stockbroker. I'm a servant of *die Volk*, remember?"

"The bloody arm of the law. I wish to God you were a stockbroker."

He picked up the phone and dialed.

Mansell left Jennifer with the Impala and the promise to meet her later that evening at Jarrad and Harriet Pruitt's in Oyster Bay. He drove the police sedan to the airport.

"The victim was sitting in this chair, in this very spot when he was shot," said the pathologist. Steenkamp brushed fly eggs and maggots away from the face. Mansell sucked smoke into his lungs, a futile attempt to combat the attack on his olfactory senses. Despite powder burns, a tattooing ring around the bullet hole, and the blackish hollow between the eyes, Mansell knew he was looking at Fredrik Steiner.

"A single bullet entered here at the base of the frontal," Steenkamp continued, "exiting a centimeter below the occipital. Extremely close range."

The chief inspector stood opposite the luggage cart. He struck a classic stance for firing a handgun: feet spread, arms extended, hands together, a finger impersonating the gun barrel.

"Sixty to eighty centimeters. A clean shot."

"It's cool enough down here," said Steenkamp, "but putrefaction is well advanced. Our friends the maggots and their busy cohorts attest to that."

Bloating from gas, darkening of the skin of the suspended arm, blisters, discoloration. All tools used to pinpoint time of death. But an unused airline ticket would probably suffice, thought Mansell. He said, "He had a plane ticket to Jo'burg at nine thirty-eight the morning of the fourth."

"Someone displayed a rather strong prejudice against his being aboard, I'd say." Steenkamp continued his examination. The pool of dried blood on the luggage rack was small, the muscles of the face slack. "He died immediately, and, I'm quite sure, without protest."

Four meters behind the victim, there stood a framed wall covered only in Sheetrock. Mansell stepped around the luggage rack, positioned himself with his back to the victim, and took four steps. He bent down. The concrete was dusted with white powder. A recent occurrence, he thought. With his fingertips, Mansell picked up fragments of the white granules. He followed the line to the wall. A puncture hole the size of a goose egg revealed itself in the Sheetrock a meter up from the floor. Using a penknife, Mansell cut away the drywall. He found the bullet embedded dead center in a stud.

"A gunman of remarkable accuracy," he said, wrapping the slug in a cotton handkerchief.

Amid the lumination of portable flood lamps, Anna Goodell photographed the scene. She completed detailed sketches from three different viewpoints. At last, they moved the body away from the luggage rack. Steenkamp checked the abdominal area and the lower extremities. Mansell searched the victim's pockets. They were, except for a single piece of paper, the size of a business card, empty. He discovered the card in Steiner's shirt pocket. He extracted it with great care. The card was blank on one side, but on the other, four words had been typed. They read "Caves of the Womb."

Mansell stared at the words like an aging philosopher convinced, beyond doubt, that he must surely be on the brink of some profound epiphany, only to find his memory failing and his mind wandering.

He passed both card and bullet to the chief of forensic science and ordered the body removed for immediate autopsy. He and Joshua proceeded with their search. They found the freight elevator inoperable, but little in the way of physical evidence.

While Forensic set about its tasks, Mansell spent fifteen minutes with Samuel Crawley. The witness was excitable, curious, and undeniably without guilt. His lack of insight into the matter was equally undeniable, and Mansell sent him back to the boiler room with a pack of cigarettes and an uneaten lunch.

A moment later, Merriman Gosani returned from upstairs with a half-eaten candy bar and a full scratch pad.

"I spent an hour with the airport chief of operations and the maintenance super," he told Mansell. "The freight elevator's been out of action all week."

"And they discovered that when?"

"Monday, the super said, but it was definitely in working order last week. The elevator stops at every floor—in the baggage-claim area on the lower level, on concourse A on the first floor, in the terminal cafeteria on two, and in an employees' lounge on three. But it's rarely used." Merry showed Mansell a typed page with ten names on it. "The elevator is key-operated. Those are the names of the people with keys, but the super said spares are available on the board in the employees' locker and in his office. I've got a man working through the list right now."

"Okay. The elevator stops at four places. Use those as your reference points," Mansell said. "Start with the employees in baggage claim and on the concourse, and anyone who might have used the lounge or the cafeteria on Friday the fourth. If nobody ever uses the elevator, then maybe someone noticed something. Use the portrait sketches we got from Lea Goduka and the manager of The Outdoorsman. Who knows?"

They started back toward the crime scene, a stage now illuminated by purple spots and flashing speedlights.

"By the way," Merry said, "didn't you have plans for this weekend, pal?"

The chief inspector raised an eyebrow, and Merry turned away, smiling. Mansell fished for a cigarette. The words wouldn't leave him alone. The Caves of the Womb, he thought, extemporizing, . . . where blue light flickers from the soul of the earth and the sun is . . . and the sun is what? . . . Damn it.

He went in search of a telephone.

Mansell harbored a strange fondness for the ballistics lab.

It was a small room with a worn tile floor and pale green cement walls. Some energetic soul had plastered the walls with posters of Table Mountain and graphics from a production of *Carmen*.

A water tank four meters long dominated the space. A marble counter filled with X-ray lamps and photographs lined one wall. The lab technician was scanning the bullet through a comparison microscope when Mansell arrived with a Styrofoam cup of hot tea and lemon.

Mansell leaned over the apparatus, adjusting the focus. Beneath the left eyepiece lay the slug he had taken from the stud at the airport. A second bullet occupied the right slide, an unfired comparison. The first was severely damaged from contact with bone, concrete, and wood.

"It's not one we see very often, Inspector," said the technician. "It's a .45-caliber manufactured primarily for an American semiautomatic. The model number is M1191 A1. It's a service weapon by and large."   *M1911A1*

"The U.S. Army pistol."

"Standard issue," he replied with a shrug that barely concealed his enthusiasm. "Check the rifling, Inspector, and the lands and grooves."

"New?"

"Brand-new. The gun hadn't been fired before, period. This was the first bullet." Mansell sipped his tea, listening. He glanced at the wall clock. Four-fifteen. The technician showed him a photo of the gun. "It's a beautiful design."

"John Browning, wasn't it?"

"That's it. Nineteen-fifteen." *Eleven* Excitement burst forth. "The United States Army has used various versions of this same gun ever since. But it hasn't been imported here to any extent since the mid-1960s. And since the '77 embargo, well, not at all."

Mansell departed ballistics at a slow gait, cursing his addiction while striking the match.

A gun that hasn't appeared in this country, legally, for over ten years, he thought. How likely is it that someone has had a brand-new .45-caliber handgun stashed in an underwear drawer in his bedroom for the last ten years? The victim knew his assailant, trusted him some—enough. Enough to follow him down a rusty freight elevator to a dingy basement three floors below the airport. Enough to sit quietly in a folding chair while the man put a bullet between his eyes. Steiner was a professional himself, and how often does a guy like that let his guard down? Mansell wondered. With a friend maybe, or an accomplice. Or his employer. Which means they were talking about what? Money? A new contract? More money?

Since homicide was the spice of their science, the specialists in Forensic always appreciated a visit from the chief inspector. The one vacuuming pockets from the victim's clothes smiled thinly. A second scraped blood samples from the luggage cart.

Chas du Toits had just returned from the airport.

"What we know for certain is what you know for certain," he

offered. A spark of mischief flashed from his eyes, for there existed a definite correlation between an inspector's consternation and the rising value of his forensic team. "The victim is definitely Fredrik Steiner. We have print confirmation. We have the shoes. We have SEM and protein analysis on the hair."

"My day is made. And how about the clothes?" Mansell hoped that a locally produced item might give a clue to Steiner's employer. "Any idea on the manufacturer or the place of purchase?"

"Playing the long odds, are we?" Du Toits turned up the collar on Steiner's long-sleeved shirt. Made in the People's Republic of China. Fifty-five percent ramie. Forty-five percent cotton. "Who knows where clothes come from in this day and age? You could find the same shirt at Sander's in Jo'burg or at La Bola here in P.E. The sweater comes from Italy, as we expected. Expensive, very nice."

"Anything on the card?"

"Standard business-card stock, available at a thousand office-supply stores from here to Cape Town. No prints. But we know that the words were typed on a 1949 Olivetti portable. I like that. A nice touch. The character *e* is mis-set, high left. We'll have more in the morning."

"Joshua will be around," Mansell replied. "Don't give him any less grief than you give me, please."

O yster Bay, by carrier pigeon, was a hundred kilometers from the heart of Port Elizabeth. Using the freeway, the drive took an hour and twenty minutes, but Mansell opted for the scenic route, the beach highway. An impending dread hung about his shoulders, and he couldn't talk himself out of it. The weekend, he told himself half sarcastically, meant putting out, facing up, and making decisions. Three of his favorite things. Absolutely. Still, he thought, Jarrad and Harriet were the kind of people you could spend a weekend with in comfort.

Jarrad Pruitt and Mansell were college chums. They had met in the dormitory at the University of Natal. They shared the same suite, the same passion for tequila and hash, the same diet-pill approach to studying, some of the same women. Mansell began his education in marketing; Jarrad ended his there. Advertising, he never tired of telling Mansell, made the world spin. "People can be sold anything." He was right, Mansell thought. The more fallacies that are applied, the more gullible people become, and the more society degenerates.

He cranked down the back windows. Cool air filled the car as he drove southeast on Humewood Drive past the Apple Express into Summerstrand. In the spring and summer, the tourists flocked here. The beaches were wide and white. The water seldom dropped below seventy degrees. The waves were tailor-made for body surfing, and the women were so scantily clad that the imagination numbed.

This evening it was quiet—a lone sailboat with a pinstripe spinnaker billowing in the breeze, a sunset washed in pinks and purples.

The report from Research Bureau lay on the passenger seat next to a bag of green grapes and two bottles of Suaza tequila. Mansell switched on the radio. Humewood Drive mutated into a numerical interchange called M4. M4 swerved westward past the golf course and the Wool Institute. The University of Port Elizabeth slipped past on the right. A broad, flat champaign of wild grass and scrub oak opened up before him. The ocean protected his flank. He felt immune.

Mansell picked up the research report. He anchored it across the steering wheel. A man, he thought, is shot down in cold blood. His body is stripped of every article except a business card with four words typed on one side. Why? Three explanations came to mind. Either the killer overlooked it, or he didn't consider it of value, or he planted the card himself.

When a dozen questions besieged him for every explanation rendered, Mansell took refuge in the report.

The Caves of the Womb, it began, *lay beneath the Pyrenees Mountains in the Basque Province of Spain, four kilometers east of the city of Tolosa. The caves were the remnants of an underground saltwater lake believed to have dried up ten million years ago. Theory suggests that the caves developed during the orogenic period of the Pyrenees. Over many millennia, underground streams from the Bay of Biscay served as the lake's source.*

Ten million years ago the border plates between France and Spain collided. Structural onslaughts of incredible power and duration followed, and violent earthquakes sealed the caves from their natural water supply. Gradual desiccation began, a drying process evidenced by the huge pockets of sodium deposits that still lingered at the base of the caves.

A mining expedition, led by a Spaniard named Diego Franco,

172

discovered the caves in the early 1930s. Interest in the area developed after archeologists digging in the area found deposits of silver and high concentrations of cobalt. The Spanish government commissioned Franco to explore further. One hundred and twenty meters below the surface, they stumbled upon the great caverns. Initial estimates suggested that the caves covered 150 acres. Later exploration revised the figure to include thirty-four connecting caves covering 425 acres.

The name, Caves of the Womb, originated from an entry in Diego Franco's journal dated 7/18/33. It read, "We have tumbled into the belly of the mountain, the heart of the world, the caves of the womb where blue light flickers from the burning soul of the earth, and the sun is but a wishful dream at the doorstep of imagination."

During the Spanish Civil War the Basques used the caves for their base of operations in support of the Loyalist movement. As a precaution against invasion by pro-Franco forces, the Basques rigged explosives at the entrances to all surface tunnels and inside all access shafts. At their peak, in 1937, the caves housed as many as twenty-five hundred Basque soldiers, but they abandoned the caves on April 1, 1939, the day the Loyalists surrendered.

The report's last notation jumped off the page at Mansell, and he read it aloud. "Today, the caves are a favorite site for the sport of spelunking (the exploration of underground caves)."

He read the whole report again, and then set it aside.

The beach along M4 dissolved into a shoreline of rocks and tide pools. The road snaked through a rugged strip of land known as The Willows and narrowed outside the tiny village of Skoenmaker-skop, the Shoemaker's Hillock. Mansell eased off the gas, enjoying the shadowy view and the fragrant scent of evening. He plucked a handful of green grapes from the bag.

At Sardinia Bay, the road turned inland. Mansell stopped for petrol at Sea View. He bought coffee and cigarettes. Here he caught the freeway and concentrated on driving. Fifteen kilometers later, he approached a narrow oiled road. The sign on the shoulder read, OYSTER BAY—6K.

Jennifer walked along the beach with Harriet, a perfect contrast. Jennifer: blond, sleek, aloof. Harriet: Latin, buxom, challenging. Mansell and Harriet had cultivated a stormy relationship during his junior year at school. It lasted two months. Back then, she wore torn T-shirts and lace panties. She needed it twice a day, and her hands were always busy. Jarrad never asked, and Mansell never volunteered. Five kids and eighteen years had taken its toll on Harriet physically. But sexually? Mansell wondered.

He and Jarrad sat on the redwood deck in the face of a gentle breeze. The air was alive with the fragrance of sea and jasmine. A waxing moon highlighted the whitecaps of tiny breakers and the foam of a rising tide. They drank tequila. Mansell listened to the ocean with one ear and Jarrad Pruitt with the other.

"So here are the Americans still talking about this bloody disinvestment bullshit like it's the black man's last great hope. Shit. But it's not just the government; you'd expect that. It's these other sanctimonious institutions—the courts, the church, the university. Now, that's a good one. Okay. Ten days ago, guess what happens? Bloody Radcliffe College threatens to sell a hundred thousand shares of its Firestone stock. Why? They're demanding the company pull out of South Africa unless, of course, we straighten up and fly right, sure, the way all red-blooded democracies do. Right, chief. Very forceful. Very impressive. Firestone refuses, of course. The next day, Phillips and Drew in London buys the whole block at a discount, and the president of Firestone rips up the letter from Radcliffe and throws it in the trash. And so what if Firestone does pull out? Ten thousand blacks out of a job. Now, that's what I call doing your civic duty. But that's okay, because then Michelin, or Mitsubishi, or somebody else who doesn't give a shit what the American Congress wants, moves in here and hires the blacks right back. Thank you very much Radcliffe College."

Jarrad was off on another tirade. Mansell put salt in the hollow between his thumb and first finger. A lime wedge in one hand, tequila in the other. Salt first, tequila, the mandatory grimace, suck the lime, feel the heat spread through your system like ripples over the water.

Mansell poured two more shots. He said, "All right. So you're Firestone. What do you do? Stay or leave?"

"It's business, Nigel. Not racial. If business stinks, get out. But tell it like it is, that's all. 'We're out of here 'cause business stinks, not because we're doing the black man a big favor.' One minute the Americans are preaching the inviolate rights of their fellow man, the next they're sticking a welfare check in his hand. Then they console the poor guy with a pat on the back and say, 'Hey, you're better off this way, believe me.'"

Nigel Mansell stared into the bottom of his shot glass. With a single motion he disposed of the tequila. He gazed out across the black shimmering sea.

"Sounds oddly familiar, Jarrad."

On the beach, Jennifer walked with arms folded over a bulky sweater. Mansell wore swimming trunks, but a long-sleeved soccer jersey felt good. The sun stood at the peak of its journey, pale and dim through a veil of clouds.

He said, "The ocean doesn't let you get away easy, does it? It talks and whispers and soothes no matter how much you fight it. It creeps under your skin and into your soul, and finally, inside your head. Three murders, a suicide, a township in flames, a killer on the loose, and the ocean still manages to relax me."

"Harriet said that Jarrad's planning to open a new branch office in Cape Town."

"He mentioned it. My ex-roomie's doing well for himself, isn't he? I told him if he's not careful some monster conglomerate's going to come in here and make him a rich man."

The tide charged up the sand, and Jennifer stepped above the rising waterline. "Did he make you an offer?" she asked.

"He always makes an offer. Harriet would kill him if he didn't."

The tide receded, and then rushed forward again, hauling forth its quota of sand. When the water withdrew it deposited the particles across the beach with a sizzling sound like bacon frying. Mansell carved deep impressions with his heels.

"So what did you say?" Jennifer asked anxiously.

"I told him there was no way he could afford me." They paused, turning, eyes locking. The sea lapped at their feet. Mansell turned aside. "Of course, then I found out he could."

"Take it. Please take it."

"And would that be the answer?"

"It would be a start."

"For who? Me, or you?"

"For us both."

"Why?"

"At least you wouldn't come home with the picture in your brain of some maniac who decided to jump out of a ten-story window. At least you wouldn't spend half your nights on a cot in some burrow hole of an office. Maybe we could go out to dinner one night a week, or to a movie. I've forgotten what that's like. Maybe we could afford a place like this on the beach, or a summer house in the mountains. Or maybe we could just afford a new car."

Clouds parted overhead. Mansell faced the sun, eyes closed. "A policeman turned advertising agent," he said. "That's a tough one."

"You could do it," Jennifer implored. "You'd be good at it. You'd learn."

"Easy."

"You don't want it."

Mansell glanced at his wife. A pout pulled at the lines around her lips. Her eyes flared like pilot lights, cold flames. Mansell wanted to say, "And in a month or a year, when the glitter wears off, will there be another Jason, another turn of the head? Or will it be my turn to get bored, my turn to point the finger?"

But he didn't.

Two sanderlings raced back and forth with the tide, plucking crabs from the settling sand. A sea gull circled overhead, drifting, landing at the peak of a dune.

They walked in silence back to the beach house.

When the telephone rang during cocktails, every eye turned in Mansell's direction. Jarrad answered it on the fifth ring, but they were right.

"Joshua. What is it?"

"Sorry to intrude, Nigel. But I thought you should know. Last Monday, two blacks were arrested outside of Johannesburg in a city called Springs."

"I know the place."

"Well, they were drunk, and they were carrying guns." Blacks were not permitted to own or carry firearms. The question of a license was a moot point. "They're also being held in connection with the alleged rape of a sixteen-year-old white girl. Evidently they were on their way to some mining job on the East Rand, and—"

"Joshua. I have three pairs of eyes boring holes in the back of my head. I know there's a point to all this."

"Three points, actually," Joshua replied. "One, they were both in possession of ANC membership cards. Not too smart. Two, the guns they were holding? American-made .45-calibers. Model M1191 A1. Yes? And third, they were both carrying blank business cards with four words typed on one side."

"What?"

"That's right. 'Caves of the Womb.' "

———

176

At dinner, Harriet drank too much.

She said, "Nigel, we've been friends for a lot of years. Sure, maybe Jen's a better friend than you, but I still care. I care a helluva lot. And for a lot of reasons." Mansell smiled remotely. Harriet leaned across the table, exposing ample breasts. "Do her a favor, huh? And yourself, for God's sake. Jarrad's offering you a future. He'd run the Cape Town office if you went down there. Things aren't so goddamn tense on the Cape, Nigel. You know that. Christ, you can't spend the rest of your days breaking heads."

Mansell tipped his head, a sudden weariness stealing the color from his face. "Breaking heads?"

"God damn it, Harry," cried Jarrad. "Save the theatrics for Sunday choir, okay?"

"It's becoming more like the Gestapo every day," Harriet exclaimed. "Jennifer deserves better."

Mansell touched a napkin to his lips. "Who might that be?" he asked quietly.

"You know what I mean."

"Don't make the mistake of grouping me with them, Harriet," he replied. Jennifer excused herself from the table. She walked out to the deck. Mansell fished for a cigarette as she disappeared down the stairs. "I'm not the enemy."

"No? The Elgin case! That boy!"

"Harriet," Jarrad intervened. "Good God, woman."

"Shut up, Jarrad." She struggled to her feet. Throwing back her shoulders, she said, "I'm not the one who voted for the Nats in the last election, am I?"

She stormed out. Jarrad threw up his hands. "Nigel, I'm sorry. Really sorry."

"It's okay," Mansell said. He reached out for the wine bottle at the center of the table, studied the contents without enthusiasm, and decided against it. "Did you really vote for the Nats in the last election?"

Five years ago at the East Fields mine, the roofs of two empty storage tanks had been converted to accommodate sliding steel plates four meters in diameter. The plates moved on hydraulic-assisted tracks, allowing access from above.

From his station atop a flatbed railroad car, Jan Koster watched as the boom arm of a derrick crane swung gracefully above the open plate at the top of the nearest tank. Slowly, the crane operator lowered cable and hooks to the crew inside.

Koster removed his cap and mopped sweat from his brow. He massaged a day-old beard. Dark circles below his eyes testified to another sleepless night spent in another cramped airplane.

He allowed his mind to drift, thinking again of the letter from his wife, Julia, worn now from so many readings. Eleven-year-old Tonya was down with the flu. She'd missed three days of school this past week. Hannah was busy with ballet lessons two mornings a week and swimming classes on the weekends. Julia's opening at the Rhine Gallery had been a rousing success. Four sculptures had already been purchased, and two commissions taken. The very idea of leaving South Africa had shocked them all. Still, toward the end of the letter, in words now etched in his brain, Julia had said that she understood. My God, he thought, what will she say when I tell her the rest of it? And I will have to tell her. And soon.

The crane's diesel engine coughed, shaking Koster from his reverie. Black smoke belched from the exhaust pipe. The cable went taut, and the cargo began its sixty-meter ascent.

Koster considered the news from Port Elizabeth without enthusiasm. If the fag can just keep his cool, he thought, we'll be all right. Koster shook his head. Fags and addicts. How did it ever get to this?

Replacing his cap, he scanned the compound and considered the state of East Fields's increasing population, now sixteen thousand strong. Wanting a drink, he settled for a cigarette.

The pallet materialized at the end of the cable. When it was centered next to fifteen similar crates, a diesel locomotive nudged the flatcar inside the huge hull of Central Access. There, a stationary boom unloaded sixteen handheld bazookas, eighteen grenade launchers, and four dozen submachine guns into a shaft elevator.

Two hundred and twenty meters belowground, the weapons began a methodical journey through man-made tunnels to the connection tunnel that linked East Fields with the White Ridge Mines. The guns were then loaded onto tunnel cars, and three hundred meters of electric track brought the cars to a deserted access shaft.

One by one the crates were hoisted by pulleys to an abandoned work station forty meters below the plant facilities of South Africa's most profitable gold mine.

Eight days out of New York—eight days of uninterrupted sailing save the refueling stop in Freetown, linkage problems three days past, and twenty-four hours of severe thunderstorms outside the Gulf of Guinea—*ARVA II* rounded the Cape of Good Hope within sighting distance of Table Mountain.

The crew worked feverishly repackaging the last twenty crates of M1191 A1 semiautomatic handguns. Andrew Van der Merve encouraged the crew with cigarettes and the promise of a cash bonus.

From the bridge deck, Captain Amil Aidoo radioed the Port Elizabeth harbor control tower to confirm their berth assignment, and the tower reaffirmed that berth number ten had indeed been reserved for his vessel. Pilotage, he was told, was scheduled for 2:30 P.M. the following day, Monday, the fourteenth day of July.

Working nights was a good excuse for Delaney Blackford to get out of the house.

She packed a briefcase with the forum outline for the General Mining Group negotiations scheduled for midweek, the arbitration proposals with the Harbour Association, and the UDW contract with International Consolidated. If all went according to plan, she thought, the contract would be finalized and signed Tuesday. In a paper bag she stowed a box of Earl Grey tea, a tomato and cheese sandwich, and an old fingerpainting that Amanda had done in kindergarten—something new for the office bulletin board.

Delaney left Gelvandale at 10:35 in her 1978 Fiat convertible. A bright moon the color of topaz lit the sky. She took the highway, to Settler's Way, and reached downtown ten minutes later. Main Street retired early on Sunday night. The bars were closed all day, the buses quit at six, and the restaurants locked their doors by ten. Streetlamps stood their lonely vigil, while tourists window-shopped. A taxi delivered its last fare. Coal smoke drifted in from New Brighton and Kwaford.

Britannia Street led Delaney beneath the overpass, across the tracks, to the waterfront and Charl Malan Quay. A frontage road paralleled a high chain link fence for a hundred meters. Spotlights illuminated the entrance. Delaney tapped the Fiat's horn, but the guardhouse was empty. She used her own key and rolled the gate aside. She drove onto the tarmac, locked the gate behind her, and then continued on. The UDW building was situated beyond a bank of storage sheds and a row of empty shipping containers.

Delaney parked in an empty lot at the side of the building. The moment she stepped out of the car she saw the light, a dim reflection coming from the rear of the office. The overhead lamps, she thought, above the filing center. She hesitated. Clarisa must have left the light on, she told herself. It happens, right? So relax.

With her briefcase in one hand and a brass-headed walking stick in the other, Delaney started toward the office. Her ankle ached more than usual, the result of a long hike in the Kouga Mountains earlier in the day. Feeling silly, but still anxious, she skirted the steps with the thought of peeking through the front window. The blinds were drawn. Butterflies invaded her stomach. "Clarisa," she whispered, "never closes the curtains."

Deliberately, Delaney stepped away from the porch. She circled to the north side of the building. A gravel lot extended from here to the bay. Black water glistened beneath the heavens.

The windows on this side were shoulder-high, squares with diamond-shaped quarrels in the center. Stretching, Delaney peered inside, and in the far corner, hunched over an open file, was Steven de Villiers.

Irritated with herself and annoyed with him, Delaney returned to the front door. Without warning, she burst in. Had she expected de Villiers to flinch, she was very much mistaken. In fact, he righted himself with such deliberateness that she was taken by a cold foreboding. He turned, showering her with stern, piercing eyes. Delaney felt a chill at the base of her spine.

Hoping to cover it, she asked, "What brings you here at this time of night?"

"I don't recall anyone mentioning your authority in matters pertaining to the Federation of Mineworkers Union, Mrs. Blackford," de Villiers replied. He closed the file unhurriedly. Delaney noticed that the top drawer of the cabinet nearest the window was ajar. The shipping manifests. "But, like you, I rather enjoy the cover of darkness."

"How did you get in here? I wasn't aware you'd been given a key to the front gate or to the office."

"Of course not. Lucas Ravele was so kind as to oblige me. I didn't think it was necessary that you knew." De Villiers turned his back to her. He slid the file into the drawer and closed it. Delaney caught sight of the red index tag on the upper-right corner—the

180

berthing insignia. A green tag was third day; a blue, second day; and a red tag indicated a vessel scheduled to dock the following day. "Lucas suggested that I familiarize myself with the filing system here in the office. And with the contracts coming up next week, you know, the union's negotiations with the Chamber and all? I thought that after hours would be more convenient for your staff."

"How thoughtful," Delaney answered evenly, but that didn't explain the shipping manifests.

De Villiers started toward her. The muscles in Delaney's shoulders tensed. She retreated a step. She dropped her briefcase on the edge of Clarisa's desk; the head of the walking stick caught the lip of a clay planter, knocking it to the floor. The pot shattered. Red lilies scattered across the floor.

De Villiers continued to weave his way through the desks, watching her. Amid the scatterings of broken clay and dirt, he paused. He bent forward. He reached out for a stray blossom. Eyes still upon her, he lowered his head to the bloom, sniffing the fragrance. Then, with the flower cradled in his palm, he arose.

Again, he approached her. This time he stopped so close that Delaney caught the sweet sick scent of cologne diluted by perspiration. He held the bloom out, but Delaney didn't move. Suddenly, his fist closed around it. His knuckles were red with exertion by the time he opened his hand again, and the crushed flower tumbled to the ground.

"Good night, Mr. de Villiers," Delaney said definitively.

A smile split de Villiers's waxen face, spreading the gray and white bristles of his moustache across hollow cheeks, but having no effect on his eyes.

"Indeed it is, Mrs. Blackford. And a splendid night to you as well."

The next morning, Joshua Brungle sat at the computer. The CRT screen flashed dot-matrix impressions of exploding fireworks. Mansell stepped into the office with the *Port Elizabeth Daily Bulletin* under his arm.

"What's this?" he asked. "A step toward early retirement or a brief return to childhood?"

Joshua reclined further in the swivel chair, stretching. He said, "This is an eager lad's first taste of what Monday morning can be like away from the mania of the Pit. You've probably forgotten what it's like down there."

"Energizing, invigorating, inspiring."

"You have forgotten."

Mansell sat behind his own desk scanning the headlines: U.S. CONSIDERS MASSIVE BOYCOTT. A subheading read, "Black Policeman Succumbs to Injuries." At last, he pointed to the simulated fireworks on the monitor. "And that?" he asked.

"That, Inspector, is the reply sent by Research Bureau and Security Branch Central when I so politely asked them for follow-up material on those two yo-yos arrested in Springs last Monday. Their names are Joseph Mokane and Amos Hlongwane. They're being held in Jo'burg at Modder Bee."

"Bad boys."

"But that's it. They're not releasing anything else. Not even department-to-department. We know that no charges have been filed, and we know that the sixteen-year-old in Springs is denying it ever happened."

"Ah. Someone's exerting some influence. Only a minister's decree can close things up that tight."

"Malan."

"Or Leistner." Mansell folded the newspaper, tossing it toward the wastebasket. "What else do we know?"

Joshua shrugged. "Not much. They both have valid passports. Their travel papers were in order. They were holding current identity cards. Labor Bureau confirms their latest work permits for the mining job I told you about, but they've been ordered to withhold any specifics." Joshua turned in his chair. He punched the "off" switch on the side of the computer and said, "So?"

"So let's make some sense out of this thing." Mansell arose. Smoking led to pacing. "Fredrik Steiner has enough of an illicit profile to be tagged and listed with Interpol. He resides in an Eastern-bloc country. And someone, here or in Europe, knows enough about the underworld, or has the contacts, to hire this guy who can pull off two murders with enough skill to damn near fool the best pathologist I've ever worked with."

"And he knows enough to realize that Steiner's the only link between himself and Elgin. With Steiner out of the way, he's in the clear. But his opportunities to take Steiner out were limited, right? Here or in Jo'burg."

182

"According to Steiner's travel plans, his stopover in Jo'burg would have been less than an hour. He had to do it here."

"Agreed." Joshua crossed the office to a small refrigerator set beneath the water cooler. Mansell hadn't used it in years. The detective removed two cans of Coke. He tossed one over the desk to the chief inspector. Mansell raised an eyebrow, but didn't comment. "The guy's smart. He lets Steiner do his dirty work for him."

"A frame job that's just short of being masterful."

"They probably made arrangements to use the airport basement for their last payoff, and while he's handing Steiner an envelope filled with English pounds, he puts a bullet between his eyes."

"And he uses a handgun that under normal circumstances would be almost impossible to trace."

"Except the exact same guns show up in a hick town outside of Jo'burg in the hands of two card-carrying drunks from the ANC. A U.S. Army pistol that hasn't been imported into this country since 1977. Not exactly a staple item in ANC's arsenal, is it?"

"I feel like I'm stumbling around in the dark with a leash around my neck," Mansell said. "All right. We know we're looking for someone with European contacts. Someone who probably travels to Europe as part of his or her job. Who knew Ian Elgin or had business dealings with him. And who figures to gain, financially or politically, from his death."

"Or someone who suffered at Elgin's hands over the course of the last few years," Joshua added. "After all, 'Revenge,' some wise man once said, 'is a temptation strong amongst poor losers.'"

"Sounds like something Julius Caesar would have said, doesn't it? And didn't he also say that even a blind marionette eventually feels the tug of the puppeteer's strings?" Mansell circled to the window. He tapped at the glass absently, and then wheeled away, saying, "Okay, let's start over with those personnel files from Durban, Jo'burg, and Cape Town. We'll use those parameters. If we're wrong, then we'll expand."

Mansell discarded the empty Coke can in favor of a cigarette. "Okay. So following his ill-timed demise, Fredrik Steiner is stripped of everything except a blank card with four enticing words on it. Two days later, a pair of ANC activists glide into Springs on their way to a mining job. They start drinking."

"That's understandable."

"They get drunk."

"That's predictable."

"Yeah, but the stupid buggers are carrying American handguns and the same blank card with the same four words on it?"

"The tug of the puppeteer's strings."

There was a knock at the door, and a uniformed policeman poked his head past the threshold. "Excuse me, Inspector. The railroad police finally got around to cleaning out Anthony Mabasu's locker down in the baggage department. They found this. I thought you might be interested."

The policeman handed Mansell an evidence bag containing the paper sleeve from a Sea Lanes bus ticket. The sleeve was empty, but the travel information had been neatly printed across the front. It read, "Time of Departure, 6:20 A.M. Date of Departure, 3 July. Destination, Butterworth, Transkei."

"The sleeve to Sylvia Mabasu's bus ticket."

"On the other side, sir."

Mansell flipped it over. The words were handwritten in red ink at the bottom. "Sylvia. Meet me. 4:30 A.M., Friday the 4th. The sleep room."

The telephone rang.

The caller was Delaney Blackford.

"I had to put in some later hours last night at the harbor," she said. The edge in her voice told Mansell that the call was strictly business. "I told you about the impending arbitration with the Association, I think."

"Charming habit," Mansell replied. "How can I complain about my work schedule if you're keeping the same hours?"

"I had a visitor. An unexpected visitor."

The tone remained—anxious, taciturn. Mansell retreated, taking a seat. "At the office?" he asked.

"Yes. Steven de Villiers."

"Elgin's temporary surrogate."

"That's right. He was rummaging through some files when I arrived around eleven," Delaney said, then described the encounter.

Mansell lit a cigarette. He laid the match on his desk. "I assume shipping manifests are not generally within a union liaison's scope of responsibility."

"Hardly."

"Can I put Detective Brungle on with us? He's harmless as long as he doesn't talk."

"Certainly."

Mansell gestured toward the extension. "Go ahead, Delaney. Please."

"You remember when Lea Goduka was telling us about her first encounter with Ian Elgin? The day they met?"

"They met at the port control tower on Charl Malan Quay. A year ago, she said. Elgin was meeting a ship."

"The point is, union negotiators and board consultants don't normally serve that function. It's probably nothing really, but. . . ."

Mansell pressed on. "The ship was a freighter. The AVA, wasn't it? Something like that."

"The *ARVA II,*" Delaney corrected. "I checked the files that de Villiers was looking through last night. *ARVA II* is red-tagged for arrival in port today."

"Synchronicity?" Joshua muttered.

Mansell tipped his head slightly. "Delaney, is there any way of knowing if Elgin was—"

She broke in. "I've already checked. ARVA's docked in P.E. five times over the last six years. I cross-checked the dates with the minutes from Affiliated Union board meetings and staff reports. Ian was in town on every occasion."

"I see. What type of cargo?"

"According to the manifests, mining equipment. On all five occasions."

"That might explain it, I suppose." Mansell crushed out his cigarette. "Could Elgin have expedited matters for an incoming vessel in terms of berthing rights, or unloading privileges, or freight services? Anything like that?"

"Absolutely."

"What about customs?" asked Joshua.

"I would have to say yes."

As *ARVA II* rounded Cape Receife, the waters of Algoa Bay reflected a lustrous ultramarine. A prevailing breeze blew temperately from the southwest at ten k.p.h. When the harbor pilot came aboard the freighter, Captain Aidoo relinquished control. Nervously, he lit a briarwood pipe and thought about the trouble resting in the belly of his ship.

At the harbor entrance, the freighter slid past an outgoing cargo ship and a South African naval cruiser. A tugboat stood watch over ARVA's stern. Berth number ten was located on the south side of number two quay, and there they cast anchor.

An assistant port captain, two customs officials, and the port systems manager met the freighter dockside. And though supervising incoming vessels was not a normal function of the systems manager, a lengthy conversation with Chief Inspector Mansell of CIB had convinced the port manager to take special note of this ship's safe harbor.

From the railing of the bridge deck, Captain Aidoo surveyed the docks. Nervousness became deep-seated concern. Holy Mother of God, he thought. Where in the hell is Mr. Elgin?

Concern, however, did not give way to panic. Before going ashore, Aidoo sent a deckhand below with a message for Andrew Van der Merve. Then he delivered an entirely new set of papers to the assistant port captain. The packet consisted of four documents. Both the export license and the export permit now listed São Paulo, Brazil, as the port of record. The sales agreement now listed the Porto Nacional Iron Works in São Paulo as the seller of record, and East Fields Mining Corporation as the buyer. And the shipping manifest now gave an itemized listing of thirty mining implements and showed the place of lading, the destination, and the passenger and crew list.

In due course, the documents were relinquished to the customs authorities, and sweat dripped from beneath Captain Aidoo's cap.

From the upper deck of the Harborhouse Tearoom, Nigel Mansell and Delaney Blackford followed the proceedings over tea and biscuits.

Moments later, they saw Steven de Villiers emerge on the pier. De Villiers walked briskly toward the gangplank. With the informality of an old acquaintance, he shook hands with the systems manager and both customs officials.

"It didn't occur to me until just now," said Delaney, watching the exchange, "but de Villiers spent most of his time this past week poking around the control tower and the Transport Service Building. Now I see why."

"Getting acquainted."

"Yes. And with some success."

De Villiers released himself from the second customs agent's grasp. He turned to the captain of the ship and extended a hand. With conspiratorial ease, he placed another hand on the larger Aidoo's shoulder, and in a gesture that seemed perfectly natural from where

Mansell sat, pulled the captain aside and whispered briefly in his ear. Laughter followed the exchange.

Twenty minutes later, the customs agents, the systems manager, and Steven de Villiers followed Captain Aidoo up the gangplank onto the main deck. A hatchway opened, and when they disappeared into the freighter's hold, Nigel Mansell called for his check.

He escorted Delaney back to her office. Then he left the waterfront on foot. On Fleming Street, two fire engines and a hook-and-ladder surrounded a wholesale-retail bakery called La Pâtisserie. Flames engulfed the building. Curiosity seekers crowded the sidewalks. Others peered from neighboring windows. Smoke caught in Mansell's throat, and he remembered now that, for the past month, the bakery had been the target of protesters and pickets—a dispute over substandard wages. Odd, he thought, that R1.25 an hour isn't enough incentive to get up at three in the morning to come bake apple turnovers. He picked up the charred remnants of a sign that read, NO BLACKS AND NO DOGS.

On Court Street, he stopped at a diner for fish-and-chips and a beer. District Prosecutor Hurst was sitting in a booth by himself, and he insisted that Mansell join him.

"Good news," Hurst said energetically. "We're clearing Anthony Mabasu's name of the Elgin murder charge. It's true he'll still be listed as a possible suspect for a time, and that the record will show both the Elgin and Mabasu cases still open, but those are standard procedures in a situation like this."

"Unfortunate that such news has no beneficiary," replied the chief inspector. Suddenly, the beer tasted flat; the texture of cotton coated the roof of his mouth. "We all know who killed Ian Elgin and Sylvia Mabasu, Peter. But then, such an obvious blot on the transparent record of our Security Branch wouldn't look right, would it? Ah, what the hell, it's just paper work at this point."

"If it's your personal record you're concerned with, Inspector, we can—"

"My personal record as chief inspector or my personal record as a human being?"

"An unblemished record is hard to maintain in a system such as ours, Nigel."

Their eyes locked. Hurst's contrite, but unyielding. Mansell's mindful, but deflated, his concentration wavering. Air escaped his lungs in a rush of exasperation. He made one last attempt, asking, "Then, will the district prosecutor consider presenting the evidence gathered by my office to a regional magistrate?"

Hurst shrugged. He dabbed his lips with the corner of a napkin. "Inspector, have you any idea of the caseload . . . ? Yes, of course you do. And, of course, you would know that I can't possibly do that." Hurst slipped from the booth, dropping two rand notes on the table. "Find me Fredrik Steiner's killer. I'll prosecute that. However, I do plan to make our new position on Anthony Mabasu public. Will that offer a measure of satisfaction?"

"I see. And what about the Police Act?" asked Mansell. He stared down into the remains of a half-eaten meal. He pushed the plate away. Slowly, he lifted his head. Pale eyes sought out the prosecutor. "And the minister of justice?"

"Leistner? Why, it was his idea."

Back at the station house, Mansell met Oliver Terreblanche in the forensic lab. The Sea Lanes ticket sleeve had been given top priority.

"We found fingerprints from four sources," du Toits told them. "Sylvia Mabasu and her husband, as expected, and two clerks at the bus depot."

"But not the bus driver," Mansell said remotely.

"Only those four, I'm afraid."

"Vinyl or rubber gloves?"

"Impossible to determine." Du Toits shrugged. "We analyzed the handwriting against John Martyn's signature on the car rental papers. Negative. We checked it against a dozen samples of Ian Elgin's writing. No way. But pen position, pressure, and shading all point to a man. A man with large, thick hands. That's a point of conjecture, of course, but one worth noting, I thought."

"Noteworthy," Terreblanche said, starting for the door, "but hardly court-worthy."

The man wore bib overalls. The bright patch on the back read, "Chelsea's Department Store." He parked the panel truck at the curb in front of the Mansell residence on Northview Avenue in Millard Grange.

He stepped down from the cab carrying a clipboard and wearing

188

sunglasses. By his size, he looked like a deliveryman. He walked past sculptured junipers and blooming birds of paradise to the front porch. He rang the bell.

As expected, no one answered. The hide-a-key was there, behind the mailbox. The unlocked door swung open easily. He glanced over his shoulder, and then stepped into the entryway. His footsteps echoed on hardwood floors. He waited—listening, watching. He knew the layout by heart. The front room: an overstuffed chair, a gentleman's rocker with cane seat, the fireplace, a Julian print hanging above the oak mantel. The living room: an oak dinette, the aquarium with three angelfish, a rolltop desk, the upright piano with sheet music from *Peer Gynt*.

The hallway led to a darkroom, a bathroom, a study, and the master bedroom at the end. Light blues and lavender washed the walls and the drapery. Stuffed pillows were neatly arranged at the head of a queen-sized bed. Framed watercolors of steep canyons and waterfalls adorned one wall, and pine furniture lined the other. A walk-in closet occupied the far corner.

The case, he'd been told, was in the closet. The man pushed aside silk blouses, cotton dresses, and corduroy pants until he discovered the pine case attached to the back wall. Behind a six-millimeter pane of glass he could see the guns. Three of them. A 1930 nine-millimeter Webley. A nine-millimeter Browning HP 35. A six-shot .38-caliber Colt Detective Special.

The man used a thin metal file to jimmy the lock. He pushed the glass panel aside. Eyeing the classic Webley, he reached instead for the Colt. Though he wore gloves, he used the file to avoid touching the barrel or the grip. Carefully, he laid the gun on a white handkerchief, folded it, and then dropped the bundle into the pocket of his overalls.

He relocked the case, fluffed the clothes, and slid the closet doors back to their original position. Sixty seconds later, he climbed back into the cab of the panel truck, started the engine, and drove slowly down the street.

ARVA *II*'s cargo cleared customs without a hitch.

At 4:41, a fifteen-ton dockside crane hoisted the first crate from inside the freighter's hold, setting it gently on the back of a Bristar

Straddle carrier. By late evening, dock workers had laid the last crate, one containing two handheld grenade launchers, inside a storage shed next to the railroad siding in front of number two quay.

At 10:30 that same night, the port systems manager unlocked the rear door to shed 4D, giving access to the newly consigned shipment to Inspector Mansell and Affiliated Union official Delaney Blackford. In the breast pocket of his sports jacket, the inspector held a search warrant obtained from Magistrate Zachary Alexander at his home an hour before. In his hands, Mansell carried a tool box and a crowbar.

Two hundred meters away, standing at the window of an unoccupied office on the sixth floor of the customs house, Steven de Villiers watched through high-powered binoculars as the pair stepped through the door into the shed. De Villiers's first impulse was to pick up the telephone and dial Pretoria. Another thought caused him to hesitate. The minister, he remembered, played bridge on Monday nights. The game broke up at eleven sharp. He would wait.

Inside the low-lying warehouse, concrete and steel beams formed a concave hull redolent of damp basements and used machine oil. Idle forklifts and winding conveyor belts sat at the foot of narrow corridors formed by stacks of cardboard cartons and wooden boxes.

The East Fields crates were stacked next to a shipment of Japanese pottery and imported wicker.

It took five minutes to dig through the polyurethane foam in the first crate and another three minutes to uncover a weighty bundle wrapped in soft cloth stashed within the hidden crate. What they found inside the cloth was a freshly oiled replica of the .45-caliber pistol used to kill Fredrik Steiner nine days before.

Mansell heard the pounding of his own heart, felt the sweat beneath his arms. He uncovered six more M1191 A1 .45-caliber pistols. And while Delaney photographed the contents with a thirty-five-millimeter camera, he set to work on another crate. Within minutes, he had unearthed a layer of M16 automatic rifles, oiled and gleaming.

A third crate contained two grenade launchers, and a fourth, ammunition.

Delaney shot a full roll of thirty-six pictures. Then Mansell began to repack. The original crates were easy. They rewrapped each gun, laid them neatly between layers of bubble paper, and nailed the lids closed.

The polyurethane was a different story. Delaney observed the irretrievable scraps of foam covering the floor.

"You're not reporting this, are you, Inspector." It was a statement. Concentration had long since replaced the initial shock of their discovery.

"I can't. Not yet. It's not enough. All we know," Mansell answered, "is that someone has smuggled two hundred and fifty crates' worth of American guns onto South African soil. What we don't know is who. The people at this mine in the Transvaal could deny it out of hand. For all we know, someone's using their name, and they don't even know it."

"And that someone is responsible for Ian's death."

"Exactly."

Steven de Villiers focused in as the two hurried away from the rear of the shed. The binoculars brought him so close to the pair that he could see the burning ash on the tip of Mansell's cigarette and the intensity etched in Delaney's conversation. They were in there too damn long, he thought as perspiration formed a narrow ridge along his forehead.

De Villiers checked his watch. It was 11:17. As he reached for the telephone, he heard the door handle turning. He set the receiver down. He shuffled nervously into the shadows. The office door squeaked as it swung slowly inward. A figure bathed in darkness stepped past the threshold. The door closed.

The man stood a full head taller than de Villiers. He wore bib overalls and gloves. Sunglasses dangled from a chain around his neck. Haven't I seen him before? de Villiers wondered. He opened his mouth to speak, but the man put a finger to his lips.

The man moved forward with long strides, saying, "A friend sent me."

De Villiers breathed. "Leistner?"

A smile cut across the man's bony face. He reached out with his left hand. De Villiers assumed he wanted the binoculars, and he held them out. He gestured toward the window. The man snatched the glasses away. With his other hand, he grabbed de Villiers by the throat. He pressed the smaller man against the wall.

De Villiers gagged. "What? What are you doing?" he mouthed inaudibly. His arms flew into the air, resisting. A hand swept back, shattering the window. He cried out. "But they know, you fool. Don't you see? They—"

The man drove the narrow end of the binoculars into de Villiers's temple. Again. A third time. His body contorted, shuddered, and fell limp.

The man hung the binoculars around his neck. He slung de Villiers over his shoulder like a rag doll. The emergency stairs led down to an alleyway between the customs house and the Immigration Building. Parked there was a maroon Saab 900. The trunk was opened. He stowed the body inside, closed the lid, and locked it.

He drove the Saab without lights south along the railroad tracks. A narrow frontage road led to an entrance ramp onto the Settler's Way overpass. The man switched on the headlamps. Observing the speed limits, he drove northeast fifty-four kilometers to the R32 exchange. Traffic dwindled as he entered the foothills. The terrain rose amid wild bush and lonely evergreens. The countryside grew choppy, mountainous. Aided by the light of a full moon, he spotted the dirt road just beyond Sheldon and turned right. The road paralleled the Fish River through wooded hills. He drove ten minutes and parked thirty meters from the bank. Before getting out of the car he changed into tennis shoes that were two sizes too small. Then he removed the body from the trunk.

A shallow grave had already been dug, hours earlier, ten meters from the river. He dumped Steven de Villiers in it. From the pocket of his overalls, he took the Colt Detective Special. Carefully, he pumped three bullets into de Villiers's chest. Blood spread across the front of his shirt. The man tossed the gun into a clump of wild grass near the bank. It took five minutes to cover the body. Finally, the man formed a barrow of broken sod and rocks.

He returned to his car and retraced his steps to R32. He drove hard all night, and by dawn, he was back in Johannesburg.

Nigel Mansell returned home well after midnight. A plan was formulating, but he didn't want to think about it. Fatigue buzzed about like an annoying fly inside his skull. A burnt-out porch light left the house dark, lifeless. He was surprised to find the front door unlocked.

Inside, a dank stuffiness overwhelmed him. He cracked the front window and switched on the attic fan. He walked halfway through the house before turning on the hallway light. He peeked into the bedroom. The bed was still made. The darkroom was locked. He called out Jennifer's name, but there was no answer.

He turned. The aquarium cast a dim blue haze over the dining room. He switched on the brass overhead. Light fell across the table. A bouquet of cut daisies drooped in a porcelain vase, tired and browning. A note was propped up against the vase, and Mansell reached for it.

My dearest Nigel,

I couldn't bear to tell you in person. I just couldn't face you. I'm sorry, so sorry, but I must leave you, Nigel. And this house and this city and a thousand memories. I must. Please forgive me. I need something out there, something inside me. Something. Peace of mind, a new beginning. I know it sounds childish. I thought we would find it together, that something. But I feel time slipping past me, Nigel, and I'm so frightened. I thought you would feel it in time too, but your work, your life, they seem to be enough for you. We've missed each other somewhere along the line, haven't we? You were right. Oh God, I'll miss your handsome face and your laughter.

I'll stay with Harriet and Jarrad, at least until I settle on something else.

Stay well,
Jen

Mansell read it again. Then he folded it slowly into the palm of his hand, crushing it until his fingers cried out from the pressure. He buried the crumpled paper in his pants pocket.

He walked numbly into the kitchen, stopping at the refrigerator. He opened the door. Cold air rushed over him. An involuntary shiver stung the back of his neck.

He had never called her "Jen." "Jennifer" had the sound of a spring flower blossoming, the heartbeat of a distant river on a summer's night.

The refrigerator was bare. He snatched a bottle of White Crown beer from the shelf and twisted the cap off. He flipped the cap toward the wastebasket, missed, and watched it tumble to the floor. The cap circled meekly on its rim, hesitated, and then collapsed.

Mansell told himself that he felt lighthearted, a lie poorly sold.

He sipped cold beer, and anger and hurt welled up inside him. His stomach bunched into a thousand tiny knots. He sucked in air, staving off panic. The air escaped in a rush, and he hurried into the study, reaching for the telephone. With increasing fever, he dialed the Pruitts' number. But after a single ring, he slammed the receiver down and shouted, "Fuck you." And then quietly, "Fuck you, Jen."

Using his private line, a hung-over Mansell dialed long-distance direct to Springs, an industrialized city on the East Rand. The switchboard operator at the Eighty-fourth Police Station answered, and Mansell asked to speak with Captain Richard Noore.

The station commander came on the line sixty seconds later.

"Mansell?" he shouted. "What's this? The major or the inspector?"

"It's the punk kid—Nigel," answered Mansell. As teen-agers, Dick Noore and Mansell's father had fought side by side in Italy at the tail end of World War II. Together they had attended the police college in Pretoria, graduating at the top of their class. Frank Mansell had been granted an early retirement last September. Noore was due in three months. "Haven't they chased your tail out of there yet, you old man?"

"Old man? Hey, kid, when I go out this whole force will probably fall apart," the captain replied. "So how's your papa doing, Inspector?"

"Ornery as ever. You know the major."

They exchanged amenities for a few minutes. At last, Noore asked, "So, is there a business side to this conversation, Inspector Mansell?"

"A week ago Monday, Dick, two blacks were arrested in your East District. They were accused of raping a sixteen-year-old white  girl. They were also carrying handguns and ANC cards," said Mansell. "Recall?"

"We were treated rather rudely by Security Branch on that one. Yeah, I remember," Noore answered brusquely. "The Lord giveth, and the Lord taketh to Jo'burg."

"We've heard the case is under a ministerial decree."

"You heard right, kid."

"Which ministry, Dick, do you know?"

"Justice. Why?"

"I think there's a connection with a case we have going down here," Mansell replied offhandedly. "They're holding information I could use but I'd rather not ask for. You know how that goes."

"So ask me," Noore retorted.

Mansell gave the veteran policeman a brief picture of the Steiner case, and then said, "He was killed with the same American gun your ANC friends were carrying."

"Yeah, the M1 something or another, wasn't it?"

"That's it. Do you remember the condition of the guns?"

Noore laughed. "I should have pistols so clean," he said. "You tell me, Inspector, where does a migrant pick up a gun that glistens like a Kruggerrand and shines like a Kimberley diamond? And I can tell you, Security was more than a little curious about that one, too."

"Curious or ecstatic," Mansell replied, encouraged by the answer. "Also, Dick, they were both en route to mining jobs somewhere in your area. Do you happen to remember where? The Labor Bureau's not handing out a thing."

"I can make a call."

"I'll wait. Thanks."

Mansell waited five minutes, smoking, massaging bloodshot eyes, studying the train routes between Port Elizabeth and the Transvaal.

At last, he heard Noore say, "I've got your answer, kid. It's a 'small.' Real small evidently. I've never heard of it. It's called East Fields."

Delaney sat on the deck of the Harborhouse Tearoom. She watched rail workers shunt a single boxcar alongside the loading platform in front of storage shed 4D. Again she checked the schedule sheet for outbound freight. The East Fields cargo was due for hookup and departure at 11:45.

When a fleet of one-ton forklifts entered the shed, Delaney made her decision. She left R2.50 on the table alongside an uneaten pastry and a forgotten mug of tea. She walked down to the waterfront, where she caught the harbor shuttle. The shuttle entered downtown at Produce Street. Delaney jumped off at the next corner. She walked a block west on Military Avenue to the police station.

Delaney had heard about the walkout last night at Ford's Neave plant and about the firebomb that set off the riot. She knew for certain that one policeman had been badly injured and that at least a dozen arrests had been made, and by 8:20, the Pit was waist-deep in bodies.

She took the front stairs to a subdued second floor. The door to Nigel Mansell's office was open. The chief inspector sat motionless at his desk, textbooks stacked like hastily constructed guard towers at each corner, a cup of coffee cradled between two hands.

"You look terrible," she said.

He glanced up. "Thank you. It always seems fitting that the visual impression attests to the state of physical discomfort. Personally, I strive for balance at all times."

"A head-to-head bout with the bottle?"

"I lost." Mansell fell back in his chair. Bloodshot eyes studied Delaney without embarrassment. She wore faded blue jeans, a cotton smock of Indian cut and color, and a solid blue scarf tied in her hair. It looked frightfully abstract and completely in vogue. She wore the ensemble, he thought, like a fashion model challenging her audience with a new style. He said, "You, on the other hand, look stunning this morning."

"Well, since I wasn't invited to the celebration last night, I was forced to seek comfort in my own pillow. I guess I should be thankful." Delaney pushed a straight-back chair alongside the desk and sat down. "And what was the occasion?"

"Freedom," Mansell answered at once. No, he realized, shaking his head, this was detachment, not indifference. Whiskey, he thought, has a marvelous way of miscoloring emotion. "Well, maybe it's a little soon to send out a declaration. Call it a celebration of survival."

"Very profound," Delaney replied, watching him. Mansell made an effort to avoid the cigarettes in his breast pocket. He was certain her oval eyes were looking right through him, but she surprised him, asking, "You okay, Inspector?"

He offered a qualified nod. "I'll make it."

Mansell knew why Delaney had come. He had thought about it himself since last night. Arms smuggling was a direct breach of internal security, and internal security took precedence over the murder investigation of three individuals. That was the law.

Yet within the delicate framework of his investigation, there were subtleties. The smuggled arms were another subtlety added without his control. If the subtleties were upset, he felt, the investigation disintegrated. If news of the arms shipment leaked, the investigation would be handed over to Security Branch, and his killer would be lost. Mansell wasn't prepared for that just yet.

The destination of the crates in storage shed 4D, he believed, was vital to his investigation. It was also vital to the security matter created by so large an amount of arms. Times five other shipments? Mansell wondered if he could achieve one end without destroying the other. Was it enough to believe the East Fields superscription at the top of a shipping manifest? There were a dozen remote stops between here and the East Rand where the transfer of the weapons would be a simple matter. He knew that. Delaney, he realized, would know it as well.

Intent on using the dilemma, he said, "Your train leaves at eleven forty-five, does it not?"

Surprise registered ever so briefly on her face. "They're holding a spare cabin for me in the crew's car."

"And you're going, why? Why would you be willing to risk your neck over this thing?"

"Because my union has a special interest in anything so illicit as arms smuggling on our rail system, that's why. Especially arms smuggling that might involve one of our own leaders." Delaney toyed with her walking stick, avoiding his eyes. "Ever since the unions became legal, Inspector, the Transport Service has been looking for some excuse to pull the rug out from under us. You know that. And the government would love it. We've worked too hard to let that happen."

"Then you've told your people about the guns?"

"No, I haven't."

Mansell studied her. He shook his head. "It's Elgin, isn't it?"

"I was with him the night he died. I feel . . . responsible."

"Don't be melodramatic. It's not that simple."

"And if news of the guns gets out, then what?"

"Then you can forget about finding out who is responsible."

"I can help, and you know it." The lines around Delaney's eyes softened. "I need to do this."

Mansell drew a deep breath. "I'll send Joshua with you."

"Joshua couldn't get near that train. They'd know in a minute. No one will give me a second glance, Inspector."

There was some truth to what she said, Mansell knew that. Self-monitoring of union projects and employees was a stipulation of trade-union law, and spot supervision by union officials was commonplace, even desirable. A union official spends a day observing the stevedores at the harbor in Durban. A union official tours a gold mine in Welkom or a diamond pit in Kimberley. A union official spot checks the computerized signaling system between Port Elizabeth and Jo'burg. She was right. It wouldn't raise an eyebrow.

"The railroad police can't know. Only Joshua will know here," he said. "This is a dangerous business, Delaney, and I won't be able to offer much help along the way."

"Yes, I know."

He passed her an I.D. card. "The train reaches Bloemfontein tomorrow at four-thirteen. If anything happens before then, call. Otherwise, we'll expect to hear from you then. Talk to Joshua or myself, no one else."

Delaney stood up, embracing a cherrywood cane. "Count on it, Inspector."

He walked her to the door. "You know, one of these days you're going to call me Nigel," he said. "I can feel it."

She flashed an expression of exaggerated shock. "Really?"

While Delaney packed a small carry-on for her journey, Nigel Mansell bought a carton of cigarettes, two candy bars, and a *London Times* at the gift shop in H. F. Verwoerd Airport.

He booked a flight on South African Airways scheduled to depart for Johannesburg at 10:59.

The flight lasted two hours and ten minutes. As the plane banked for its descent, Mansell studied a skyline so dense with skyscrapers and high rises that an American journalist had once called the city South Africa's Manhattan Island. Other sobriquets were equally apropos. The natives called it Egoli, the City of Gold. English speakers called it the City of Big Deals and Fast Bucks.

From the air, Mansell counted sixteen derrick cranes hovering above new buildings. For every brick or adobe bilevel he saw in the city proper, he saw two shacks made of sheet metal and cardboard in outlying townships.

At 1:10, the plane set down at Jan Smuts International, east of the city. Mansell hailed a taxi. He gave the driver an address in lower downtown, and they set out. The cabby switched on the radio. While they drove, Mansell gazed blankly at the scenery and wondered at the circumstances that must have led Ian Elgin's fellow conspirators to consider him either a liability or an expendable. Purpose, if purpose could be placed on an act of murder, was taking shape.

As they approached the inner city, Mansell found himself trapped among cubicle high-rise apartments, thirty-story office buildings, smart shops with expensive prices, and the roar of jackhammers, construction crews, and cars.

On Commissioner Avenue bumper-to-bumper traffic encapsulated them. The taxi escaped onto Loveday Street, where a rear-end collision brought traffic to a standstill. Accepting the obvious, Mansell paid his fare and joined what remained of the lunch-hour crowd.

Instantly, the winter chill of the Transvaal struck him. His breath turned to shafts of steam as it left his lungs. Coal smoke burned his eyes. Hunching his shoulders against a gusting wind, Mansell buried his hands in his jacket pockets and walked three blocks west to the public library on President Street.

Inside, the ninety-five-year-old building contained three museums, two galleries, and one of the most complete collections of books in the world. He consulted the directory. The business department was located on the fourth floor.

A staff worker directed Mansell to a caged area housing government documents, library reference books, and the business guides he was seeking. Two services in Jo'burg provided subscribers and members with information about public companies in the Transvaal. The first was called the *Nationwide Exchange Telegraph, NET*, and the other was *Moody's Industrial Manual*.

Impressed by their size, Mansell selected the most recent edition of *Moody's*. He hauled the thick volume to an empty table. Under "e" *Moody's* listed sixteen companies whose corporate names began with the word *East*. No East Fields.

That, Mansell thought, suggested three possibilities. One, East Fields wasn't a public corporation at all. Two, the mine was no longer in business—though that hypothesis failed to explain the two natives arrested in Springs. And three, East Fields was a masterful fabrication designed solely as a false front for smuggling guns.

Undaunted, Mansell tried a back issue, the 1985 edition. Again, no East Fields. Stymied, he hailed the staff worker and explained his problem.

"A service like *Moody's* or *NET* lists active companies only," the staffer told him. "A defunct company doesn't earn revenues. It doesn't pay income taxes. Now, they may be starting up a new business, in which case they're probably a subsidiary of a larger company. Or they may be reentering the business. Unlikely, but that would explain the new employees."

It would, Mansell thought and, working on that premise, he selected editions from 1975, 1965, and 1955. He drew a blank with the first two. Deflation gave way to resignation. Still, he thumbed through the '55 edition, and there it was. East Fields Mining Corpora-

200

tion, an incorporated gold mine located in Brakpan County. A footnote indicated that 1955 represented the company's first year of operation.

Mansell spent another five minutes learning that *Moody's* listed the company for only three years. A bust, he thought. An expensive bust for someone.

He departed the public library with intentions of finding out who that someone was.

Three blocks away on Harrison Street, a man dressed in a topcoat and homburg entered the stately lobby of the First Industrial Bank of Johannesburg. He went directly to the elevators. The brokerage offices of Stobbs and Brimblecombe were located on the sixteenth floor. He was five minutes early, and thus, by Afrikaner standards, punctual. He was admitted at once to the office of a Mr. M. H. du Buisson, the firm's senior vice-president and the man's personal account executive.

"Mr. Montana," du Buisson said. "It's a pleasure to see you again, sir. Please sit down."

"Thank you."

"The transfer papers are all in order." Du Buisson spread two forms in front of his client and offered him a fountain pen. The first document authorized the transfer of R50,000 from the joint account of Martin and Christina Montana to a similar account at Citicorp in New York. The second form authorized the transfer of R32,000 from the First Industrial Investment Trust to the same New York bank. Instructions would be forwarded with the transferrals requesting that the funds be placed immediately into government certificates of accrual and treasury bonds. The transactions represented the third, and final, such transfer over the course of the last twenty-four months.

The client signed both documents. He passed du Buisson a waiver with Christina Montana's signature acknowledging the joint account transfer. He stood up. The two men shook hands.

"It's been a pleasure doing business with you, Mr. Montana," said the broker.

"Thank you. You've treated me well," he said. "I won't forget it."

A taxi was waiting at the curb for the man when he emerged from the bank five minutes later. He jumped into the backseat.

"Pretoria, please. The Union Building."

A city bus delivered Mansell to a restored colonial building on Van Brandis Avenue. Out front sycamores and jacarandas formed a graceful arch above a circular fountain. Marble steps led past a colonnaded entry to the Provincial Courthouse.

Mosaic tiles and a high arching ceiling highlighted the foyer. Footsteps echoed with a percussive hollowness. Mansell rode the elevator to the basement, where the vaults of Companies House, a public-domain facility giving the ordinary citizen rights to a public company's complete documentation, were located. At the front desk, he filled out a card with the East Fields information. He presented the card to the archivist, paying his statutory fee in cash.

The archivist returned with a thin file. Mansell found a seat and started reading. In 1955, the year East Fields incorporated, they filed a prospectus with the Securities Board of the Johannesburg Stock Exchange. They contracted with the brokerage house of Clare, May, and Seymour to present a public offering of ten million shares of common stock, priced at R3 a share. The initial offering sold 200,000 shares. A second offering at R1.50 a share netted 125,000, and a final offering in 1957 at R.75 sold an additional 195,000.

The total amounted to a mere fraction of the three million shares listed as outstanding. All, Mansell thought, surely forgotten in deed boxes and safety deposits across the land. Five board members accounted for the remaining 2,480,000 shares outstanding. Mansell surveyed the list, noting that three of the five now lived far from Johannesburg, one in Sussex in England. Each owned 100,000 shares.

A fourth director, the company's treasurer and secretary, was a member of an old established law firm, whose offices at 235 Jeppe Street in Johannesburg were given as East Fields's company address.

The fifth was Cyprian Alfred Jurgen; total holdings of two million shares. His positions included chairman of the board and president of operations. Last known address: 49 St. Mark Street, Houghton Estates, Johannesburg.

Mansell closed the file. Houghton Estates rang a bell. One of Jo'burg's wealthier suburbs, if he remembered correctly. He felt confident. People didn't move away from a neighborhood like Houghton. And tomorrow morning, he thought, with luck, Mr. Cyprian Jurgen will be entertaining an unexpected guest.

Mansell checked into an antiquated, thriving hotel on Hanover Street called The Joubert. That afternoon, he toured the Johannesburg Art Gallery in Joubert Park. When he returned, he placed a phone call to Mrs. Ian Elgin.

Mrs. Elgin was in the middle of preparing dinner, and not eager to talk about her husband's demise. Mansell explained in oblique terms about the internal security matter that had arisen because of the arms, and a deep-seated concern about the safety of several high-ranking government officials. As part of the investigation, they were searching deeper into Elgin's past, and could she remember when Ian and the minister of justice had first met?

"I suggest you ask the minister, if it's his life you're so worried about," she replied.

"The minister is in France at the moment, Mrs. Elgin. And I might add that the person we're seeking is almost certainly responsible for your husband's death."

"Meaning I should be grateful, correct?" She punctuated the words with a sarcastic chuckle. "My dear Ian and Minister Leistner met in Durban, Inspector, in 1975 during the harbor strikes my husband was so proud of. Cecil saved Ian's neck from the chopping block, didn't you know? He also managed to get Ian transferred here, which, I suppose, sealed their friendship, and—"

"Thank you, Mrs. Elgin, I appreciate it."

"I assign a simple task," Cecil Leistner said, "to the most powerful bunch of hooligans in Africa, and they bring me excuses."

The conference room reeked of smoke and discarded cold cuts. But for now, it was quiet. The commissioner and his staff had departed. Oliver Neff sat opposite Leistner in a leather-bound club chair, absorbing his employer's fury.

"Minister, Fredrik Steiner was dead days before anyone even knew he existed. Your own Security Branch included."

"Is that supposed to make me feel better? I've got fifty headhunters looking for the guy who offed Steiner, and this small-town constable from Port Elizabeth, Mansell, keeps beating them to the punch at every turn."

It had come to Leistner's attention that Delaney Blackford had been seen in the inspector's company on at least one social occasion, and he wondered now if that bit of gossip was contributing to his consternation. The phone call from Jo'burg earlier this morning should have squelched any such sophistry, but it hadn't.

The minister of justice sucked on the tip of his pipe, staving off a feeling he knew to be far more acute than simple irritation.

"Oliver, if there's a connection between Fredrik Steiner's death and those ANC bastards we arrested last week in Springs, we'd damn well better find—"

At that moment, Jan Koster appeared at the door, and the minister paused in midsentence. What in the name of God, Leistner wondered, is he doing here?

"My apologies, Minister. I was told your meeting had ended," Koster said. "Shall I—?"

"Come in now that you're in," Leistner said. He pushed away from the table and stood up. Oliver Neff bowed his head and excused himself without looking at the newcomer.

"I'm surprised by your visit, Jan Koster," Leistner said as they climbed the stairs to the second floor. "Has something happened? It was my understanding that Christopher Zuma arrived today. Am I wrong?"

"He arrives tonight, Minister. And I'll be there when he does, but my own department also requires a certain amount of attention here, if only for appearance's sake. And there's news that you should know about. I've heard from Van der Merve."

Leistner responded to the announcement with narrowed eyes, and Koster said, "Andrew Van der Merve, Minister. From ARVA II."

"Yes, how foolish," said the minister. "Nothing quite so annoying as a nasty dose of preoccupation, is there?"

"Which leads me to wonder, Cecil, if it's wise to be pushing your Security people quite so hard right now. Those ANC bastards, as I overheard you calling them, were carrying permits for our mine, if you recall. True, the evidence has been taken care of, but the people in Springs know, and so do the people at the Labor Bureau. It's not just our secret. All it would take is one of your overachievers to start asking the wrong questions."

They entered Leistner's office, and Koster asked, "What have you heard from Port Elizabeth? Anything?"

"I've heard there's a killer on the loose out there, that's what I've heard," Leistner replied. "And the winds have a suspicious smell to them."

"I agree," was all Koster said. "And we don't need a can of worms we can't handle right now, do we?"

Leistner grunted. He retreated to his desk and shed his suit coat. "Very well. I'll call the dogs off. Now tell me about Van der Merve."

By train, the route from Port Elizabeth to Bloemfontein measured 692 kilometers, another 410 to Jo'burg. Their schedule included nine additional stops along the way. If all went according to schedule, train number 407 would arrive in Johannesburg Wednesday morning at 8:12.

Delaney reported to the chief engineer, a leathery Afrikaner captain named T. L. Smit, at eleven. The "hogger," a nickname often endured by chief engineers, assigned her a closet-sized cabin adjacent to his own in the train's employee car.

With an overnight bag across her shoulder, a briefcase in one hand and walking stick in the other, Delaney informed Captain Smit of her plans to keep a rigid file on computerized signaling and crew performance. The latter elicited a stern glare, but it confirmed Delaney's authenticity.

For the next thirty minutes, she introduced herself to the crew, asking perfunctory questions in order to update each member's union file.

Like every railroad, the South African system employed men known as watchdogs. The watchdog's primary function was to rid his particular train of any excess baggage that might attach itself before or after the train left the station. This excess baggage assumed many labels in many different parts of the world, but in the train business, every name translated into the same thing, a bum looking for a free ride.

Like those of every railroad, the watchdogs of the South African railways were generally burly, rugged, and truculent.

The watchdog on train number 407 was Boy Sixpence. Boy was thirty-one-years old, as tall as a phone booth and nearly as wide.

His father was Zulu. But his mother being of a lesser tribe called the Shangaan, Boy entered the world a bastard. The doctor who delivered Boy into the world announced his arrival by saying, "It's a boy and a half, and his mama done died in the process. I'll take a sixpence and a bottle for my trouble. Thank you and good-bye." Thus the name.

There were worse things than being raised an orphan among the Shangaan, but not many. At the ripe age of nine, Boy dug coal seven days a week. Every cent of his wages went into the tribe's coffer. At sixteen, he went to work for the railroad, shoveling coal into hungry locomotives.

Things changed.

When a thief armed with a butcher knife tried to rob Boy of his first week's paycheck, he bludgeoned the man with a single punch to the face and a knee to the groin. The docile Shangaans decided Boy was old enough to keep his own pay from then on. They expelled him from the tribe. Boy moved to New Brighton. He built a house with chicken wire, barrel staves, and sheet metal.

The railroad promoted him to watchdog. He proved reliable and effective. Boy never used his fists. Most times the pikers jumped train when they saw him coming. Otherwise, Boy threw them off when the train slowed for a sharp bend or a steep grade.

Five minutes before departure, Boy Sixpence was inspecting the train one last time. A man dressed in blue jeans, a sailor's shirt, and a windbreaker, and holding an army duffle bag at his side, approached him with a friendly wave. Boy's guileless expression never changed. The man hailed him in Afrikaans first, English second. Boy understood neither and both, bits and pieces. He didn't even bother to shake his head.

The man reached into his back pocket and pulled out a fistful of rand notes. This, Boy understood. The railroad paid Boy R125 a month, plus food and a boxcar to sleep in while he worked. He watched the man count out two hundred rand's worth of the bills.

Silently, the man pointed to a sealed boxcar. Then he said, "Johannesburg."

Casually, the way he did everything, Boy surveyed the train yard. He stuck his hand out. The man passed him the money. Boy cracked the boxcar door, and Andrew Van der Merve clambered aboard.

Boy finished his rounds minutes later, and with a nod of his head, gave Captain Smit the go-ahead.

———

Ten minutes later, as the carillon of bells in the Campanile celebrated the arrival of noon, eighty-two train cars, laden with automobiles from General Motors, rubber goods from Firestone, wool from Cape Angora goats, citrus from Kirkwood, steel from Japan, and oil from Saudi Arabia, cleared the Port Elizabeth city limits.

Standing on a platform outside the employees' cab, Delaney counted backward from the caboose until she came to the East Fields boxcar. She watched it sway in unison with the other cars until the features of its exterior were etched in her brain.

Later, she walked from the sleeping compartment to the locomotive, where she climbed a steel ladder into a cozy, modern control booth. The chief engineer and the fireman were hunched over a geographical chart. Columns of smoke lingered above them.

They both looked up in surprise.

"Gentlemen," she said.

"Ma'am," said the fireman. "Do we cut the mustard so far?"

"A model of efficiency," she replied.

"Have a cigar, Mrs. Blackford," Smit said curtly.

"After dinner, perhaps."

The fireman threw back his head, laughing. The hogger grunted.

Delaney cracked a window and leaned out. They were fifty kilometers from the coast now. The train steamed over a suspension bridge spanning the Sundays River. North lay the Suurberg, the Sour Mountains. Climbing, they swept through the Addo bush, a hardy land of drought-toughened shrubs and stunted, bent trees.

The broken mountains of the Olifantskop loomed ahead. Valleys fed by itinerant rivers grew in richness. Wisps of coal smoke ascended from beehive-shaped huts, and thatched-roof rondavels hid beneath the bows of cottonwoods and acacia. Cattle pens and harvested mealie patches surrounded native kraals. Sheep grazed in fields of stubby grass. Delaney fancied a sense of peace foreign to the shantytowns of New Brighton and Zwide, and she wondered if it was real or imaginary.

She made short notes concerning the signaling systems at Middleton, Cookhouse, and Eastport. And finally, a steep, rocky gorge that paralleled the Great Fish River and cut through the mountains of the Winterberge and the Bankberg led to their first stop, the bustling rail center of Cradock.

It was 5:18, early evening of the fifteenth day of July.

The helicopter circled the mine slowly and then set down upon an improvised helipad next to the control tower. Within minutes, rumors were running in wild streaks throughout East Fields. He had arrived.

The excitement and the anticipation infected every black man. Leaders, they all knew, were rare enough among the tribes of South Africa. Those who chanced stepping forward had a way of disappearing: prison, exile, death.

Christopher Zuma, the estranged leader of the African National Congress, had been living underground in Botswana for more than a decade. Still, despite distance and the persistent rumors of his demise, his power base had continued to grow. Where Mandela and Tambo still captured the fancy of the public and the attention of the Security Branch, Zuma was the acknowledged choice of the ANC's rank and file.

Jan Koster had been quick to recognize this. Zuma had been his first choice in selecting a candidate to lead the movement following the East Fields operation. His charisma and poise in dealing with the white hierarchy were secondary only to his ability to light a fire under his own kind.

Cecil Leistner had never mentioned it to Koster, but Moscow had opposed Zuma's selection from the beginning. The minister of justice had only met Zuma once, but he had been quick to detect the black man's indignation at any outside interference in his affairs. It was an "unacceptable" quality, and he had been surprised that Koster had overlooked it. But it didn't matter. Moscow had also determined Koster's expendability, and Zuma's replacement was already being groomed.

An early morning phone call shook Joshua Brungle out of a deep slumber. He knew, before answering, who the caller would be.

"Nigel," he said. "How's the big city?"

"Sorry about the hour, Joshua. I owe you lunch at the Pic."

"The Pic, is it?" Joshua scrounged through the mess on top of his nightstand until he found a pad and pencil. "You must need a favor. What is it?"

"The name is Cyprian Alfred Jurgen." Mansell relayed Jurgen's current address and explained about his status with East Fields. "Can you draw up a profile without causing a ruckus at Research?"

"With my charm, good looks, and insidious cunning? Of course. Give me an hour."

Mansell left Joshua with the direct-dial number of his room, and then ordered melon, biscuits, and hot tea from room service.

Fifty-five minutes later, the phone rang.

"Cyprian Alfred Jurgen. Born 1916 in Johannesburg." Joshua capsulized Jurgen's family history and his current holdings in real estate, construction, and oil, adding, "No mention of any mining interests, though. He sat on the Transvaal Provincial Council for sixteen years, and served as an adviser to Verwoerd for a year back in the early sixties. His Broederbond number is an ancient 4276."

"Ah. That makes him an old hand," replied Mansell.

"Not somebody to be messing around with, if that's what you mean." Joshua mentioned several of Jurgen's social connections, his religious affiliations, and gave an update on his current situation, saying, "More or less retired at this point, it seems. He owns houses in southern France near Cannes and in the Bahamas. He smokes cigars and bets the horses. He grows roses and raises beagles."

"A well-rounded chap, isn't he?"

"Money does that."

"What kind of cigars?"

"Christ sake, man. Havanas? Upmanns? How should I know?"

They broke the connection. Mansell dressed in a clean white shirt, a maroon knit tie, and a charcoal sports jacket. He clipped the pen microphone to the breast pocket of his jacket and slipped the cigarette-case-sized recorder inside his pocket.

Downstairs in the lobby, he sought out the head bellman. The man was suitably stiff and somber with a portly front and snow-white hair. In response to Mansell's inquiry as to the location of the nearest tobacconist, he said, "You're in luck, young man. The Princeville Pipe and Tobacco it's called. Two blocks south on Twist at the corner of Union Square."

Mansell debated between a box of Macanudos from Jamaica at R2.10 apiece and the Te-Amos from Mexico at R1.80. He settled on the Macanudos, disliking the aroma, but falling for the eccentric silver containers in which each cigar came.

At the Budget Master next to the hotel, Mansell rented a Cressida. He drove up Banket Street to Catherine, past the Girls' School to Tudhope, and beneath the Louis Botha Highway to St. John's Way.

A three-meter-high stone wall enclosed the whole of Houghton

Estates. Ancient ivies covered the wall and jacarandas adorned the parkway out front. Wrought iron gates and a circular guardhouse obstructed the entryway on Elm Street, and Mansell flashed his I.D. to a uniformed guard. He was admitted without questions.

The Estates reeked of Old World money. Narrow roads wound past sprawling houses of colonial, Old English, and Victorian architecture. Towering alders and gangly eucalyptus dotted every lawn, hibiscus and roses every garden.

A circular cobblestone drive fronted the colonial mansion at 49 St. Mark Street. Mansell parked at the curb. A flagstone walk led him to the entrance, where white colonnades supported symmetrical arches and a rooftop belvedere overlooked the grounds.

He leaned on the doorbell. Moments later, a butler in black tails answered.

"May I help you, sir?"

"Yes, you may," Mansell answered in brusque Afrikaans. It wouldn't do to be English in this instance, he realized, nor from Port Elizabeth; too obscure. Pretoria always indicated something official, something urgent. It also wouldn't do to merely be from CIB. Mansell flipped open his badge, obscuring the nameplate. "My name is Mitchell Wenn. Captain Mitchell Wenn. South African Police, Security Branch, Pretoria. I'd very much like a word with Mr. Jurgen. It's a matter of some importance. And if you could present these to him, I would be appreciative."

Mansell offered the box of Macanudos, and the butler eyed him with suspicious regard. Mansell responded with silent gravity.

"If you'll be so kind as to wait," the butler replied, allowing Mansell inside. "I'll see if Sir's schedule will allow him a moment."

From the entryway, Mansell's eyes drifted from English floor tiles to a crystal chandelier to a framed Picasso at the head of a circular staircase. He took note of the cameras positioned overhead and the red lights signifying their employment.

The butler returned shortly, saying, "If you will follow me, Captain."

Cyprian Jurgen received his visitor in the billiards room. Rich oil paintings of clipper ships and seafaring galleons lent a masculine air to the room. A walk-in bar filled one wall. Gaming tables for pool, billiards, and snooker, and an octagonal poker table dominated the room. Drop lamps hung above each.

A wiry old man, with a cue stick in his hands, stalked about the pool table like a lioness on the prowl. The feline metaphor was compounded by a slender sunken face, a conspicuous hook nose, and busy, piercing eyes.

"Captain Wenn, is it?" Jurgen said eventually, his eyes leaving the table for only an instant. He spoke Afrikaans with thick German inflections. The voice, Mansell thought, sounded bored. "Pool is such a refined game in the correct setting, don't you think? Do you play?"

"I was quite good at one time," Mansell answered. "May I?"

Jurgen gestured toward the cue sticks. The balls were racked for straight pool. Jurgen broke. He cleared the table in three minutes, broke down his cue stick, and withdrew to the bar.

Mansell set the balls up again. "You shoot a good game, sir," he said deferentially.

Sipping straight Scotch, Jurgen said, "Normally, Captain Wenn, I would have been informed in advance of a visit from SB. Perhaps I should have a closer look at your identification, please."

Mansell ignored the request. Instead, he launched the cue ball. It hit the one ball with a loud crack, and the others scattered. When the table was still again, Mansell leaned on his stick. This was the moment. All his calculations, all the hints and innuendos that had formulated in his brain over the past twelve days would either expose him now or bear fruit. He circled the table, studying the balls.

"This is rather more of a personal matter, sir," he said. "With regards to East Fields."

"Oh." Jurgen intended that the word be spoken without commitment, but the edge in his voice betrayed him.

Mansell faced him now. "Yes, sir. What I mean to say is that the minister sent me personally."

"A phone call wouldn't have sufficed?" Jurgen touched the glass to his lips. "Cecil knows my number, I believe."

A door opens, Mansell thought. He took his wallet from his back pocket and opened it to the shield. He said, "A phone call may have caused . . . more concern than necessary. Not to mention the . . . safety factor."

"There's a problem?"

"Yes, actually." Mansell started forward slowly, offering Jurgen his credentials while saying, "I'm afraid there is a problem, Mr. Jurgen. One of considerable concern."

"A problem with our lease agreement? Or the property?" Jurgen snapped. He waved Mansell away, pulling vigorously on his Scotch and leaning on the bar. "If Cecil wants some consideration or changes in our arrangement, or—"

Mansell held up a hand. He offered a sympathetic smile. "No, sir, not at all." He replaced his wallet casually and withdrew. Jurgen's earlier confidence was veneer, he thought, bolstered by his prowess at pool. "The problem, Mr. Jurgen, concerns . . . a matter of internal security. And my visit is simply exploratory, shall we say? Precautionary."

Mansell stretched across the pool table. He tapped the cue ball against the six, and the green ball dropped into the side pocket. Then he approached the bar again.

In a lower voice, he said, "Some individual, or some group, no doubt the ANC or the SACP, has been smuggling guns into the country. They disguise the cargo with mining equipment. They've been using the corporate names and addresses of several small mining companies for shipping purposes, to legitimize the freight. It's quite a sophisticated operation, and it came to our attention that one of their fronts is East Fields. There's some muck flying about, as it were, in Pretoria, and the minister doesn't want you involved."

"But it's his group that's leasing the land, not—"

"Your name, sir. Your good name is still listed on the property. You are still listed as the chairman and major stockholder. The minister doesn't want a friend implicated in any way. You know how the press preys upon formal hearings, the committee probes, the inquisitions. All that. We have leads, and . . . we are pursuing them."

"Leistner controls these things," Jurgen protested. "Why in the name of—"

"It's Malan, sir. The minister of police is putting the pressure on."

"That ungrateful bastard. On the prowl, as usual."

"Yes, I'm afraid so."

"Shall I take action?" asked Jurgen, suddenly anxious.

Mansell sidled over to the cue rack. Casually, he replaced the stick. "Perhaps, you could . . . Do you still winter in the south of France, Mr. Jurgen?"

Cyprian Jurgen sipped his drink thoughtfully.

"Margaret has been complaining lately. The usual. Politics, the servants, the coal smoke," he replied. "That's a good indication that Jo'burg is getting to her. I could surprise her with the idea.

Call ahead and have the house ready. Not that many loose ends to tidy up anymore."

"Expediency and a certain stealth would be helpful," Mansell hinted.

Jurgen warmed to the idea, drumming the bar top with one hand, replenishing his drink with the other.

"I could have a few trunks packed and shipped up after us. After all, a servant's only as good as his ability to take a simple instruction or two."

"So true. However, if there were a way to limit the number of people who knew—"

"Yes, indeed," Jurgen cut in eagerly.

Mansell returned to his car. He drove half a block, stopped at the corner beneath a sprawling eucalyptus, and consulted his map.

In Bedfordview, on Beau Valley Street, he found an OK Bazaars Discount Store. He bought blue jeans, tennis shoes, a flannel shirt, and sweat shirt from the seconds bin for R16, and binoculars on sale for R13. From the grocery section, he selected red plums, club crackers, and a liter of seltzer water.

At 12:15 in the afternoon, Mansell set out east from Jo'burg on Highway R24. He lit a cigarette and munched on a plum. He thought about Cyprian Jurgen, wondering if a man like that would really drop everything and ship off for the south of France without making, at the very least, punitive inquiries as to the legitimacy of his brief encounter?

An addressee adjustor certificate is simply a form which indicates that the original shipping address on a package or parcel has been changed to some other locale. To obtain such a form for cargo shipped from outside the country, a letter of transmittal and acknowledgment, as it is called in South Africa, is required from the original addressor abroad. Normally, such a letter is sent to the port authority in the first city of receipt, where new freight tags are applied as the parcels are discharged from the shipping vessel. This letter is then transferred to the port goods officer and verified by customs.

Andrew Van der Merve bypassed these normal channels, having the letter of transmittal sent instead from the Porto Nacional Iron

Works in São Paulo direct to the stationmaster in Cradock. The letter requested a "discharge transferral" only, meaning that the goods were still destined for the original addressee, but that transfer to a secondary shipper would occur en route. The letter also requested that Andrew Van der Merve of Benori act as the subagent for both the seller and the buyer. The letter had arrived on the evening of the fourteenth, adding to its authenticity.

In Cradock, Van der Merve presented himself at the stationmaster's office, where the formalities were completed, but not without creating a stir. A bloody nuisance, the assistant stationmaster called it. And it was, of course, Van der Merve agreed. Retagging 253 crates would require the better part of an entire shift, a four-man work crew, and reassigning the boxcar to another train. A bloody nuisance.

Van der Merve, as he had done five times before, in various towns, offered a solution. If the adjustor certificates could be provided now, he suggested, the forms could be assigned to the crates as they were unloaded in Kroonstad. If the East Fields office in Brakpan County and the stationmaster in Kroonstad were notified beforehand, that might solve the dilemma.

It never failed to amaze him. Such a transaction, Van der Merve knew, would have been impossible back home. Black marketeering would have been immediately suspected, and every participant would have faced certain arrest. Ian Elgin had assured him from the outset that no such entanglements would occur here.

None ever had.

The assistant stationmaster reacted to the suggestion with relief and enthusiasm. He placed two long-distance phone calls. He received assent from both East Fields and Kroonstad. Van der Merve signed the discharge transferral, and the assistant placed the necessary forms trustingly in his hands.

As he exited the office, Van der Merve nearly collided with a striking young woman walking with the aid of a cane. He juggled his papers, apologized, and hurried out. He had seen her before. In Port Elizabeth talking with the chief engineer. Why was she here now? he wondered. Alarm set in. It had to be the arms, he thought. But then, she had hardly looked at him. In fact, she'd displayed no signs of recognition at all. And if she did know, then where were the Intelligence people or Security Branch?

Inside the stationmaster's office, Delaney confirmed that only two auto transport cars, two boxcars loaded with auto parts and rubber goods, and a flatcar of processed wool had been deposited here in Cradock.

From his station inside the East Fields boxcar, Andrew Van der Merve studied Delaney as she returned to the employees' car at the head of the train. Ten minutes later, train number 407 set out again, and he breathed a temporary sigh of relief.

Between standing watch over the East Fields cargo during stopovers in Rosmead and Noupoort and the undulation of the steel wheels, Delaney Blackford felt stiff and groggy by 7:30 Wednesday morning when the freighter pulled into Colesberg.

A farming town of ninety-six hundred, Colesberg lay on the outskirts of the Great Plateau. In the distance, bleak, rambling kopjes stretched as far as the eye could see. Cattle and sheep scrounged among tussock and plowed fields. Delaney devoured the crisp morning air, walking briskly along the tracks until the fatigue in her legs and arms disappeared.

The chief engineer suggested breakfast at the station diner. Inside, the smell of steaks grilling, eggs frying, and coffee brewing set her stomach on fire. They sat at a dinette with a vinyl top and simple wooden chairs. Purposely, Delaney sat opposite the window with a view of the train yard.

The waitress served coffee and tea. Smit recommended the house specialty, sirloin and eggs.

When they were alone, Delaney said, "This is fabulous country on the hinterland."

"Big country, for sure," Smit replied warily. "The problems seem smaller for the size, but they're still here. The waitress is black and so is the cook. But the owner is an Afrikaner. The shepherds and the farmhands are all black, and they live in grass huts in the valley. The farm and the sheep are owned by an Afrikaner who lives in a fifteen-room mansion on the hill."

"There are worse things," Delaney said. She didn't want to talk politics. She glanced outside. The train began to roll forward, and her eyes widened. It stopped with a jolt.

"They won't leave without us," the engineer said, seeing her reaction. "We're dropping seven cars here, picking up five others."

Delaney blushed. "Of course. We are in the delivery business, aren't we?" she said, looking aside.

Out of the corner of her eye, she saw the door to the East Fields boxcar open. Delaney immediately recognized the man stepping down from the car, and she marveled more at her own self-control than at the turn of her discovery. It's him, she thought, almost passively. The guy who nearly ran me over in Cradock.

Delaney felt the chief engineer's eyes on her, and she recovered, saying, "I'm famished, aren't you?"

The food arrived. "The steak sauce is homemade," the hogger said. "Try some."

The steak was cooked to perfection. "It's delicious," Delaney said, thinking, He's the escort, of course.

"It's the same old story," Smit was saying. "It's not the vote that's important. They're not ready for that, yet. Education's the bloody answer. We think they're stupid. Hell, they're stifled, not stupid."

Delaney listened to the engineer with one part of her brain while theorizing with the other. The smugglers wouldn't leave the guns unattended, she thought. That's just common sense. But why was he in the stationmaster's office in Cradock?

The waitress refilled their mugs and left a check.

Delaney watched as Boy Sixpence lumbered past the boxcar, his head pivoting, eyes searching. He doesn't know, she thought. She considered the pros and cons of informing Boy of their uninvited guest and decided almost at once against it.

Captain Smit continued to talk. Delaney regretted having lost the thread of his conversation.

"I was in love with a black woman once," he said. Delaney caught the sweet and sorrowful glint in his eyes. "She was a smart, funny woman. A wonderful storyteller. She spoke three languages without a hitch. We lived together for seventeen months before Security Branch found out her work permit was invalid. They relocated her one day without so much as a word to me. That was ten years ago."

Smit lit a cigar and grunted. Delaney saw a shadow materialize next to the boxcar. A crack appeared in the door, and the escort scrambled in. A second set of hands closed the door behind him.

"The watchdog!" The words escaped Delaney's mouth in a diluted whisper, and the engineer peered intently across the table.

"Pardon me, miss?"

"I'm sorry," Delaney replied shyly. "Thinking out loud."

Grunting again, Smit excused himself. Delaney searched her purse until she found a bottle of aspirin. She swallowed three with water. Then, staring out the window, following the line of a sparrowhawk as it soared ever higher into the air, she decided on a course of action.

Outside of Springs, Mansell fell in behind a convoy of migrant workers, panel trucks and flatbeds overflowing with shivering kids and dogged parents. At a crossroads two kilometers out of town, Mansell pulled alongside one of the trucks. He passed the plums and the club crackers out the window to one of the women. He tossed a pack of cigarettes and matches to an old man.

He drove ahead. Wild grass and sage covered the hills of the East Rand. Farmhouses and low-lying barns huddled in broad valleys. Lazy cattle grazed in the company of tall horses in the vales of unseen streams.

Mansell watched as gray thunderheads rumbled toward him from the north, becoming ever darker with their passage. At a junction off R555, a large signpost on the left read, HOMESTAKE MINING INCORPORATED. PRIVATE PROPERTY. TRESPASSERS WILL BE PROSECUTED. Barbed-wire fence enclosed the property.

Mansell parked on the soft shoulder next to the sign. According to the geological map he had acquired in Springs, East Fields lay northeast of Homestake 4.5 kilometers.

He put the car in gear and drove on. A light drizzle sprinkled the windshield. Mansell rolled down his window. The grass shimmered. The air smelled of honeydew.

Three kilometers further on, he turned left onto a narrow dirt road. The road meandered between two plots of fenced land, that on the left, according to a large sign, belonging to Highland Vaal Mining.

Similar No Trespassing signs assaulted him from both properties.

The road ascended a steep grade, dropping, in turn, into a lush valley. Ore dumps appeared on either side. Plumes of smoke drifted into the air. At the base of the valley, the road forked. Mansell parked here. He changed hurriedly into the work clothes he'd bought. He hung the binoculars and a thirty-five-millimeter camera around his neck and forced an opening between the barbed wire.

A stand of evergreens covered the crest of the first hill. Mansell sought shelter here as the drizzle gained strength. The hill tapered off into a broad plateau broken only by symmetrical mountains of dump tailings. To his left, four kilometers away, loomed the facilities of Homestake Mining, and with the aid of the binoculars, he focused on a plant of breathtaking dimensions. Smoke belched from the stacks of the reduction plant. Steam seethed from the ducts of the refinery. Blue flames licked at the sky from gas portals. A dozen mineral cars waited on railroad tracks alongside conveying platforms. Flat warehouses and brick dormitories extended over acres.

Highland Vaal, further off to Mansell's right, was obscured in some measure by ridges of ore, but directly in front of him, dwarfed by its neighbors, lay East Fields. A working farm surrounded the facility; tractors plowed, dairy cows grazed, and workers painted an old barn white.

Stretching out on a dry spot beneath the trees, Mansell used his arms to form a stand for the binoculars. At the heart of the complex was Central Access. Beyond were barracks and warehouses. There were no flames, no steam, and no smoke. Lines of black men, the first signs of life at the mine, carried backpacks and pushed dollies from the warehouses to Central Access, while flatbed trucks and forklifts performed the same function with pallets of cardboard boxes and wooden crates. Mansell kept expecting to see grubby faces, miners' hats, and work belts, but there were none.

Then he saw signs of a military presence. The group was twenty-five or thirty strong. Running between the barracks and the largest of the warehouses, they carried automatic rifles over their shoulders. They wore black windbreakers over olive green camouflage fatigues slashed with brown, paramilitary jackboots on their feet, and camouflage berets on their heads. Mansell switched to his camera in time to flash a half dozen pictures with an inadequate zoom.

Then he returned to the binoculars and studied the warehouse again. A similarly dressed pair, fingering holstered sidearms, stood in the doorway, smoking, peering beneath combat helmets that shook with the rhythm of their conversation.

He surveyed the perimeter of the warehouse and found, within a fenced enclosure, two satellite dishes, each pointing in an opposite direction. At the peak of a tall radio tower, he saw a radar screen, air-to-surface, scanning the horizon, and thirty meters further on, atop a steel derrick, a second screen, larger and slower in its rotation. The discoveries, he decided, warranted a return to his camera.

Frustrated by the lack of people, Mansell scribbled notes and focused again on a silolike structure, fifty meters high, located directly behind the warehouse. Descending a circular staircase were four men, dressed as the others had been and carrying the same make

218

of weapons. Mansell snapped a single picture. Then he raised the camera to the top of the silo, only to find sheets of olive green canvas covering the entire surface.

Drizzle turned to rain. A clap of thunder echoed to the north. Mansell looked for lightning but saw none. He took up the binoculars again. Behind Central Access lay idle conveyors and a shipping yard, equally idle. A long ridge of dump tailings separated these from a field of storage cylinders and a generating station. Mansell zeroed in on one of the storage tanks. He noticed a circular opening at the top. A crane, stationed behind the tank, centered its boom above the opening. Cables were dropped into the tank's belly. A white man in a billed cap stood on a flatcar giving hand signals to the operator. A crew of black workers huddled around eight wooden crates.

These Mansell studied in earnest. They were similar, he told himself. Larger than those he and Delaney had opened, yes, but similar in construction. And though the distance was too great for positive identification, he snapped two pictures. Another crate emerged from the tank. The crane maneuvered it gracefully onto the train car. And when the supervisor removed his cap, Mansell ripped off two more shots—one profile, one straight on.

He studied the face. The supervisor wiped his brow. He lit a cigarette, cupping the match against the rain. His shoulders sagged. In time, he replaced the cap, and Mansell looked elsewhere.

Far across the compound, a convoy of trucks entered the main gate and stopped. Workers piled out. Mansell focused the camera. Behind him, he heard the crack of a rifle bolt as a bullet fell into the chamber, wondering how he could have missed the footsteps.

"Good day to you, sir." The accent was British, cockney. Mansell lowered the camera. "Turn over very, very slowly, if you would."

Mansell turned, head and shoulders, and began to stand. The barrel of the gun, a service carbine of some type, pressed in on him. "Don't get up, sir. Not at all. I said, roll over. Legs and arms spread, right? Like an eager maiden on her weddin' night."

This time, Mansell followed the instructions, and the man withdrew, saying, "You, sir, are trespassing on the private property of the Homestake Mining company. It may well be that your reading skills aren't what they should be. And it may well be that you're going to regret that educational deficiency, sir."

"And perhaps you'd better check my identification before you get too free with your threats, guv'ner."

"That a fact, sir?"

He towered above Mansell, grinning. A red handlebar moustache bobbed against a background of weatherbeaten skin. A cue-ball-smooth head glistened with water, and a rain-soaked T-shirt stretched across a thick torso.

"I'm Chief Homicide Inspector Mansell. Criminal Investigation Bureau." Mansell gestured toward his back pocket, and the barrel closed in on him again.

"Slow, laddie. Slow like molasses oozing from a stiff prick. Hear?"

Mansell touched an empty pocket. Bloody hell, he thought. "My I.D.'s in my other clothes. In the car at the bottom—"

"Sure thing, laddie. Sure thing. And my dear old mum's still a virgin. No, sir, you'll come with me now, I think."

"Do yourself a favor and listen. CIB is investigating the murder of a mining-union official. The case has been deemed a matter of particular importance by the minister of justice, and your interference will not be taken lightly. Does this make any sense to you?" The tree above Mansell no longer sheltered him from the rain. His pants and shirt absorbed water like a sponge. "You're an employee of Homestake. True?"

"True enough, sir," he answered, enjoying himself. "A caretaker of sorts, you might say. Guardian of the jade gate, if you get my drift. And on their land, I'm the law."

"Don't flatter yourself."

"Stand up real slowlike, laddie."

Mansell did so. He said, "Let's walk down to my car and finish this, can we?"

Suddenly, the caretaker lunged forward, and the rifle butt landed squarely in Mansell's abdomen. He doubled over. A second blow penetrated his rib cage. And a third his sternum. Pain, like splintering glass, rippled through his upper body. He collapsed.

"That's just what I had in mind," the man said, frisking Mansell while he was down. With his free hand, he grasped the back of Mansell's shirt, lifting him with ease, and propelling him with a shove down the hill. Mansell stumbled. He slipped on the wet grass. His feet gave way. He tumbled, half skidding, half rolling. The pain in his chest caused him to cry out. He heard laughter.

At the bottom of the hill, the caretaker separated the barbed wire with the barrel of the carbine. He shoved Mansell through, and Mansell's shirt snagged on a barb. The material ripped. He felt burning and sudden wetness along his ribs.

"Spread 'em laddie," the man ordered, pressing Mansell against the front bumper of the Cressida.

Breathing shallowly, Mansell uttered, "In my jacket. In the backseat."

The caretaker snorted. The back door was locked, so he leveled the carbine at Mansell's chest and leaned into the car through the window. When he glanced away, Mansell reared up. He leapt forward, swept aside the gun barrel, and brought an elbow down into the caretaker's kidney. The gun discharged, echoing like the bellow of an angry moose throughout the valley. The man's knees buckled. From behind, Mansell drove a toe heavily into his groin.

The caretaker slumped forward in the mud. The rifle fell from his grip, and Mansell snapped it up. With an angry swing, he propelled it far into the brush. Then he clambered into the front seat. His shoulder harness was on the floor, and he loosened the strap just as the caretaker was struggling to his feet.

Mansell scrambled out of the car. He leveled the gun at the man's head.

"Very professional, guv'ner." Mansell winced, tasting blood in his mouth. He picked through his sports coat until he found his wallet. He flashed his badge. "Very stylish."

The man groaned. "You'd a done the same thing as me, Inspector. My job is my job, and you were the one trespassing."

"A serious threat lying up there under a tree, wasn't I?" Mansell pointed with the gun toward the east fork in the road. "Start walking."

When the caretaker was fifty meters away, Mansell fished out a cigarette. He smoked until he felt dizzy. The pain subsided some. He retrieved his camera and struggled into the Cressida.

He drove back to Springs, bought aspirin and Suprine, swallowed two of each, and then a third aspirin. He sat in the car waiting to be sick. He ran the heater and toyed with the radio dial. He fashioned an image of Delaney Blackford in his brain, the subtle curve of her hips, the dark pools in her eyes, and suddenly, the nausea passed.

In a gas-station rest room, Mansell washed and changed out of his wet clothes. In the mirror, he studied the gross discoloration along his stomach and the bluish swelling around his rib cage. The cut from the barbed wire oozed blood.

He stopped at a liquor store. A pint of cheap brandy cost R5.50. Mansell sipped the elixir until he made it back to the airport.

It wasn't until he was sitting in the airplane awaiting takeoff that he began to question the significance of his findings. Questions gave rise to doubt, but he couldn't think. The Suprine and brandy took hold. He slumped back in his seat and dozed.

Train number 407 crossed into the Orange Free State at 10:05 Wednesday morning.

To the unobservant eye, Delaney imagined, the southern part of the Great Plateau, known as the highveld, no doubt represented a monotonous expanse of flat, barren land, in which wide, dry river valleys and the occasional outcropping of dolerite provided the only variation. She fancied it a rugged terrain of simple elegance, uncompromised space, and loneliness.

The dual locomotives sped across this empty prairie through Trompsburg and Edenburg, picking up as many cars as it dispensed, and arrived in Bloemfontein at 4:01 P.M., twelve minutes ahead of schedule.

Delaney discovered a phone booth at the end of the passenger loading platform amid gift shops, restaurants, and newsstands. She dialed the number Mansell had given her at the Port Elizabeth Police Station, and Joshua Brungle answered on the second ring.

"It's Delaney Blackford."

"Are we still on schedule?"

"Yes. I'm in Bloemfontein."

"You sound tired, lady."

"Exhausted." The very word sent shock waves through her entire system. "The cargo is still on board, but it weighs slightly more than when it was loaded."

"Meaning?"

Andrew Van der Merve followed the woman with the cane across the tracks to a loading platform filled with milling crowds and harried travelers. Two Blue Trains had just entered the station, and the flood of disembarking tourists, farmers, and businessmen provided him with perfect cover.

She walked at a steady pace, dodging a baby carriage here, a baggage cart there. The cane providing balance and support. She was a shapely woman, dark and mysterious. She reminded Van der Merve of his own Valeria and so many winter nights huddled beside a blazing fire drinking peppered vodka and making love until

222

exhaustion and alcohol led to deep slumber. Four months, he thought, watching the swaying hips and imagining the scent of her long black hair.

If this one knows, he thought, she will have to die. Such a pity; such a sweet pleasure.

He would see it in her face.

When she entered the telephone booth, Van der Merve bought a copy of *Die Transvaaler*. He stood with his back to the newsstand. She talked for sixty seconds. When she turned aside, he folded the paper, slipped it under his arm, and started for the telephone booth.

"We should have anticipated that. Damn it," Joshua said following Delaney's explanation. "Does he know you're with the train?"

"He must. I've made my presence known."

"Good. Good. That's to your advantage, I think, but he mustn't suspect that you know anything about the arms."

"I agree, believe me."

"It could be bloody dangerous if he does."

Delaney expelled a heavy sigh. Her ankle throbbed. She leaned heavily on her walking stick, turning as she did so. And when she looked up, the escort was outside the door, his face inches from the glass, dark eyes staring straight into hers. Delaney froze.

"Joshua, he's standing right outside the booth," she whispered.

"Smile. Smile," he shouted. Delaney forced a brief grin through clenched jaws. "Hold up two fingers. Fast. Tell him you'll be right out."

Delaney placed a damp palm over the mouth of the receiver. She held up her hand. "I won't be long," she said, surprised at her own equanimity.

She nodded. The smile came easier this time. The escort looked away.

"My God," she said into the phone.

"You did good," Joshua said. "What's he doing now?"

"Pacing. Reading a newspaper."

"When you walk out, say, 'It's all yours,' or, 'Sorry it took so long.' Something clever like that." Joshua heard the squeal of train brakes, the tension in Delaney's breathing. "Your next major stop is Kroonstad. Check in from there. Please."

Delaney replaced the phone. Brandishing her walking stick, she stepped out of the booth. A folded newspaper obscured the escort's face, and she hurried away.

The newspaper dropped. Van der Merve studied the exaggerated gait as the woman scurried across the platform.

He stepped into the phone booth. A hint of perfume lingered, and he inhaled deeply. He closed his eyes, thinking of Valeria again. Finally, he dropped two coins into the phone and dialed the operator.

She, in turn, dialed three long-distance numbers in three different cities. All without success. She tried the first number again, and a familiar voice answered.

"A woman is riding on our train," Van der Merve explained. "She boarded in Port Elizabeth. It's my guess that she's a railroad official. A suspicious railroad official."

"Describe her."

"Thirty years old. Dark complexion. Black hair, quite long. Attractive. She walks with a cane."

"Mrs. Delaney Blackford. She's a union official."

"I suspect she knows about our cargo."

"You suspect?" the voice challenged. "Do you have proof?"

"In my business, proof is deciphered by the look in someone's eye. The way they walk. A hint of perspiration on a chilly night. The hesitation in their voice."

"Yes, your intuitions are well founded. No one's arguing that."

"We can't afford the risk."

"We?" the voice replied sharply. "Your job is to see to it that the arms reach their destination safely. The woman is our responsibility."

"It would be very easy from this end. Very easy."

"Yes, I'm sure. Proceed with the plan as is. I'll see to it that Mrs. Blackford is taken care of."

A BLACK-AND-WHITE MET MANSELL AT THE AIRPORT. HE HAD EX-
pected Joshua, but the patrolman explained. "There's been some
trouble at the Industrial Park."

"The Ford protest?"

"You got it, chief. The usual stuff. Bonfires, fist waving, short
tempers. Ford closed its Neave plant today. Laid off five hundred
workers—temporarily, they say. I guess now
the Kaffirs'll find out what low pay is all
about, huh? Anyway, the mayor sent in the
local commandos this afternoon."

Mansell sighed. He touched the congested
mass beneath his shirt and winced. "Great.
The usual stuff. Billy clubs, tear gas, rubber
bullets. And a grand time for all."

That ended the discussion. They drove
in silence. Mansell gazed out at the harbor. Algoa Bay glistened
purple and black. The sea stretched out before him, a void of eternal,
kinetic energy, disappearing at last into the maternal hands of night.
At the station, he used the back entrance to his office. He dialed
Captain Terreblanche's private line, and found his superior still on
duty.

A minute later, Mansell descended the stairs to the Pit, where
his reappearance was met with conspiratorial ribbing and theories
of early retirement. Amid this packed house vying for elbow room
and attention, it took Mansell several minutes to track down Joshua.
He found him in a small glass cubicle cloistered with two blacks,
wearing red-and-white baseball caps, and a public defender, who
Mansell recognized for his lack of talent.

He knocked once, cracked the door, and stuck his head in. He
said, "I'm meeting with Terreblanche in fifteen minutes."

"I'll be there," Joshua replied.

Gingerly, Mansell walked downstairs to the pathology lab. Steenkamp sat at his desk studying a backgammon board. Mansell slumped
into a chair without speaking.

The pathologist stared at him for ten seconds, bemused. "You
look . . . well, *shitty* is the only word that comes to mind."

Mansell unbuttoned his shirt with difficulty. It was cold in the basement.

"Sit up and breathe," Steenkamp said, running chilly fingers over the bruised ribs and inflamed abdomen. He studied the puncture wound, hissing. "A night-long siege with some illicit barrio queen, no doubt. I'm jealous."

"I went to Jo'burg for a round of sightseeing and culture shock, and ended up mud wrestling with a moustachioed Goliath."

"Oh, not sadistically induced orgasms, then?"

"You should see the other guy. He paid for his pleasure."

"Mmm." Steenkamp returned to his desk. "Even David needed a breather now and again, I imagine."

He unlocked the door to a cabinet and came away with a bottle of white pills. From a desk drawer he produced a bottle of Martell and two teacups.

"Codeine," he said, passing the pills to Mansell. He read the label. "Take one every four to six hours." Steenkamp laughed. "You'll take two, of course."

Mansell washed down the pills with cognac. The pathologist scribbled on a prescription pad. He pushed the paper across the desk.

"This will get you some antibiotics," he said. "Do have it filled, please. I haven't an empty table available for at least a week."

Mansell climbed the stairs believing he could feel the medicine taking effect. Joshua was standing in the hall outside his office. The chief inspector saw surprise and amusement spread across the detective's face, and he held up a hand.

"Yeah, I know. I know," he said, "I look a bit ruffled."

"Ruffled?" Joshua replied, chuckling. "You're good, man, you know that? You, no doubt, would have described the *Hindenburg* as looking a bit toasted. Trouble?"

"I ran into a jackhammer."

They strolled down the corridor, up another flight of stairs.

"We have four possibilities from our suspects list," Joshua said in reference to the files from Durban, Cape Town, and Johannesburg. "Two from the Jo'burg-Pretoria area, big money losers in the mining business. One from Cape Town, a government official from Mineral Resources and Energy Affairs, and a union guy from Durban who didn't fare too well under Ian Elgin's tutelage. Piet Richter's in Durban right now."

"Good."

"And I heard from Mrs. Blackford." Joshua relayed the developments from Bloemfontein in brief.

They opened the door to the station commander's domain. Captain Oliver Terreblanche sat alone behind a tidied desk. Fatigue and a graven scowl masked his oval face.

"Where have you been, Inspector?"

"In Johannesburg since noon yesterday."

"On company time?"

"On company business." Mansell dug for a cigarette. "I decided the matter was better off kept under wraps."

Terreblanche showered them both with a quizzical glare. He said, "This had better read like a Dashiell Hammett mystery, boys."

At a loss for a suitable beginning point, Mansell started with Lea Goduka and his introduction to the freighter *ARVA II.* From there, he painted Ian Elgin and the arms into the picture. Finally, he recounted his and Delaney's discovery in the harbor's storage shed the night of the fourteenth.

"You entered a harbor storage shed and opened secured and bonded cargo without a warrant?"

"Captain, I had a warrant."

"How thoughtful. Yet you casually allow a cache of arms—what did you say?—two hundred and fifty crates' worth into this country without informing me or Security? Can you imagine the effect this is going to have on your career, Mansell?"

Terreblanche reached out for the telephone, but Mansell covered the receiver with his own hand first.

"Oliver, maybe we've both had a rough day, all right? And maybe I should have consulted with you before taking off for Jo'burg. But I think you'd better hear what I have to say before calling out the firing squad. Would you like to grant your chief inspector that one small courtesy, please?"

Terreblanche relented. "All right. Talk."

"Ian Elgin knew about the guns. Elgin was a part of it from the very beginning. He was the link between the arms, the harbor, and the railroad. He was their guarantee." Bit by bit, Mansell felt his body surrendering to the effects of codeine and exhaustion. He stripped off his jacket and stood up. "Why he was killed, we can only guess. Because he knew too much? Because he'd outlived his usefulness? Maybe he was getting cold feet. I don't think so. I think that after six years, whatever those guns are being used for, whatever it is the people behind this whole thing are planning, it's close.

My guess is that maybe Elgin was demanding a bigger piece of the action, maybe even threatening to expose the whole operation."

"What the hell operation are we talking about, Nigel?"

Mansell sidestepped the question. He responded, instead, by working his way step by step through the case, carefully alluding now to every possible connection between the minister of justice, Ian Elgin, the arms, and East Fields. He saw the effect each reference had on both Terreblanche and Joshua. It wasn't encouraging.

This led to Cyprian Jurgen. Mansell related the encounter and said, "It's on tape. All of it. Jurgen confirms that our minister of justice is part of whatever the hell is going on at that mine, Oliver."

"Really? He used those words? Exactly?" Beads of sweat collected on Terreblanche's forehead. "Well?"

"He said, 'Leistner's group is leasing the land from me.' That's reasonably close, don't you think?"

"For what purpose?"

"My guess is that Jurgen doesn't know. And I wasn't about to ask. That's why I went to East Fields myself this afternoon."

Mansell consulted his notes, describing the scene in detail up to the point of his untimely confrontation with the Homestake caretaker.

"So?" Terreblanche turned his palms upward. "What do we have? A newly opened mine displaying a bit of overkill in its security measures."

Mansell tipped his head. "A mine that's due to receive an illegal shipment of guns from America within two days. A mine that may well have received five similar shipments over the last six years."

"Are you certain the arms are headed for this East Fields mine? Could it be that the smugglers are using the name as a cover?"

"It's possible."

"Could you identify the guns the guards there were carrying? Were they M16s? Were the pistols American?"

"Not from that distance."

Terreblanche massaged a day-old beard. He yawned. "Is there any evidence that this freighter—what did you call it?"

"ARVA II," answered Joshua, impassively.

"Indeed. Is there any reason to believe that this ARVA II brought anything other than mining supplies into the country on its previous trips here?"

"Only Ian Elgin's presence at the time of each visit," Mansell answered.

"In other words, none. Okay. The one thing we do know for certain is that a cache of arms has been brought into the country illegally. Correct?" Terreblanche raised an eyebrow, looking from inspector to detective. "Okay. Whether these guns are related to Ian Elgin's murder or not, it's still a Security Branch matter. A damn serious one. And whether the guns end up at this East Fields mine or in the Kalahari Desert, it's still Security's problem."

"I wish it were that simple. If the arms are destined for East Fields, then a certain amount of suspicion falls on the very man who controls Security."

"Do we know that he knows? The most powerful goddamn minister in the country? What would he have to gain from such temerity, Inspector?"

"If the prime minister falters, or if he's forced to step down at some point, who do you think the job belongs to?"

Terreblanche struggled to his feet. "Now you listen, mister. No one else had better hear those charges, do you hear? No one. You can save your political speculations for after-hour bull sessions at the bar. Your job is homicide investigation. Now, there's a corpse in the morgue with a bullet hole between its eyes, and your twenty-four-hour purge of Johannesburg provided this office with exactly zero information about who put that hole there."

Terreblanche snatched a glass from his desk and poured water from a nearby pitcher. He sipped it briefly and then sat down again. Composed, he said, "My chief inspector isn't particularly fond of Security Branch. Fine. I understand. Your contempt and flippancy are overlooked because of certain talents that you possess. But don't push it, Nigel. You start pointing a finger at the highest legal authority in this land and you'll end up sweeping floors at the local high school."

"Oliver, listen—"

"You listen. Now, I've got to think about this one, Nigel. I mean I can't deny that you might be on to something, but it's damn fantastic. And like you said, we've both had a pretty rough day." Terreblanche leaned across the table. Gesturing with his glass, he said, "Okay. It stays in this office for the night. Just between the three of us. Agreed? Nigel, go home and get some sleep. You look done in. Check in with me first thing in the morning. We'll make a move then. Joshua, the same."

The attendant at the police garage handed Mansell the keys to a gray Chevelle. "Tight clutch," he said as Mansell turned the engine over.

The soporifics were winning. Mansell cranked down all four windows. He drove slowly. A cool breeze and fragmentary thought kept him from succumbing.

An English union official is killed by an East German thug. The thug also kills an innocent woman, whose husband is purposely framed for both murders. Still, the setup is only temporary; poison is discovered. Later, the hit man himself is disposed of. The body is put on display; the killer leaves a note. Facts? Or convenient rationale for a cop in dire need of explanations? The justice minister complains about the need for a solution. Demands results. Is that unusual involvement, natural concern for a friend, or is he just doing his job? The cop uncovers a shipment of illegal weapons. He suppresses the information. Tells himself it's the only avenue left to his killer. Why? Is a perfect record that important to him? Or is the cop really trying to convince someone else of its importance? Maybe convince that someone enough so that she'll come back home? Maybe it's time the cop got on with his own life. Maybe it's time the cop tried being more of a human being and less of a cop.

By some stroke, Mansell found himself on Cherrywood Parkway. Two blocks further on, he turned right onto Northview. He parked at the curb. He peered out at the house. Reluctance overwhelmed him. He switched on the radio and heard the pedal steel guitar of King Sonny Ade.

Another possibility struck him. Maybe the cop is looking for an excuse to have himself bumped from the force? Dismissal meant avoiding the decision himself. Mansell could just imagine Delaney's response to that. But if Security Branch was forced into a case built of sticks and straw, then someone would have to answer for it. Except, he thought, switching the radio off, the guns in those crates weren't made of straw, and the automatic rifles and radar screens at East Fields weren't built of sticks.

This last thought propelled him out of the car.

Shafts of moonlight cut through the sycamores, illuminating the street. Lights glowed from the dining room, bathroom, and pantry, giving the house a lived-in look. Suddenly, Mansell felt lighthearted, almost at ease. Halfway up the walk, he paused to light a cigarette.

A car crept down the street. Mansell watched it approach. Ray Thompson's Ford, he thought. But then it pulled into the next-door neighbor's drive. Jason Smith worked the swing shift at the Wool Exchange. Mansell couldn't see his face, but he raised a hand, waiting.

The driver killed the headlights, but not the engine. The door opened. Mansell saw the gleam of black steel. A pistol. He threw himself on the ground. He heard a muffled thud, followed instantly by lead ricocheting off the sidewalk. He rolled to his knees, madly fumbling for his own gun. He saw a large figure wearing a ski mask, feet spread, arms extended. Mansell dove behind a forsythia bush. A second shot hissed past. A third struck a terra-cotta planter on the porch, shattering it.

Mansell fired off two rounds, wildly. He came to his feet, scrambling toward the side entrance to the garage. A fourth shot ripped through his jacket. He felt a burning sensation. That was good. He lunged for the door. A fifth bullet punched a hole in the front picture window. A sixth whizzed past his head, embedding in brick. The door opened. Mansell tripped over the top step and collapsed on the garage floor. He heard the roar of an engine, the squeal of tires.

He hurried back to the porch. Peering around the corner of the garage, he saw brake lights and heard the protest of tires as the car swerved violently onto the parkway and was gone.

Six shots, a broken planter, a shattered window, a grazed shoulder. A brutal warning or an unfortunate assassin? Mansell wondered. No. The gunman's actions were well planned, his timing exact. He had used a silencer. No, he thought, those were not warning shots.

Weakened by drugs and spent adrenaline, Mansell threw himself down on the porch. The police would be here soon. Drifting, he imagined the tinnient chiming of bells, a ringing. He shook his head. The sound grew in volume, and something in his brain made the connection. The telephone.

He entered the house with his gun raised, crept into the study, where the phone seemed to be screaming at him, and grasped the receiver, holding it silently to his ear.

"It's Delaney."

"Delaney. Hold on."

Mansell raced back through the house to the front door, bolting it. He switched off lights in the dining room and pantry and carried the phone from the study to the back porch. He settled into a rattan chair with a view of the backyard and the front rooms.

"Good of you to call."

"Something's wrong."

"Yes. We've impressed someone."

"What's happened?"

Mansell thought about that. Who actually knew? Who had he talked to in the last twenty-four hours that could possibly know? Mansell dismissed the caretaker from Homestake out of hand, and Ian Elgin's wife had seemed more bitter about his call than concerned about its repercussions. He thought about Cyprian Jurgen, the sprawling mansion, and the cameras that followed him from room to room. Had Jurgen decided to talk with Cecil Leistner after all? Could he have been followed to East Fields? It was possible. Mansell shook his head. That left Terreblanche and Joseph Steenkamp. He reviewed their conversations and shook his head again. It didn't add up. There must be someone else. "Joshua." Mansell said the name aloud. "No, not Joshua."

"Inspector?"

"I'm sorry," he said quickly. "Delaney, they know about you. They'll be looking for you now."

"I don't think so."

"The escort will know soon enough, if he doesn't already."

"Are you sure? What's happened?"

Mansell felt himself drifting again. He stood up. Pacing helped. He explained in brief about his visit to the East Rand, and about the turn of events since his return. "This isn't union business anymore."

"I know that."

"Where are you now?"

"In Kroonstad."

"I want you to get away from there, Delaney. . . ."

"They're unloading the weapons."

Mansell hesitated. He perched on the edge of the chair, massaging his eyes, thinking. "You're sure."

"The boxcar's been dropped at a loading platform."

"They'll use trucks from there."

"I've rented a car."

"Good, then. Get as far away from there as you can."

"Do you . . . know for sure?" she asked. "Do you have the proof you need?"

"No. Not yet," he admitted.

Her voice softened. "I'm following those guns. I have to."

"You're no good to my investigation dead."

"Is that your way of saying be careful?"

"That's my way of saying I'd like to see your incredible face again."

"I'll settle for that," she replied. "Where will you be?"

Mansell hadn't thought that far ahead. The light was dimming. He needed sleep. "I don't know yet."

He heard Delaney stirring on the other end of the line. He heard the edge in her voice when she said, "I have to go. There's a key to my place under the strawberry planter in the backyard. I'll call there at ten tomorrow morning."

She broke the connection. Mansell stared at the receiver, eventually guiding it back to the cradle. He ordered himself to move, but the caverns behind his eyes were suddenly filled with darkness, and his chin, like a lead weight, fell upon his chest.

In Johannesburg, a thousand kilometers away, another man in an equally deep slumber was wrenched awake by a telephone that possessed a ringing sound oddly like that of a warbler during mating season.

He groped for the receiver, staring at it, calculating his response. "Montana," he muttered.

"Someone just made a play for Inspector Mansell on his own front porch, Mr. Montana," the caller said.

Blood drained from his face, but he managed to control the tone of his reply. "And?"

"He's alive. That much I'm sure of."

"Who? Do you have any idea?" He swung his legs onto the floor. His watch read 1:15 A.M.

"Not at the moment."

"Where's Mansell now?"

"Unless he's stupid, which he isn't, he won't be hanging around his own place for long."

"Let's hope not."

"It gets worse," the caller continued. "Tomorrow morning a federal warrant will be issued for Mansell's arrest."

"A federal warrant? On what charge?"

"In connection with the murder of Steven de Villiers. His body was discovered this morning near Sheldon, off R32. Very dead."

My God, he thought. "Discovered by whom?"

He heard a short, dull cackle. "Your guess is as good as mine, and probably the same as mine. I'll know more in the morning."

Kroonstad was a nineteenth-century town bent on preserving itself against a rash of twentieth-century excess. An agricultural center, it was inhabited mostly by farmers, ranchers, and miners. The whites were furiously Afrikaner, the blacks underpaid, well fed, and contented. The Dutch Reformed Church, as always, continued to wield a strong hand here, and history, as always, continued to grip the architecture, the politics, and the people.

The railroad station reminded Delaney of a sprawling Dutch farmhouse. Blunt windmills flanked the terminal on either end. Stone chimneys rose from the rooftop.

The night was cool under thick clouds, thunderheads gliding in the wind like mercury and the same black-gray hue. The air smelled of rain and livestock.

Rail workers had shunted the East Fields boxcar to a loading dock at the north end of the yard. Now, from a warehouse located behind the docks, sliding doors opened. Two four-ton forklifts motored toward the car. Beneath the glow of yellow floodlights, two empty tractor trailers maneuvered dockside. The drivers climbed out of the cabs, and the exchange of cargo began.

From the balcony off the depot's all-night lounge, Delaney studied Andrew Van der Merve as he huddled with one of the truck drivers. Beneath the power of the telephoto lens attached to her thirty-five-millimeter Minolta, the faces came to life. Van der Merve talked, gesturing with his hands and a black cigarette; the other man's head bobbed in response. Delaney snapped four pictures.

Then she took the stairs down to the main terminal. She found the stationmaster's office next to the ticket counter. Inside, a stripling in dungarees and a skimmer greeted her with a sheepish grin. Delaney introduced herself, presenting identification and a radiant smile in return.

"The boxcar on platform number sixteen. That is the mining equipment bound for the East Rand, isn't it?" she asked.

"Righto," he answered. "She's been tagged with adjustor certificates issued in Cradock."

"Yes, I know." Delaney offered the white lie with another, equally magnetic smile. The clerk blushed. "I seem to have lost my copy of the transaction, and, just for my records, I was hoping you could tell me if the adjustment was for a change of receivership or just a shipping transferal."

"Destination's the same," the boy beamed. "Sometimes it's easier than goin' all the way to Jo'burg, I guess."

"Easier for them. Just a lot of extra paperwork for us." Delaney exchanged a knowing glance with the clerk. "By the way, could I ask a small favor?"

"Just name it."

Delaney scribbled a message for Captain Smit explaining her departure and offering her thanks. She left the note with the clerk and went outside to the parking lot. She slipped behind the wheel of a Volkswagen Jetta.

Across the frontage road from the train station was a Checker's hamburger stand and a gas station. Delaney bought two large coffees and a bowl of chili. She parked at the corner of the station lot with a clear view of the loading docks. She ate the chili greedily, and then, resigned to a long wait, sipped at the coffee.

An hour and twenty minutes later, Andrew Van der Merve and his drivers piled into the cabs of two Hinos. The trucks rolled out of the train yard onto the frontage road that connected with N1 Freeway. Delaney followed at a distance. Two kilometers further on, they exchanged N1 for the R34 highway. Traffic was sparse. Delaney settled in behind a beat-up Toyota, keeping sight of the trucks' taillights a kilometer ahead.

A light rain fell. Delaney cracked the wind-wings, hoping to stay alert. She searched the radio until she discovered a Johannesburg jazz station that was more static than music. In her imagination she composed brief fantasies about the guns and their purpose: ghost riders on horseback robbing a gold-laden stagecoach, mercenaries hijacking a diamond shipment out of Kimberley, vigilantes prowling the borders between Gondor and Mordor in search of orcs and trolls. In the end, anxiety displaced imagination.

The trucks sped through Liberty and circumvented the dim lights of Heilbron, where the Toyota turned off at a rest stop. When the trucks veered east into the hills, Delaney closed the gap. She lost sight of the trucks in a deep river valley and then again when the road swept around a steep escarpment.

When the trucks reappeared at the crest of the next hill, Delaney saw brake lights. As they broached the peak, the trucks continued to slow. Delaney downshifted. At the base of the valley, she doused her lights. With mixed emotions, she urged the Jetta to the crest of the hill. Halfway down the other side, she saw stationary dots of red and plumes of exhaust. Her heart skipped a beat.

The trucks had stopped.

Nigel Mansell was still sleeping in the rattan chair on his back porch when the phone in his lap rang. He reared up. The phone tumbled to the floor. The ringing ceased. He breathed a sigh of relief, wondering how long he'd been out. In time, he heard a distant voice, and only then did he realize that the receiver had disconnected from the cradle.

He gathered up the phone, raised the receiver, and heard his name. "Mansell. Nigel Mansell. Are you there?"

"Who is this?"

"A friend. And you could use one just now."

"Fuck you." Mansell slammed the receiver down.

He stood up, gazing out the back window. The porch light washed a redwood deck and empty lawn chairs. The police never came, he thought. In the back of his mind he doused an indiscernible flicker of panic.

The phone rang again. Without knowing why, he answered it again and heard the same voice say, "Thought one, Inspector. You're due for arrest in the morning. Got that? A federal warrant. If you're still alive. You'd be a little less conspicuous someplace other than your own house, don't you think? And thought two. Remember your history lesson. The Caves. The Caves of the Womb."

Ten minutes passed.

Delaney stepped out of the car. In a vain effort to suppress mounting anxiety, she gulped huge amounts of air. Cool rain sent shivers down her spine. She heard Mansell's voice pounding in her head.

236

"They'll be looking for you now. . . . You're no good to my investigation dead."

She circled the car, eyes glued to the highway. She searched the tarmac and the gulleys alongside. Scrub oak rustled in the rain; a prairie dog scampered up the bank into the woods; a coyote howled.

Suddenly, the Hino engines turned over. The roar traveled across the valley like thunder. In seconds, the trucks were plunging down to the valley floor, across, and up the other side. Delaney scrambled into the driver's seat. The Jetta sprang to life.

She was a kilometer and a half back and crossing the valley floor when the trucks reached the summit of the next rise and disappeared. Caution intervened, and Delaney tapped her brakes. The Jetta struggled to the ridgetop.

Only then did it become clear what had occurred.

From here, the backside of the hill descended down a long, shallow bowl into a lush plateau dotted with farms and beehive huts. The plateau stretched for ten kilometers to the foot of the Drakensberg Mountains and the Liebenbergs Vlei River. Dim lights and coal fires shone from the town of Frankfort on the river's far bank. Railroad tracks, running north and south, bisected the plateau, intersecting the highway a kilometer this side of the river.

Off to her right, Delaney saw a powerful beacon, the headlight of an approaching coal train. She calculated its speed, in the same breath complimenting the smugglers on their ingenuity.

The trucks were still a kilometer ahead. Delaney glanced at the speedometer, seventy k.p.h. She pressed the gas pedal to the floor. The Jetta leapt forward. The highway glistened with rain and oil.

Red and green warning lights flashed at the train crossing. The train's whistle echoed throughout the valley. Smoke belched from the chimneys of three old diesel locomotives. The whistle sounded again, shrill and cold. The trucks powered across the tracks. The Jetta was a half kilometer behind and closing.

Delaney saw the crossroad arm descending slowly across the highway. She punched the gas one second, and a second later, jumped on the brakes with all her strength.

The Jetta lurched, skidding violently. The rear end fishtailed, sending the car into a languishing tailspin. Delaney grappled with the steering wheel. She pumped the brakes. The earth shuddered as the train rumbled past. The car slid sideways, lurched again, and came to rest an arm's length from the crossroads.

Delaney clung to the steering wheel. Her heart slammed against the walls of her chest. Sweat pooled around her temples. Her breathing came in sharp, labored gasps. The hydraulic brakes of the train hissed time and time again as it prepared for its stopover in Frankfort. Delaney glanced out at steel coal cars; aloof, unperturbed, immune.

She covered her face and laughed. *My God.* Nausea raced through her system. Bile filled her mouth. The rumble of the train invaded the car.

Delaney tried the engine a half dozen times and finally pumped it back to life. She backed the Jetta away from the tracks.

Her legs shook as she climbed out, and her ankle throbbed. The train slowed to a crawl. Coal trains on the Great Plateau, Delaney remembered, resigned to the inevitable wait, were often three hundred and fifty cars long.

The rain fizzled out. Broken clouds revealed a slender, pale moon. Delaney thought about Nigel Mansell.

In time, her heart quieted. The quivering in her legs subsided. She retrieved a map and a flashlight from the glove compartment of the car. She laid the map across the front hood. There were a dozen routes leading from Frankfort to the East Rand, she realized, and all the photos and notes she'd taken until now wouldn't be worth much if she didn't confirm the final destination.

With two tractor trailers, Delaney reasoned, they'd be looking for speed and directness without entanglements. The delay at the crossing had given them nine or ten minutes, at least. She glanced back at the train and the box-cut shadow of the caboose was now in sight.

Directness, Delaney decided as she folded the map, was also her single ally now. The freeway gave access to two interchanges that led directly to the heart of the East Rand.

She returned to the car. The caboose nudged forlornly past, and the barricade rose. She crossed the tracks. Fully awake, Delaney chose speed over prudence. Merging onto the freeway, she pushed the Jetta to a hundred and twenty-five k.p.h. Traffic was practically nonexistent.

Fifteen minutes later, she exited N3 for another secondary highway, R43. The road was straight, flat, and freshly paved. When the highway skirted the city limits of Balfour, she cut her speed. Fifty kilometers to her left, Johannesburg emitted a luciferous glow. Directly ahead, the East Rand opened up before her.

Another worry, Delaney thought as she glanced at the gas gauge. An eighth of a tank. In Balfour, she remembered, there had been a flashing Gas sign, but it was too late for that now. Her blouse clung to the back of the seatcover. Her hands were suddenly clammy on the steering wheel. She opened the window on the passenger side. "We'll make it," she whispered.

In Devon, fate shone upon her. Delaney discovered an all-night self-service station. After setting the gas pump, she pored over the map again, facing a last decision. The R29 exchange out of Jo'burg led to several major mines; of these, the map indicated Maritime and AmAfrica, and the road to Delmas several others—Homestake and Highland Vaal among them. But East Fields was not included in this select group.

When Delaney paid the station attendant, she asked the obvious question, but the attendant had never heard of the mine.

It didn't matter.

As she was walking back to the car, the decision was made for her. Off to her right, two tractor trailers rolled slowly down R29 into town. Green cabs shimmered lemon and lime beneath yellow streetlamps. Entranced, Delaney watched as the trucks stopped for a red light at the intersection. Recovering, she ducked inside the Jetta and took the lens cap off the camera. The light changed, and she snapped two quick pictures.

The convoy rumbled around the corner onto R50, headed for Delmas. Delaney took the last picture on the roll. She started the engine.

The digital clock in the kitchen read 1:38 A.M.

Nigel Mansell crept slowly through the house into his bedroom. He went straight to the walk-in closet, switched on the overhead light, and pushed aside the clothes hanging on the closet rod.

He stared at the gun case. The Colt Detective Special was missing. Jennifer's gun. Mansell had given it to her years ago, and they had spent several weekends on the department's firing range familiarizing her with it. It hadn't been used since, though Mansell had cleaned and oiled it a year or so ago. "I thought she'd forgotten about it," he whispered. "She must have packed it."

He opened the case with the hide-a-key. Ignoring the Webley, he removed the 9-millimeter Browning HP, a Belgian gun, that had been a gift from the station house gang. He checked the chamber and the trigger mechanism; cleaned and oiled. He found the shoulder harness and cartridge magazines in a shoebox on the top shelf. He locked the case and closed the closet.

Standing in the darkness of his bedroom, Mansell stripped off his rumpled sports coat. Gingerly, he removed the harness that held his .38 Police Special. He changed into fresh undergarments, a clean shirt, and gray denim pants. He put the .38 back over his shoulder before putting on a charcoal jacket. He packed a small duffel bag with a change of clothes. He left the bedroom carrying the harnessed Browning, an empty briefcase, two sets of keys, and the duffel bag.

Mansell toured the house at a brisk pace. He switched on lights in the kitchen and pantry. In the bathroom, he washed down two codeine pills with water. He turned on the transistor radio to Jennifer's classical station, left the light burning, and wedged a laundry hamper between the door and the threshold. He crossed to the living room, dropped the window shades, and turned on the television to a rerun of "The Lost City of the Kalahari." He set the volume a little above normal.

Mansell left the house through the garage, where his own Impala was parked. Outside, a night owl called out from a distant tree. Wind swept dead leaves across the pavement. He climbed openly into the police sedan and started the engine. Mansell drove the car around a dozen blocks and through as many alleys checking for tails.

Satisfied that the gunman was done for the night, he returned to Northview Avenue. He parked six doors down from his own bungalow in front of the Clavers' Tudor two-story. John Claver worked as a bond broker for Sherrill, Barnswell. He made R100,000 a year selling munis, corporate issues, and junk bonds. Traditionally, the Clavers spent July in Florida. They always left keys and instructions with their best neighbors, the Mansells, but the house was better protected by twenty-five hundred rand's worth of burglar devices.

Using a passkey and a code combination, Mansell shut down the alarm system to the garage. The door rose automatically. Parked inside was a Porsche 911 and an Audi 5000. Mansell drove the Audi down the drive into the street. He parked the police sedan in the garage. Then he maneuvered the Porsche into the driveway directly behind the sedan.

He walked casually back to his own house, removed the Impala from the garage, and drove it back to the Clavers'. The Impala fit neatly in their garage next to the police car. Mansell let the garage door down and reset the alarm.

Adrenaline ceased to be a factor. The mechanics of driving the Audi seemed to come from a distant source, like a drunkard who survives the trip home but can't recall how. Cool air from the air-conditioner washed over him, but it wasn't cool enough. The Browning lay coiled in its leather sheath on the seat next to him. Mansell observed that the weapon served not as a source of comfort, but as a reminder of a recently acquired state of paranoia. The empty briefcase and the hastily packed duffel bag served as blunt exclamation marks.

The Audi was spotless, a glossy patina the color of bronze. They would know him by his automobile as much as by his face. A South African policeman in a German luxury car, he thought, was like a black wig and thick glasses on Queen Elizabeth—a ridiculous but effective disguise.

At the first stop sign, the car staggered and nearly died. Idling, Mansell revived himself by massaging weighted eyelids and grooming slack hair. An unidentified crank caller, he thought, sends the vaunted homicide inspector into a state of trepidation by pushing exactly the right buttons. So be it.

The car seemingly steered itself from Millard Grange to the coloured township of Gelvandale. He remembered Trevenna Avenue and recognized the house more by the yellowwood trees than by the address or the stuccoed exterior.

Delaney's red Fiat was parked out front. Mansell had to move two bicycles and an unfinished picnic table from the center of the garage to make room for the Audi.

The back gate squeaked when he pushed it aside. Across the back fence two dogs began to howl. Mansell crouched behind a lawn chair, eyeing the strawberry planter. A porch light came on in the neighbor's yard. Someone yelled, "Get in here."

It was dark again and quiet. He waited two minutes, easily outlasting the most conscientious neighbor at 2:30 in the morning. He found the key and unlocked the door to the back porch. The layout came back to him. The butcher-block table in the center of the kitchen; African violets above the sink. The china cabinet in the dining room. In the sitting room, Mansell was drawn to the photographs of Amanda lining the piano. Off the hallway was a study, a bathroom, and a bedroom. Her bedroom, he thought. It smelled of potpourri and perfume. A satin spread and silk pillows adorned a queen-sized bed. He couldn't stay in here.

Mansell fled to the living room. The wicker chair, the couch, the oak table with the empty porcelain vase—all brought back memories of his first visit. He took off his shoes and coat. The harness for the Browning fit neatly over the arm of the couch. Folded across the back of the couch was an afghan, and Mansell wrapped it around his shoulders. He stretched out on soft cushions, closed his eyes, and fell into a deep, dreamless sleep.

While the red flecks of the second tractor trailer's taillights dimmed, Delaney reloaded her camera. When the flecks were nothing more than illusionary pinpoints on a sheet of glossy blackness, she set out in pursuit.

At the edge of town she crossed a trestle bridge spanning a dry creek bed. The highway widened, rising steadily into the heart of the Witwatersrand. Darkness closed in about her. Solitary lights from lonely farmhouses were lifelines to the world of the living.

Delaney ordered herself not to hurry. Still shaken by the incident at the train crossing, she realized now how close she had come to death. She realized in the same moment the foolishness that had ruled her life since that night three years ago. And she was aware, all at once, of a new will to live, a new reason: a policeman, of all things. Following the guns made less sense all of sudden; but for the same reason, turning back was out of the question.

She stared out at the hypnotic pools of light leading her deeper into the night. Yellow highway lines were tongues of fire licking at the car as it swept hurriedly past. Road markers were armless dwarves staring back at her with marionette eyes. And for an instant, Delaney was transported back to that night three years ago and the memories. The shocking rumble of rock sweeping across the highway. The hollowness in her own screams. The lifeless body of her only daughter tucked beneath a gray blanket stained a reddish brown by blood and grime. She saw the headlights of an onrushing semi and cringed at the bellow of its horn. The car rocked in the truck's wake, shaking the image from her head, and the village lights of Delmas, set at the crest of the rise, rescued her.

The road veered left, intersecting R555, and there, a half kilometer ahead, were the red flecks of her prey.

On her right, farmhouses and chalets perched among pines and junipers overlooking the road. On her left, gentle slopes and broad plateaus, enclosed by chain link and barbed-wire fences, served as the domicile of gold mines and wheat fields. Slip trails of bright lights and blue flames punctuated the shadowy works of Highland Vaal a stone's throw away.

Five kilometers further on, Delaney saw the red lights multiply and brighten as the drivers applied their brakes. Billows of smoke rose from the exhaust pipes as they dropped into lower gears. Delaney touched her brakes. She eased off onto the shoulder of the road and stopped.

Ahead, floodlights illuminated an entrance a hundred meters away. The trucks stopped momentarily in the center of the highway, obstructing traffic in both directions, and then eased into the light. Delaney mounted the camera atop the steering wheel. She peeked into the viewfinder, and the automatic winder ripped off a half dozen pictures.

Then she pulled back onto the road and closed the gap between herself and the trucks. Stopping again, she could see a circular guardhouse enclosed by lofty chain link gates. Attached to one of the gates was a rectangular sign, green lettering on white. It read, EAST FIELDS MINING CORPORATION—PRIVATE PROPERTY. Delaney cranked her window down halfway. She balanced the lens on the glass. Armed guards gathered at the gates, and she managed a single close-up.

Up ahead a man stepped into the road. He wore a fluorescent orange vest and carried two white flags. He motioned in Delaney's direction, waving her forward. As the Jetta inched ahead, Delaney glanced toward the entrance. She saw the gates opening, swinging outward in a wide arc. She heard shouting. The entrance was too shallow, the arc too wide. The trucks were forced to retreat. The back-up lights on the second trailer illuminated. The traffic controller held up his flags. The truck's warning bell sounded, and it nudged back across the road.

Delaney readied the camera. She glanced into the viewfinder. The East Fields sign, a profile of the first truck, and four armed guards were fixed within the lens. As she adjusted the focus, another man stepped around the huge cab into the picture. It was the escort— intent, anxious, a black cigarette clamped between tight lips. Narrowed eyes looked straight into the camera, and Delaney snapped three pictures. Discarding the cigarette, the escort started toward her. He held up a hand. He broke into a run, yelling. Delaney stepped on the gas. The traffic controller's eyes widened as the Jetta lunged forward, and he leapt aside.

Delaney steered the car in a tight circle around the rear of the trailer. She heard the truck's warning bell again. The Jetta's right wheels plunged onto the soft shoulder. Clouds of dust filled the air. The rear end fishtailed. Delaney glanced into the rear-view mirror and saw the escort and two guards a step behind. She punched the gas, and the Jetta forged back onto the highway.

An hour and ten minutes later, Delaney pulled into a We Deal used-car lot off of R29 on Johannesburg's east side. She parked the Jetta in an empty space next to the service garage between a Nova and a Subaru station wagon. She left the key in the ignition and studied the highway for ten minutes. Satisfied, she got out and walked across the road with her carry-on, briefcase, and camera bag to a Motor West motel: FIFTEEN RAND PER NIGHT, CABLE TV, SWIMMING POOL.

She registered under her mother's maiden name and paid cash. Minutes later, she unlocked the door to room 343, engaged the dead bolt behind her, and collapsed on a wickedly hard bed.

Sleep was another matter.

While her body protested against the hours spent behind the wheel, her brain churned out tales of hitmen and smugglers. Delaney comforted herself with the rationalization that she was on the side of right. One of the good guys, she told herself, remember? Still, she didn't feel like one of the good guys; the fantasies continued.

She stripped off dank clothes, took four Bufferin, and turned on the shower until steam billowed like whipping cream throughout the tiny bathroom. The water bit deliciously into her skin. Steam cleared her lungs. Twenty minutes beneath the hot jets of water gradually soothed the jagged edges. Delaney scrubbed and lathered until her entire body tingled with pleasure.

She toweled herself in front of a full-length mirror wondering if Nigel Mansell was, at that minute, in her house, perhaps in her own bed.

Naked, she crawled between cool sheets; hazy, fading. Another worry eclipsed the advent of sleep. She tossed off the covers and slipped into a robe.

The camera bag was sitting on the nightstand next to the telephone.

Delaney took the Minolta from its case, rewound the exposed film, and stored it in a plastic canister. She buried the canister at the bottom of her carry-on along with the other two rolls. That won't do, she thought, turning on the light. She retrieved all three rolls.

Meticulously, Delaney scanned the room for a suitable hiding place.

The drop ceiling with yellowing tiles and layers of dust seemed too obvious. In the base of the desk lamp seemed amateurish. Taped inside the dresser drawer? The toe of her shoe? In the bottom of the wastebasket? Delaney knelt on the floor and glanced under the bed. Between the mattress and the box springs? No, even a child would look there. Beneath the box springs, she thought. She could pull away an inch or two of the stapled material on the bottom, set the canisters on the wooden frame, and then reset the staples. "Don't be ridiculous," she whispered. Inside the air-conditioning vent? Not without a screwdriver. In her dirty clothes?

Delaney opened a bare closet, studied the entryway, and dismissed the bathroom. Wishing she had never started the whole charade, she opened the front door.

Buzzing fluorescent tubes lit the hallway. Indoor-outdoor carpeting and sterile tan walls smelled of cigarettes and ammonia. The maid's closet was located directly across the hall, and Delaney tried the door. It wasn't locked. She stepped inside. A forty-watt bulb showered dim light over stacks of bed linen, towels, and hand cloths, mops and buckets, squirt bottles and dusters, three cases of toilet paper, and cartons of complimentary Motor West soap.

Delaney set two cases of toilet paper in the doorway. She pulled at the corners of the third case, and flaps sealed with hot glue separated with a sharp pop. Inside were layers of generic toilet paper wrapped in tissue. Delaney dug down to the second layer. She removed the center roll and unwrapped the tissue until she could see the tube. She dropped all three canisters inside. Then she rewrapped the roll, replaced the contents neatly, and stacked the cases exactly as they had been.

A distracted Cecil Leistner stirred cream and a half cube of sugar into hot coffee. He donned half glasses and read the document one last time.

FEDERAL WARRANT ORDER #6141

For: Nigel Morgan Mansell
253 Northview Avenue
Port Elizabeth, Cape Province,
South Africa

Notice. IN TERMS OF PARAGRAPH A, OF SUBSECTION
201 OF SECTION D . . . OF THE CONSTITUTION OF THE
REPUBLIC OF SOUTH AFRICA

Whereas, I, Cecil Andrew Leistner, Minister of
Justice, am satisfied as to the preliminary
evidence presented by the legal authorities of said
district . . . do hereby warrant that the aforementioned
individual shall be . . . subjected to immediate
arrest and detention . . . in conjunction with
the violent death of one Steven Edward de Villiers. . . .

Given under my hand at Pretoria on this 17th
day of July . . .
/s/ C. A. Leistner
Minister of Justice

Leistner removed his spectacles and massaged the bridge of his nose absently.

He was not pleased about the warrant. It signaled an element of discord—another element of discord. His signature would formalize a nationwide manhunt, he knew that. Some considered his signature at the bottom of a federal arrest warrant tantamount to a declaration of war. The minister of justice would have been content to forget Mansell's name forever. He was more concerned with the fate of Fredrik Steiner and the formalization of a state of emergency. True, the cabinet was nearly unanimous in its favor now, but the P.M., for some reason, continued to stall.

Leistner knew that Mansell would be picked up first thing this morning, and he knew that the histrionics of a manhunt would be avoided. But now, he thought, there was this damn mess with Delaney. How in the hell had she become so involved? It was impossible. Worse, it was impossible that she could have gotten as far as she had. Koster had known far enough in advance. He had been warned. Why, Leistner thought, hadn't he taken the necessary action?

The intercom came to life, and Leistner acknowledged it.

His secretary said, "Deputy Minister Koster of Mineral Resources and Energy Affairs is here to see you, sir."

Good, Leistner thought, we'll find out why right now. He said, "Sara, come in here first, please."

Sara entered the room, refilling coffee while Leistner signed the last copy of the federal warrant.

"Have these sent off to all nineteen police divisions immediately, will you please?" He passed the secretary all but two copies. "And send in the deputy minister on your way out. He'll drink tea, I'm quite sure."

Mansell called in his one and only marker.

He, actually, had never considered it a marker, but Merriman Gosani always had.

The funeral on June 10, one year ago, had been for three factory workers employed by Alford Steel in Uitenhage. The three men worked the night shift at the plant's foundry. A gas leak from canisters stored belowground and reportedly labeled, two months before, "Dangerous—Immediate Action Required," had killed the three and blinded a fourth.

The dead were black. The outcry that followed the accident led to a wildcat strike, and demonstrations consumed four days and set the stage for further calamity.

It was chilly and gusty the day of the funeral. The service was staged in the township of Kwaford in a stadium built of pine—in a stadium built for high school soccer and track, not funerals; in a stadium meant to hold six thousand, not five times six thousand.

Every cop within fifty kilometers was on duty that day. The local commando unit and an infantry squadron from the South African Defense Force were engaged.

Mansell, Merry, and Piet Richter were patrolling a parking lot east of the stadium. From where they were parked they could see the smoke from the ceremonial bonfire. No one really knew how the other fire started, only that it began in the bleachers behind the east end zone, only that the pine exploded like a tinderbox, only that panic spread like an epidemic. The bleachers collapsed;

six people were crushed. Army troops dispersed. A frightened mass stormed onto the parking lot.

Mansell remembered the woman with the infant strapped to her back and the three-year-old tugging at her skirt. He remembered seeing her trip in the face of the mob, and he remembered Merry sprinting across the lot and herding the three of them to a place of safety. But what he remembered more clearly than anything was the vengeance of the crowd when they recognized the black cop and the hatred when they started pelting him with stones.

When Mansell saw Merry go under, he clambered onto the hood of their car with two tear-gas canisters and his .38 raised. After that it was a blur. Piet Richter driving headlong into the throng. The horn blasting. Bodies caroming off the hood. Tear gas filling his lungs. The warning shots ringing in his ears. Mansell remembered scampering off the hood and hoisting the unconscious detective over his shoulder, but the trip to the hospital was a blank.

Still, the look on Merry's face when he regained consciousness an hour later was the best memory. It didn't matter that Piet Richter recounted the events in what Mansell felt sure was an overly colorful fashion. Merry was alive.

At 9:15, Mansell telephoned Merry at his private cubicle at the rear of the Pit, a crackerbox squashed between the men's room and a deserted holding cell. At that moment, Merry was interviewing a potential witness about the bakery fire on Fleming Street.

"Son of a bitch, Nigel. Where are you?" the detective whispered. The tumult from the Pit eclipsed Merry's voice, but Mansell heard him say, "Don't move, Mr. Jacob. I'll be right back. Help yourself to some tea."

Merry carried the telephone into the holding cell and closed the door. He said, "All hell's broken loose, pal. What in God's name is going on?"

The tone of the detective's voice conveyed only friendship, and Mansell loosened his guard. "Merry, I heard the good news about the federal warrant. No details, though. What do you know?"

"Are you kidding? It's bad, man. Murder one. Murder one."

The onslaught was more physical than mental: the constriction of his chest muscles, the swelling in his throat, the loss of breathable air. "Who?" he forced himself to ask.

"Does the name de Villiers mean anything? Steven de Villiers?"

"The temporary union liaison for the miners and dockers?" he replied disconcertedly. "We never met."

"Murdered. Beaten about the head with a blunt instrument. Gunshot wounds in the chest. The ETD hasn't been fixed yet, but he was buried near the Fish River east of Sheldon. A little strange, though. Very professional in one sense, yeah, but damn unprofessional in another. I mean, they found the gun ten meters from the grave."

"And?"

"And your prints are all over it, pal."

The Colt Detective, he thought. Jennifer hadn't taken it after all. How stupid. Rhetorically, he asked, "Model?"

"A six-shot .38. A Colt Detective Special. Know it?"

"I know it," answered Mansell. "What about the report?"

"A phone tip. Yesterday. Somebody notified Security. And guess what? Wolffe's in charge."

"Merry. For the record, I—"

"Hey, pal, you don't have to say that to me," Merry cut in. "You're on to something, aren't you? The Elgin thing."

"I need help, Merry. Quiet help. Dangerous help, maybe. The department can't know."

"You came to the right place, you know that." Merry's eyes darted across the Pit. At the foot of the stairs he saw the district prosecutor talking in earnest with Captain Terreblanche and Joshua. "But I'll need to know it all, Nigel. The works."

Mansell hesitated. Disobeying a federal warrant could spell the end to a cop's career. But Merry knew that, too.

"All right, then," he said at last. "I'll need the complete file on the Elgin-Mabasu murders. It should be in my office. Can you get to it?"

"Meet me at my place in an hour."

"Thanks, Merry," Mansell said, but the connection had already been broken.

Mansell showered. He made English tea and toast.

On a yellow legal pad he started a systematic daily log dating from the early morning of July 4.

At ten o'clock, the phone rang.

"Delaney?"

"Hello. Did you sleep?"

"Like a baby. You have the most comfortable couch in the world."

"The couch? I'm disappointed."

"What?"

"Nothing."

"Where are you?" he asked. "Are you all right?"

"Yes. I'm in Johannesburg. Our friends made their drop. On location. I have it all on film."

"Don't pass the film on to anyone but me. Please. Joshua included."

"I don't understand. Joshua?"

"You will." Mansell gave Delaney a telephone number at the Clavers' residence, an answering machine and its coded message return. "I'll be away from P.E. for two or three days. Wait for my call."

In the systematic assignment of residential areas that placed Port Elizabeth's whites at the foot of the harbor, the coloureds in the central corridor between highways and greenbelts, and the blacks enclosed by factories to the north, there was a flaw. Not a flaw really; an exception. The township of Stuart.

Stuart was a parcel of land two kilometers square. It was located at the southernmost border of the city, across from the mansions of Walmer and Mill Park and adjacent to the airport. The streets were paved and lined in yellow. Small plots were terraced with grass and shrubs. Electricity lit the interior of brick houses, and plumbing was used instead of night soil tractors. Yet the residents were black. A corporate lawyer in a brick tri-level on Cooper Street. A textile exporter in a Spanish two-story on Ocean View. A police detective in a framed one-story on Fairplay Avenue.

Mansell toured the neighborhood by car, scouting for telltale signs of entrapment. Then he parked the Audi a block away. He walked down the alley behind Merry's house, reconnoitering. He pushed aside a picket gate and stepped between two hibernating rosebushes. A sagging badminton net bisected a lawn in need of mowing. Old-fashioned clothespins perched on a clothesline like emaciated sparrows. The siding on the back of the house was half painted, light blue over white, but the incomplete job served only to call attention to the graffiti it had been intended to cover. "Black Beans and White Bread. . . . Pig Soup. . . . Die You Mo. . . ."

Mansell stared at the words until they became a blur, until a car churning sand in the back alley cut into this foggy retreat and he forced himself to move. An opened screen door led to a tiled porch. Two opened beers sat on an oval coffee table between deck chairs.

"Merry."

A short chuckle accompanied approaching footsteps. "Hey, it's the back-door man," Merry replied. "You must be hiding from the law or something, pal."

Merry extended a hand, and Mansell grasped it. "Still trying to get used to this outlaw image," he said, gesturing with his thumb toward the backyard. "Nice paint job. The neighbors are green with envy, right?"

"Yeah, they're just dying to get hold of my decorator."

Mansell put a hand on Merry's shoulder. "I wouldn't mind getting ahold of the bastard myself."

Merry gestured to the deck chairs. They made themselves comfortable and drank White Crown beer while Mansell related the entire story. Merry interrupted only once, frowning as the chief inspector recounted the aborted hit that followed his meeting with Terreblanche and Joshua.

"It had to be Jurgen," Merry said. "The old bastard probably has a thousand connections."

"I don't know," Mansell replied. He gazed out at the backyard. A stiff breeze shook the badminton net. "I don't know. It could've been."

Merry looked grim. "Terreblanche has Joshua in charge of this de Villiers thing."

Mansell toyed with the label on his beer. "He'll do a good job," he said flatly.

He finished the narrative, concluding with Delaney's news that morning, and Merry went into the kitchen for another round. Mansell followed. He sat on the counter, while Merry retreated to a high seat next to the telephone. The detective tugged pensively at his beer.

"You want me to go into that mine, don't you, pal?"

Mansell drew a deep breath.

The sudden, shrill ring of the telephone filled the room, and Mansell noticed Merry's momentary start. Good, he thought, the call was not expected. It rang again.

"Bloody hell, Merry, it's probably one of your pining lady friends. Go ahead and answer it."

Merry drank beer, ignoring the phone. "How do I get in?"

"You walk straight through the front gate." The ringing ceased. Silence stepped eagerly into the void. Merry peered down at the phone, and Mansell followed his eyes. He said, "Remember the Boyer investigation? Ten months ago?"

Merry nodded. "Yeah, I remember." Leonard Boyer had been the Labor Bureau's chief commissioner until his death the previous October. He had been accused of selling forged work permits and falsified identity cards to blacks facing relocation. "What was he getting? A thousand rand apiece for the permits? Half that for the cards? A real class act."

"Acquitted on a technicality."

"Yeah, and a week later convicted and executed by a conscientious maniac with a firebomb. Poor bastard."

"We confiscated sixty-five I.D. cards and a hundred work permits from the 'poor bastard's' office. All blank. All officially stamped and initialed. All ready for use. And they're still in a filing cabinet in my office."

Merry slumped into his chair, striking a pose of deep thought. Mansell accommodated him, sipping beer, studying the kitchen of a bachelor. Dirty dishes stacked in the sink; trash accumulating in paper bags beside a crusty stove; a refrigerator stocked with beer and TV dinners instead of broccoli and milk.

"You know, I would like to find out why Sylvia Mabasu died the way she did," Merry said at last. "I've got the weekend off. I'll report in tomorrow. Say I'm following up on a lead out in Uitenhage. Something about the bakery fire. I can take R32 straight out of town."

Mansell shook his head. He dug a roll of hundred-rand notes from his jacket pocket, the result of a reckless trip to the bank on his way here. He counted off ten bills, crossed the floor, and set the bundle next to the phone.

"Take a plane. Have a drink on me." Mansell took a pen from his jacket and scribbled seven numbers on a note pad. He passed the paper to Merry, saying, "This is a phone number. Very safe. It's an answering machine at a neighbor's. They're away. Use it, please."

Merry studied the number and then shredded the paper. He stashed the money in his shirt. "If getting out's as easy as getting in," he said, valiantly, "I'll be back on the beat by Monday morning."

Delaney stuffed a toothbrush, a hair comb, and a jar of facial balm into the side pocket of her carry-on. Humming a classical melody, she checked her wristwatch. It was 10:22. Her plane was scheduled for departure in an hour and ten minutes. A taxi was on the way.

She locked her briefcase and was in the process of storing her camera gear when a heavy knock shook the front door. Her first thought was maid service, the planned distractions of motel living. Go away. The intruder knocked a second time.

Reaching for her walking stick, Delaney crossed to the door. She opened it. Standing in the hall were two business suits occupied by sterile men with grave faces. The younger face cracked a smile revealing straight, polished teeth.

"Good day, Mrs. Blackford. How are you this morning?" Courtesy laced with condescension. He produced a wallet from his slacks. He opened it long enough for Delaney to glimpse the silver-and-gold shield. "I'm Lieutenant Baumgartner. District Two Security Police. This is Sergeant Linder. May we come in for a moment, please?"

Delaney reached out with her hand, and the lieutenant shook it. She corrected him. "Your I.D. May I look at it?"

"Oh, do tell. So sorry." He grinned, sheepishly this time. His partner exuded morose boredom.

The photo depicted Lieutenant J. R. Baumgartner of Pretoria Police District Number Two in a criminal pose. The description was a perfect fit, the credentials genuine. Delaney composed herself.

"Come in," she said, returning the wallet.

"The film," said Baumgartner, drumming fingers over the dresser top. "We'd like it, please."

"I'm sorry?" Delaney understood Security Branch. A smile backed by a sword. A sword backed by three hundred pieces of suffocating legislation that granted SS liberties to men in leisure suits like the lieutenant and his enforcer. Prosaic, insecure, and thus, she thought, extremely dangerous.

"You've exceeded your authority as a union official, Mrs. Blackford. Not only have you infringed upon the rights of interprovincial trade, but you were seen taking photographs of an East Rand mine last night without the consent of the rightful owners."

"Was I?" she countered. "And if I was, is that now an infraction of the law, Lieutenant? Photographing property owned by a publicly held corporation?"

The polished smile evaporated. Now the threat, Delaney thought. Baumgartner crossed his arms. He leaned back against the dresser and said, "I don't intend quoting constitutional law, Mrs. Blackford. We can search the premises if need be. The motel owner has given his consent."

"Did he? For film that doesn't exist? Such a model citizen. And tell me, Lieutenant, presuming I am guilty as charged—and I'm sure you are presuming—why wasn't I stopped in the act?" Delaney walked from the entryway to the bed. She unzipped her camera bag, removed the thirty-five-millimeter camera, the light meter, the speedlight, the telephoto lens, and two canisters of film. She laid each neatly on the spread. "Since you're chomping at the bit to do so, why don't you start with these? Sergeant Linder, I imagine this is your specialty."

The rotund Linder, whose flat, oval face was scarred by a poorly manicured moustache and drooping eyes, was standing in the bathroom doorway with hands locked about a protruding girth. Baumgartner nodded curtly, and the sergeant trudged forward. He bent over the bed. Stubby fingers opened the back of the Minolta. He emptied batteries from the speedlight and dissected the light meter. He tossed the lens aside. He ripped the film from each reel.

"Unexposed," he announced.

"Let's take a closer look," ordered the lieutenant.

Sergeant Angus Linder was a fettered bulldozer awaiting emancipation. He concentrated, initially, on the bed. Using the long blade of a pocket knife, he shredded two pillows. Goose down filled the air like shedding cottonwoods in summer. Gathering steam, he set loose the steel blade on the mattress, slicing diagonally, spewing foam rubber from one end of the room to the other.

Baumgartner, in the meantime, dismantled the dresser, searching for false bottoms and loose panels. He picked up the table lamp and casually smashed the base against the edge of the dresser. Shards of porcelain tumbled to the floor.

Drawn by the escalating tumult, the motel operator hurried into the room. He stopped cold two steps past the threshold. His mouth hung agape. Hands covered his cheeks. He whispered, "Oh, dear Lord," and walked out.

Neither officer seemed to notice. Baumgartner was fumbling through Delaney's overnight bag, strewing clothes from one end of the dresser to the other. He reached for the briefcase. Delaney offered him the key, mutely feigning indifference.

254

Linder, having disposed of the mattress, set his sights on the box springs. He stood it on edge, ripped away the undercovering, and hand-searched the interior. Delaney saw Baumgartner retreating to the bathroom, but she couldn't move. She was far too fascinated and repelled by the heated sergeant, who traded the box springs for the room's one overstuffed chair. He dissected it front to back, cushion to armrests, wielding the knife like a crazed blacksmith. The baseboard heater came next and then the air-conditioning.

Delaney turned aside as the carnage consumed the entryway, the closet, and the nightstand. She repacked her clothes, stowed her camera equipment, and filed wayward documents back into her briefcase.

By the time they'd finished, sweat beads were rolling down Linder's nose and chin, and Baumgartner was forced to loosen his tie and top button against the bulging veins in his neck.

Delaney surveyed each with disgust and amazement. "Was that stimulating, gentlemen?"

The detention order unfolded from Lieutenant Baumgartner's breast pocket. He held it up. "Come with us."

Castle Drug was located on the corner of Castle Drive and Apple. It was owned by an elderly Jewish couple and open to all race groups. Judith Goldstein, the pharmacist, glanced up from her platform scale when Nigel Mansell entered. A jocose grin creased her face.

"Ah, the inspector. The skinny one with no cheeks." Mrs. Goldstein was amused by what she considered underfed men. She had married one thirty-two years ago and had been trying to fatten him up ever since. Without much success, Mansell thought, remembering her frail husband. "Has that wife of yours learned anything yet about the art of cooking?"

"No, Mrs. G., I'm still on the same starvation diet." The chief inspector couldn't help but admire the Goldsteins. Nineteen years ago, they'd left the security of a prominent Jewish community in Johannesburg to seek a quieter existence here in Port Elizabeth. They'd bought an abandoned market across from the Industrial Park and a thriving pharmacy now included a delicatessen and a photo lab. The gray-haired matriarch ran the deli and the pharmacy. The reclusive old man did the developing. "How's the Mister?"

Mrs. Goldstein followed Mansell around the store, telling him about Jacob Goldstein's bronchitis and her hip injury. Glancing out a side window at a passing patrol car, Mansell ordered a roast beef sandwich to go, set a carton of Camels on the counter, and then crossed to the photo department. He filled in the information on the red envelope and stashed the film from his trip to the East Rand inside.

"I need blowups of four shots, Mrs. G.," he told her, gesturing toward the film. "Toward the end of the roll. Two of a white man standing on a railroad flatcar, just the face, and two of the wooden crates on the same car. Can they be done by Saturday?"

"Can they be done by Saturday, he asks." Mrs. Goldstein patted Mansell's cheek. "For the inspector with no cheeks, why not?"

Affiliated Union President Daniel Masi Hunter reminded Cecil Leistner, morbidly so, of Idi Amin. The features of his coal-black face were uncanny in their resemblance. And the vastness of his girth, Leistner thought, only serves to enhance the specter, while the manner in which he plunders his food only helps to explain it.

In the company of the Federation of Mineworkers Union President Lucas Ravele, they dined in a private room at Café Alessandria on Storrar Avenue in Pretoria. The menu of the day included baked apples, samoosas, smoked snoek, sauteed salmon, and blueberry cheesecake.

The waiter brought a second bottle of French Chardonnay.

Table conversation centered on the stalled contract negotiations between the FMU and the Chamber of Mines, and the pending arbitration between the General Union of Stevedores and the Harbour Association. Leistner was ecstatic. Privately, he was urging members of the Chamber to take a harder stance on union benefits such as housing and family boarding, and proposed dental and medical plans—all key issues in the miners' negotiations.

"Arbitration favors the union in this day and age, Minister," Daniel Hunter boasted. "Damnation, our demands for retirement benefits and a shorter workweek are more than fair. The bloody Harbour Association hasn't a leg to stand on, and I think they know it."

"They're talking a twenty percent across-the-board raise, Daniel," said Leistner. "Seems damn generous."

"The Harbour Association's idea of generosity is a new Coke machine in the employees' shack, a used dart board in the men's locker, and a ten-minute break in the afternoon. But pay equalization?" The fat man was enjoying himself, pecking at morsels of samoosas and slurping wine. "Damnation, Minister, the bloody white forklift operator still makes three times what the black doing the same job does."

He's leading right into it, thought Lucas Ravele as his counterparts continued to debate. Ravele was eager to see it all out in the open. Since his first meeting with the minister twelve days ago, and the lengthy follow-up on Monday, deep concern had been replaced by a sense of anticipation, opportunity.

"The situation is not unique, Daniel," Ravele said, filling the minister's wineglass. "We all know that. A black miner sleeps alone on a straw pallet in a prefab compartment, while his white buddy hangs his hat in a carpeted apartment and sleeps on a firm mattress with clean sheets."

"With his hands tucked comfortably between the legs of his warm wife," Hunter added. He raised his palms, shrugging.

"Gentlemen, you're breaking my heart!" Leistner exclaimed. A brief chortle contained little humor. He leaned across the table and formed a steeple with his hands. With eyes uncommonly dark, he looked straight at Daniel Masi Hunter. "So we change things. Now."

The heady declaration caused Hunter's tiny eyes to widen, and the fixation in his dining companions' eyes left him adrift. He searched for a suitable riposte, saying in time, "A bold statement, Minister. Very bold."

"Boldness will be a considerable factor in all our lives this next week, Mr. Hunter. I assure you."

The fat man found his desire for fish and wine suddenly diminished. His hand unconsciously sought out the pipe stored in his suit-coat pocket.

"On Tuesday, July twenty-second, Mr. Hunter, four major events will occur. Four events which will alter the course of South Africa's history," said the minister of justice calmly. "The first of these will actually transpire on Monday the twenty-first, when the prime minister will announce a nationwide state of emergency. You can imagine the reaction. Trusted friends and bitter enemies alike will call it an act of totalitarianism. Political and economic barometers will plunge. The second event is an outside operation, military in nature and seven years in its conception. An operation which will send the gold-mining industry into a tailspin. Third. On Tuesday evening, the Federation of Mineworkers Union and its associate members will announce total work stoppages by their entire memberships. And finally, all factions of the Affiliated Union of Dockers, Stevedores, and Rail Workers will announce a simultaneous sympathy strike, also scheduled for midnight of the same day."

Daniel Hunter dared not look at the minister. Such a proclamation, coming from the second highest authority in the country, was madness, tantamount to treason. He concentrated on his pipe, tamping the tobacco, torching it with care.

Finally, when this prop no longer sufficed as an alibi for silence, Hunter cleared his throat. "Minister, this second event of which you speak. The outside operation. Please elaborate."

Leistner attacked the question. "Elaboration is impossible. The project's truest ally is secrecy. It concerns several mines on the Witwatersrand. That is sharing too much, except to say that its impact will be unparalleled."

The fat man thought rapidly. "A military operation of such magnitude," he said. "The ANC perhaps. Could that be? Hardly. Their operations are generally hit-and-run affairs. Generally executed by bungling idiots. True, they've had successes, I grant you. Firebombing the synthetic petroleum plants outside of Jo'burg, now that was a bit of a coup. What, nine million worth of damage? Impressive, for their lot. Oh, yes, and then there was the refinery job in Pretoria last year. Most impressive breaking through their security system. Killed two people, pissed off a lot of others, and the refinery never did shut down. I'm dubious, Minister. With apologies."

Leistner smiled obligingly. "Your caution is admirable, Daniel."

Coffee and brandy followed dessert, and when Leistner faced his bulbous guest again, his eyes were cold, businesslike.

"The ANC is a tool. Anyone with a bit of intelligence can read between the lines of their operations. Properly controlled, any tool can serve a function."

"I didn't mean to imply—"

"Of course you didn't, Daniel." The justice minister pulled away, lips pursed. He drew a cigar lazily from his breast pocket. When the ash glowed amber, he said, "The ANC is an army. You would be surprised at its size and discipline. Yet an army is only as good as its leaders, its plans of operation, its equipment. You would agree, I'm sure."

Hunter nodded, as if to say, "Of course," while his brain measured the depth of the hole being dug beneath his feet.

"This project has all three of those ingredients, Mr. Hunter, in quality as well as quantity. My word will have to suffice on that."

"And yet," Hunter replied, drawing on his pipe, "my union is needed to back the whole operation."

"Perhaps a slight misnomer, using the word *my.*" Like a sculptor, Cecil Leistner chiseled a final accent onto his masterpiece. "You see, Daniel, over the years, Ian Elgin failed to mention certain things to you. The Affiliated Union has been a part of the whole operation since the very beginning."

With me or without me? the fat man nearly blurted out. But the answer was obvious. The minister wasn't asking. How long, Hunter wondered, had they been using him? Was it necessary to save himself now? To consent without some discussion would be an absolute sign of weakness, he decided.

"To suggest an across-the-board workers' strike by three major unions within five days, especially after agreeing to arbitration, will be a difficult task, Minister. I'm sure Lucas here will vouch for that."

Leistner chuckled. "Daniel, unions are impetuous creatures. Impulse is part of their personality. Part of their strength." His voice dropped in volume and tone, a diminuendo in a sullen requiem. "You will consult with each union head at once. Outline your proposal. Make your position known. Use the rumor of an impending miners' strike as leverage. Of course, under no circumstance will you mention this meeting or any part of this discussion."

The implication was clear. Leistner set the final peg. "Have you the influence to carry this off unaided?"

"I do," answered Daniel Masi Hunter soberly.

Time and circumstance dictated a foray into frontiers uncharted, in search of game best left undisturbed. . . .

Mansell thought about the warrant for his arrest as he drove up R32 out of Port Elizabeth. Initially, a federal warrant would be issued only to the nineteen division headquarters throughout the country. Division Number Six, headquartered in Port Elizabeth, would act on the assumption that he was still in the city, unaware of his impending arrest. Therefore, until his disappearance became apparent, local police districts would not be notified of the warrant.

Mansell figured he could count on twenty-four hours before that happened. Red tape and competition being what they were, it might be another day before the information sifted down to all 931 police stations and 39 border-control posts across the land.

The rationale was supposed to give Mansell a degree of comfort, but it didn't.

At the city limits of Sheldon, he pulled off to the side of the road. He stared for the longest time at a road sign set at the foot of a narrow trestle bridge. The sign read, THE GREAT FISH RIVER. The river glistened a lusty blue in the noonday sun. A dirt road shadowed the water's eastbound passage for as far as Mansell could see. So this is where I buried Steven de Villiers, he thought savagely. This I should see for myself.

He started the engine again, cut the wheel to the right, and punched the gas. Momentarily, he slammed on the brakes. Idiot, he thought, take care of your ego later. He put the gear shift into reverse, swung the Audi back onto the highway, and pressed on toward Somerset-East.

Somerset-East, 130 kilometers north of Port Elizabeth, proved to be a nondescript farming town boasting of one principal thoroughfare devoid of trees and character. Still, Mansell thought, the view of the Boschburg Mountains in the background, patches of pine forests and lazuline waterfalls, made the trip worthwhile.

He located the police station a block off Oos-Main Street, behind the courthouse. The building was a fortress, six stories of granite with a crenellated roof line and a marble arch over the entrance.

He parked across the street. Stone steps led through revolving doors into a room the size of a hotel lobby, and equally ornate. It was cool, quiet, and nearly deserted. Along one wall, a uniformed man, wearing half glasses and reading a newspaper, sat behind a high pedestal desk.

Mansell approached him. The officer glanced up. "What can I do you for?" he asked.

"Chief Homicide Inspector Mansell from Port Elizabeth." Mansell produced his shield. "Where is everyone?"

"Sergeant McCarty," he said, extending his hand. McCarty removed his specs and panned the room, shrugging. "This is it, Inspector. Oh, Major Boutsen's office is upstairs. I'll ring him."

"No, don't bother. We've got a bloody mess over Sheldon way.

I'm in need of some computer time, rather urgent. I've heard Somerset's particularly well equipped."

"All the latest. That's a fact." McCarty climbed down from his perch. He looked like a koala bear but moved like a penguin, and Mansell had to hurry just to keep up. "We're up on the second floor. Research and Communications. Suzanne's our computer expert. She'll set you up."

When they entered, Suzanne was standing, arms akimbo, a pencil between her teeth, staring down at a data sheet. She was fortyish, dressed in blue jeans and a soccer jersey. She possessed a farm girl's wholesomeness and a chorus girl's figure. McCarty introduced them, and a smile lit Suzanne's angular face at the prospect of working with a big-city inspector.

Mansell let her down gently. "In P.E., you see, we live and die by the computer. If you can't run your own unit," he exaggerated, "you don't work there. Would you mind terribly if I spend some time with the IBM over there?"

Suzanne laughed. "If you insist." She helped Mansell patch into the main research banks in Pretoria. "I'll get some tea."

The profile on Cecil Andrew Leistner was, as with those of most Nationalist officials, sparse and protectively worded.

Leistner was born in Pampoenpoort, a remote farming community on the Great Karoo in Cape Province. His father, Peter, farmed wheat and raised sheep. His mother, Anna Kathleen, taught school and played the organ and violin. Both were deceased. No brothers or sisters. Leistner's great-grandparents, farmers as well, immigrated from Germany in 1861, settling in Calvinia. Thirty years later, Leistner's grandfather, a schoolteacher, received an offer to open a new school in Pampoenpoort. He built the two-room schoolhouse with his own hands and named it after his wife, Virginia. The Virginia Pampoenpoort School of Education.

The file included a copy of Leistner's birth certificate, but his childhood years were not mentioned. He graduated from high school, from the V.P. School of Education, in June of '49. One month later, he enlisted in the South African Air Force. He trained as a navigator, bomber division. When the Korean conflict erupted in 1950, Leistner volunteered for the Number Two Squadron SAAF to aid the UN forces supporting the South Koreans. His squad was attached to the United States Air Force's Eighteenth Fighter Bomber wing.

261

He left for Korea in March of 1950, flew thirteen sorties into enemy territory, and was shot down and captured on the first day of May. A second plane was shot down during the same raid, and reports indicated that five parachutes were seen opening moments before the planes exploded. Seven months passed before the North Koreans issued an updated casualty and prisoner list. Two of the five, Captain Andrew Crooker and Private P. L. Fourie, were reportedly killed in action, while the other three, Leistner, Private Jaap Schwedler, and Lieutenant Chaney du Plessis, were listed as prisoners of war. Schwedler and Fourie, the file noted, also hailed from the Pampoenpoort area.

Two weeks after the list was published, Christmas Day 1950, Cecil Leistner and twelve other South African prisoners were quietly released. Neither Private Schwedler nor Lieutenant du Plessis, Mansell noted, were among the other twelve. The Red Cross supervised the exchange through civilian channels, and Leistner arrived in Cape Town on January 6, 1951. He was twenty years old.

One week prior to their son's scheduled return, on December 31, Peter and Anna Leistner were killed in a one-car automobile accident. No details were given in the profile.

Mansell read the last paragraph again. He shook his head, tasting the bitter irony and sympathizing with the man whose life he was now probing. He glanced over his shoulder. Suzanne was watching him. Mansell smiled, and she looked away, blushing. He sipped his tea, waiting. He lit a cigarette and peeked back again. Finally, he returned to the file.

After a month's convalescence in Van Riebeeck Military Hospital, Leistner was decorated and given his honorable discharge. He enrolled for the summer session at the University of Cape Town under the service bill. He took a flat on Kinga Street two blocks from campus. In June, Leistner joined the Junior Wing of the National party. By September, he was secretary of the organization, and the following January was elected president.

During his rise in the Junior Wing, in which he emerged as a highly regarded party organizer, Leistner studied pre-law. He graduated with honors in three years. While in law school, he clerked at the parliamentary office of the current prime minister. After graduating second in his law-school class, Leistner apprenticed under the P.M.'s watchful eye for another two years.

In 1956, at the minimum required age of twenty-five, Cecil Leistner was indoctrinated into the Broederbond; #5921. It was, Mansell thought, a rare achievement for one so young.

Leistner won election to the House of Assembly in 1962 as a member of the George, Cape Province, constituency. Four years later, the prime minister, then minister of defense, named Leistner as his deputy. The following year, Leistner also accepted, voluntarily, the portfolio responsibilities for the Agency of Policy and Security Development. The vacancy occurred after the deputy minister of justice, Ira Baldwin, was killed in a mountain-climbing accident in Royal Natal National Park. Leistner, the profile noted, had also been a member of that expedition, but was unhurt in the accident.

As head of Policy and Security Development, Leistner's innovations in the Security Branch and in the border patrols won him acclaim from his peers in the face of rising terrorist activities. Most notable among these, Mansell thought, remembering the early seventies, was the increased power of arrest granted to Security and the "immunity clause" given them in interrogation and investigative matters. The innovations, he thought, no doubt increased Leistner's powers far beyond those granted by his positions.

Following the 1978 Department of Information scandal, during which then prime minister Vorster was forced to resign, the current P.M. won election. Cecil Leistner accepted his present cabinet position as minister of justice.

Mansell remembered the rumors. The prime minister, it was said, had offered Leistner the head post in the Defense Ministry. Leistner declined, holding out for the more prestigious Justice position instead. An internal squabble erupted between certain key House of Assembly members and the prime minister over Leistner's qualifications. Ulterior motives were also mentioned. In the end, Mansell thought, the dispute only served to enhance Leistner's already considerable influence.

Leistner's profile contained only minor references to his personal life. He was not married. He was a deacon in the Dutch Reformed Church. His special interests were listed as rock climbing, spelunking, and Afrikaner history. His current address had been deleted in favor of a mailing address at the Union Building.

Mansell copied the file on a daisy-wheel printer. He erased the transaction from the computer's memory, bade farewell to Suzanne and Sergeant McCarty, and left without encountering another soul.

———

On his way out of town, Mansell stopped at the Somerset-East Public Library. He went straight to the sociology department, hailed the nearest clerk, and requested a copy of the current *Who's Who in South Africa*. On page 312, he found a half-page official government photo of Cecil Leistner sitting at his desk, preparing to sign some document or other, and staring serenely back at the camera.

It occurred to Mansell that he hardly recognized the face. He remembered seeing an interview with the minister on public television, perhaps two years ago, but couldn't recall the last time he'd seen Leistner's photo in either the newspaper or any recent periodical.

Scanning the empty corridor, and feeling like a purse snatcher with a conscience, Mansell quickly ripped the page from its binding. This he put in his briefcase along with Leistner's personal profile, the Elgin-Mabasu file, and the daily log he'd started while at Delaney's house.

Pretoria was cold this day.

Coal smoke hung heavily above the valley. Outside, the smell reminded Delaney of the old gravity furnace her folks once had in the basement of their first house. Inside the car the stench of stale cigarettes filled her nostrils.

In time, they came upon a checkerboard park in the center of the city known as Church Square. Here, two hundred years ago, the Voortrekkers had built their first church. Now a bronze statue of former president Paul Kruger marked the spot. Palm trees and street vendors encircled it. Corner to corner, history surrounded the square: the Old Raadsaal, the South African Bank, and the Palace of Justice. It was here, in a narrow drive fronting the palace, that Sergeant Linder now parked.

Lieutenant Baumgartner escorted Delaney past an entrance of stone and brick into an interior of similar elegance: marble stairways and turned banisters, domed ceilings and turn-of-the-century reliefs.

The east wing of the palace housed the Transvaal Supreme Court; the west, segments of the South African Police. It was the steps of this wing they now mounted. On the second floor, Baumgartner opened a heavy mahogany door that led into a lofty chamber. At the head of a long conference table sat a man smoking a pipe and reading. The pose, Delaney thought, was still familiar, still engaging.

Cecil Leistner arose. A smile creased his face as he hurried across the floor to greet her.

"Delaney," he said, taking her hand. "It's been ages."

"Two years."

"Two years, one month, and eight days," he corrected.

"Ancient history."

"Not so ancient. I haven't cared for anyone since."

Delaney threw her head back, laughing. "Minister, you always did have a flair for the dramatic."

The laughter was contagious. Leistner joined in, grasping her by the shoulders. He noticed Baumgartner. "Lieutenant, if you'll make yourself scarce for a time, please."

The door closed behind them. Leistner took Delaney by the arm, guiding her toward a chair. "You look terrific," he said.

"I've changed tailors."

"How's the ankle?" he asked, glancing at the walking stick.

"Stronger."

Leistner gestured toward the porcelain serving set at the center of the table. "Tea?"

"Thank you."

"Cream but no sugar, if I remember correctly."

"You always remember correctly," she teased.

"You haven't remarried," Leistner said, pouring for them both.

"I'm married to my work these days." Delaney stirred cream into her cup. "It's so much less combative."

Leistner studied Delaney over the rim of his cup, reminiscing, wondering. They talked for a time like long-lost friends meeting on a street corner. Finally, he tapped the sheaf of papers stacked before him. He said, "You've done well for yourself, Mrs. Blackford."

The use of Delaney's surname signaled an end to the amenities. Old styles that never vary, she thought. Was she grateful or disappointed?

"Thank you. As have you by all accounts. Though there is a motel owner in Johannesburg who no doubt has a complaint or two about some of your hired help."

"The motel owner in Jo'burg will be suitably compensated, I'm sure," Leistner countered. "I am bothered more by the fact that someone in your position suspects that a quantity of American arms has been smuggled into the country, but for some reason, you've failed to transmit such information to the proper authorities."

"And I'm bothered by the fact that such information might be used to undermine my union."

"Come now, Delaney. Some of my colleagues, some of my less creative colleagues that is, have gone so far as to suspect fraud, or, if the facts are true, then at least complicity on your part."

"Come now, Minister," Delaney remarked, though beads of perspiration were collecting at the base of her spine. "Three, maybe four people have died because of those guns, and one of them was a friend. I'd like to find out why."

"Ian was my friend as well. A very good friend," said Leistner. For a moment, he seemed to languish over a memory. The moment passed. "So, also, was Steven de Villiers."

"Yes, I'm aware that Mr. de Villiers works in your office, and if I—"

"Worked in my office, Delaney. Worked. Steven de Villiers is dead."

"Dead? My God, when? How?"

"It's my fault, really. Misjudgments. Sloppy work. Two good men dead, and for what purpose?" he said, regretfully. "You see, Delaney, it was I who enlisted Ian's help nearly five years ago when we first heard about the possibility of arms coming in through Algoa Bay."

"You? You knew about the arms smuggling five years ago?"

"Suspicions more than knowledge, unfortunately."

"Then Ian wasn't . . . wasn't part of it after all?"

"Arms smuggling is NIS business, by and large. And it was only a rumor then, as I said. The dockers were trying to organize. So were the stevedores and the rail workers. It was a delicate situation. A situation too delicate to upset with negative publicity, and Ian was eager to help. You know how he was."

"I know he liked being where the action was."

Leistner ran a finger absently around the rim of his cup, musing again. "Our information said it was a freighter, midsized, possibly flying a Maltese or Liberian flag. It wasn't much, but Ian still managed to identify the ship."

"*ARVA II*," Delaney muttered.

"Yes. That was more than three years ago. It was a small shipment, but NIS bungled the trace. The ship didn't come back again for thirteen months. This time it was clean, legitimate mining stuff. NIS shelved the matter. They figured the ANC or the Democratic Front had worked a couple of deals, their source dried up, and it was finished. I told Ian to let the matter go. He wouldn't. He was

266

there the next time the ship came into port. This was a year or so ago."

"A year ago June. The last time ARVA was here."

"I was in Rome at the time. Ian told me later there were two hundred crates or so. He inspected several and called my office. My idiot deputy refused to authorize a surveillance team. Instead, he called NIS and they sent someone out the next morning. It was too late. The guns had been moved by then. Ian tried to follow by car, which was a mistake. He lost the trail near Kimberley."

"Kimberley? Are you certain?"

Leistner pushed a handwritten report across the table. Delaney studied it. The script was stilted and labored, exactly like Ian's.

"The shipment," he explained, "was tagged, like all the others, for the East Fields mine. Adjustor certificates were issued in Noupoort, a shipping change. As far as we can make out, the goods were loaded on trucks in Kimberley and diverted somewhere in transit. NIS staked out the route to East Fields, but the arms never arrived. Probably ended up in some ANC camp in Botswana. We don't know if Ian's death was related, but it would be difficult to refute. I thought I had to follow up for his sake. I sent another man down there."

"De Villiers."

"Yes, with Lucas Ravele's help. Perhaps we should have let you in on the matter, but . . ." Carefully, Leistner warmed Delaney's tea, offering condiments, smiling. "Anyway, Ian knew the ARVA was scheduled to dock sometime in July. By that time, NIS had managed to track down the shipper—according to the shipping manifests, a manufacturing concern in Brazil. As we suspected, it was a front. I knew Ian was too close to the situation. His interest was too obvious, especially to the trained eye. After he was dead, I tried to find someone inconspicuous, someone without direct union ties. Steven knew his business, but he got careless."

Delaney shook her head. "I don't know if it was carelessness or just dumb luck."

"Meaning . . . what?" Leistner leaned closer. A show of concentration etched his face.

Delaney recounted the night she had discovered de Villiers in her office sorting through the shipping manifests. "By then, I'd heard the ARVA mentioned in relation to Ian. It wasn't hard to put the two together."

"Truly. Then perhaps dumb luck is right." A mask of indignation covered Cecil Leistner's face. "And you shared this information with Inspector Mansell."

Leistner noted Delaney's reaction, a minute penetration of well-honed defenses. "That next morning," she replied.

"You see, Steven was killed the night the arms arrived in Port Elizabeth. His body was discovered in a shallow hole on the banks of the Fish River, near Sheldon. He was killed by a .38-caliber pistol found near the burial site. The gun is registered in Chief Inspector Mansell's name and the fingerprints found on the weapon are his."

Blood drained from Delaney's face. "Are you saying—?"

"You're unaware of the federal warrant out for the inspector's arrest, I assume." Delaney shook her head. The minister passed her a copy of the warrant.

Delaney read through the arrest order, pushed it aside, and then sipped pensively on her tea. "He's in custody, then?"

"I'm afraid he's eluded us to this point."

"Too bad," she replied, sullenly. "And what about the arms? They were being escorted. By one man. He was—"

Leistner raised a hand, nodding. "Yes. His name is Van der Merve. Colonel Andrew Van der Merve. The colonel is an NIS officer. Eighteen months ago, he signed on with the ARVA as a crew member. He was on board when the freighter arrived in port, Delaney."

"That's why he was so curious about me. Mutual suspicion. Utterly brilliant." Delaney buried her hands in her hair, nervously pushing it away from her face. "And then I passed the information on to the inspector in Bloemfontein."

"To his detective, yes."

Delaney's mouth was parched. She arose, slowly, stretching her legs. Her ankle throbbed. "Then the guns would have been intercepted before they actually reached East Fields had everything gone according to plan?"

Leistner fielded the theory routinely. "We can only presume. The route was monitored, of course, but without success. The trucks were impounded at the mine, and the drivers were arrested. A half a loaf is better than none at all, I suppose," he said with a resigned shrug. "Where is Mansell now, do you know, Delaney?"

Delaney leaned heavily on her walking stick. Don't play games, she told herself. They know by now. At last, she answered. "As of this morning, he was in P.E. Fool that I am, I gave him permission to use my house last night. I didn't know—"

"You couldn't have known," Leistner said. Delaney sat down again and Leistner took her hand. "But his apprehension is vital, Delaney. Can you see that?"

"I wouldn't mind having a word or two with him myself, Minister."

"He's fond of you. He'll want to see you again. Help me. Please."

It was a request. Delaney was better prepared for importunity. Her voice husky and low, she said, "I'm expecting a call, either this evening or tomorrow."

"At your home?" Delaney answered with an exasperated nod, and Leistner offered her a business card. "The telephone number on the back is a private line. Leave a message. I'll be back in touch within ten minutes."

Behind them, the chamber door opened. Lieutenant Baumgartner entered seemingly without notice.

"I'll make certain that you're adequately . . . protected when you reach Port Elizabeth," Leistner told her. He arose and offered his hand. "The lieutenant here will see you to the airport."

Northeast of Somerset-East, the abrupt cliffs of the Sneeuberg and Suurberg mountains punched wickedly toward the sky—the heart of the Great Escarpment. The Klien Vis, Vogel, and Sundays rivers and a hundred tributaries dug deep gorges into dolerite rock. Evergreens four hundred years old and boscages thick with willow and sage blanketed the hillsides.

In Graaf-Reinet, amid rugged mountains of sandstone and shale, Mansell consulted the map. He filled the Audi's tank at the local gas station and bought hot tea at the market across the road. The clock behind the counter read 3:08.

Beyond the Sneeubergs, the Great Escarpment ceased with the rapidity of a shooting star. Beyond lay the Upper Karoo, the word *karoo* being derived from an ancient Hottentot phrase meaning "dry" or "barren." And the Upper Karoo was both of these for as far as the eye could see.

Mansell pushed the Audi now at a steady clip, and R63 drew out before him. The highway seemed to sway beneath the sun's bleak rays, an iridescence glimmering hypnotically in the distance. The radio spat gospel music and static. Mansell smoked for companionship.

Past Victoria West the farms diminished in size. Sheep grazed in brown pastures enclosed by tired barbed wire. Towns centered around one-pump gas stations, wind-weary diners, and mom-and-pop grocery stores.

Thus, too, was Pampoenpoort—an unlikely oasis in a sea of sand. While pondering the reason for the town's existence, Mansell heard the train whistle. Two kilometers away, he saw clouds of diesel smoke spewing from the chimneys of overworked locomotives. Exhaust beats sent tremors through the ground. Mansell checked his watch. It was 6:18. To the west, the horizon hid behind a veil of golds and oranges.

He toured the town, calculating, fantasizing. The one-room schoolhouse and the steepled church, the feedlot and the silo, the drive-up diner and the laundromat. The village farmer who rose at dawn six mornings a week to tend his wheat and mealie and coax life from a land parched three hundred and sixty-five days a year by a cruel sun and a meager fifty centimeters of rain. The sheep rancher whose stamina was matched only by that of the stupid, lovable animal that produced wool for the market and mutton for the table. The soldier who fled the life of his forefathers in hopes of glory, freedom, and an easier way. The barn dances, the sheep-shearing contests, the frosted mugs of beer, the home-distilled sour mash.

There were worse fates, Mansell thought as he parked the car in front of Mattie's Inn and Restaurant. He stepped out and surveyed the main drag. Farmers, sheepherders, soldiers. The boundaries of birth, he thought. But a politician? Mansell locked the car and walked inside.

Mattie's lobby reminded him of a cramped, comfortable living room. Hardwood floors, a raging fire, a mantel crammed with clay figurines and thimbles, overstuffed chairs occupied by pipe-smoking farmers. Heads turned as he entered, and Mansell nodded. A hush followed. He approached the registration desk. A chatty woman of fifty with wire-rimmed glasses and gray bangs bade him welcome.

"Good evening," he replied. Afrikaans was the language of the Karoo, not English. "You have to be Mattie."

"That I do," she said.

"I need a comfortable bed, a hot shower, and a good meal."

"Then you've come to the right place."

Mansell paid for a single night. Mattie led him to the second floor. "What brings a handsome gentleman like yourself to these parts, I'm wondering."

Mansell understood that his arrival would be the source of some discussion among the patrons downstairs, and he wasn't anxious to raise any eyebrows. "The railroad, actually," he answered. "I'm with Transport Services. We're computerizing some of the system between the Cape and the Orange Free State. I'm checking the line out. Surveying some land. That kind of thing. Boring stuff, if you want to know the truth."

Mattie turned down the bed and fluffed the pillow. "And Pampoenpoort?"

"Won't be affected," Mansell assured her. "Though I could use some legal advice on a matter or two which came up in Victoria West. Is there a reputable lawyer here in town?"

"One and only one. On the corner of this very block, as a matter of fact. An English-speaker like yourself, but a good chap nonetheless. Named Chesney. Lloyd Chesney."

From the pocket of her apron, Mattie produced a copy of the restaurant's menu. She recommended the house specialty, lamb chops and fried potatoes. Finally, she cracked the room's only window and left her guest alone.

Mansell stripped off his jacket. He lit a cigarette. Laughing and shouting drifted up from the street. He walked to the window, parted the shades, and gazed down. A tractor crossing the road interrupted four boys kicking a soccer ball. The sound of a guitar filtered up from the tavern next door. The last light of day touched the hood of the Audi, now caked with the dust and grime of a six-hundred-kilometer journey. A dark Impala pulled into the parking space next to it. Fumes spewed from the car's tailpipe. The beam of a flashlight filled the interior. From Mansell's vantage point he could see the dashboard, the steering wheel, and the movements of the flashlight. For an instant, an arm appeared outside the front window. Mansell noticed a momentary reflection, like a wristwatch or a bracelet. The beam from the flashlight scanned the outside of the Audi, and then lit its interior. Just as quickly, the arm withdrew. The light was extinguished. The car backed away from the space and started down the street. Mansell pressed against the window, squinting, but darkness obscured the license plate. Gloves, he thought, remembering the reflection. The bastard wore gloves.

Flight 691 from Johannesburg to Port Elizabeth was scheduled for departure at 4:15. Delaney Blackford declined Lieutenant Baumgartner's invitation for a drink, and he escorted her to the boarding gate. He watched the stewardess accept Delaney's boarding pass, waited until she was aboard, and then strolled back to the coffee shop. He ordered blueberry pie and black coffee.

Delaney waited ten minutes before deplaning. She waited another five minutes in the boarding corridor until the plane began to taxi. Finally, she sidled back into the waiting area, peered along the concourse, and then slipped through an Emergency Exit Only door that led down to the airfield.

From there, she followed an empty baggage wagon back underneath the terminal into a shed filled with conveyor belts, baggage handlers, and luggage. Swinging doors led to the baggage-claim department, revolving carousels, and weary travelers. An escalator led to the passenger pickup area. Delaney hailed a cab.

A fifteen-minute drive east on R29 brought them to the entrance of the Motor West motel in Edenvale. The No Vacancy sign flashed its neon message in red and yellow. Delaney studied the parking lot of the We Deal used-car dealership across the road; the Jetta was gone. She pressed a twenty-rand note into the cabby's hand and told him to wait ten minutes.

She climbed two flights of outside stairs to the third floor. The corridor was empty. Delaney started down the hall. A television blared from an opened door on the right, a "Mystery Theater" rerun. The sounds of a party resounded from another; laughing, loud voices, pulsing reggae. A door opened. A robust man dressed in baggy slacks and a wrinkled shirt swept into the hall with his arm draped around a working girl with a painted face and tombstone eyes.

Outside room 343, Delaney scanned the corridor. Hastily, she opened the maid's closet, pulled the light cord, and stepped inside. She closed the door behind her. She waited fifteen seconds, holding her breath, listening, looking. Something was wrong, she thought. It didn't look the same. Hadn't the bed linen been on this side? Weren't the mops and brooms in this corner? One thing was certain; only two cartons of toilet paper remained.

Delaney pushed the top carton aside. The box below had a familiar bend in the flap, and it gave way without resistance. She peered inside, remembering. Quickly, she tossed a half dozen rolls from the top layer onto the floor. She stabbed a roll from the center of the second layer and ripped away the tissue. Wrong roll. Delaney

272

exposed a second and third roll with the same results. No film canisters.

Suddenly, her heart was thumping against the walls of her chest. Shredding tissue paper indiscriminately, Delaney searched the entire second layer. No film. She paused long enough to collect herself, breathing deeply, drying damp palms. Methodically now, she checked every roll in the box. And then the first box, roll by roll.

The canisters were gone.

The door opened behind her. Framed by the doorway and illuminated by the dim light of the hall stood SB Sergeant Angus Linder.

He held out a hand. "I'll take the film now, I think."

THE DARK IMPALA WAS NOWHERE TO BE SEEN. MANSELL TOOK THE back alley to Third Street and walked briskly to the corner. The shingle outside the single-story office read, LLOYD FOSTER CHESNEY— ATTORNEY-AT-LAW.

Mr. Chesney had just arrived. Mansell presented his official police identification to the receptionist, referred vaguely to his position with the South African Police, and asked for a few minutes with the lawyer. The secretary buzzed Mr. Chesney on the intercom, and Mansell was ushered into a comfortable office. The lawyer wore a gray suit, wire-rimmed glasses, and a genuine smile.

"I've come as an envoy from the Office of Internal Affairs in Pretoria, Mr. Chesney," Mansell said. The lawyer's eyes widened, fulfilling the chief inspector's expectations, and he added, "No, no. No problems here, sir. We're simply conducting an official review of several cabinet members. Minister Leistner in this case. Historical background, personal profiles, that type of thing, you know. Strictly confidential, however. It seems that the recent media rage for government witch-hunting has hit several of the larger Afrikaner tabloids, and they're uncovering a few more skele-  tons than is comfortable. If you understand my meaning. May I ask a few questions of you?"

"Please sit down, Inspector." With a wave of his hand, Chesney guided Mansell to a chair. "Ask away."

"You weren't practicing law in 1951, were you, Mr. Chesney?"

"What? Why no, I was only twenty-one years old in 1951. Law school was still a year away."

"Of course. And who would the attorney of record have been in Pampoenpoort then, would you know?"

Chesney chuckled. "Why, my very own Uncle Jason."

"Still alive?"

"And kicking. Yes, indeed."

"Anna Kathleen and Peter Leistner, the minister's parents, died

December thirty-first, 1950. Would your uncle have been the chief executor of their will, by chance?"

"Let's find out," Chesney answered. He picked up the telephone and asked the switchboard operator to dial a local number. The conversation lasted sixty seconds. Then Chesney excused himself. He disappeared into the outer office. He returned shortly, carrying a sealed file and a tray of tea and sweet rolls.

"If you don't mind," he said, serving for them both, "we'll wait for Uncle Jason."

Not five minutes later, Jason Chesney shuffled through the door complaining about the wind and the dust. He was bald and bespectacled, with the profile of a vulture. He supported himself with a cane, but his eyes glowed like slow-burning butane and his handshake was firm. He shooed his nephew away from the desk and sat down.

Mansell reiterated his purpose, and the elder said, "Peter Leistner, yes. A quiet, hardworking farmer. His wife baked the best rhubarb pie in the province. Now his boy's some power packer back in the Transvaal. Huh. Leaves me all aquiver. Sure it does."

Lloyd Chesney opened the file. He spread papers out in front of his uncle, saying, "Not much to show for it."

"Enough," said the elder, adjusting his specs. "I took care of the will, all right, but the minister, if I recall, was away when his folks died. Korea or something."

"A car accident, wasn't it?" asked Mansell.

"Out on the county highway. On their way home from a hoopla of some kind or another, celebrating the new year and their new-found son, I suspect," said Jason Chesney. "No one's real sure what happened, except that they went off the highway at a fair clip. No skid marks, nothing. Just a ball of flames and a scrap heap in the middle of a wheat field."

"Terrible thing," said Mansell slowly. "And the bequests from the will?"

"It was your standard last will and testament. In two parts, if I recall. Upon Peter's death everything transferred to Anna. In the case of both parties dying, it all went to the minister," answered the uncle, reading, grunting. "There were some small cash gifts to employees and the like, all that hogwash. Let's see. A player piano to Anna's friend Julia Littner. A gold locket and a silver set to the old schoolmistress, Sheena Goosen, and a hunting rifle to Peter's godchild, a friend of Lloyd's here in fact, named Jaap Schwedler."

"All of which was destroyed in the fire," added the nephew.

"Fire?"

"A flash fire the night after the parents died. Destroyed the old schoolhouse Peter's father had built in 1892, and the house Peter himself built thirty-five years later as an attachment. Two lives and sixty years of history snuffed out in two heinous nights of disaster."

The words echoed in Mansell's brain. Fire, he thought, the claw with no arm. He grappled with a cigarette, inhaling until his lungs ached.

"What about personal effects from the house? Strongboxes, photo cases, safes. Things of that nature," he asked. "And from the school. Personal records, filing cabinets, medical charts from the nurse's office. Surely something survived."

The two lawyers looked at each other woefully. The elder requested water, and his nephew fetched a tall glass. In time, Jason Chesney said, "Inspector, I remember that fire like a ten-year-old remembers the fireworks on Independence Day. Pete musta stored lamp fuel or kerosene somewhere in the house. There were explosions and heat something fierce. A bona fide conflagration, sir. And Pete and Anna didn't store things in safes or strongboxes. No, everything that could burn, did."

"I see. And Minister Leistner disposed of the property when he returned for the funeral?" asked Mansell.

"He never returned," answered Uncle Jason, coughing. "Ah hell, would you? He's a bigwig now. Pampoenpoort's a forgotten memory. There was land, of course. Farm equipment and a fine herd of sheep, if I recall. Enough to start fresh on for sure. But I received a letter from young Cecil from an army convalescence center in, hm, near the Cape somewhere. Sell what we could, he said. Send him anything that was left after expenses. Thank you very much. But you probably know all that."

"They didn't tell me much, I'm afraid," Mansell said, shaking his head. "Was Jaap Schwedler a friend of the minister's?"

"Indeed," said the nephew. "They signed on for Korea together. Part of the Number Two Squadron. Shot down in the same raid."

"Did Schwedler come back?"

"Shell-shocked some say. Others say brainwashed. Jaap lives on his son's ranch near Carnarvon."

"And the other two recipients of record? Julia Littner and the schoolmistress? What about them?"

Lloyd Chesney fielded the question as his uncle slipped into a reverie of days gone by. He said, "Mrs. Littner moved away soon after the funeral. To Bloemfontein. We heard she died of cancer ten years ago. Miss Goosen, bless her heart, still lives here in Pampoenpoort. In Logan, actually, on the edge of town. She's near deaf, but sharp enough."

The nephew scribbled addresses for both Sheena Goosen and Jaap Schwedler on a card. Mansell stood up. He shook hands with both Chesneys, asking again that a certain confidentiality be placed on his visit.

"Ah. And one last question, Mr. Chesney, if I may be permitted?" Mansell turned his attention to the elder attorney. "Where did most of the folks here in town go for their dental work back in the forties, do you recall?"

Jason Chesney's eyes narrowed, benignly studying the inspector. "Recall? Huh. Old Bailey the Butcher we call him. Still at it. Still damn good, too, but don't tell him I said that. I'll deny every word."

A dentist, much like a lawyer or a barber in a town of this size, held a virtual monopoly on his trade. But unlike some monopolies, a profit margin couldn't be guaranteed. Oh, payment for services rendered could usually be counted on, and sometimes it was even in cash.

In Pampoenpoort, the dentist and the barber happened to be one and the same, Dr. Dominic Bailey. Doc Bailey was a shoestring type with a shock of slick gray hair, a Vincent Price moustache, and a rubicund complexion.

The doctor was sitting bolt upright in an old-fashioned barber's chair studying X rays with a magnifying glass when Mansell entered the shop. Bailey reacted to Mansell's identification and explanation with much the same alacrity as had the younger Chesney.

"Shall we retreat into my inner sanctum, Inspector?"

Doc Bailey breezed from the barber shop to the dentist's office like the Shadow on the prowl. Mansell wondered if the sobriquet "the Butcher" alluded to Bailey's dental practice or his salon expertise.

The facilities and equipment were of a vintage fifteen years past, but spotless and gleaming. Beyond the dentist chair and the drills, and past a curtain-covered doorway, was Bailey's office. A rolltop desk dwarfed all else except for a bank of wooden filing cabinets that lined the back wall.

"How's this for memory," said the Butcher, striking a Shakespearean pose before the files. "Pete Leistner had a lower bridge, root-canal work topside, and gum problems. Anna had perfect teeth. Never a cavity, but I did remove four wisdom teeth one winter. And the kid? Well, now. He needed braces for an overbite, but they couldn't afford it. He had a chipped cuspid lower left. We pulled two soft molars on the bottom to allow the wisdom teeth some room to come in proper, and . . . Oh, hell's bells, let's check me out."

The files were labeled "Active," "Inactive," and "Inactive—Backdated." The dentist used a skeleton key to trip the lock on the cabinet labeled "Inactive—Backdated 1945–1955." Bailey tugged at the drawer, but it wouldn't budge. Mansell lent a hand, and eventually, the outdated tracking yielded, creaking in protest. Manila folders and yellowing paper overflowed from the drawer.

Doc Bailey thumbed from file to file, mumbling. "Aha," he exclaimed in time, removing three folders. "Leistner P. L., Leistner A. K., Leistner C. A."

Mansell leaned across the desk as the dentist picked over Peter Leistner's records. "Did I tell you. The bridge. The root canal. I was proud of that work." He turned to the mother's file. "Not bad. Well, I forgot about the gold cap. Not a single cavity, though. Terrible patient."

They both laughed. Bailey opened Cecil Leistner's folder, and his joviality toppled.

"I can't understand it," he said, staring at the chart and two X rays.

"What is it?"

"I must've been thinking of someone else's mouth. There's no overbite, and all four wisdom teeth have been pulled." He pointed disconcertedly at one of the X rays. "There's a chipped tooth all right, but it's a lateral, not a cuspid. And look at this."

Mansell followed the dentist's finger to a jagged edge along the upper jawbone. "It's a screw implant," said Bailey. "Developed by a French dentist named Chercheve in the forties. The part of the implant that went into the jaw was essentially a helix-type screw. A square shaft extended outside the gum line and an artificial tooth was attached to that."

"Clever."

"Clever yes, except the screw didn't allow the bone to grow back, and there was generally not enough bone left to support the screw."

"So?"

"So I've never performed a screw implant, Inspector. I don't know

278

a dentist in the country who used implants at all until after 1950. The first implants used here, as far as I know, were called vent plants. That wasn't until '52 or '53. This file dates to 1949, when Cecil left for the air force."

"Is this your handwriting, Doctor?"

"Yes. Yes it is."

"The minister must have traveled abroad at some point."

"Inspector, with all due respect, Pete Leistner could hardly afford a train ticket to Beaufort-West, much less plane fare to Europe," countered Doc Bailey. "You see, I've been blessed with this memory. I can remember the haircuts I gave back in 1945."

"Well," said Mansell in a placating voice, "there must be some explanation. I'd like to take these files with me if I could, Doctor. Just to update our records. Double-check a couple of facts. To be returned very shortly. You have my word on that. . . . And a favor, if I might, sir. This discrepancy in the minister's record. Until I check it out with him, could we keep this whole matter sort of hush-hush? Just you and me? I'm sure Minister Leistner would take it as a personal favor."

Nigel Mansell climbed into the Audi. He sat behind the wheel, gripping it, staring down the windblown street, wrestling with his imagination and hurling commands at his logic.

The last flight from Johannesburg to Port Elizabeth departed Jan Smuts International at 1:15 A.M. Sergeant Angus Linder sat in the first-class seat next to Delaney. He slept, snoring, while she worried. With stops in Bloemfontein and Grahamstown, they arrived at H. F. Verwoerd Airport at 5:25 in the morning.

A Security Branch officer met them on the concourse. Delaney took one half-dosage of a sleeping pill in the car, while the officer drove and Linder slurped hot tea. She took the other half with water in her own bathroom and fell into a deep sleep by six. The Security officer parked out front by the curb, while Linder reconnoitered the alley out back. They drank more tea and ate day-old donuts until replacements arrived at ten.

Delaney awoke with a dull headache at 1:20 in the afternoon. She washed three aspirin down with apple juice. A cold shower set her mind in motion: Nigel Mansell, Cecil Leistner, Steven de Villiers, the pending arbitration with the Harbour Association.

Acting on impulse, she picked up the telephone in her bedroom and began to dial. Not so fast, she thought, replacing the receiver. She wrapped herself in a full-length robe, returned to the bathroom, and peeked through the Levolors to the front yard. The car was there. Nothing covert. A man, dressed in tweed and smoking, circled the car. He surveyed the street. He glanced toward the back of the house and exchanged nods with an unseen partner. Delaney stepped away from the window. And they'll be listening in on my phone, too, she thought. Lousy bastards.

In the kitchen, Delaney brewed Costa Rican coffee. She dressed while drinking the first cup. From the kitchen cupboard she took an empty measuring cup, walked purposely out the front door, and crossed the lawn to her next-door neighbor's. Sally Claybourne answered the door, holding her three-month-old daughter.

"Sal, hi. I'm in the middle of a corn-bread recipe, and I ran out of flour." Delaney held out the empty cup, and Sally snatched it away, smiling. They went inside the house. "Listen, I'm having some trouble with my phone, too. Can I make a quick call while I'm here?"

"Girl, of course you can. Use the phone in my room. I'll get your flour."

Delaney dialed the message return at the Clavers' house, hoping to hear from Mansell. There were no messages. She took a deep breath, composing herself, and then dialed again; the answering machine. "This is John Clavers. We're not in. . . . Please leave a message at the sound of the tone, and we'll be sure to get back to you. Thanks."

"Nigel Mansell," Delaney said following the beep. "I'm back. Need to see you. Need to talk. I . . . It's . . . Nigel, it's been a long time since I've made love to a man. Please call. Soon. Don't use my home phone. Delaney."

She hung up, hating herself for being so forward, wondering why she had been. Hating herself more because she knew the truth of the matter, wanting him and despising him in the same breath.

Ignoring the sentry at the curb, Delaney returned to her own house with a cup of flour. She dialed the phone number Cecil Leistner had given her. A woman's voice; another answering machine. Delaney said, "No contact as of two P.M. Friday. Will be in touch again tonight. Mrs. Blackford."

A knot tightened in her chest. She stared down at the phone, frantic about the missing film, picturing the body of a man she

280

hadn't even liked in a grave on the banks of a river she'd never seen.

After drinking another cup of coffee and eating banana yogurt, Delaney placed a scheduled call to the office of Daniel Masi Hunter in Durban. The Affiliated Union potentate took the call himself, and Delaney detected a note of urgency in his voice.

"We meet tonight at Huron's place. Confidential. Seven o'clock," he said. Percy Huron was the acting president of the United Dock Workers and an adviser to the Affiliated board.

"Who is 'we'?" Delaney asked.

"Just the three of us."

"The arbitration schedule. Should I bring it?"

"Never mind that. Our plans have changed," said Hunter. And the connection was broken.

Fifty meters belowground, directly beneath an abandoned storage shed of Homestake Mining, Inc., Target Three, Jan Koster heard the creaking sound of the dilapidated transport elevator as it descended. With a jolt, it came to a halt. A line foreman pushed aside the screen and stepped out. The foreman wore a pale green jump suit and a hard hat with the gold Homestake insignia on the front. He'd been employed by the huge mine now for thirteen months.

"It doesn't sound worth a shit," Koster said, gesturing toward the elevator.

"We'll lube and oil it," the foreman replied. "The engine's been overhauled and the cables reinforced. Come the twenty-second, she'll hold a hundred men, easy. Armed men. I'll get things started at exactly eleven-forty, no problem; but don't forget that my shift ends at midnight, and they'll be sending somebody around, sure as hell."

"We'll make it," Koster assured him. He ran the calculations through his head for the hundredth time. The initial strike team consisted of fifteen hundred men. From this point, it would take ten minutes to transfer the heavy artillery up to the storage shed and another ten to fifteen for the team. It was too long, but there was nothing they could do.

Twenty minutes later, in a tiny office attached to the command center, he expressed another concern to Colonel Rolf Lamouline and to Christopher Zuma, the black leader whose impact at East Fields had amazed even Koster.

"Gentlemen, I see us with a small problem. Too many cooks in a kitchen built for a single chef. Too much dead weight." Koster made a point of directing his comments at both men. These two, he thought, understand one another. "Our European engineers have served their purpose, I think. It remains a matter of whether our military operations can survive without the aid of our Cuban advisers at this point. Colonel?"

"You're asking me? My men call them the Caribbean Peasant Corps."

"Is that a yes?"

"They won't be missed, if that's what you're asking."

"Fine. Mr. Zuma, can you see to the evacuation of this 'nonessential personnel'?"

"With pleasure."

While lunching in his room on braaivelis and potato soup, Mansell opened the Elgin-Mabasu murder file. He studied the sketch of the man who'd bought the nylon-rayon rope at The Outdoorsman almost a week before Elgin's death, and the one of the man who reportedly hit Lea Goduka's car the night Elgin died. There was no comparison. The first was a man of average height, a narrow face, dressed in a three-piece suit and a fedora. The second was a large-boned man with an oval face, wearing glasses, a raincoat and a golfer's hat. Undistinguished, Mansell thought, but somehow familiar. And, he recalled, he wore gloves. Tan leather gloves with gold buckles across the wrists.

At 12:30, Mansell set out in the Audi for Logan. He kept an eye out for the Impala and used the flat, empty Karoo as a visual buffer, much like the cheetah uses the flat, empty grasslands in northern Africa.

Logan, as it turned out, was located six kilometers east of Pampoenpoort. The center of the village lay beneath a single roof housing a grocery store and a gas pump and resting along a two-lane road that had never been paved.

The clerk at the store gave Mansell directions to Route 76 at Die Kill, which proved to be not a street at all, but a shallow stream flanked on either bank by willow and locust trees. A two-story, kelly green farmhouse huddled within walking distance of the water.

A sward of browning grass stretched from the road to a split-rail fence. A yawning sheep dog met Mansell at the gate. A walkway made of tree-trunk slabs led to a screen-enclosed porch. A black woman, dressed in a gaily colored shift and wearing a white bandana over her hair, dozed in the porch swing.

Mansell tapped on the door. "Excuse me, lovely lady."

The woman stirred. Her eyes popped open, and she sneezed. "Hmpph. By the looks of you, there's no excuse," she said, rising and picking up the broom that lay at her feet. "And since I get plenty nervous seeing a strange face dressed in city duds, maybe you'd best tell me your business."

"I've come to see Sheena Goosen. Is she about today?"

"Who's askin'?"

Mansell pressed his shield against the screen, and this subdued her.

"I'm Miss Goosen's live-in," she said. "I'm afraid you caught her napping. But you're welcome to wait."

Beneath a giant willow at the foot of the stream, Mansell sipped lemonade and watched the sheep graze. An hour later, he joined Sheena Goosen on the back porch for tea. In her eighties now, the old schoolmistress smiled, her oval face crinkling like a walnut shell. She wore hearing aids in both ears, was confined to a wheel-chair, and her legs were swaddled in a wool blanket.

After hearing Mansell's well-rehearsed preamble, Miss Goosen said, "I retired after the new schoolhouse was finished—1953 that was. I was still a youngster at the time, but by then I had a little nest egg set aside and a healthy flock of sheep. And, without Anna, it lost some of its magic. That woman, God rest her soul, could turn a lesson in brushing your teeth into an adventure, young fellow."

"I understand. A terrible loss." They discussed the accident and Cecil Leistner's background for fifteen minutes, and then Mansell asked, "Was there ever any attempt made to restore any of the old school's records?"

"I don't see how." Miss Goosen drank her tea, and then, quite furtively, inquired as to the possibility of the inspector having any tobacco. Mansell offered his Camels. The old lady glanced about for the prying eyes of her maid, tucked the pack beneath her blanket, and winked. Finally, she said, "We were a small school. Records weren't as important as learning."

"I see. A good philosophy. Did the old school have yearbooks or class pictures? Anything like that?"

"You can forget the yearbook. No money. We did have a display case, though, outside my office on the wall. Every year old Doc Bailey would take pictures of everyone in the senior class. Then we'd put copies of those in the display case until the next year. 'Class of '48.' 'Class of '49.' Like that."

"What became of the pictures when the next class went into the display case?"

Her answer was taciturn. "I was the headmistress. I kept the pictures, of course." Cut-and-dried. Mansell grinned. "And now you want to steal the 1949 photo of young Cecil right out from under me, don't you, young fellow? Well, I'm a believer in the barter system myself. It is a one-of-a-kind, after all."

The deal cost Nigel Mansell a half carton of cigarettes and a solemn vow of eternal silence. It was near evening when he left Logan with a black-and-white snapshot of Cecil Leistner, smiling coyly, wearing knickers and knee socks, a high collar, and a sleeveless sweater. He was standing behind a sagging tennis net swinging an old wooden tennis racquet.

Mansell calculated. Pampoenpoort's telephone system still operated out of a central switchboard. As a precaution, it wouldn't do to place a call back to Port Elizabeth from here. A call from a switchboard might well raise eyebrows, and worse, could easily be traced.

Carnarvon was located seventy-five kilometers away, an hour's drive.

Mansell returned to the inn. He made an obvious display of reserving his room for a second and third night. He left Pampoenpoort at 6:50, alert for the Impala and more concerned now with the coming of night. Despite road construction fifteen kilometers out of town, he still arrived in Carnarvon by eight.

At the first public telephone, outside a fast-food joint called Whimpy's, Mansell pulled over. He entered the restaurant, approached the counter, and ordered a soft ice cream. He asked for three rand's worth of change.

Graffiti scribbled on the inside of the booth read, "Slug It Out with Becky Jo. Six-to-One Odds. First Come. Best Two Out of Three. Call RE6–1921."

An angel in hobnail boots, thought Mansell.

He rang the message return at the Clavers'. Delaney's message played through so quickly that he wasn't sure he'd heard it right. He dialed again. No message. There had to be a way of rewinding the tape, Mansell told himself. He played it through in his own mind, re-creating. ". . . Nigel, it's been a long time since I've made love to a man. Please call. . . ."

He sagged against the glass, repeating the words. He felt a stirring in his loins, a shortness of breath. He tried the number again. Same result. Why didn't she want me to use her home phone? he wondered. The answer was obvious.

He looked at Becky Jo's phone number and hissed.

Mansell booked a room at the Kareeberge Lodge at the foot of the low-lying Kareeberge Mountains. He parked the Audi in the underground garage beneath the lodge. In his room, he consulted the local directory. He found that Jaap Schwedler's son, Anson, still resided at the same address the attorney had given him.

When the main desk informed him that room service operated only "in season," Mansell walked a half kilometer into town. At a food-and-drug called Shelley's, he bought cheese, crackers, biltong, and hot peppers. At the Karoo Liquor Mart he selected a pint of Canadian whiskey, and then carried his purchases back to the lodge.

He ate first and then showered. Thirty minutes later, he heard someone tapping at the door. Mansell scurried across the room to the bed, unleashed the Browning from its harness, and crouched alongside the entry. With a flick of his wrist, he swung the door open. There at the threshold, with hands dug deep in his pockets, stood Joshua Brungle.

Detective Merriman Gosani chose a dry creek bed at the west edge of the East Fields property. Thickets of willow and stands of evergreen lined one side of the wash, while a four-meter-high fence with coils of barbed wire along the top lined the other. The wash provided Merry with sufficient cover and a view of the road—for the moment, his primary needs. He hid the Honda 150 motorcycle, a rental from the Johannesburg airport, in a ravine beneath the trestle bridge spanning R555. He used tree limbs and willow branches as camouflage. Next to the bike, he put a small backpack and a large thermos.

Within an hour of sunset, the temperature dropped ten degrees. By midnight, it would broach the freezing mark.

285

Merry reconned the perimeter of the East Fields property on foot. Beyond the fence, he discovered roving patrols every hundred meters. Well armed and in teams of two.

The news wasn't surprising, nor was it defeating; Merry didn't consider forced entry into the mine a viable option. Still, it had occurred to him that the forged work permit and identity card he'd gotten from Mansell's office would probably not be sufficient to see him past the guard towers at the entrance.

Any military or paramilitary operation worth its salt, Merry thought, would, by necessity, have built-in safeguards. A password. A code. A checklist. Something. Which meant he might have to assume another identity.

Right. And whose identity would that be? he asked himself. Convoys of black men, workers supposedly, were arriving at the mine at regular intervals. He knew that. But arriving how? On foot? By truck? And from where? How often? How many?

It could, Merry thought dejectedly, take days just to formulate a safe plan for getting inside. So we wait, he told himself. We wait and watch and freeze our tail off and try not to wonder why in the motherfuck we're here because a friend who saved our black ass is up to his white ass in trouble and now it's time for us to set the record straight. Dig it? It's as simple as that. So.

So Merry checked his map. The wind howled. He thanked his mama for the long underwear she'd sent him last Christmas from Klerksdorp, where it got damn cold in the winter without electricity. He'd laughed then, yeah, but something had told him to find a corner in his closet just in case. He'd send her flowers later.

At 9:15, Merry heard the rumble of trucks. He scrambled up the bank on his stomach. He saw headlights bearing down R555 from the west. Three flatbed trucks with wooden guard rails. As they crossed the bridge, Merry saw migrant workers, black bodies packed like sardines in a can. He clambered out of the wash. He ran down the shoulder of the road until he saw brake lights.

When he was certain the trucks had turned at the East Fields entrance, Merry walked back to the wash. He turned up the collar on his denim jacket and pulled a stocking cap over his ears.

Ten minutes later, the empty trucks steamed back down the road. Merry checked his watch, considering. The trucks, he decided, were the key. Should they return again tonight, and the tempo of their departure indicated that they might, then he would follow them back to their pickup station. Using a pencil flash and a red marker,

Merry studied the map again. Benori, Brakpan, and Springs were the closest train depots of any size, and size, Merry knew, meant less attention. The buses stopped closer yet, in Welgedacht, Delmas, and Geduld.

He munched an apple and a thick slab of dried biltong.

The convoy appeared again at 11:35. Merry climbed to the edge of the bank. Same trucks, less crowded. He used binoculars to follow their progress. Brake lights illuminated; dogged figures scrambled to the ground. The trucks drove through the entrance and disappeared. A bad sign, Merry thought, crouching in the wash again. He opened his thermos.

Fifteen minutes passed. A half hour. At 12:40, Merry packed his gear. The closest town was Delmas. He'd spend the night there. Abruptly, he changed his mind. Hell with it, he told himself, another hour. That felt better.

A transparent mist settled in the wash as the temperature bottomed out at a couple of degrees below freezing. Merry felt the weight of his eyelids. He was pacing in circles and chewing through toothpicks when he heard voices. In an instant, he checked the camouflage around his motorcycle and flattened himself against the bridge support.

The voices grew louder. The echo of footsteps. Laughter. The *click, click* sound of a dialect Merry didn't recognize. The volume indicated a large procession. But from where? he wondered, beginning a count. Springs was twenty kilometers away, Welgedacht half as far. Still, a healthy walk.

Those at the head of the pack were beyond the bridge now, marching at a brisk pace against the cold. Merry heard two other dialects, Zulu and Xhosa, both of which he spoke fluently. But the procession strung out for a half kilometer, the later marchers less spirited, struggling, grumbling. Merry saw the bottles passing between them. He counted eighty-five workers in all.

When the last straggler lumbered by, Merry scrambled out of the wash, hunched his shoulders, and set out in pursuit. The last half dozen workers were in single file, the gaps between them widening, their pace waning. Merry was considering a play for the last straggler when a worker further up the line stopped.

Merry hesitated. He was fifty meters back. The man staggered. He moved onto the shoulder of the road. He unzipped his pants. The last worker passed him by without a word. The man started peeing into the rain ditch off the side of the road. He turned his head as Merry approached. Merry flashed a broad smile, nodded, and punched the unsuspecting man as hard as he could. The blow drove the man into the ditch. Merry punched him a second time.

He stripped off the man's coat and beret, exchanging these for his own. He searched every pocket, exchanging work permits and identity cards, pocketing the man's travel papers, a pocket knife, a crumpled deck of playing cards, and a folded business card with the words *Caves of the Womb* typed on the back.

Quickly, he dragged the man behind a thatch of juniper. With his belt and handcuffs, Merry harnessed the body to the trunk of a tree. A thick piece of bark and a bandana proved an effective gag.

Returning to the road, Merry jogged ahead until the gap between himself and the last worker closed to within fifty meters. He was whistling softly when he reached the entrance. The group was bunched up in front of a chain link gate beneath bright spotlights. No one gave him a passing glance. Merry stamped his feet, tugged at the crusty black beret, and nudged forward. By the time he reached the guardhouse, he was tenth from the rear.

Two white guards armed with pistols and automatic rifles stood before the gates. Merry held out his identity card, work permit, travel papers, the playing cards, and the business card. One of the guards glanced quickly at the words on the business card. Then he snatched away the identity card. He studied the photo and stuck a flashlight in Merry's face. Merry had seen the look a thousand times—denigration tinged with fear. His eyes never wavered. By this time in the night, the guard had seen seven hundred dirty black faces, and they all looked the same. The moment passed. He relinquished the card and spat on the ground. The other guard studied the work permit, the job description, and the labor bureau's seal. He flipped the papers over to the last page. He passed a flashlight over it, and Merry saw something on the page give off a blue reflection.

Wordlessly, the guard returned the document, and Merry passed through the gates into East Fields.

Joshua glanced down at the weapon dangling from Mansell's hand.

"There's something about these wide-open spaces on the Karoo," the detective said. "Small towns, clean fresh air, springboks and antelope. Everyone knows everyone else. Gossip, cliques. Animosity, suspicion."

"The good life," replied the inspector. "I'll buy you a drink."

The room was smoky, curtains drawn tight. The television flashed an underwear commercial, but no sound.

"All we need's a stripper and a saxophone," said Joshua, parting the curtains. "Bloody hell, we'd have ourselves a party."

He cracked the window. Cool air filtered in. Mansell perched on the corner of the dresser, watching. A nine-millimeter Browning, he told himself gallantly, can put a hole the size of a cantaloupe in a human body.

Joshua pointed to the whiskey bottle on the nightstand next to the television. "A drink?"

"There's ice in the bathroom. Make it two."

As he stepped into the bath, Joshua glanced back over his shoulder. He disappeared. Mansell heard the tingle of ice meeting glass.

"You figured it had to be me or Terreblanche," he heard Joshua say.

Muscles taut, Mansell circled to the window, leaning heavily against the sill. "Jurgen, maybe."

"A long shot," Joshua said. He emerged from the bathroom carrying two stubby glasses packed with ice. "Jurgen's a wimp. He'd run before he'd investigate. Who was it that said, 'The path of least resistance is a road heavily traveled'?"

"That sounds like one of mine."

Joshua chuckled. He poured two ounces of whiskey into each glass. "Yeah, but you probably stole it from Jean-Paul Sartre or Marcel Proust. Somebody earthy, deep, you know."

"I think it was Empedocles, actually."

"Ah, a student of Greek essentialism." Joshua set the glasses on the edge of the dining table. He kicked out a plastic-covered club chair and dropped into it. He sipped his drink epicureally. Then he said, "There is another possibility, other than myself or Terreblanche. Other than Cyprian Jurgen. But it's not a pleasant one. It seems that Delaney Blackford and Minister of Justice Leistner have been . . . or became . . . involved about two years back. Word has it that it's over, but. . . . It may be coincidence, probably is, but they were introduced by—"

"Ian Elgin."

"Yes."

"So." Mansell looked aside as the seeds of betrayal invaded his stomach. "And is there more?"

Joshua shook his head. "But I thought you should know."

"You've told me."

Joshua returned to his drink. Ice swirled at the touch of his finger. Whiskey sent tentacles of heat throughout his body. He said, "It wasn't me, Nigel."

"Oh?"

"Six shots from fifteen meters? Six misses?"

"You ever see me move when I'm dodging bullets?"

Joshua chuckled. "You played goalie in soccer, not halfback. I've seen you run," he replied. Seconds passed. His voice changed. "And besides, I seem to recall that you're my best friend."

Mansell studied the handsome profile, seemingly at ease, watching the silent tube. Mansell followed the line of his vision. A game show. People stomping their feet and screaming in the name of petty greed and eternal degradation. He pushed away from the sill, crossed the room, and punched the "off" button on the set.

Finally, he put the gun back in the shoulder harness and laid it at the head of the bed. Joshua used the heel of his shoe to push a chair out for him. Memories of similar scenes swept over Mansell. He accepted the chair and the drink.

"To Deacon Blue," Joshua said, hoisting his glass. "Smoky bars, saxophones, naked women, and whiskey."

"How'd you find me, Joshua?"

"I had a good teacher. Remember?" The detective tapped the lapels of his sports coat. He opened the jacket with two fingers. The shoulder harness was missing. "Inside pocket."

Mansell nodded, and three plastic film canisters materialized from the pocket. Joshua stacked them on the table, saying, "These were in my box at the station this morning."

Mansell checked the contents: 135-millimeter film, twenty-four shots per, all three rolls exposed. "Any indications?"

"Express-mailed from downtown Jo'burg yesterday afternoon. The main annex. The prints on the envelope belong to the clerk at the post office. The prints on the canisters and the reels belong to Delaney Blackford. No others."

A rush of air escaped Mansell's lungs. "Delaney didn't mention anything about sending the film through the mail. I talked to her two hours before her plane was to leave."

"I don't know." Joshua shrugged, raising an eyebrow. "Maybe. . . . Do you know if she's back in P.E. yet?"

"She left a message on her answering machine this morning."

Joshua needn't know about the Clavers. Not yet. "She didn't mention the film. She's waiting for my call."

"Then you haven't talked to her?"

"Not yet." Whiskey provided a momentary diversion. On the one hand, Mansell thought, Joshua was as good a friend as he had; believing was easier than disbelieving. On the other hand, had Joshua strayed to the other side, it was a masterful stroke of insidiousness. And if he *had* strayed, then he wouldn't come in here with guns blazing. Questions needed answering. Like, how much the fugitive had learned. Like, what was the fugitive planning? Mansell drained his glass. He changed the subject, asking, "How far has the federal warrant gotten, Joshua?"

"Division was still sitting on it as of last night, but Terreblanche was getting nervous. District stations will have it by now. The locals, they might have it by tomorrow morning." Joshua freshened their drinks. He pulled enthusiastically on his own, and said, "De Villiers wasn't a pretty sight. He'd sustained multiple head injuries from a blunt instrument of some kind, but we still don't know where the beating took place. Steenkamp has established that de Villiers was in a comatose state when the bullets from your gun were fired into the body. Time of death around one A.M. Tuesday morning. We found tire-tread and shoe prints. Both in mint condition. Security traced the car to a Budget Master in P.E. The car was rented in your name."

Mansell didn't even wince. "Traces?"

"Clean, except for the trunk. Blood, hair, tissue. All de Villiers's." Joshua touched whiskey to his lips. He glanced across the table. "And we found a ball-point pen. Your fingerprints. And the shoe prints at the scene came from running shoes, size 11D. Security checked your locker at the station. Your Nikes were missing. Worse, they were discovered in a trash bin at the Budget Master in Jo'burg where the car was returned on Tuesday, the fifteenth."

"The same day I happened to be in Johannesburg." Mansell glared at two spent matches lying at his fingertips on the table. He lit a cigarette with a third. "Well done. Very well done."

"Yes, but there is this," Joshua said directly. "The countergirl at the Budget Master in P.E. won't identify you. She says the guy that rented the car was big. A hand taller than me and bulkier. That makes him nearly two meters tall. Okay? And second. Janis Warren? Know her?"

"A policewoman from the Summerstrand district."

"That's her. Well, Monday evening, the night de Villiers bought it, she sees this guy on the back stairs of the station house. Again, a big guy. He's going up. Janis is heading down to the Pit with coffee in her hand. But she thinks he stops on the second floor. All right, a couple minutes later something clicks. She runs back up. The guy's gone, of course. But her description and the counter-girl's are just too similar to ignore."

"So this guy lifts a pen from my desk and running shoes from my locker. He breaks into my house. He knows about the gun case in my bedroom, and he takes Jennifer's Colt .38 Special figuring that I'll think she took it with her when she left."

"The point is, Wolffe has himself a pretty strong case. And he has a witness who swears he saw you talking to de Villiers on the docks the night of the murder. Anything to that?"

"Delaney mentioned de Villiers a couple of times, but I never met him," Mansell answered impassively. "Have you talked to this . . . witness?"

Joshua shook his head. "I'm letting him have a taste of Security Branch for a while. Then we'll see."

"Do me a favor. Don't wait too long." Mansell drank whiskey straight from the bottle, wincing. "I need some sleep. In the morning, you can see about that film while I have a talk with a friend of a friend."

"Of our distinguished minister?"

Mansell didn't reply. Instead, he made a magnanimous gesture toward the bed, wrapped himself in an extra blanket from the closet, and stretched out on the couch.

Before long, Joshua was curled up in the bed, and his breathing deepened. Mansell watched his chest rise and fall in the steady rhythm of deep slumber.

Sleep, Mansell told himself, a fool's paradise, an unnecessary luxury. He didn't remember dozing. Told himself he hadn't. At dawn, he went into the bathroom, locked the door, and showered beneath a cold, hard spray.

In the bedroom, Joshua tossed the covers off, rolled quietly out of bed, and pulled on his trousers. He moved swiftly to the door and outside. The police sedan was parked across the lot and the revolver and harness lay beneath the seat on the passenger side.

In the motel room, he screwed the blunt-nosed silencer onto the end of the barrel and slipped the harness over his arm. The hit, he knew, was inevitable; Mansell had brought it on himself. It was a question of where. Joshua had made his presence known at the front desk, which made the motel room a bad choice. But it was still a possibility. When he heard the shower turn off in the bathroom, he crawled back beneath the covers.

The pocket calendar next to his cot read, Saturday, July 19. Two words were handwritten in red ink under the date: "Day Four."

Jan Koster struggled to a sitting position, massaged bloodshot eyes and a two-day-old beard, and staggered over to the washbasin. Carefully, without looking too closely at the cadaverous reflection, he shaved. He splashed the last drops of aftershave into the palm of his hand, patting cheeks and neck, and welcoming the sting.

Sighing, he tossed the empty bottle into the waste can and returned to his cot.

He opened a small notebook that contained the letters he had begun the night before. The first of these was destined for the eyes of General Alexander Becker, the chief of South Africa's National Intelligence Service.

Sending the letter to Becker was the result of far more than a logical guess; "a sophisticated projection" described it better. For the last six months, Koster had composed a hundred different scenarios for these next four days. Each scenario, drawn to its most suitable conclusion, included Becker's interaction. Yet drawing him into the action, Koster realized, would take inducement, convincing. As catalysts, he meant to rely on two disturbing elements from the general's past. One being the unresolved controversy surrounding his father's death in 1978, a prelude to the scandal that led to the resignation of then prime minister Vorster. The other being the NIS chief's deep-seated and long-standing prejudice against the rival Security Branch.

Koster labored over the letter for another thirty minutes, decided that a fictionalized signature would do more harm than no signature, and addressed the envelope to NIS headquarters in Pretoria.

The second letter proved more formidable, the recipient, his wife, Julia, more vulnerable, more important. So many days, he thought, had slipped away from them, so many unspoken feelings. Over the last month Koster had written two other letters preparing her and the family. Still. . . .

293

Dear Julia, he thought, *I've been working for the Soviet Union for the past seven years; to say nothing of the sixteen years that came before. Yes, treason. So sorry. Please forgive me.* Very creative, very redeeming.

He tore off the page, crumpled it, and tossed it toward the trash. Then he stared again at the red ink on his calendar, and the words he sought came at last.

The name in Merry's reference book read "Uzo Egonu." The faded picture showed a thick man wearing a black beret. The physical description was not noticeably out of line. Still, the blue reflector badge on the back page of the work permit had proved the most essential commodity thus far.

Merry Gosani was, as of 1:15 on the morning of the nineteenth, an official member of the Blue Strike Team.

He'd been assigned a bunk in a cramped barrack and spent a sleepless night on a straw pallet. Breakfast, served cafeteria-style to shifts of a thousand men, consisted of powdered eggs, beans, hard rolls, and coffee.

At seven, his unit received orders to attend a briefing session in a long low-lying warehouse known as the command center.

Inside, the warehouse had been converted into a gigantic lecture hall. Row after row of folding chairs lay at the foot of a broad platform. A small podium stood at the center of the stage. A series of land and geological maps hung from wooden stands to the right of the podium, and a blank movie screen stood to the left.

Merry chose a seat near the back. He fondled the real Uzo Egonu's pocket knife and gnawed a toothpick. For thirty minutes, the warehouse filled. Conversation and expectation split the air.

Eventually a tall man in full military dress approached the podium. He introduced himself as Colonel Rolf Lamouline. A moment later, another man, spry, slender, wearing thick eyeglasses and dressed in a brown business suit, mounted the stage. Uncontrollable cheering filled the hall. *My God*, Merry thought, *Zuma. Christopher Zuma.* The cheers amplified. Zuma bowed serenely to the audience. Merry found himself standing, applauding, heard his own voice joining the celebration.

It could have lasted indefinitely, but in time, Zuma took a seat behind the podium, and Lamouline raised a hand. The hall fell silent. The lights were dimmed, and the briefing began. Spotlights illuminated maps of the East Rand and the Witwatersrand. Slides highlighted the plant facilities of Highland Vaal, the White Ridge mines, Brakpan Holdings, and Homestake Mining. In awe, Merry listened as seven years of planning and preparation unfolded before him.

Lamouline gestured with a pointer toward one of the maps and a blue circle enclosing the Homestake property. He said, "Three days from today, on Tuesday the twenty-second at midnight, Blue Strike Team will be responsible for the initial thrust into this baby right here. Homestake Mining."

Then, jabbing the pointer at a cross-section rendering of the tunnel system beneath East Fields, he outlined the step-by-step process of underground infiltration; the supply centers, the primary tunnels, the connection tunnel, the dead access shaft below Homestake, the work station, and the eventual ascent by elevator into the deserted storage shed inside the plant itself.

"At eleven-forty P.M. that night, you will begin your ascent. You will be well armed as you know, and you may well meet with some resistance, armed resistance. But understand this, gentlemen, our intent is not destruction. Nor death. Got it? Our intent is control, leverage. Bad blood has no place in this operation. Don't forget it."

Merry stared at Christopher Zuma's placid face. The dark eyes were closed, as if meditating, but his head nodded slowly in agreement. Despite himself, Merry thought of Nigel Mansell and Sylvia Mabasu, and from that point on, he seemed only to catch bits and pieces of the lecture.

". . . At three Tuesday afternoon, Blue Strike Team will descend into the tunnels below East Fields for the last time . . ." he heard the colonel saying.

". . . You will enter the connection tunnel here by nine. Do not rush, gentlemen. . . . From there, you will proceed to the access shaft . . . and ladders here, here, and here which lead to this work station. Now, it'll be crowded as hell in there, people, but cool and well lit, right? So do not panic."

The work station, Merry noted, was only thirty meters below the surface. It was impossible.

". . . The work station, the primary tunnel, and the surface elevator have all been reinforced, and . . ."

Not impossible, he thought, fucking brilliant.

". . . Eleven-forty, gentlemen. That's our magic number. . . ."

". . . your objectives are. First, the control tower, here. Second, the refinery substation and the reduction plant substation here and here. Third . . ."

It might actually work, Merry thought.

". . . All positions inside the targets will be supported by infantry and artillery based here at East Fields. Radio contact will be maintained at all times. . . ."

When Christopher Zuma stepped up to the microphone ten minutes later, a wave of electricity swept over the hall again. Merry welcomed the emotion.

Zuma raised a hand into the air. In a clear voice, he said, "Do not forget the goals that we have set for ourselves. Do not forget the means we have chosen to achieve those goals. Enough people have been made to suffer. Do not forget that in all true causes there is hope, and in all just fights there is victory. . . ."

Merry filed out of the warehouse with two concerns. He had anticipated the first: how to communicate with Nigel Mansell. But not the second: what to communicate once he did make contact. And more, how to accomplish both without dying in the process.

With a last glance at Joshua's inert form, Nigel Mansell closed the door to his room behind him and stepped gratefully into the face of a crisp morning breeze.

The main street of Carnarvon was wide and freshly paved, the buildings staggered and square. Concrete walks with wooden park benches fronted cluttered storefronts. Parking meters stood guard over diagonal parking spaces.

A block off the main drag, next to the Karoo National Monument, Mansell discovered The Breakfast Nook. A sward of browning grass with a banyan tree set at its heart formed an esplanade leading to a large log cabin. Smoke billowed invitingly from the chimney. WELCOME TO THE NOOK—BREAKFAST AND LUNCH—WHITE RACE ONLY, PLEASE.

"Right," Mansell muttered. "Prepared for your pleasure by our famous nigger chef and served by our sturdy coloured waitress."

He set out again.

The smell of baking bread led him to a flat-roofed building that resembled a converted wheat shed. A sign out front read, THE SHIRE. Mansell ventured inside. The tiny restaurant was crowded, but Mansell found a stool at the end of an old-fashioned bar. A man in a white T-shirt, starched apron, and chef's hat greeted him with tea and a single-page menu. Mansell asked for a telephone, and the proprietor pointed down the hall next to the rest rooms.

Mansell stared at the phone thinking about the news Joshua had dropped in his lap the night before. Delaney and Leistner. But that was two years ago, he told himself. Yeah, and it was three days ago that someone nearly blew you off your own front porch, remember? Delaney was the one person he hadn't suspected. She was the one person he couldn't face suspecting.

Mansell understood that by now either Security Branch or CIB was watching Delaney's house, that her phone was also tapped. Why, he could only guess. He knew that suggesting a rendezvous made no sense. He also knew it didn't matter.

He punched R3 worth of coins into the phone and dialed the Clavers' number. After two rings, the answering machine took over. He said, "Delaney. Hello. It's Nigel. I got your message, and. . . . Can we meet? Soon? Tonight, at the Clavers'? I know it's dangerous. I know. . . ."

Mansell explained about the guest entrance on the northeast corner of the house, and the key she would find above the gas meter next to the door. The inside stairway, he said, led to a small studio in the basement. Should he mention the film canisters? He didn't. Should he mention the federal warrant? It wasn't necessary, Mansell thought. She knows. Somehow, she knows.

He rang off, deflated, alone. He slumped down in the phone booth for nearly a minute, stoking the low fires of adrenaline and resolve. Turning back entered his mind, but turning back was out of the question.

Cecil Leistner returned Delaney's call fifteen minutes later.

"You've heard from the inspector." His voice exuded the warmth of diplomacy, but the firmness of an expectant master.

"This morning," Delaney confided. Returning the cup of flour to her neighbor had provided Delaney with the perfect cover for dialing the Clavers' message return again.

"But not on your own telephone," the minister commented.

"No, not on my own telephone," Delaney retaliated. "It's tapped, in case you hadn't heard. I know it, and so does he, evidently. And I don't like it, Cecil. I'm not one of your second-class terrorists. And I don't like your leisure-suit flunkies hanging around outside my house either. They give the neighborhood a bad name."

"They serve their purpose."

"And what would that be? The reinforcement of your personal insecurity? I offered you my help. Harassing my home life wasn't part of the bargain."

"Delaney, please. We're searching for a killer. A federal warrant is a serious matter. I know the leisure suits and the phone tap are an annoyance, but they're not meant to be an embarrassment. And they're certainly not measures taken against you. If anything, they're meant for your own protection."

"How thoughtful."

"Now, please. Where is he?"

"He left a message on my secretary's answering machine at the office," Delaney heard herself say. She'd anticipated the lie all along, but not the mettle it took to convey it. "Mansell didn't say where he was, but he did say he was on his way back to Port Elizabeth."

"Did he say when?"

"Sunday night." This time the fabrication came easier. She needed time alone with Mansell. A day couldn't matter. "We're to meet as soon as he gets to town."

"Good girl. Excellent. Where? At your home?"

"I doubt it. He said he'd call the minute he arrives, but he's being extremely cautious, Cecil."

"We should expect that. And we should expect him to use any means necessary to accomplish his ends, Delaney. Please be careful." Leistner's tone hardened almost immeasurably when he added, "I'll expect a call from you the moment you hear from the inspector on Sunday."

The town of Carnarvon, though abutting the rugged Kareeberge mountain range on the north, was embraced on three sides by endless acres of farms, ranchland, and desert. It took a special breed of craziness, Mansell thought, to try to draw life from the Karoo. But for those who did, dry crops like wheat and mealie predominated. For those less bent on masochism, sheep and cattle provided meager livelihoods.

Anson Schwedler, a logical masochist, had chosen both courses.

Mansell followed a gravel road thirty-eight kilometers out of town until he happened upon Trinity Road. The younger Schwedler owned 620 acres here. Half he devoted to wheat, the remainder to sheep.

Trinity Road led to a three-story farmhouse, white with blue trim, with a full-length porch and a tire swing dangling from the branch of a huge elm. Chickens wandered aimlessly about pecking at seeds and complaining. A sheep dog slept on the steps. Out back stood a Dutch-style barn and a red brick silo.

Despite a chilly breeze, five boys were playing soccer on the front lawn, but they stopped in midstride when the Audi appeared. The chickens scattered. The sheep dog barked. Four of the boys gathered around to admire the bronze finish of the 5000. The youngest, a stout, freckled lad with a crew cut and faded dungarees, held the soccer ball at his side and stared at the stranger dressed in a sports jacket and tie.

"Your daddy around this morning?"

"In the house," the boy answered, motioning with his arm. "I'll fetch him for ya."

Mansell followed him to the front porch. The chickens ignored him. The dog sniffed his pant legs, and a moment later the father appeared. No mistaking it: stocky, boyish. He wore dungarees and a plaid shirt. Smoke rose from the carved churchwarden clamped tight between his lips.

"We've been expecting you," he said, offering a meaty hand. "I'm Anson Schwedler. Come on in."

Schwedler led Mansell through a narrow entryway made narrower by two antique half trees, into a living room dimly lit behind lace curtains. The room was homey and cluttered. An antique tabouret in one corner, an oval china closet filled with English porcelain in another. A mahogany library case against one wall, a pressed chiffonier against the other. A small fire burned within a granite fireplace, and sitting on a velour davenport facing the blaze was an old man.

"This is my papa, Jaap Schwedler," Anson said. The older man stuck out a hand. Mansell felt the rigid bones of age and the thrifty grip of the tired. He had to remind himself that Jaap Schwedler was of the same vintage as Cecil Leistner and Lloyd Chesney. The years hadn't been as kind. "The womenfolk have gone off shopping someplace, so Dad and I are having a bit of an eye-opener. Join us."

"Thanks. I will," said Mansell reluctantly. He sat down in a spindled rocker adjacent to the davenport.

"So you've come about the minister, have you?" said Jaap. "Funny, no one ever has before. Old Lloyd Chesney called up to prepare me. See, everyone thinks I came back from the big shoot-out a little tipped."

Anson the younger chuckled. He poured straight vodka into a shot glass. Mansell explained his assignment.

Then he said, "You were in Korea with Minister Leistner."

"A bombardier in the Number Two Squadron, that's right," the elder answered. "We went down together and lost each other in the process."

Mansell studied the old man, who studied the fire, and asked, "Where were you shot down, Mr. Schwedler?"

"We were there almost from the beginning," Jaap answered instead. "Protectors of the Republic of Korea. Except the ROK buildup was a farce. Yeah, they had fifty thousand men hanging around the thirty-eighth parallel toting American rifles. Sure. Fifty thousand farmers who just wanted to go home to their families and their rice paddies. War? Shit. But the Chinks and the Russkies, now they'd built up the Korean People's Army in the north with seven or eight infantry divisions, a couple of armored brigades, and about ten thousand independent advisers. That's what they called the Russian and Chinese bastards who ran the whole show.

"Hell, they blew down the Uijongbu corridor like shit runnin' through a goose. Took Seoul by the end of the first day. By nightfall they'd advanced twenty kilometers inside the parallel from one end of the front to the other. Ten thousand dead, another thirty thousand instant refugees. Kids without dads, wives without husbands. Straw houses and farms that disappeared in a puff of black smoke."

Jaap Schwedler paused, his face red from exertion. He drank vodka in stingy sips, coughing and sucking air.

But his voice was strong when he started up again. "The U.S. and the dumb-fuck ROK got caught with their pants down around their knees. They sure enough did. And we all paid the price. Amazing, it was. No one could believe that Mao and Stalin might have an agreement, even though Mao was holed up in Moscow swizzling peppered vodka and stuffing his face with caviar.

"The guns, the artillery, the tanks—all Russian. The Chinks, well they provided the waves and the Russkies the brains. By the spring of '50 every key position in the Korean People's Army was held by a Russian, and the slant-eyes—"

"Dad!"

"Oh, sorry. Chinks, slant-eyes, what's the difference? Anyway, it was a helluva way to run a police action, I'll tell you that much, Inspector. It was hit-and-run those first months. The Number Two . . . we were part of the Eighteenth Bomber wing. Well, we ran raids up and down the coast of the Sea of Japan for two months. The KPA had a full division pushing down along the Taebaek San-maek Mountains. The bastards had anti-aircraft guns by the hundreds and rocket launchers and . . .

"They shot us down near Kumgang in the mountains. Two planes. Five of us made the ground. Captain Crooker and Fourie, they made a run for it. Lucky bastards were mowed down clean as a whistle. They took the three of us to a prison everyone called Magic Mountain. They snipped off Chaney du Plessis' little finger that first day with trimming shears. They pulled out two of my teeth with pliers when I couldn't tell them the strength of the Eighteenth Bomber group. Me and Chaney were separated for a while, and neither of us ever saw Cecil again after that first day."

"Where was the minister taken, do you know?"

"You came all this way to ask me that?" snapped the old man. He glared at Mansell and then looked back at the fire. "Why the blazes don't you ask the high and mighty man himself?"

Mansell leaned forward. He stroked his chin and in a low voice said, "Frankly, Mr. Schwedler, the minister isn't prepared to say. He has long spaces where there is . . . no memory. The obvious explanation might be drug-induced interrogation. Something like that. Do you, by chance, have any idea?"

Jaap Schwedler snorted. He sounded pleased. "We heard he was taken to Anbyon or Wonsan," answered the veteran. "We heard he'd agreed to cooperate. We heard he was eating fresh chicken and vegetables every day and drinking wine every night. They told us we'd get the same treatment if we'd cooperate, like Cecil. Ever eaten rat meat, Inspector? Rat meat cooked in a rusted tin can over a fire made from pieces of your own shirt?"

"Dad, for crying out loud!" exclaimed the son.

The elder Schwedler seemed unfazed. "We ate cracked corn and millet once a day. On good days we'd have soya beans. Rats, they were a luxury. I watched five hundred men die that winter," he said, lifting a pipe from the ashtray. "And they said we were lucky, you know that? Everyone said that we were the luckiest bastards in Korea."

"Lucky?" asked Mansell. "Why was that, Mr. Schwedler?"

Ancient rheumy eyes peered back at him. Jaap Schwedler said, "See, we were captured in a Russian-occupied sector of North Korea, Inspector. Fifteen kilometers further west and we'd a been in a Chinese sector. See, rumor had it that the Chinese forbade their prisoners from killing any rats. Rumor had it that the Chinese served their prisoners *to* the rats."

The clerk at the registration desk of the Kareeberge Lodge handed Mansell a note as he prepared to pay his bill.

The note was from Joshua. It read, "The developed film is in the dresser, top drawer. I'm heading back to Port Elizabeth. I have a witness that needs talking to. Thanks for the bed and the booze. Ciao. Deacon Blue."

The film was there, in the top drawer, just as Joshua said it would be. Mansell thumbed through the prints, impressed by the quality of Delaney's photography, but unable to muster the proper enthusiasm. As evidence, Mansell thought, the photos could be easily refuted. It could be argued that the initial sequence showing the M1191 A1 pistols and the M16 rifles in the storage shed at the harbor had been staged, a fabrication of their own devising. It was a foolish mistake; he and Delaney were the only witnesses. And the sequence following the crates from Port Elizabeth to Kroonstad? A good defense lawyer would have a field day with that one. The truck caravan from Kroonstad to East Fields proved only that 253 crates had been transferred from a boxcar to two tractor trailers. How could it be proved that those same crates contained pistols and rifles and not pneumatic drills and pickaxes? he asked himself. Answer: it couldn't.

Mansell left his key in the room. With his briefcase in one hand and a duffel bag in the other, he walked down the corridor to the exit at the rear of the building. He climbed down the back stairs to the underground parking garage.

His footsteps echoed on iron stairs that led to the second level. The metal door that led into the garage squealed like a fox caught in a bear trap. Concrete radiated a permanent cool, like the catacombs of ancient Rome. The air smelled of machine oil and exhaust fumes.

A generator kicked on overhead. Escaping steam hissed. Water pipes shuddered.

Mansell glanced cautiously over his shoulder. He paused, peering the length of the garage in both directions.

Concrete cylinder supports, sporadically placed, stood guard over a sparse array of lonely automobiles. Fords, Chevys, Toyotas. A gold Mercedes-Benz, a white Cadillac, a silver BMW. White paint formed symmetrical parking spaces. Steel girders formed a prison wall overhead. Bare sixty-watt bulbs sprinkled insufficient light and formed pockets of dark shadows. There were no attendants.

Capital letters had been painted on each support, a reminder to forgetful motorists. Row C was at the far end of the garage. Fifty meters away, Mansell saw the Audi. Dreading the drive home, he stopped to light a cigarette. The matchbook was empty. He set down the duffel bag, unzipped the side pocket, and dug out a lighter. Smoke invaded his lungs. He thought of Delaney and the fragrance of her bedroom. He touched the handle on the Browning. Half assured, he hoisted the bag again.

Twenty-five meters from the car, he heard footsteps. Where? Up ahead? No. He glanced to his left and then to the rear. He lengthened his stride.

Directly ahead, Joshua Brungle stepped from behind a concrete pillar. He held a service pistol in both hands. Mansell froze. He recognized the blunt cylinder on the end, a silencer. Joshua spread his legs. He raised the gun, arms extended. His handsome face was calm, ghostlike.

"Joshua." The duffel bag dropped from Mansell's hand to the floor, a dull thud. "Joshua, no!"

The cry stuck in Mansell's throat. He saw an orange flash at the end of the barrel. He heard the muffled pop of the bullet leaving the chamber, braced himself, and then stumbled. At first, there was no pain. A clean hit, he thought. Bad sign. The groan in his ear seemed to come from a distant source. He heard a clatter, like iron hitting concrete. He saw Joshua darting forward, gun poised.

But Joshua didn't stop. He skirted past, eyes feverish with concentration, and, at last, Mansell understood. The groan. The absence of pain. The clatter. He turned. Twenty meters behind, curled in a ball at the rear end of an Impala, lay a body, blood pooling about the head. Joshua hunched over it. Mansell broke into a run.

The eyes were opened wide with surprise. The mouth agape. Blood dripped from the bullet hole dead-center in the forehead. A pistol lay on the floor next to the face, a .45-caliber American-made M1191 A1 pistol. Gloved hands still gripped the stock. The gloves were a tan leather with gold buckles across the wrists.

"Bloody hell," gasped Mansell as he stared down at the contorted features of Captain Oliver Terreblanche.

Calmly, Joshua dragged the body behind a row of parked cars. He tried the trunk latches on several. On the fourth, a Ford Maverick, the latch disengaged and the trunk opened. He lifted the body inside and closed the lid.

"My car's at the edge of town," Joshua said. He grabbed Mansell by the elbow and steered him back to the Audi. "There's no hurry."

The engine turned over. "You knew he was here," Mansell said. "How?"

A steep incline led to the garage exit. "I had a good teacher. Remember?" Joshua said for the second time.

"I'm learning a few things myself."

They located Joshua's GM sedan parked at the rear of a gas station at the city limits.

Joshua opened the door, but Mansell caught him by the wrist. Their eyes met. "Thanks," he said.

Joshua shrugged. "What are friends for?"

Delaney stood at the front door leaning on her walking stick.

With her free hand she motioned to the Security Branch officer, who was, at that moment, slouching in the front seat of the unmarked car parked at the curb. He sat up with a start, opened the door, and clambered out.

"Tea?" she called out. "I just made a fresh pot."

He hesitated. Delaney walked halfway down the walk, exaggerating her limp. "Sitting in that car can get a little boring, I imagine."

"I'm used to it," he answered with bravado.

"I'm sure. Still, I think we're supposed to be on the same side." Delaney threw back her shoulders and smiled. She turned and started back to the house. "I'll leave the door open in case you change your mind."

"I guess you're right," he said, following.

His partner was already seated at the kitchen table. Delaney poured three cups. She set a box of donuts next to the cream and sugar.

"Help yourself, but save me one of the chocolates," she said, smiling again. "I have to make a visit to the little girls' room."

In the bathroom, Delaney pushed aside wooden shutters and looked across the front lawn. She watched her neighbor, Sally Claybourne, cross the street, open the front door of the Security officers' car, and lean inside. Sally rolled up all the windows. She locked both doors. She climbed out, held up the keys triumphantly, and scurried back to her own house.

Back in the kitchen, Delaney refilled the officers' cups. She turned on the radio and started humming.

"We're eating all your donuts," the partner said.

"Eat," replied Delaney, taking a chocolate one from the box. "They'll only go stale if you don't. I'll see if the newspaper has come yet."

Silently, she took her purse and coat from the hall closet. She stepped outside, and reset the dead bolt behind her. The Fiat was parked in the driveway.

When the Security men heard the engine, they sprang for the front door, one of them pulling unsuccessfully at the handle. Frantically, they raced through the house to the back door and outside. By the time they reached their locked car, the Fiat was out of sight.

In the city, Delaney parked in an underground lot below the Port Elizabeth National Bank. She returned to the street and hailed a taxi.

Afterward collecting his East Fields photographs from Castle Drug, Mansell returned to Millard Grange. He parked the car off Lancaster Avenue and set out on foot for his own neighborhood.

Once there he crept furtively through the alley behind Northview Avenue. A cedarwood fence separated the grounds of the Clavers' house from the alleyway. He walked the length of the alley, using the neighbors' backyards for reconnaissance. As far as Mansell could tell, they were using one car and three men to watch his own house six doors up. He returned to the Clavers' fence. He pushed aside a tall gate. Like a nervous doe at the edge of a forest, Mansell stood, poised, studying. The house was shrouded in darkness except for the time-activated lights in a bathroom upstairs and a bedroom on the main floor.

The door to the guest entrance was not locked.

Mansell closed it behind him. His hand touched the key left in the lock, and he turned it. He felt his way down a flight of stairs.

He followed a glow of yellow light through a narrow hallway into a room filled with wooden furniture and thick carpet. Delaney was there, seated on the edge of the sofa. A bottle of champagne and two crystal goblets sat on the end table next to her. Lighted candles cast soft shadows across her face. A silk dressing gown reflected the dancing flames. She arose.

Without speaking, Mansell stepped across the floor. He took her in his arms. Her gown opened, and their lips met. Delaney's arms surrounded him. Her hands darted from his head to his back, drawing him closer. Slowly, through the flood of their kisses and the urgency of their caresses, Mansell lowered her to the edge of the couch.

"I wanted you to love me that very first day in my office," she said afterward. "It seems like an eternity since then."

The tips of her breasts were still hard with fever. Mansell touched her lightly in the hollow below her ribs. "You didn't look up when I stopped at the door. I felt like a schoolboy standing there, but I wanted that more than anything."

Her eyes closed. "I couldn't," she said. "You were the enemy."

The sheets lay upon them like the cool ripples of a lake never ended. Delaney sipped champagne, wanting him again.

"You were wrong, you know," he said. "Policemen aren't policemen every minute of every day. Look at me."

"You are different. Yes, but . . ."

"But what? Tell me." He kissed her hair, her shoulders, her neck.

"I know about the warrant for your arrest." Her voice was low, turbulent, cautious. "I've pictured Steven de Villiers's face a hundred times lying there in that grave."

"And do you believe it?"

"I don't know."

"Did they tell you why?"

"Why?"

"Because I'm close. Close to their secrets. Which is why we shouldn't be here, together. Because if they find out how close, and if they find out about this . . ."

———

306

He wanted to tell her. Needed to.

"Today," he whispered slowly. "I almost died today."

"Nigel . . . ?"

He touched her lips, assuring her. "A friend saved me. You know, I'm not sure I couldn't have faced it then." He touched her breasts, wanting her. "Now I feel like I never want to face it. You saved me from that."

The first songbird offered a subtle hint of the impending break of day.

At last, Delaney told him about the arms, and the film, and the long arm of Security. But she resisted mentioning the minister. Why? she asked herself. Wasn't it too late?

"I went back to the motel. The film was gone. Linder had followed me, expecting it to be there, too."

"Meaning Security doesn't have the film either," Mansell suggested. "Meaning they haven't seen it."

"I don't know," she answered. "I'm sorry."

Then why do I have it? he asked himself. Why do I have the film? Could she know? Could Delaney know?

From twelve midnight until five a.m., Blue Strike Team conducted underground maneuvers, perfecting their skills with electric cable cars, winch-rope transports, and shaft-elevator operations.

After a breakfast of powdered eggs and canned fruit, and an hour-long briefing, the fifteen-hundred-man unit was given the morning off.

Detective Merriman Gosani left the barracks at 7:25. He wandered into an office complex whose main floor had been converted into a recreation hall. Despite the hour, men lingered everywhere, bored warriors awaiting the call of the bugle. Card games flourished beside improvised crap games. Darts, chess, and daydreaming. The level of noise testified to the fact that zero hour was still a day and a half away.

A lecture hall had been converted into a movie theater. Merry stepped over and around bodies squashed together like sheep at shearing time. Cigarette smoke formed thick columns against the ceiling. The smell of stale beer hung in the air. The movie was American, presented in English. *Butch Cassidy and the Sundance Kid*. Merry wondered how many in this largely Bantu audience understood the language. No one seemed to care.

He waited ten minutes in line for a beer, watched the movie until Butch and Sundance sailed off a cliff into a raging river, and then slipped out a side door onto a courtyard that led to the control tower.

Merry peeled the paper off his last toothpick. Guards, in teams of two, patrolled without any apparent pattern. Had they seen Merry, or cared, the beer and toothpick would have seemed a sufficient explanation. No one questioned him. They were, after all, on the same side; the thought came upon him without warning and felt too good to dismiss.

Still, he crossed the courtyard with a certain caution.

Beyond the control tower were three huge cooling tanks made of concrete. Between the tower and the tanks lay a patch of brown grass and a stand of naked fruit trees. Here, three black Africans dozed in the grass, while a fourth read. Merry propped against the trunk of a tree. He sipped beer and studied the lay of transmission lines that crisscrossed the facility, noticing, as he had yesterday, that a single line was strung to a small, freestanding house located to the south just beyond a bank of storage units. As far as he could tell, the storage units had been abandoned; the patrols, by and large, ignored the area.

Merry went back to the movie room for a second beer. When he returned, he sat beneath the same tree, slack and relaxed, his eyes forever busy.

At 10:30, the first lunch whistle sounded.

At the sound of the second whistle, fifteen minutes later, Merry clambered to his feet. He crossed beneath the steel supports of the cooling tanks to the storage area. Shuffling between two units, he slipped along the rear walls and stopped. He pressed against the cool brick and waited sixty seconds.

Then, hands in his pockets, he strolled across thirty meters of drive to the flat-roofed house. He peered through the front window. The door was locked. He circled the house, checking for patrols with lazy side-glances. On the west side, furthest from the plant, he paused. The windows were metal-framed. No screens. Merry tugged at the first, expecting it to be locked, and it was. As was the second.

He stripped off his shirt. He wrapped it tightly about his fist. With the flick of his wrist he punched at the lower corner of the window. The glass splintered. He tapped at it again, and the shards fell silently onto a carpeted floor inside.

Hurriedly, Merry pushed aside the bolt. The window opened without protest. He climbed through, closed the window behind him, and drew the shade.

Perfect, Merry thought. He sat on the floor for a moment surveying the remains of an old medical clinic. Two narrow beds, in whose mattresses inquisitive rats had ripped gaping holes, were shrouded in flakes of white paint. Sterilization paper, now yellow with age and curling at the edges, still covered the examination table. A medicine cabinet had fallen prey to hopeful thieves. Water dripped from a rusted faucet, and the basin was stained yellow.

Merry came to his feet. He scurried from this room into a tiny cubicle that had once surely been a reception area.

Beyond a narrow counter lay the office. An overturned file cabinet blocked the doorway from the inside, so Merry scrambled over the counter. A sign-in board and two yellow files were stacked neatly next to an adding machine and a forgotten coffee mug. Along one wall was a metal desk, an empty in/out tray, a burnt-out desk lamp, and two telephones.

Merry picked up one of the receivers and a severed cord swung disconsolately in the air. Feverishly, he tried the other, and the sweet sound of a healthy dial tone filled his ear. He dialed the number Mansell had given him. It rang three times, and the answering machine at the Clavers' came on the line asking the caller to leave a message at the sound of the tone.

Beads of sweat glistened on Merry's brow. He pounded the desk top.

Finally, he heard the tone and said, "Nigel, you were right. Some group is planning a major military operation against the four gold mines surrounding this joint. Targets: Highland Vaal, Homestake, White Ridge, and Brakpan Holdings. Mode of operation: underground infiltration. Fifteen thousand men, maybe more. It's incredible, pal, and well planned. But there's something here. Something . . . Christopher Zuma's behind it, Nigel. I saw him. I heard his plan. It might work. I'm not so sure it shouldn't, man. You know where Zuma stands. I . . . ."

Merry heard the outer door slam. Footsteps, running. Voices, shouting. He wheeled around. Two men appeared at the counter; one pointed a submachine gun directly at him.

"All right, you. Put the phone down," he yelled. "I order you to put the—"

"Nigel," Merry shouted. "It's not what you—"

The gun exploded. Bullets traveling eleven hundred meters a second ripped into Merry's chest, driving him against the back wall. The phone fell from his hand. Blood erupted from gaping wounds. He crumpled atop the metal desk and slipped down to the floor. He whispered the words "*Sala Kahle*. Don't let me down, pal," and died.

Jaap Schwedler consulted his copy of *A Veteran's Guide to Fellow Vets*. It was a thin volume distributed every five years by the South African Defense Force to veterans of wars gone by. The forgotten remembered; the hidden uncovered.

And therein lay the irony. The irony of overplanning. The irony of overcompensation. For there were no more than three places in the country where Justice Minister Cecil Leistner's private residences or telephone numbers were actually listed. The numbers were not listed with the phone company. Neither Leistner's residence in Pretoria nor his country estate in the mountains near Kruger National Park was listed in any government directory. Not fifteen people, close friends only, knew the estate existed at all.

Certainly Leistner was listed in *Who's Who*, and in the *South African Year Book*, and the *Pretoria Social Register*, and in another hundred different government and social guides. But by name and title only.

The *Veteran's Guide* was an exception. In South Africa, the war veteran was inviolate, sacrosanct. The last bastion of the Voortrekkers and the Boers.

The elder Schwedler found his copy among dusty volumes of L'Amour westerns, the poetry of James Matthews (disguised in brown slipcovers), Alan Paton's *Cry, the Beloved Country*, the plays of Athol Fugard, and the Bible. These were Jaap's personal escapes from a world that had kicked him around for too many years.

It took the old man nearly an hour to summon the courage to dial the number in Capital Park, and he was on the verge of hanging up when a stern voice answered.

"Yes?"

"If I could speak with Cecil, please," Jaap said, clearing his throat. "I mean Minister Leistner."

"The minister is not available, I'm afraid. Who's calling, please?"

"This is Jaap Schwedler from Pampoenpoort. We fought in Korea together. He'll remember. He'll remember."

When Leistner first heard the name, he was puzzled, irritated. And then the knot formed in his throat. History swept before him like the windblown pages of a lost book. A thousand hours of forsaken study welled up in his brain.

"Jaap Schwedler," he said in a hardy voice. "Jaap Schwedler, my old comrade. How are you, Jaap? How are you?"

"Old and decrepit, Cecil," he answered. " 'Minister,' it is now."

"Not to you, old friend." Leistner loosened his collar.

"Sure. Thanks," replied the veteran. "It's been since the fire, hasn't it? No, before. You didn't come back."

What's this all about? Leistner wondered. Why is he calling me?

311

He said, "Sometimes you can't, Jaap. So what can I do for an old friend?"

Schwedler stammered. "Well, it's about that personal file. The one they're doing on you, Cecil. Some of the things I said. Well, I mean about the camps and all. I mean, I was caught off guard and . . . and I sure didn't mean no harm to you or—"

"Hold on, old friend. Slow down." Leistner felt the heat building on the back of his neck. "Now, what in the blazes are you talking about, Jaap? Personal file? What personal file?"

"Well, you know, the investigator from Internal Affairs or something. The one you sent down here to do the update on your life. He said you couldn't remember about Korea. Drugs or some such thing."

"Oh, that. Christ, Jaap, of course. It slipped my mind." Think now, Leistner ordered himself. Think. An investigator in Pampoenpoort? "Can't remember the man's name, Jaap. What was it?"

"Manson, I think, or Mansell maybe. Some bloody English name or another. You know some of those. Anyway, about the war. I didn't mean to imply that you might have—"

"Jaap, Jaap," said the minister in a soothing voice that masked the shock waves flooding his brain. "Of course you didn't, old friend. War, Jaap. It was war. We were all just trying to get out with our skins intact. I know that."

"That's right, isn't it?" Relief filled Jaap Schwedler's voice. "Thanks, Cecil. Thanks for listening."

The minister of justice forced himself into a straight-back chair. He gripped the armrest with such force that blood vessels surfaced in protest. How? he asked himself. It was perfect. It was goddamn perfect.

A chauffeured limousine took Leistner directly to the helipad on Church Street. The Westland-TL landed at the Springs County airport twenty-five minutes later.

The airport manager met the minister at the gate and escorted him to a private lounge above the main terminal. Minutes later, Jan Koster arrived wearing blue jeans, a denim work shirt, and circles beneath his eyes.

Leistner skipped the amenities. "Chief Inspector Mansell has been to Pampoenpoort. There can only be one reason."

"I agree," replied Koster. So, it's begun, he thought. He ordered

312

himself to move with caution. He gestured to a table overlooking the airfield. "I need coffee. Can I pour you some?"

"Tea," Leistner answered.

"How much can he find out?" Koster implored, glancing at the implant scar on Leistner's upper jaw.

"Enough to cause problems, especially now. He's got to be stopped."

"Yes. Unfortunately, it doesn't stop there, I'm afraid," Koster announced. "We have a second problem. And it's certainly related. We've been infiltrated."

Leistner's head jerked up in response. Tea sloshed over the rim of his cup onto his fingers, but he seemed oblivious.

"Explain," he said.

Koster did so, adding, "We found the real Uzo Egonu outside the property at about eleven this morning. He had the impersonator's I.D. The bad news? He was a P.E. cop."

Leistner shook his head. "And has Blue Strike Team been briefed in the last thirty-six hours?"

"Saturday. So he knew plenty," answered Koster. "We know he made his connection, and we know Mansell was the target; he used his name. But the call was picked up by an answering machine, and we're fairly certain he didn't finish his message."

"How reassuring." Leistner sucked vigorously on the tip of his pipe, strumming at the tabletop with his fingers. Aggravated lungs revolted in a spate of harsh coughing. "All right, if he did make his connection, then you should've been able to trace the call. Has that been done?"

"It came through just as I was arriving here."

"And?"

"And it's a private residence on Northview Avenue in Port Elizabeth. The owner's name is John Claver. Records indicate that he and his family have been out of the country since June twenty-seventh. But the house is just six doors down from Mansell's own place and—"

"Good God, man." Leistner set aside his pipe and jumped to his feet.

"There's a squad of policemen standing by in P.E. right now. They're waiting for orders."

Leistner set out for the door. The porter was stationed outside in the hall, and the minister of justice ordered a telephone brought to the room at once.

The house smelled of bacon and eggs.

It was ludicrous. Mansell knew that. Yet it all seemed so natural. They awoke an hour before noon. They made love, leisurely at first, like a sailboat on a still lake, pushed by a gentle breeze; a gentle breeze that grows with each passing breath, becomes a wind, and then a storm, which, at its peak, stretches each sail to its outer limits.

Mansell threatened her with his "famous" french toast, as he called it, but Delaney boasted about her matchless omelets. Impossible to pass up. Mansell brewed tea. They sipped day-old champagne. While Delaney cracked eggs into the pan, Mansell kissed the back of her neck and ran his hands over the gentle slopes of her hips.

"Don't you realize what a delicate operation this is?" she said, pushing him away.

"But we're on vacation," he replied. "Free-floating balloons sailing over the ocean. A magic carpet leaping from castle to castle over the snowy peaks of the Alps. Mere mortal eggs would never think of burning. Not today, at least."

Delaney faced him. Her downturned mouth confessed to the fact that such fantasies were difficult for her to imagine. But last night was no fantasy, she told herself, as Mansell bounced from cabinet to cabinet seeking teacups. Delaney watched him, caught in a thousand confusing thoughts. She moved nearer. She put her arms around his waist and kissed him lightly.

"Not today, at least," she whispered. "Shall we eat these merely mortal omelets before they get cold?"

They carried paper plates and champagne into the family room. They huddled on the floor around a mahogany tea table.

"Music," Mansell said suddenly, jumping up. Stereo components and album-filled racks lined one wall. Mansell thumbed through the records and selected two. He held them up. "Debussy or Juluka? 'Tis the fair lady's choice."

"Debussy, of course."

"After all," he said, laughing. It was then that he saw the telephone and the answering machine, on a stand next to the stereo. He hesitated, shaking his head.

Delaney noticed. "Business before pleasure. I know the feeling. Go ahead."

Mansell cued the replay. The tape ran for ten seconds, blank. He was reaching for the stop button when the tone sounded. The connection was poor, obscured further by the sound of labored breathing, but the voice was unmistakable.

"Nigel, you were right. Some group is planning a major military operation against the four gold mines surrounding this joint. Targets: Highland Vaal, Homestake, White Ridge, and Brakpan Holdings. Mode of operation: underground infiltration. Fifteen thousand men, maybe more. It's incredible, pal, and well planned. But there's something here. Something . . . Christopher Zuma's behind it, Nigel. I saw him. I heard his plan. It might work. I'm not so sure it shouldn't, man. You know where Zuma stands. I . . ."

Merry's voice faded. Mansell touched the volume control. Delaney reached for her walking stick and stood up. Suddenly, they heard another voice. "All right, you. Put the phone down. I order you to put the—"

"Nigel," they heard Merry cry. "It's not what you—"

An explosion of gunfire drowned out the words. A deafening blow of silence followed. And then the crack of the telephone hitting the metal desk, shuffling feet, indistinguishable voices, an unseen hand replacing the receiver on the cradle, the hum of a broken connection.

"My God," Delaney whispered. She grasped Mansell's hands.

"He's dead. Just like that. Dead. And he couldn't even finish his goddamn message. We don't even know when. He died for nothing."

"No. No, that's not true," Delaney said coolly. She drew away, peering into his eyes. "It's Tuesday. The strikes. My God, Nigel, they're all striking. The miners, the dockers, all of them. Tuesday night. I should have said something, but . . ."

Momentarily forgotten, the answering machine had continued to play, and Delaney was interrupted by the sounding of the tone.

"Mansell," the tape began, "the house you're standing in will be under siege in a matter of minutes. I would suggest that you get out of there now. Erase this segment of the tape and get the hell out of there."

"That voice!" Mansell exclaimed, realizing the truth of the message. "I know that voice."

Quickly, he rewound the tape. He listened to the message a second time, took the cassette out of the machine without erasing either segment, and slipped it into his pocket.

He took Delaney's hand and led her down the stairs to the guest room. "They'll trace Merry's message. And if I know Security, it won't take long."

They gathered clothes, a briefcase, and a handbag. They raced up the stairs to the rear entrance.

"No," Mansell decided. "The other way."

Hands clasped, they retraced their steps to the front room. Peering through the curtains, Mansell surveyed the street and found it deserted. Keys readied, they stepped out the front door and walked down the drive to the Clavers' Porsche. One key unlocked the doors. A second key engaged the engine. "Don't rush," Mansell whispered.

He backed into the street and headed north. At the intersection of Northview and Cherrywood, they were forced to the side of the road as two police cars with lights flashing swept around the corner.

Once they had passed, Mansell pulled into the intersection. He saw two unmarked cars dashing down the alley. In the rearview mirror, he watched as four black-and-whites formed a barricade around John Claver's house.

Two blocks further on, he turned left onto Lancaster and then again onto Burton. As they approached Newton Park, Mansell bypassed the N2 freeway exchange in favor of the M15 secondary road a kilometer ahead. He swept brashly around the arm of the cloverleaf and headed southeast out of town.

"You didn't kill Steven de Villiers, did you?" Delaney said, the words catching in her throat.

"No, Delaney, I didn't," Mansell answered woodenly. The horizon captured his attention. Heat mirage danced across the highway, mesmerizing him. He explained about the stolen gun, the rental car, and the phony witness, and, for the first time, he considered what probably happened that day in Johannesburg when Delaney was accosted by Security Branch. He glanced in her direction. "I imagine the minister of justice is a highly persuasive man."

Delaney hid her surprise. "Don't embarrass me."

"There's nothing to be embarrassed about."

"Then don't patronize me."

"I think it's more than patronization, Delaney."

"I know. I know. But . . ." She touched his arm. "After Amanda died. After my husband fell in love with the bottle. And before I forgot what a miserable ally self-pity can be, I was introduced to Cecil Leistner. At a cocktail party in Durban. He . . . we . . ."

"Yes, I know . . . about that." He peered into dark, sad eyes.

316

Had anything ever mattered less than that, he thought, or more than this? "I understand."

She touched his arm again. "Nigel. What Merry said. About the mines. He died believing in it. You know?"

Mansell kept his eyes on the road. No, I don't know, he told himself, fishing for a cigarette.

The Porsche breezed through a hairpin turn, and M15 dropped into a low, flat plain with fertile farms and grazing horses. Delaney said no more about it. Ahead, a thick stand of cottonwoods hovered along the banks of the Baakens River. A narrow bridge signaled their exit from Sunridge Park into the township of Lorraine. They followed the highway for another two kilometers until they came to Theescombe. At the edge of this tiny town, Mansell pulled into the gas station where Joshua had first located the Honda Civic used by Fredrik Steiner.

He parked the Porsche toward the rear of the station next to the rest rooms. As they were climbing out, Bobby Verwaal sauntered around the corner wiping grease from his hands and chewing on the short end of a stogie.

He gave the Porsche an indifferent stare and grunted. "So it's you again."

"Yes, Inspector Mansell." They shook hands. Mansell introduced Delaney, and a crooked smile split the Afrikaner's face.

"Saw in the papers that you found that hustler you was looking for, except it looked like somebody else found him first."

"Vigilantes," Mansell said, putting an arm around the attendant's shoulders. "Tell me about the narrow-gauge, Mr. Verwaal. When does the next outbound train leave, do you know?"

Bobby Verwaal peeked shyly over at Delaney. His crooked smile turned into a broken laugh. "You're in luck, Inspector. Not long. Let's go inside and get the pretty lady something cold to drink and we'll check the schedule."

"Not long" meant fifteen minutes, and the 1:20 out of Port Elizabeth was always on time, Bobby Verwaal told them.

"Fine," Mansell said, peeling off R25 from his money clip. "The Porsche. Can I store it with you for a couple of days? It's a bit of a sticky matter, I'm afraid. You know how a car like that draws attention."

"I do indeed," said the attendant, accepting the money with the proper dose of reluctance. "Just happen to have an empty stall out

317

back. Probably keep away most of the nosy folk that might come snooping hereabouts."

Mansell extracted another twenty-five rand from the clip. "Will this cover a lock and key?"

"And a lift to the train depot," answered Bobby Verwaal.

"I'm afraid he slipped through their fingers," Leistner said. "He knew. Somehow, he knew."

"Mansell's no fool," Koster said carefully. "If he heard the message, which we can assume he did, then he probably anticipated the trace, too."

Their eyes met. "The eggs on their plates were still warm."

"He's not alone, then."

"Apparently not. The police are taking prints now." It had to be Delaney, Leistner knew that. Could I have misjudged her? he wondered. No, she's not the kind to let an opportunity slip away, and if she's still with him, then there's still a chance. Yes. I must not miss her call tonight. "He escaped in a metallic-blue Porsche. Arrogant bastard."

"Not for long. It's too obvious."

"We'll have men at every artery leading out of Port Elizabeth by now, and choppers watching the roads. The train stations, the airports, the ports. They'll all be under surveillance. We'll find him."

"Yes, but the question is not how he's traveling, but where. The man's under a federal warrant for first-degree murder. That puts him at odds with every cop in the country."

"He'll go to the media, of course. One of the English papers. *The Argus* or the *Daily Mail*. Or somebody from the west, perhaps. *Time* or *Newsweek*."

Koster took his time, shrugging. "But with what? He's dealing in rumors, not facts. How much can he really know?"

"He knew enough to dig out Jaap Schwedler in Pampoenpoort, and he knew enough to dig out Cyprian Jurgen in Pretoria. He's heard my name mentioned in connection with East Fields, and he knows that American weapons were smuggled into Port Elizabeth and taken to East Fields." Leistner toyed with his pipe, almost leisurely. He struck a match and smoke mushroomed overhead. "He knows plenty, but the guns might just be his weak spot. Mansell,

318

for all his cleverness, never did report the discovery of those guns, did he?"

One hundred and forty kilometers out of Port Elizabeth, on the floor of a wide vale alive with cactus, aloes, and herds of Angora goats, the train slowed. The town of Klipplaat, population 3,121, prepared for the afternoon arrival of the narrow-gauge.

The conductor made his announcement, and the train stopped a half kilometer from the station beside a water tower. Mansell cracked the window and peered out at the station ahead. He saw six uniformed policemen pacing uneasily along the platform. His trained eye also spotted a pair of plainclothesmen braced against a pillar, scanning folded newspapers and chewing toothpicks.

He took Delaney by the hand. They stepped onto the platform between cars and jumped off the train on the left side. Directly across the tracks was a huge feedlot, a corral filled with Herefords, three grain elevators, and a series of broken-down sheds. Beyond the sheds stood a brick warehouse and a four-story office building, and, further yet, tree-lined streets and clapboard houses built on rolling knolls.

The train moved again just as they reached the far side of the feedlot. A dirt path littered with sheep manure led past the sheds to the office building. An Office Space for Rent sign was plastered across the lobby window.

They went inside. The walls were a dusty cream color. A water stain shaped like an oil derrick sagged beneath a whining air-conditioner. The receptionist wore curlers in her hair, turquoise jewelry on every finger, and was reading *Sun City* magazine.

Delaney offered a cool smile. "The office space for rent. How large is that, please?"

The receptionist blew her nose. "A hundred and twenty square meters, as is."

"We'll take a look, if we may?"

Exuding exasperation, the receptionist propelled her chair across the floor to a filing cabinet. She produced a key from inside, rolled back to the counter, and handed it to Delaney. "Third floor. Room 303. Help yourself."

The empty office looked down on the station. A dozen passengers disembarked. Seven or eight others boarded. Four of the uniformed policemen circled the train. The plainclothesmen boarded near the locomotive, while the other uniforms worked their way through from the caboose.

Ten minutes later, both pairs emerged near the center of the train. One plainclothesman waved in the direction of the locomotive, and Mansell saw the engineer signal in return. The whistle sounded. The train lurched forward. When it cleared the station yard, the policemen dispersed.

Delaney returned the key, announcing that the space wasn't quite what they were looking for. They located a phone booth, and Mansell checked the local directory. The nearest car dealership was in Jansenville. Reasoning that the local police would be under orders to keep tabs on all car-rental establishments, he set out for the center of town in search of a garage or a gas station.

It was early evening when he came upon a ramshackle garage with the sign TURLEY'S AUTOMOTIVE—BODY WORK AND ENGINE REPAIR. The stalls were empty. Two men in greasy overalls sat in a small office smoking. A wall calendar from A-G Parts Supply featured a buxom blonde in a two-piece bathing suit holding a wrench next to her crotch.

Mansell tapped on the door and walked in. "Good evening, gentlemen."

The two men—an Afrikaner, by his oval, reddish face, and a lanky black—stared at one another. The Afrikaner said, "He talking to us?"

"Gentlemen, he said," answered the black.

"Must be us, then."

They both howled. Mansell endured the joke with a thin smile, and then said, "I need to hire a car to Jansenville."

"Hire?" asked the Afrikaner suspiciously.

"Someone to drive two people as far as Jansenville. My car's there now. The rental agency won't give me a one-way. Bastards tried to rape me for seventy-five rand for a driver. I thought I could do better."

"How much better?" inquired the black man, standing.

Mansell offered him a Camel. He lit one himself. "Twenty-five rand is my offer."

"Fifty and you've got a deal."

320

Shaking his head, Mansell countered, "Twenty-five plus gas both ways."

"Let's take a ride."

Cecil Leistner sat in a leather-bound chair surrounded by oak bookshelves filled with hardbound books and a library of classic film originals. A Waterford tumbler, set atop a marble-faced side table, held twelve-year-old K.W.V. brandy, heated to perfection.

A call from the police commissioner, ten minutes earlier, had informed Leistner that John Claver's Audi 5000 had been located in an alley off Lancaster Avenue in Port Elizabeth. The blue Porsche 911 had been found in storage in Theescombe. The commissioner also said that Mansell and a female companion had boarded an eastbound train there at 1:20 in the afternoon. Security Branch offices along the route had been notified and a full-scale search was now proceeding from Kirkwood east to Klipplaat and as far north as Graaf-Reinet. Both were still at large.

Leistner pushed aside the brandy, grimacing. He checked the clock on the far wall. It was 9:10. He glanced at the telephone sitting on the side table an arm's length away and it rang.

"At last," he whispered.

Leistner activated the tracing module and the tape machine and picked up the receiver.

"Delaney, I've been waiting for your call," he said.

"It's Daniel Hunter, Minister."

"Hunter? Excuse me." Leistner deactivated the tracing device. He drank from his brandy, heavy gulps that pushed the tentacles of panic momentarily from his stomach. "My apologies, Daniel. I was expecting another call."

"You asked me to call on Sunday, I believe, sir."

"Yes I did, of course. What news?"

"Our appointment for Tuesday evening has been confirmed, Minister," the Affiliated Union president said. "Every preparation that can be made, has."

"Very good, Daniel. Likewise from this end. Thank you."

The two-lane road between Klipplaat and Jansenville spanned twenty-nine kilometers of low-lying hills covered with sage and cactus.

321

The '64 pickup covered the distance in forty minutes. Mansell paid the driver R30 and was extremely pleased to see him stop in front of the White Owl Tavern on his way back down the main drag.

Jansenville was, in many ways, a carbon copy of its neighbor, though not on the route of the narrow-gauge and thus a shade less prosperous.

Mansell found the city's one and only car dealership, a Ford New and Used, on the edge of town next to the Angora Inn. The blue-and-white oval sign out front was a mere shadow in the dark. A padlock hung from the door. A Closed sign dangled across the window.

Delaney shaded her eyes and peered through the front window. A single light illuminated a shoe-box office beyond the showroom, and she saw a man leaning across a metal desk going through the drawers.

"There's someone in there," she announced, knocking on the glass. "A nonchalant thief or a disorganized proprietor. I can't tell which."

The man struggled up from the desk, walked halfway across the showroom floor, and squinted toward the window. Finally, he waddled penguinlike toward the door, an immense girth jiggling as he moved. He waved his hands and shook his head.

"We're closed," he hollered, pointing at the sign. "I'm sorry. Closed for the night."

He wheeled away, and Mansell banged heavily on the window. The glass shook in protest. The proprietor pulled up and glanced over his shoulder. Mansell pressed his shield against the pane.

"Open the door," he ordered.

The man lumbered forward. Keys rattled nervously in the lock, and the door caved in. "What is it, officer? We're closed for the night."

Mansell shook his head. He replaced the badge, and said, "Inspector Mansell, Security Branch, Cape Province. Mr. . . . ?"

"Nathan Wolfaardt." Beads of perspiration, like dew on a chilled bottle of beer, popped off the proprietor's brow. He smelled of cheese popcorn and sudden paranoia.

"Mr. Wolfaardt. It's late, I know that." Placate, but never apologize: a Security Branch maxim. "We've got some problems over in Klipplaat. I need an automobile for the night. The department will rent it at full price, insured and guaranteed."

"For what purpose, Inspector? Can't you get a vehicle from the

322

local department? It's just down the street. We're not prepared to handle rentals. Budget Master is only six blocks away. They'll be open first thing in the morning, I'm quite sure."

"There might not be a Budget Master in the morning, Mr. Wolfaardt. A white man, an Afrikaner businessman just like yourself, was killed two hours ago in Klipplaat. Stoned to death."

Lapidation: the black man's sword, the white man's dread.

"Bloody Kaffirs," he murmured, backpedaling.

"A mob scene." Mansell stepped inside. "A dozen businesses have been overrun. A white woman's been taken hostage, and it's spreading. If they reach Jansenville, we'll have more of the same. They firebombed my car, and every police car that's available is already on the road."

"But risk one of my cars? I can't."

Mansell pressed forward. "You can rent me the vehicle, or I can requisition it. Your choice. You have five seconds."

While the proprietor wrote out the order in the half light of his office, Mansell pulled Delaney aside. "You'll stay here tonight, at the inn next door," he said, avoiding her gaze. "Leistner's expecting a call. If you fail to make contact you'll automatically be implicated."

"Don't be foolish!" Delaney exclaimed. She shook free of his grasp. "By now, they know I was in that house with you last night. I'm already implicated."

"Aiding and abetting a suspected killer carries a minimum five-year sentence. You'll tell the minister that you accompanied me under duress."

"If I nearly betrayed myself and you before, that's my business. I have to live with it. Don't ask me to disgrace myself again. And how would you know if I had an arrangement to call the minister?"

"I know," he whispered. He touched her hair, her cheeks, he kissed her lips. Then he withdrew and wrestled a cigarette from his jacket. "You can't help me, Delaney. Not by your presence."

"Nigel, what the hell is going on? You know, you haven't told me one damn thing, really." The proprietor's head popped up, and Delaney lowered her voice. "This thing with the guns. And the strikes. And now the mines. Where does it go from here? You say the minister of justice is behind it all. He says you're a cold-blooded murderer, and a federal warrant is issued for your arrest. Why?"

"Because he's scared. And when a man like Cecil Leistner tastes fear, he becomes dangerous. Dangerous enough to ruin your life, Delaney. And I won't let that happen." Mansell took Delaney's face in his hands. "In one hour you'll place your call. It will be traced, so tell him exactly where you are. Tell him, as far as you know, I'm on my way to Cape Town. Leistner's only real enemies are there, so he might just believe it. But don't mention the tape. If he knows what I know, he'll call off the whole operation."

Delaney stared anxiously into Mansell's pale eyes. She took his hand. "Nigel. . . ."

"Shh. Don't say it. We'll get through this."

In Cradock, a hundred-and-twenty-kilometer drive northeast from Jansenville over an oiled truck route, Mansell stopped at a phone booth across from an empty farmer's market. He dialed Joshua's home phone in Port Elizabeth.

The bearer of good tidings, Joshua said, "When I got back from the Karoo I did some checking on that Sea Lanes bus sleeve, remember? From Anthony Mabasu's locker? The handwriting on the back? Captain Terreblanche's."

"Oliver. Bloody hell."

"And I showed a photograph of Terreblanche to Lea Goduka, Ian Elgin's locker-room sweetheart? Remember the guy who plowed into her car the night Elgin died? Positive I.D."

"I don't get it. How did he get in so deep?" The rumors, Mansell thought. Maybe they weren't rumors after all. Maybe the bastards found out and that's how they got to him. A sudden wind sent chills down his spine, and he asked, "Any progress on the de Villiers thing, Joshua?"

"It seems that Wolffe's principal witness, the dock inspector who said he saw you and de Villiers together the night of his death? It seems he might've had his arm twisted a little. A matter of job security, if you get my drift. I convinced him there were greater powers in the world than our demented Major Wolffe. If you get my drift."

"Charmer."

"There's more," Joshua said. "We found the place where Steven de Villiers was first assaulted. A vacant sixth-floor office in the customs house. Chas du Toits found a series of muddy boot prints. Size 13-E. In the alley behind the building we found another print, same boot, same size. And a tire tread. The tread is a match for the rental that was used to haul the body to the burial site near Sheldon."

"So the killer changed into my shoes there at the river."

324

"Chas found a heel mark from the boot next to where the car was parked. The district prosecutor thinks it might be enough."

"Give Chas my congratulations."

"He'll be thrilled, I'm sure. You know Chas," Joshua replied. "But, we're not out of the woods yet."

"I knew there had to be a darker side."

"Yeah, well, we painted you into a corner with this arms thing by failing to file any kind of a report, even a contingency statement. Leistner's filed a second warrant. This one's a conspiracy charge involving the illegal importation of weapons into the country. Some bullshit like that. But this time their witness is legit. The port systems manager, Von Tonder. Remember him? He's saying you pretty much insisted the crates from ARVA II slide through customs without proper inspection." Joshua paused, and in the silence that followed he could well imagine the look on Mansell's face. He added, "Yeah, and what's worse is this: Delancy's name is on the same charge."

Mansell stared out into barren city streets. A semi roared past. A police car cruised among the boarded-up stalls of the farmer's market.

"Joshua," he said in time, "I need two favors. Delaney's at an inn in Jansenville. Don't ask me to explain. It was a mistake. She'll be picked up before the night's out. Do what you can for her, will you? And your report on the de Villiers murder. I need you to file it, in full, with NIS headquarters in Pretoria. Personal attention to Becker himself. It's got to be on his desk by nine tomorrow morning. And make a note of my impending visit. Can you do that?"

"Consider it done," Joshua replied.

Mansell dialed the Angora Inn in Jansenville. The phone in Delaney's room was busy. He dialed again three minutes later, and the operator answered. She informed him that the number was temporarily out of service.

A t midnight, in a rare television speech that would be flashed around the world throughout the coming day, the South African prime minister announced the formalization of an unrestricted, nationwide state of emergency, to be effective at once.

By way of explanation, the prime minister cited increased anti-government, anti-apartheid rioting, a state of widespread civil unrest, and a marked escalation of violence. The state of emergency, he announced, would empower police to make arrests without warrants, impose strict curfews, seize property unilaterally, and limit press coverage in areas of unrest. Furthermore, persons detained for the inciting of anti-apartheid demonstrations would now face an automatic five-year banning order upon their release. Riot police would henceforth be armed exclusively with live ammunition, and township quarantines would be enforced through the issuance of new "Residence Passes."

While the state of emergency would have no formal boundaries as to its implementation, the prime minister cited Port Elizabeth, Johannesburg, Durban, and Cape Town as areas of particular concern.

Following the announcement, Minister of Justice Cecil Leistner ordered all commando units and Security Branch personnel stationed in the East Rand, with emphasis on the mining corridor surrounding the East Fields Mining Corporation and its neighbors, to new assignments west of Johannesburg near the black townships of Soweto and Duduza.

The motel door shook.

"Open it, Mrs. Blackford." It was more of a hiss than a shout.

Delaney swung her feet off the bed. She stood up and seized her walking stick. The door shook again, the handle rattled, and it opened. Major Hymie Wolffe stepped inside. The gray-and-blue uniform hugged his squat body. Wire-rimmed glasses punctuated layered jowls. Wet ruby lips parted in a thin smile.

He removed black gloves, closing in on her. "Good evening."

"It was," she answered, holding her ground.

Wolffe laughed through his nose; pale cheeks reddened.

"Mansell. Where is he, missy?"

"Gathering roses. I think he smelled you coming."

The fleshy part of Wolffe's hand crashed into Delaney's cheek, driving her onto the bed. "Something tells me you'll remember your manners once we get you to Port Elizabeth, missy."

Principal truck routes led Nigel Mansell from Cradock to the mountain resort city of Bethlehem on the banks of the Liebenbergs Vlei

River north of Lesotho. He stopped, filled the car with gasoline, and drank black coffee.

He set out again without rest, momentum being his sole ally.

Dawn arrived, painting iridescent purples across acres of coniferous forests. Rain cried silver drops that within weeks would touch the trees with snow. Mansell drove in a vacuum of cigarettes and caffeine and saw none of it. What he did see was a drugged-out policeman sitting on his back porch with a telephone in his lap, the survivor of six errant gunshots. What he heard was a single ring and an unfamiliar voice telling him about the warrant for his arrest and urging him to get the hell out of his own house. And what he remembered was that the voice he'd heard that night was the same voice on the tape he now carried in his jacket pocket. And now he couldn't help wondering: how many other warnings and clues had there been along the way?

Mansell entered Pretoria at 10:05 Monday morning without encountering a single roadblock, a positive side effect of the state of emergency, though he was unaware of it at that moment. He parked in an underground lot on Vermeulen Street and found a donut shop one block away overlooking the Apies River. He ordered hot tea and an apple turnover, sat in a corner booth with a view, and opened his briefcase on the table.

Numbly, he extracted paper and pen. Chain-smoking, he began with his personal file on the murder of Ian Elgin, consolidating it to a single sheet of paper and correlating the murder with that of Sylvia Mabasu and, eventually, that of Fredrik Steiner.

Then Mansell constructed a timetable showing each connection between the union leader and the minister of justice. He began with their initial meeting in Durban, in April of 1975, following the harbor strikes there. Subsequent to that, Leistner influenced Elgin's transfer to Johannesburg and the promotions that followed. The next year, 1976, Leistner appointed Elgin to his staff with the Agency on Policy and Security Development. Three years later, Leistner nominated Elgin for the Wiehahn Commission. In 1981, Leistner recommended Elgin for his positions with the Federation of Mineworkers Union. In 1986, his letters of reference secured Elgin's position as board consultant to the Affiliated Union. And finally, the minister's personal involvement—uncommon pressure from above, Mansell called it—in the Elgin-Mabasu murder investigation.

Following that, Mansell chronicled the gun-smuggling operation, beginning with ARVA's first appearance in Port Elizabeth six years ago and ending with the arrival of the last shipment at East Fields five days ago.

The events leading Mansell to Cyprian Jurgen came next. Mansell included the taped conversation in which Jurgen confirmed the minister's lease agreement for the East Fields property, and a recounting of his own visit to the mine site, including photos.

Mansell noted Merry's infiltration into the mine, the taped message, and his death. He wrote the message out in full. Inexplicably, he omitted the warning that followed and left the cassette in his jacket pocket.

And finally, he documented the search into Cecil Leistner's background: the computer room in Somerset-East, the townspeople of Pampoenpoort (here making a special note to validate old Doc Bailey's handwriting on the questionable dental chart), and the Korean veteran in Carnarvon, Jaap Schwedler.

Then, a barrow of half-smoked cigarettes having accumulated in the ashtray like fallen soldiers, Mansell reread his mosaic of speculation and fact. As court-worthy evidence you could forget it. But then, Mansell thought, no one's on trial. Yet.

Outside, fifty kilometers from Pretoria, a cold rain obscured the flashing neon sign that read, THE WITBANK MOTOR INN—VACANCIES.

Inside, beneath the hazy overhead light in room 215, Jan Koster unlocked a slender attaché case. Years ago, the hand-stitched leather case had been a gift from his wife. Tomorrow, he hoped the contents inside might be a gift to her.

Koster extracted, from among dozens of documents, four passports, collaborating visas, and a packet of travel papers. These, Koster knew, represented the bare skeleton of a fictitious family and its fictitious history so totally supported by legitimacy as to be born again.

The names on the passports were Martin Robert Montana, age forty-two, Christina Marie, age thirty-nine, and their daughters, Gabriela Marie, age twelve, and Olivia Lee, age ten. The photographs on the passports belonged to Jan Koster, his wife, Julia, and their own daughters, Tonya and Hannah.

To understand the roots of this masquerade, one had to journey back in time to a January in 1976, when the real Martin Montana

328

was a debt-ridden dairy farmer and the owner of a fledgling trucking firm on the outskirts of Lisbon, Portugal.

Two months before, on November 11, 1975, the Portuguese government had granted its last colonial province, the African nation of Angola, its independence. But independence had not come easily. Years of revolutionary war and months of civil war had devastated Angola. Two-thirds of the country's white populace, most being of Portuguese descent, had fled. The exodus sent Angola's economy tumbling. Stagnation and starvation were rampant.

By January of 1976, a Soviet-backed faction called the MPLA controlled the country, but victory did not solve the problems. The country's new leader, Dr. Agostinho Neto, sent out an urgent plea inviting the Portuguese to return to Africa. As an inducement, all emigrants would be allowed to retain both their Portuguese citizenship and their passports until such time as they themselves saw fit to do otherwise.

It was a generous offer.

The Montanas, weary of Lisbon's military tyranny and Europe's most depressed economy, accepted Neto's offer. On March 16, 1976, they emigrated. They settled in Luanda, the coastal capital dying a slow death. Yet Martin Montana recognized the essential problem at once. The soil along the coast was nearly infertile, the climate dry and stingy. One hundred and twenty kilometers inland, the lowlands ended in a series of abrupt escarpments, and the highlands that lay beyond were fertile and generous. Luanda had always been dependent on the highlands for food, but with the exodus of the white man, transportation of cattle, fruit, grain, and vegetables had ceased.

The MPLA offered Martin Montana a 50 percent working interest in a trucking firm with five idle tractor trailers. Montana opened his first route between the capital and the highland city of Malange.

Eight years later, he owned fourteen trucks and ran three different routes. He bought out his government partners. A long-awaited vacation to Victoria Falls in Zimbabwe was planned. The children, six and four at the time, were old enough to travel, and the train seemed the ideal means. The Benguela Line, a British-built rail system connecting the coast with the African interior and a survivor of years of war, had been reopened to passenger service three months before.

On May 1, 1984, the Montanas departed.

But 1984 was a deceptive time in Angola, peace a mirage. The

MPLA was still locked in a fierce guerrilla war with Jonas Savimbi's UNITA forces and two thousand mercenaries. A sabotaged trestle bridge sent the train in which the Montanas were traveling plunging into a gorge a hundred meters deep. All four perished.

One might call it an odd case of synchronicity that caused Jan Koster to be in Angola that same May. He had come to meet with a mercenary soldier named Colonel Rolf Lamouline. He had come with the intent of recruiting Lamouline for the project at East Fields. As it happened, it was the colonel's squadron that first happened upon the tragic train crash.

Instinct and training drew Jan Koster to read the fatality list. The family of four from Luanda lit a spark he could not ignore. The ages and descriptions were too similar. Koster checked back. Spawned by the MPLA's generous offer in 1976, the Montanas had not yet abandoned their Portuguese passports.

Thus Jan Koster brought the four back to life again.

With Lamouline's assistance, the Montanas were listed among the survivors. After their vacation in Victoria Falls, it seemed the family continued on to South Africa. Pretoria caught their fancy. Their extended vacation became a sabbatical. Letters were exchanged with friends and business associates in Luanda.

Then, through a friend, one deeply indebted to Koster and at that time stationed in the Soviet embassy in Lisbon, unseen hands withdrew copies of four birth certificates from the Social Affairs Office. Postal applications were sent to the Central State House in Lisbon for new passports. A checklist was duly processed. The applications were automatically granted.

Koster received the new passports and birth certificates in August of the same year. Methodically, he pumped life into the Montanas. Drivers' licenses were applied for, bank accounts opened, credit cards issued. Koster purchased and sold a car so the computers at Motor Vehicle would show the Montanas' name. He wrote a contract on a new home in Sunnyside.

He negotiated the sale of Martin Montana's trucking business to a European conglomerate in exchange for stock options. These options he exercised over the years. The proceeds were deposited with the First Industrial Bank of South Africa. Over time, the funds were transferred, at Martin Montana's request, to Citicorp in New York City, and transferred again to government certificates of accrual and Treasury bonds. Property was purchased, in Christina Montana's name, along the coast of Maine.

Then, six months ago, Martin Montana applied for an extended travel permit to Zimbabwe and the United States. The Ministry of Travel and Tourism granted the permit ten weeks later.

Now Jan Koster rechecked the date of departure.

He closed the attaché case, locked the motel door behind him, and drove two kilometers to the Witbank Municipal Airport.

Four years ago, Koster, using his Martin Montana identification, had responded to a Witbank classified ad for an eight-seat Cessna 164. It was a used 1979 model, but the engine had been rebuilt and the price was satisfactory, and Koster made his first payment that day. He rented docking and shed space at the Witbank airport. Over the next year he earned his pilot's license. For the last three years, he had used the Cessna to commute between cities where buying a ticket in a major airport might have aroused curiosity.

Today, Koster filed a flight plan for the following afternoon.

The tower manager knew Koster well by this time, and he raised an eyebrow at the plan. "A bit of an odd one for yourself, eh Mr. Montana? Weather being what it is up there this time of year."

Koster curbed his annoyance. "Vacation. A vacation begins where the people leave off. What better place than the mountains?"

The tower manager booked the Cessna into the Members Only hangar to be gassed up, tuned, and lubricated. The overhaul, he promised, would be completed by noon the following day.

An hour and twenty-five minutes after his arrival at the donut shop, Nigel Mansell stood on a narrow footbridge staring down into the gray waters of the Apies River. Absently, he thumbed through the pages of the completed file. And then he saw those same pages drifting, like falling leaves, into the waiting arms of the river. He saw them riding the rapids. And at the very moment when he saw them disappearing beneath the water forever, a passing patrol car's siren wiped the image from his brain, and he locked the file back inside his briefcase.

Finally, he marched down Edmund Avenue to the vast esplanade fronting the Union Building. He spent five minutes reconnoitering but found nothing out of the ordinary. Still, he felt the warning signs, the wetness along his lower back and the angry fist inside his gut; but there was nothing to justify it.

Inside, he presented his credentials at the reception desk and explained his desire for an audience with General Alexander Becker, the head of the National Intelligence Service.

The receptionist studied her daily log and then peered back at him. "I'm sorry, Inspector, but my log doesn't show that you have an appointment."

Mansell shook his head. "It wouldn't, no. The telephone. You'll have to use it, I think."

The receptionist did as Mansell suggested, and five minutes later, two uniformed officers materialized. Without preamble, they escorted Mansell to the top floor of the west wing. Corridors adorned in civil service brown-and-cream motif meandered to the furthest reaches of the third floor.

Glass cubicles occupied by curious staff officers and busy secretaries flanked a narrow hall leading to the general's office. The escorts knocked. A brief grunt came from the other side of the door, and they led Mansell inside. Too easy, he thought, anxiety having by now given way to a state of flimsy resolve.

General Becker unfolded from behind a sparse, neatly arranged desk. He was a heavyset man with large flanks and an impervious, sunburnt face.

"I appreciate you seeing me unannounced, General," Mansell said. "I think it's important, sir. Very important."

Becker snorted. He dismissed the escorts with a brief toss of his head, and they were alone.

" 'Unannounced' is not a particularly accurate description, Inspector Mansell." The general held up an official CIB file from Port Elizabeth with Joshua's broken seal, and a handwritten letter, which Mansell stared at but did not recognize. "Your benefactors, it seems, believe it fitting that I know of your existence. An unsigned letter, very convincing, vouching for your good intent and suggesting that in all fantasy there exist elements of truth. Very noble. And a homicide investigation report from a junior detective in P.E. Most impressive. I asked myself, 'Why am I being deluged by junk mail?' When lo and behold, the advertised product shows up at my front door.

"Out of curiosity, I have one of my loyal assistants check into this mysterious entity, and guess what my boy finds out in his travels via the computer circuit? He finds out that our unexpected guest is wanted under a federal warrant for murder." Becker spread his arms, palms up, shoulders hunched. "A mark of excellence? An indisputable recommendation? Well, at the very least, a curious footnote.

"And what else do we know about our cryptic inspector, I ask?

We know your record is without peer. Not a single failure since being elevated to chief inspector. We know you were in charge of the Elgin murder case. We know you thumbed your nose at the incompetents in Security Branch and went out and found the real killer. Except that he'd had an unfortunate encounter with a .45-caliber bullet." The general gestured again, eyebrows raised in mock amazement. "People dropping like flies and the chief inspector is canned from the case? One might say . . . interesting.

"And just a pinch of spice to an already tangy stew. This morning our distinguished minister of justice issues a second complaint against our uninvited guest. Gun running? You, Inspector Nigel Mansell, are certainly a puzzle with many pieces."

Mansell drew a deep breath. "Tip of the iceberg, I'm afraid, General."

An icy chuckle indicated the uselessness of Mansell's statement, and Becker said, "Some tiny bird told me I might expect that, Inspector."

"General. Those men out front," said Mansell, gesturing toward the door. "Would they be from Security Branch, sir?"

Brow furrowed with annoyance, General Becker punched his intercom button. Mansell tugged at the knot of his tie.

"Yes, sir?" answered a secretary.

"Miss Miller, bring in some tea, if you would." Becker punched at the button again, and the two men gazed at one another. "NIS functions of its own accord, Inspector Mansell. If I want your head broken, I'll use my own head breakers. Call it egocentric, if you will, but Security Branch is not the first name in our directory. Understood?"

"An eloquent explanation. Thank you," said Mansell, hoisting his briefcase onto the desk top.

"But understand this," Becker said, after Miss Miller had delivered a tray filled with hot tea, honey cakes, and ice water. "This office is not in the habit of harboring suspected criminals of any kind. You're fortunate indeed to have a sharp detective and an even sharper forensic scientist for friends. They've stuck their necks out for you, Inspector. Now maybe you'd better tell me why."

Mansell ran a hand through his hair. "It is my belief, General, that Minister of Justice Cecil Leistner is somehow involved in a plot to . . . jeopardize the current structure of our government here in South Africa. Perhaps . . . overthrow it, sir."

Thirty-two years of intelligence work prepared a man for a great many shocks, but this statement nearly unraveled Alexander Becker. He scurried for a prop and found a half-smoked cigar in his top drawer. He considered the man seated before him—his record, his possible motives. He considered the minister—what he knew about Leistner, what he didn't.

"A little restructuring might be in order," he said. "But I doubt our esteemed minister is the man for the job. Present your case, Inspector."

"For the last six and a half years, Minister Leistner has had a working lease agreement for an inactive gold mine called East Fields, located on the East Rand. Over the course of the last five years, East Fields has been the recipient of six large shipments of American weapons, all smuggled into the country on a Liberian freighter called *ARVA II*. Ian Elgin was the link between the freighter and safe passage through customs in Port Elizabeth."

Mansell passed Becker the written statement concerning the mine and the cassette tape from his meeting with Cyprian Jurgen. Becker ordered his secretary to bring in a tape player and read the statement aloud. When the tape player arrived, Becker listened soberly to the Jurgen conversation.

"The last shipment of guns arrived on the fourteenth. Elgin wasn't there, but I was." Mansell used Delaney's photos and his own from East Fields to supplement the account of the shipment's transferral.

Becker held two of these aside, the first showing Andrew Van der Merve standing next to a Hino tractor trailer in front of the East Fields entrance and the other of an unidentified man standing on a flatcar inside East Fields. "These two. Who would they be?"

Mansell explained to the fullness of his knowledge, and Becker used his intercom again. A staff officer entered the office ten seconds later. "Find me these faces," Becker snapped. "Priority one. Handle it yourself, Sean. They could be nationals, but chances are they're not. No assumptions."

Sean departed. Mansell passed the transcript of Merry's taped message across the desk. "A friend sacrificed his life to find out what was going on in that mine." He gestured sullenly at the transcript. "Not a very fitting epitaph, is it?"

Becker ignored the remark. "Zuma? You're sure of that?"

"It's him."

Becker tugged at his ear. "Zuma and Leistner. It's a bad fit, Inspector. Not logical." The general drew a deep breath and slapped the desk top. "And you say that D-day is the twenty-second. Tomorrow. Why?"

"Because a million and a half black workers will walk off their jobs tomorrow night, at midnight," Mansell replied, elaborating. "Infiltration will occur simultaneously. Not a half-bad plan, is it?"

"Truly? Quite a revelation considering the number of yo-yos Security Branch has lurking around inside every union in the country, don't you think? One might question your source."

"Affiliated Union President Daniel Masi Hunter."

"Indeed? And how did you pry this information out of our ebullient fat man, Inspector?"

"A woman in a position of power hears things, General." Reluctantly, Mansell brought Delaney into the picture again.

"A resourceful lady, your Mrs. Blackford," mused Becker, "but hardly reliable considering her current status, don't you agree?"

"No I don't agree, General, considering the current position our minister of justice finds himself in."

"And the minister is behind all of this?"

At last, Mansell fell victim to the need for a cigarette. He brushed aside slack hair again and sighed. "General, it is my . . . suspicion, sir, that Cecil Leistner is not the man he claims to be. I have reason to believe that the minister is not the same person who grew up in Pampoenpoort during the thirties and forties, nor the same person who went to Korea in 1950 as a navigator and who was shot down and taken captive in Communist-held North Korea."

Without hesitating, Mansell laid two photographs of Cecil Leistner on the desk in front of the general. The first, from the current *Who's Who in South Africa*, showed the minister seated behind his desk, glaring soberly at the camera, poised, with a pen in his right hand, to sign a document. The second, from the schoolmistress in Pampoenpoort, showed a smiling youth behind a drooping tennis net. He was swinging an old wooden racquet, with his left hand.

"They're not the same man, General." Mansell gestured at the signature at the bottom of the high school photo. "According to Miss Goosen, young Cecil did everything left-handed. In her words, he couldn't eat an apple with his right hand if he was starving to death."

During the next hour, the general rarely spoke. He borrowed cigarettes from Mansell and ordered more tea. Mansell related what he had learned from his visit with Lloyd Chesney and his Uncle

Jason—the death of Leistner's parents a week before his return from Korea, the fire that destroyed family and school records, the funeral, the son who never returned—and his visit with Doc Bailey, and the dental file that had left the dentist so nonplussed.

Becker sent out the dental file and the photograph of the tennis player for handwriting analysis at Central Forensic, and Mansell explained about Sheena Goosen and Jaap Schwedler, about Korea and the prisoner who never returned.

"The real Cecil Leistner was killed in Russian-occupied North Korea shortly after his capture in May of 1950. His mother and father were murdered the week before his apparent release, on December 31, 1950, and the better part of his history perished in a fire the following day. His replacement entered South Africa, unencumbered, days later, and he now resides in an office in this same building."

"It occurs to me, Inspector," Becker implored, pulling absently at his ear, "that you're, no doubt, quite pleased not to be presenting this fascinating account in a court of law."

"In all honesty, there's not another person in the country I could have presented this case to, General. I'm not seeking indictment. Simply action. Investigation. Someone who can read between the lines."

Becker's head bounced rhythmically in response, and his eyes fell upon a photograph on the far wall. A tall man, older, with a bushy moustache, dressed in the uniform of a brigadier. "Remember the Muldergate scandal, Inspector?"

"Of course," Mansell said, curbing his impatience. "Prime Minister Vorster's feeble attempt to buy support for his party's racial policies."

"Feeble? Not really. The Department of Information had a secret slush fund worth about two hundred million rand. They were planting stories in every major newspaper in the world. Bribing journalists, blackmailing unsympathetic politicians, murdering uncooperative businessmen. They were a day away from buying the *Washington Star* newspaper for eighty million dollars when my papa got wind of the whole affair. Papa was with Military Intelligence at the time. He blew the whistle. And died a week later in a car accident. An 'apparent' heart attack, they said. Except I couldn't get them to do an autopsy. . . . No, they had him killed, all right, but I couldn't prove it. I got promoted instead."

Mansell glanced now at the photograph, and he was taken by a certain . . . vitality in the elder Becker's eyes. "I'm sorry."

"Papa was a fool. He thought we could work this race thing out in peace. You know, like intelligent human beings." Becker tapped an unlit cigarette against the desk top and then tossed it aside. "No, Inspector. We stood face-to-face with the harbinger, heard the foretelling of our own dim future, and then proceeded to ignore every word."

What Mansell wanted to say was that it sounded like something Jennifer would have said five years ago, but he didn't.

"General, we don't have much time."

"Accusing a cabinet minister of treason requires time, I dare say."

A last report, the timetable underscoring the connections between Leistner and Ian Elgin, passed into Becker's hands. He read it slowly, grunting twice and chuckling once.

"It fits," Mansell said. "Within six months of Elgin's appointment to the Wiehahn Commission, they presented strong recommendations in favor of black unions."

"True. But it was long overdue. It proves nothing except that a scared white ruling minority moves damn slow." A knock echoed from the office door, and Becker growled, "Enter."

The staff officer named Sean tossed the photo of the man standing on the flatcar at East Fields onto the desk. "We're still working on this one. No criminal record here or outside the country. We're running it through the photo bank now."

Sean scratched his nose. He set Delaney's photo of Andrew Van der Merve and a ream of computer paper on the desk. Becker ignored both. "And the other? Am I supposed to read your mind?"

"They slipped one past us, sir," Sean said, finally. "The man's name is Alexis Chervanak. We list him as a major with Soviet GRU, Military Intelligence. Interpol confirms. Last seen in 1984 at an embassy function in West Berlin in honor of our own Foreign Minister Botha. Chervanak was born in Leningrad in . . ."

Languidly, Becker raised a hand. "Thank you, Sean. That's sufficient. Stay in the office. I'll need you later."

Ten minutes later, the dental files from Doc Bailey and the tennis photo returned. This officer was younger than Sean—upright, serious, confident. A crew cut, narrow print tie, wing-tipped shoes, and, Mansell thought, a definite future in the spy business.

"Most significant," the officer explained, "is the screw implant. A new tooth is actually connected to the end. . . ."

He saw the general shaking his head. "Thank you, Mr. Whittner. The handwriting?"

"On the dental chart in question, a masterful forgery. Dressler down in Forensic says it's as good as you'll ever see. Slight distortions in pen pressure and on the terminal strokes were the only flaws. As for the signature at the bottom of the tennis photo, well, Dressler said the person was obviously left-handed, and was that all you wanted to know."

Becker nodded briskly, crushing out a cigarette. Mr. Whittner recognized the dismissal and departed.

They sat in silence. Mansell closed his eyes. A stillness near sleep filled his brain. He listened to his heart beat, an old stakeout trick. He returned to the room moments later and a wall clock that read 4:12. Had they been at it that long? he wondered. Less drained than he had been in days, Mansell smoked for pleasure. He glanced at Becker, lost in thought, his fingers drumming the desk top. Suddenly, the fingers stopped, the hand froze in midair. A moment later, the meaty paw slapped the desk and then punched the intercom.

"Miss Miller, send in Sean and Mr. Whittner, please."

"What now, General?" asked Mansell.

"You'll stay with us for a time, I believe, Inspector."

Alarm slashed through short-lived relief. "In what capacity?"

"Inspector Mansell, you are in the dubious position of being a wanted man. Wanted, no less, in connection with two felonies." Becker arose. He patted his stomach and straightened his tie. "Your presence on the street would be a dereliction of my duty, would it not?"

"You're detaining me."

"Such a stringent term, 'detention.' But, yes, for a time."

"So it seems," Mansell said as the door opened behind them, "that the split between Security Branch and Intelligence isn't so complete after all. Maybe you'll have the minister pop over for a visit. Later, after tea, of course."

"Ah, yes. The South African Conflict, Inspector. Never forget it. It rules our lives like the absence of water rules the desert. Unto thine own self be forever partial. Unto thy neighbor, whatever his color, be forever suspicious.

"You see, Inspector, he who says that a saint is a saint until he proves himself a rogue has not lived in South Africa. Gentlemen,"

Becker said to his assistants, "please escort our guest to chamber 320."

In an interrogation room on the tenth floor of the Hall of Justice, Major Hymie Wolffe stripped off a gray shirt yellowed by perspiration. He stirred sugar into chifir. A bead of sweat rolled down the bridge of his nose, lingering at the tip.

He approached the suspect, who was seated beneath incandescent spotlights, a cedar walking stick clutched between her legs.

"Where did Chief Inspector Mansell go after he so ungraciously dumped you in that motel room in Jansenville, Mrs. Blackford?"

"He said something about fly fishing for anchovies off the coast of Cape Town. I wasn't interested."

Wolffe rushed forward. Hot tea spilled on Delaney's thigh, causing her to cry out. He wrenched the walking stick out of her grasp.

"Drink," he shouted, forcing the teacup into her hands. Wolffe held the stick at each end. He raised it high in the air. With a thick groan he brought it down across his knee, and the cedar shaft splintered. "Drink your tea, missy."

Chamber 320 wasn't a jail cell, nor a dungeon, nor even a keep. Comparatively speaking, Mansell thought, it resembled a hospital room. Freshly painted white walls, clean sheets, a private bath, a television set. Yes, all except for the solid door, the dual dead bolts, and the wrought-iron bars across the window.

A carton of cigarettes, his brand, lay in the middle of the bed. A tiny refrigerator was stocked with bottles of Castle Lager. Signs of a well-laid plan.

Enraged by the futility and the deception, Mansell slumped on the windowsill, gazing through checkerboard bars to the south, past the valley to the dirty brown hills on the highveld. The Voortrekker Monument, a squat tribute to General Alexander Becker's cynical views, stood atop the highest of these.

Cynical though his views were, Becker was right about one thing, though, Mansell thought. The black unions were probably long overdue back in '79. He remembered Jennifer lobbying in their favor. He remembered feigning indifference, but when pressed, arguing intellectually against the idea. He'd cite the decay and decline of Nigeria, Zaire, Chad, or Uganda. Black African nations freed from colonialist rulers, thrust into civil war and eventually into tyranny. Military suppression, the black market, fallen bridges, idle factories, starving babies, bankrupt economies propped up by the Western countries they so conveniently disdained.

God, he thought, the arguments sounded so shallow now. Yeah, it was his usual devil's advocate routine—they would argue for hours, sipping wine and watching the stars—but now all he could feel was embarrassment.

Mansell slid off the windowsill and stretched out on the bed. The room paled as evening wrestled another day away from the setting sun. He tucked a pillow beneath his head and lit a cigarette. But there was no solace in either physical comfort or nicotine, and he crushed the cigarette out in an ashtray. He closed his eyelids in self-defense. Merry's face assaulted him from within. His voice stung Mansell's ears. *It might work. I'm not so sure it shouldn't, man.*

He felt the touch of Delaney's hand on his shoulder. The words were reflected in her oval eyes, but he couldn't understand the smile on her lips. They'd both been through it, she and Merry. And now he was dead, and Delaney . . .

Mansell fell asleep picturing the jail cell, the real jail cell in which Delaney was most assuredly now confined.

General Alexander Becker stood alone in the dark gloom of the NIS filing room in front of the paper shredder. He opened Nigel Mansell's briefcase and carefully laid the contents on the wooden table off to his right. He switched on the pencil flash and stuck it between his teeth. Methodically, he worked his way through the stack, page by page, reading each in full.

The Elgin-Mabasu murder records were essential, and he set these back in the briefcase. The documents and timetable connecting Cecil Leistner and Ian Elgin were also of use, and these he laid on top of the murder records.

From Mansell's chronicles on the gun-smuggling operation Becker extracted any and all information that might indicate a connection with the East Fields mine. These he placed in the mouth of the shredder. What remained went into the briefcase.

The tape and all documentation citing Cyprian Jurgen and his lease agreement with Leistner, and the photos and notes Mansell had taken at the mine, were also placed in the shredder's waiting mouth. Details surrounding Merriman Gosani's infiltration into East Fields and all evidence of his message and death were also fodder for the shredder.

Finally, all that remained was the evidence proving that Cecil Leistner was, in fact, not Cecil Leistner, and this Becker tucked neatly back into the briefcase, which he locked.

Then he turned on the shredder, and all matters pertaining to East Fields ceased to exist.

When he was seated behind his desk again, General Becker hailed Mr. Whittner and the NIS officer named Sean. It was well after midnight by now, but the two were still on call.

"Mr. Whittner. Contact our office in Gaborone in Botswana if you will. The illustrious Christopher Zuma has been holed up there for some time, is this not true?"

"In Moshupa, actually, sir."

"Ah, yes, thank you. I'd like a status report on Mr. Zuma's recent activities, please. Let's say over the last three months, shall we?"

"Something to do with Inspector Mansell, sir?"

Becker was busy rearranging an already well-tended desk. "What? No, hardly. Something else." His eyes widened now in anticipation, his head bobbed. "Tonight, Mr. Whittner, if you would."

When the younger man had departed, the general offered Sean tea, which he declined out of hand. It was a signal; what was to follow would be kept between the two of them, a matter to be handled out of the office and in confidence.

"Sean, I'd like you to contact the SDECE in Paris, please. Section Five. Talk to Colonel Guy Montclair. Drag the old fart out of bed if you have to. Tell him I'm afeared for the life of one Cyprian Jurgen, a prominent South African citizen. Jurgen has a home in Cannes, I'm told, and if the colonel would be so kind as to see to Mr. Jurgen's well-being for the next several days, I would be grateful. Give him my respects and my thanks, and please tell the colonel that a bit of caution is in order unless I'm very much mistaken."

A light tapping at the door nudged its way into the dream he was enjoying, and Becker's eyes popped open. He glanced at the digital clock on his desk and was pleased to see he'd slept less than an hour. It didn't surprise the general that he'd been dreaming about his papa. What surprised him was that it hadn't been the old dream, the broken body inside a demolished car. They were fishing, just the two of them, off East London for garrick, just like in the old days, elfish bait and all.

Refreshed, the general arose. Mr. Whittner, on the other hand, wore an expression caught somewhere between obvious dismay and something that looked like controlled irritation.

"So?"

"It appears we've had a communications foul-up somewhere along the line, General. Over the last three months, except for two day trips to Gaborone, one in late May and another in early June, Zuma never left Moshupa. Not until three weeks ago. The day trips were seen as pleasure. He stayed at the Kensington Hotel on both occasions and received a visit from the same black woman both times. A working girl as far as—"

"Until three weeks ago."

Mr. Whittner sighed. "We lost him, General. He was seen leaving Moshupa by car on the third. An apparent boat switch on the Limpopo River was the last contact of record. Speculation—"

"Is worthless. Thank you, Mr. Whittner. Alert the border-control posts in the area, maybe they've heard something. Continue monitoring Gaborone and Moshupa. He'll show up, I'm quite sure. That's all."

When the door had closed, Becker peeked at the photograph on the far wall once more and nodded his head.

The intercom sounded. The night desk. "Yes."

"Your plane's ready, sir. A car's waiting out front."

"I HADN'T EXPECTED YOUR CALL UNTIL THIS AFTERNOON," SAID Jan Koster, opening the car door for the minister.

Morning stretched its arms around a tawny sun. Coal smoke, the product of last night's near freezing temperatures, added a wisp of reddishness to the eastern horizon. Inside the diner, two policemen drank coffee, and a milkman celebrated the end of his route. The diner smelled of sausage and biscuits.

"A change of plans," replied Leistner. "This will be our last visit together for some time. The wheels cannot be stopped now, Mr. Koster. Inspector Mansell has been taken into custody by NIS. I've heard from Lucas Ravele and Daniel Masi Hunter. Their plans have been greeted with more enthusiasm than even I anticipated. But then power, or the scent of power, is completely corruptible, isn't it? And they all sense it."

"Naturally."

"The announcements will be made at organizational meetings this evening, as planned, and the shutdowns will follow at midnight. News releases for the Western press have already been prepared, of course. Oliver Neff will see to it that they're released shortly after the takeover tonight. Cyprian Jurgen will be killed resisting arrest in France Wednesday morning. I have men standing by. The state of emergency has provided us with an unoccupied East Rand, and,

more important, the justification we were seeking."

"Yes. Truly."

"I will be out of touch until Wednesday night. Out of the city altogether."

"Should I know where?" asked Koster, peering over the rim of his teacup. He knew where already, but the question was required.

"It's not necessary that you know," answered the minister. "I will contact you in Cape Town on Thursday as planned. Pretoria will have Christopher Zuma's demands by then."

Leistner stifled a yawn. He accepted a refill and used the moment to think. His long-range plans included three possible exits from the country should anything go amiss. The information stored in his head alone would be invaluable. Privately, he almost hoped it would fall apart at the last, and he would be ushered home. But the image was tainted, and he knew it; there could be no hero's welcome if this thing failed.

"I can't think of anything else," he said.

"We've created a monster, Cecil."

"The world is full of monsters," countered the minister of justice, laughing.

Leistner placed his call in a phone booth outside the diner. The recipient was a big man who favored bib overalls and dark sunglasses.

"Mr. Koster must not reach Cape Town, is that clear?"

"It can be done as soon as he leaves the mine tonight," the man answered. "The road between Welgedacht and Springs would be perfect."

"Fine," Leistner replied. "Make it look like an accident."

"How will I know him?"

"He'll be driving the blue-and-red Land Rover. The one he always uses."

At 12:45 in the afternoon, General Becker himself delivered lunch. Outside, a storm was brewing. Thunderheads were busy forming jagged shores in which sporadic blue lakes blossomed, grew, and then shrank again.

"You look a little like a ghost after a long Halloween, General," commented Mansell dully, his back pressed against the window.

"I feel more like a poker player after an all-night game and too many martinis."

Becker's normally ruddy complexion was pasty over a day-old shadow. The circles below his eyes accentuated the blood lines in his eyes.

He set a tray of steaming clam chowder, corn bread, a small salad, and hot tea on the stand next to the bed. It smelled marvelous, but Mansell didn't budge.

"A last meal, General?" he suggested. "No thanks."

"Eat, Mansell. You'll need your strength before this day is out. And I need a shave." At the door, he glanced over his shoulder. "I'll be back in thirty minutes. Save me some of that tea."

Becker left the door ajar. Mansell listened to his footsteps, a hollow diminuendo fading down the length of the corridor. He scrambled away from the window, hustled across the cell, and stopped short at the door. Within every overt action, he thought, there lies an overt message. The message was clear enough. There was no place left to run. Mansell walked back to the unmade bed. He devoured the food in minutes, and then decided a shave wouldn't do him any harm either.

General Becker returned dressed in a new suit and smelling of cologne.

"First I fly to Carnarvon and then I drive to Pampoenpoort," he said without preamble. Mansell poured tea. Becker used two sugars and most of the cream. He borrowed a cigarette. "You were very thorough, even a bit creative. Except you discounted the vulnerability of your interviewees. The fear factor, Inspector. It appears the war veteran phoned the minister to apologize for calling him a coward."

"How very human of him."

"Yes. I thought so," Becker said, nodding. "Do you know who Dr. Hendrik Bellof is, Inspector?"

"The plastic surgeon. From Jo'burg."

"Ah, much more than that, really. An anthropologist of some note and an ethnologist as well. His specialty is reconstruction. Animal and human. An old school chum of mine, actually. Had the doctor take a look at some blowups of those photos you dropped in my lap yesterday. The ones of Leistner the tennis player and Leistner the minister. It seems the good doctor agrees with you. They aren't the same person."

"You've detained him, then?"

"It seems our esteemed minister is not available today. His office doesn't know where he is. His housemaid informs us that her employer is out of town, but also doesn't know where."

"But—"

"Does the name Koster mean anything to you?" Becker held up the photo Mansell had taken at East Fields—the man standing astride the flatcar. "Jan Koster?"

For a split second, the hair on the back of Mansell's neck stood up. "We've talked. It was Koster who let slip that Leistner was responsible for Ian Elgin's positions with the FMU. Mr. Koster, the minister, and Elgin all had a common interest. Spelunking. A cave. The perfect setting for discussing matters of—"

"Yes, a triad of considerable influence," Becker agreed. "We've issued a bulletin for Mr. Koster—"

"A bulletin? Why? You know where he is. Just send in a god-damn—"

"Last night I had an air-force Night Scout make a reconnaissance flight over the East Rand. Routine stuff." Becker dropped a manila envelope on the bed. "These are infrared photos of the East Fields mine. I did the blowups myself. I didn't think we needed the extra attention. If you look closely you'll see some tractors, some trucks, a few boxcars, a half dozen flatcars. Forty or fifty men. Armed, yes. But then, armed guards are the rule, not the exception, among gold-mining operations in this country."

"General, this is an underground operation, remember? When Leistner heard from Jaap Schwedler, he probably put a blanket over the whole operation."

"As you might have guessed, I also thought of that."

"Then you've warned the other mines."

"No, I haven't, Inspector Mansell. Yesterday, you mentioned the fact that you couldn't see yourself presenting this case to anyone other than myself. Your decision was a wise one. Trust your instincts." The general arose like a Caesar from his throne. He smoothed his tie and buttoned his jacket. "And now I think it's time for a phone call."

From inside a locked safe in his own office, General Becker extracted Mansell's briefcase. He set it on the desk and returned the key to its rightful owner.

"Excuse me, Inspector, but as I said, there's a call that needs to be made. I'll use my private suite if you don't mind. Make yourself comfortable." There was a door at the rear of the office, and before he reached for the handle, Becker turned and nodded at the briefcase. "There've been some changes made."

Becker's "suite" was a windowless cubicle with a single metal desk, a secretary's chair, two direct-dial telephones, and a telex machine.

The number he dialed was known by only nine others within the South African government and perhaps a dozen others worldwide, a number that connected the caller to a white telephone in the office of the nation's highest-ranking official. It was known, jocosely, as "the white line." The exchange lasted an eternal twenty-five minutes. At the end of the conversation, the telex machine spat out two formal replies, both with the undaunted scrawl of the prime minister at the bottom next to his official seal.

346

When he returned to the office, the contents of the briefcase were laid out upon the desk. Mansell was standing at the window smoking a cigarette. Outside, thunder rumbled dully. Rain painted the streets with liquid coal smoke. Mansell turned and their eyes met.

Becker borrowed a cigarette. Silently, he laid a yellow telex sheet on the conference table, tapped the paper with his index finger, and nodded. Mansell scooped it up. It read:

ORDER #1001

For: Minister of Justice
Cecil Andrew Leistner
203 Cottonwood Road
Pilgrim's Rest, Eastern Transvaal, South Africa

Notice in Terms of Sections [inclusive] of; The Suppression of Communism Act, 1950 [Act #44 of 1950]. . . .

Whereas, I, . . . Prime Minister and State President of the Republic of South Africa, am satisfied that you have engaged in activities deemed suspicious in the furthering, and calculating to further, of the achievement of any of the objects of Communism . . . that your hand may have been involved in the furthering, and calculating to further, of terrorism within the Republic . . . I hereby tender notice subjecting you to immediate detention and questioning by official members of the South African Police Force [SAP] . . . as of this day, the 22nd of July. . . .

Given under my hand at Pretoria on this, the 22nd day of July. . . .

/s/. . . . . .
Prime Minister and State President

"Official members of the SAP, it says." Becker draped his jacket over the back of a chair. "I believe that includes you."

The telex drifted irreverently from Mansell's hand back to the desk top. "I'm not concerned with revenge, General."

"Revenge?" growled Becker. "The man sets you up for slaughter three times. Do I care? Hell, it goes with the job. You got lucky. Now the shoe's on the other foot. This is an arrest order. You carry a CIB shield. Do you want the job or don't you?"

"I've never been moved by flattery, General. No thanks."

Becker's huge head tipped backward and a hearty pistol-report laugh bellowed forth. Then he turned, as if embarrassed, and peered out the window. In time, he returned to the room, business as usual.

"Listen, Inspector. You're as good in your field as they come. Your record speaks for itself. You see things that others don't." Becker punched a finger at the address on the arrest order beneath Leistner's name. "I don't know where the prime minister came by this locale. Hell's bells, man, I didn't even know it existed myself, and that's going some. But the P.M. seemed reasonably certain.

"It's just me and you, Inspector," Becker continued. He glanced at the briefcase. Then he held out the arrest order. "I can't order you about this. Bloody hell, I look at you and I can just imagine your answer if the P.M. himself tried to order you. I need help, Mansell. There's a plane leaving in one hour for Nelspruit, a town right outside of Kruger National. I'd like you to be on it. Find Leistner. The rest is my responsibility."

Mansell glanced outside. Vertical shafts of lightning exploded on the horizon.

"A law officer under federal warrant is automatically stripped of all authority," he said.

"Ah, but I have been remiss, haven't I?" Becker drew the other telex from his breast pocket. "This might interest you."

Mansell read the executive order overriding all federal warrants against Delaney and himself. "Given under my hand," it read. Sure, the hand that slipped the ring on Leistner's finger all those years ago and brought him into the brotherhood, thought Mansell. One good deed deserves a loophole. One misdeed, several.

"At this moment, General, Mrs. Blackford is sitting in a jail cell in Port Elizabeth. A Security Branch jail cell known for more than a few indiscretions." Mansell's fingers curled around the yellow telex. He held it up. "Do they know about this?"

"I'll see to it, Inspector. Count on it."

Mansell tipped his head. He folded both orders and filed them in the breast pocket of his jacket. The general mentioned a military carrier at Jan Smuts Airport and the helicopter waiting downstairs. Becker bummed a last cigarette, and Mansell walked out into the rain.

The evensong of the swallow belied the feverish buildup pervasive throughout East Fields.

Uniformed soldiers lay wide-eyed on bunks smoking cigarettes, sat hunchbacked in the cafeteria drinking coffee, paced with shortened breath and the tangy hue of fever on their cheeks, awaiting orders.

Three hundred meters belowground, six thousand men, soldiers of the initial strike teams, took up their positions in the Weapons Supply Center. M16 rifles and American-made .45-caliber pistols were distributed in an orderly fashion.

In a small office attached to the command center sat Jan Koster. He wore civilian clothes. A small suitcase lay at his feet. Opposite him sat Colonel Rolf Lamouline, in full-dress combat fatigues; a nattily attired Christopher Zuma; and Andrew Van der Merve, a travel bag at his side.

According to their plan, Van der Merve would disappear and Koster would return to Cape Town. He would resume his normal functions with the Ministry of Mineral Resources and Energy Affairs. They would not be in touch again.

Koster hoisted his travel bag. He tossed a set of keys to Van der Merve. "You take the Land Rover. The red-and-blue one parked outside. I'll take the jeep."

"Thanks," said Van der Merve. They all shook hands.

Without fanfare, Koster slipped behind the wheel of the jeep. He watched for a moment as four yellow buses filed out of the compound with the last of the East German engineers and two groups of Cuban advisers.

When the buses were out of sight, Van der Merve pointed the Land Rover for the gate and turned west on R555. Koster followed at a distance. Once past Welgedacht, he saw the flatbed truck ease onto the highway ahead of him.

It wasn't a pretty sight. The flatbed bore down on the Land Rover with such a fury that there would have been no time to react. An instant later, Koster saw the Land Rover crash through the guardrail into a deep ravine, where it exploded into a towering fountain of orange flame.

The flatbed hurried on, and Koster pulled off to the side of the road. He leaned out the window until the nausea passed. Then he made a U-turn and pushed the jeep east until he reached R42. Forty kilometers later he found himself on the freeway, and Witbank was only eight minutes away.

The crackerbox waiting room at the Witbank Municipal Airport was bleak in the last fragments of evening and nearly deserted. The ticket counter had been abandoned an hour ago. A bored clerk sat in the Budget Master rent-a-car booth reading *Rooi Rose* magazine. An out-of-order candy machine and a partially illuminated Coke machine stood watch from the far corner.

His wife and children sat in fiberglass chairs watching the airfield. Koster called out their names. The girls raced into his arms, and he lifted them into the air. He kissed the warm lips of his wife. She touched his face. Survival, he thought wearily, at the price of a last deed.

The Cessna lifted off twenty minutes later. Rain battered the twin engines until it reached altitude above the clouds. Koster checked his flight plan. With a last glance at the East Rand, he explained to his family that the trip to Zimbabwe included a single refueling stop.

Alexander Becker entered the lobby of the Broadstreet International Hotel in Johannesburg at 5:29 P.M. The Federation of Mineworkers Union meeting of local union heads was not scheduled to begin for an hour yet. The convention room on the second floor bustled with last-minute anticipation; sound checks, early arrivals, gossip, a wet bar. Red velvet carpet and crystal chandeliers led him to the platform, where he accosted the general secretary of the union with a single inquiry.

He returned to the corridor. An elevator, glass-enclosed and overlooking lobby fountains lit with gold and white spots and a formally attired woman playing Chopin on a grand piano, carried him to the thirteenth floor.

Gray-suited sentinels flanked each door leading to suites 1301 and 1302. The general flashed his plastic I.D. card, and they stepped mutely aside.

As a matter of courtesy, he knocked, but didn't wait for an answer. Lucas Ravele, the Federation president, sat at a round tea table drinking champagne cocktails with two other FMU officials and a barefooted secretary showing more cleavage than necessary. The sound of laughter and busy glasses ceased as the stranger approached the table.

Becker displayed his magical card again. The three men arose. "Becker!" exclaimed Ravele.

"General Becker," he replied coolly. "I'll need five minutes of your time, Ravele. You and your associates here. In private. It seems there will be an addition to your agenda tonight."

Ravele's eyes widened. Hurriedly, he dismissed the secretary. A bedroom with peach-colored walls and a round bed provided them with privacy.

When the door closed, Ravele said, "General? You said something about our agenda for the night?"

"Well, then you haven't shared the information with your friends." Becker borrowed a cigarette from one of Ravele's comrades and then passed the FMU president a knowing glance. "You'll be looking for a new president tonight, gentlemen. Lucas has tired of union work. He'll be tendering his resignation tonight. Either that or spending a considerable amount of time in Modder Bee Prison. I like to offer a man a choice."

"Meaning what?" blurted out one of the associates.

Becker showered the man with a look of seasoned annoyance. Then he focused again on Ravele. Ravele removed his glasses. With a monogrammed handkerchief he dabbed at the drops forming on his upper lip. He sank forlornly into a nearby chair.

"I was meaning to announce it tonight," Ravele said. He glanced from Becker to his associates. "I'll be accompanying the general when he leaves."

"But the strike," his associate protested. "Lucas, the strike."

Ravele looked in Becker's direction.

"It's a free country, gentlemen," the general said, shrugging. "A union's got the right to strike, doesn't it?"

A fuel leak delayed the departure of the Jetstream TMK for twenty minutes.

The pilot, a grizzly air force veteran named Arthur, barked orders at a frenzied mechanical crew and paced fitfully. Thunder shook rain from black clouds, and night absorbed it like a sponge.

Nigel Mansell borrowed a copy of *The Citizen* from a magazine rack in the hangar. He took an opened can of Coke on board and waited. Nerve ends tingled as each minute passed. He pictured Cecil Leistner getting into the back of a Mercedes limousine and driving to the Indian Ocean. He pictured the fishing trawler off Kosi Bay, rusted and laden with tackle, whisking the minister out to sea. There, off Cape Sainte Marie on the tip of Madagascar, they would rendezvous with a waiting U-boat, and he would disappear along the ocean's vast floor. . . .

The image burst like an iridescent soap bubble as the pilot's menacing growl penetrated the cabin. Mansell stooped to cigarette smoking. New images assaulted him.

He pictured Delaney in an interrogation room with Hymie Wolffe, he in a sweat-soaked undershirt with wide suspenders hoisting baggy pants, his thick jowls pulsating red under her resistance, his bamboo stave cutting through the air. . . .

He saw the squashed remains of Anthony Mabasu in a puddle of red, the lacerated soles of his feet, the twitch of his hand as he died, the shattered window ten stories above. . . .

He saw two bottles of beer, bedewed and green like wild grass on a cool dawn in the fall. Two bottles greeting him on the back porch that day. He heard Merry's voice, chiding him, calling out from the kitchen, *Hey, it's the back-door man.* Then his hand involuntarily sought out the cassette in his coat pocket, the taped replay of Merry's death, bullets tearing away at the image of his face, and the beer bottles exploding in his brain. . . .

Mansell's eyes snapped open. Coke spilled from the overturned can onto his pants, cold and sticky on his thigh. A thick ash broke away from his cigarette, tumbling onto the seat cover. Impatiently, Mansell swept it aside. He glanced through the rain-scarred window and his own reflection peered back.

You see things that others don't, he heard Becker saying. Definitely a cut above, thought Mansell, cursing himself. An investigator's investigator. Indeed. Dead bodies strewn like broken matches along his inglorious path, the chief inspector stumbles from one enlightened clue to the next, pasting them together like a child's collage to be displayed, after a little parental praise, for a day on the refrigerator. Thrilled, the inspector bungles on until, at last, he finds his place in a leaky craft without wings. A marvel of modern police science.

Maybe, he thought, looking for grains of conciliation, if the General can—

He felt a hand on his shoulder. The hiss of jet engines filled his brain. The copilot's voice called out, saying, "We're out of here, Inspector. Buckle up and stash that pop can."

The Jetstream taxied momentarily. A touch of the throttle sent ripples of G-force against Mansell's chest, and relief washed over him. They lifted into the air at an abnormally steep angle. Clouds smothered the craft briefly, and then he saw stars.

"**R**ead this."

The Durban headquarters of the Affiliated Union of Dockers, Stevedores, and Rail Workers on Point Street reeked of cigar smoke, expensive whiskey, and fat wallets. The National Intelligence Service officer, a captain in rank named Sean, shoved a piece of foolscap in front of Daniel Masi Hunter's massive face.

Sean raised his voice. "You do read Afrikaans?"

The clamor in the room paused on a precipice between shock and indignation.

Hunter glared back at the smiling face. The Harbour Association, he thought undaunted, had indeed played a weak hand, sending a hatchet man into his arena. Were they seeking to enrage or simply embarrass?

"It may be wise, sir," the fat man interjected, "for you to identify yourself, lest you find yourself being removed from the premises like a common criminal. But then, the choice is yours, I suppose."

Feigning embarrassment, Sean said, "How rude of me. Of course. I do apologize." A smile, this time briefly displayed, fell away like breaking glass. The NIS card materialized from inside his wallet. He tapped the paper dangling from Daniel Hunter's hand. "Read it."

While the Affiliated Union president read through the short communiqué, Sean poured whiskey into a shot glass. He surveyed the room without apprehension. The general had told him to do it alone. Sideline work, he called it. Which meant The Company didn't know. Which meant the general was out on a limb and asking for a good measure of trust. He only needed to ask once. Sean swallowed the shot in one neat motion.

"Plans change, Hunter," he said. "You're a resourceful SOB, you'll find another line of work."

Calmly, Hunter passed the paper to an associate. "I was hoping to choose my own successor."

"Well, there's always the strike," Sean said. He watched the message take effect. Hunter offered a brief nod.

"My legacy. I see." Hunter saw the paper moving among his

retinue. Quickly, he shook a half dozen hands and whispered in a half dozen ears. Then he finished his drink and followed the NIS officer to the door. "Shall we go?"

By nine o'clock, Blue Strike Team was armed and in position in the vast hull that was Supply Central. By 10:30, the connection tunnel leading to Target Three was filling with sweat-soaked men wearing combat helmets and camouflage fatigues.

At the tunnel's entrance, a lonely man, appointed to a lonely task, took up his station at the detonator box attached to the explosives in the access shaft, completely unaware of the fact that the detonator had been defused days before.

Inside the tunnel, long strands of incandescent bulbs illuminated craggy stone walls. Generators toiled endlessly, pumping cool air throughout the system.

Ten minutes later, like their counterparts lying in wait beneath three other targets, the first soldiers started up the iron ladders that hung from the walls of the dead access shaft. In the work station forty meters below the Homestake Mining complex, they would await the final signal.

By day, Nelspruit was a flourishing farm community. Fertile plains and temperate weather combined to produce citrus groves laden with oranges and lemons and subtropical farms rich in papaya and guava.

By night, most of Nelspruit's twelve thousand inhabitants slept a contented sleep. The comings and goings of a military turboprop concerned them not, nor the blustery crosscurrent that shook the plane as it made its approach. When the tires finally touched ground, Mansell relinquished his grip on the armrests. He searched his pockets for a cigarette. A single runway led to a terminal built as low to the ground as the countryside it served.

Mansell descended the ramp to the runway, where a military car awaited him. He dismissed the driver and slid behind the wheel. Having spent the last half hour of the flight absorbing a road map of the eastern Transvaal, he pointed the car north on a meager two-lane road called R37.

Almost at once, the Drakensberg consumed him. The road narrowed, climbed, and meandered. A black sky exploded with starlight. Steep slopes laden with blue gum trees and capped by Black Reef quartzite surrounded him. Lush valleys opened up at the base of the mountains to wide floors strewn with beehive huts and rondavels. Small fires were visible here and about, smoke rising from thatch-roofed huts. Mansell glimpsed the checkerboard outline of mealie gardens and herds of cattle dozing within their pens.

Night deepened. The mountains grew in ruggedness and mystery. Traffic, heavy with tourists during spring and summer, dwindled. Beyond Sabie, Mansell passed a tractor, a semi, and a half dozen cars. At a diner outside of Mac Mac, he saw a highway patrol car, two campers, and a pickup filled with migrants. Slowly, adrenaline seeped into his system.

Like a circular staircase, hairpin turns led Mansell to the verge of a great divide eighty kilometers from Nelspruit. A narrow tunnel brought him to the other side high above a wooden glen. He parked in an alcove overlooking the valley. He climbed out of the car, fished for a cigarette, and hopped onto the hood. Below, antique lamps twinkled softly. Smoke rose from an occasional stone chimney.

Pilgrim's Rest, like much of South Africa, was a product of gold. The first discovery there was made in 1873. Easy gold diminished twenty-five years later, and the village was declared a national monument. Still, prospectors continued to mine the hills, and trout and perch continued to inhabit the red waters of the Blyde River. In time, the wealthy discovered the town. Now manors hid in the hills, estates blossomed on the valley floor.

Mansell studied the view for five minutes, seeking a logical plan for the arrest of the country's highest legal authority. The flimsy yellow telex containing the arrest order didn't feel very substantial in this wilderness. He was, quite suddenly, aware of the vague tentacle creeping through his system, the moisture gathering, despite the chill in the air, at the base of his spine, and it was almost a relief identifying its source. Fear, Mansell knew, was a tonic. Dreaded or not, it still served its purpose. His one ally, he decided, would be the minister's desire for anonymity. The veil of secrecy. Or would it? Would subterfuge take a backseat to security? He prepared himself for the obvious—armed guards, electrified fences, dobermans, a helicopter pad—and hoped his experience would seek out the less obvious, the trapdoors. He was drawn to the nine-millimeter Browning sagging uncomfortably beneath his arm. He tightened the harness. It was still uncomfortable, still of very little comfort. He jumped down from the hood and climbed behind the wheel again.

As he stood in the dark beneath a leafless tree somewhere in the heart of the East Rand, his hair matted from the rain, alone, cigarette butts collecting at his feet, General Alexander Becker felt about as lonely as he ever expected to feel. What in the name of God had he done? There was no one to put the question to. It would stay within him, a condemned prisoner gnawing at hardened steel bars, for the rest of his life.

There was nothing to do but wait, and think. . . . A memory took him momentarily back to the dirty streets of Soweto, in '76, when the Zulu clashed with Security Branch. Homemade spears were no match for the bullets and the tear gas. A baby died in his arms that day. He saw a black woman with a diesel-filled tire around her neck, burning to death. He tried dousing the flames as black smoke ate away at her lungs. He tried pulling away the molten rubber as it ate away at her skin. Twenty minutes it took. And her screams. . . . Such memories were unforgettable, but today Becker was grateful; today they served their purpose.

He cleared his eyes, a mingling of his own sweat with the rain, and trained high-powered binoculars on the East Fields facility four kilometers away.

The first hint of activity was an added glow within the hull of Central Access. Suddenly, plumes of diesel smoke billowed from the building's exhaust portals. A huge wall opened across its face. Four flatcars emerged from the building along tracks laid atop the ridge of a huge ore dump. Upon the backs of each car were identical long-range rocket launchers. Artillery teams assembled around each weapon.

Becker's chest tightened. Prayers raced through his brain as he thought about the thousands of unaware people working merrily away in the mines upon which those guns were now aimed.

Adjacent to Central Access, at the face of a huge warehouse, three panel doors opened. Shafts of light preceded a convoy of flatbed trucks and two columns of soldiers. Methodically, the trucks formed a circle in a vacant shipping yard, and the soldiers broke into well-coordinated teams. Sheets of dark canvas, draped over the trucks like dustcloths covering antique furniture, fell away revealing anti-aircraft guns, portable rocket launchers, and a host of long-range mortars. Squad after squad of foot soldiers followed the trucks out of the warehouse, each dispersing in orderly fashion toward the perimeter of the East Fields property.

Mansell followed the steep gradient into Pilgrim's Rest past the timber mill and the fishery. Cottonwoods formed a tall hedge along the Blyde River. On his left, beneath abandoned mines, ore tailings cascaded down the mountainsides like frozen waterfalls.

Along the main street of town, gas lamps sprayed sidewalks and street corners with soft yellow light. Vacancy signs flashed conspicuous invitations in front of motels and inns, and most of the cafés and shops had Closed for the Season signs hanging in their windows. Mansell found an all-night café called The Impala in the heart of town. He went inside. A pretty black girl attended an empty counter. Two men, hunters by their orange caps and mackintosh coats, hunched over steaks and eggs in the corner beneath the mounted head of the reddish antelope that had lent its name to the diner.

"Good evening," Mansell said, using Afrikaans now instead of English. He took a barstool. "Black coffee, please, and some much needed advice, if you would."

"Where's the best hunting, right?"

"No, no," he answered, laughing. "I'm staying with a friend for a while. His place is on Cottonwood Road, and for the life of me, I can't find it."

Dark eyes studied him. "Kinda late to be looking."

"Car trouble." Mansell slid two rand notes under the saucer. "Know where it is?"

"Go north of town, maybe a half kilometer. On the left you'll see the Grandfather Tree. All by itself. You can't miss it. It's a huge cottonwood. Some folks say it's five hundred years old. You can't miss it."

The Grandfather Tree stood sentinel-like, gnarled and foreboding beneath a waning moon, at the junction of a narrow macadam road. Opposite the tree were three mailboxes. Two were freshly painted, names and addresses. Upon the third, stenciled in black paint, was the number 203, but no name. Mansell turned left. He doused the car's lights.

Plowed fields and farmhouses flanked the road for a half kilometer on either side. Beyond the fields were thick forests of spruce and pine. In time, the trees left of the road gave way to an enclosed estate. The grounds were terraced and landscaped, eventually abutting a wide ark in the Blyde River. A stone wall, three meters high, separated the estate from the road. Chain link fencing separated it from the forest.

Mansell parked the car well off the road among the spruce on the right. He slid quietly out. Using the forest for cover, he walked parallel to the road for a hundred meters, studying the wall. Coils of barbed wire perched along the top for the entire length. The wall itself was unbroken except for tall iron gates at the entrance. These were four meters high and neatly enclosed by a stone arch. Gas-burning torches lit the entrance from iron sconces. Beyond the gates was a circular watchtower. A dim bulb lit the interior, but there were no guards.

A narrow drive led away from the gates in a straight line to an old country house. Spotlights illuminated an aristocratic portico with white columns, a peaked roof, and french doors. Lights burned from a first-floor window and from a garden patio off the south side of the house.

The solitude was disquieting, unnerving. The wind stirred, hissing between the branches. A night hunter crept through the woods behind him. Overburdened storm clouds anointed the forest with a cool drizzle. Mansell turned his collar up. He craved a cigarette, but instead, found a sheltered vantage point among the trees and waited.

Dressed in a silk smoking jacket and cradling a snifter of K.W.V. brandy, Minister of Justice Cecil Leistner paced in front of a roaring fire. The library represented one of but four rooms made livable by a harried caretaker over the weekend. The minister's abrupt decision to visit the summer retreat had been met with consternation. The staff had already been dismissed for the season. The caretaker and his wife had been preparing for a vacation in East London.

Still, dust covers had been removed, the four rooms aired, and the cupboards hastily stocked. The other twenty rooms, with the minister's approval, remained closed.

Further, Leistner had insisted the caretaker's vacation plans not be altered. He was alone in the house except for Jeremy, his butler from Pretoria, who was asleep in the caretaker's cottage, and the two guards and their dogs. He felt naked. Leistner was a believer in the old adage about security in numbers. And without people, he thought to himself now, power meant nothing.

He stoked the fire. He added pine chips and another log. He sought out the humidor, stored, as it had been for years, above the liquor cabinet nestled among book-filled shelves. Was it possible Charles might have remembered?

The minister cracked the lid to the humidor and beamed. It was chock-full of Te-Amos, pungent and suitably moist. He drew out one. He was snipping the end off when a soft tapping came from the outside door.

Leistner started, nearly dropping the cigar. Then he cursed himself, remembering the guards were due to check in. He crossed the floor, released the dead bolt, and opened the door.

"Good God. You!" he blurted out. "How can . . . Why are you here?"

Leistner backed away. Jan Koster crossed the threshold, saying, "I should have called first. Forgive me."

"Something's happened." Brandy sent waves of heat and a struggling element of calm throughout Leistner's system.

"Yes, something's happened. The plan has been unearthed. Becker."

"Becker? That's impossible."

Koster shrugged. "One plan fails, another succeeds."

Retreating further, the minister said, "How did you know I was here? I never—"

"I made a point of knowing everything there was to know about you, Minister. I had to. All except that insane plan of yours to kill Ian Elgin. That I almost missed."

"You . . . ? You knew about—?"

"Yes. Very theatrical." Koster tapped the tip of his wet umbrella on the terra-cotta tiled floor. He moved liquidly, smiling. "Very theatrical. But then, theatrics is one of your weaknesses, isn't it?"

"That's impossible. I—"

"You've forgotten Ian's letter, then. Destroyed, I imagine. Oh, but you couldn't know. I have a copy. You see, your press secretary—"

"Neff?"

"Yes. A drug addict can be a dangerous ally, Minister." Koster took a tiny reel of tape from his pants pocket and held it up. "We've talked, Oliver and I. More than once. Oliver would do anything to guard his secrets. You told him far too much, Minister. And what he knew, I knew. Steiner, the poison, the mock strangulation. Oliver was eager to vindicate himself. True, there were missing pieces. The time. The place. The bloody reason."

"Elgin was a liability. He knew too much for his own good."

"Translated, he was making threats. That was foolish."

Bleak revelation spread across Cecil Leistner's face. "Then it was you. You killed Fredrik Steiner."

"Of course not," Koster replied. "Well, I did provide the gun. That's true. But then it wasn't too difficult to convince your very own Captain Terreblanche that Steiner had become a problem. I merely suggested that unless the captain did something to prevent Steiner from leaving the country, I would be forced to reveal *his* darkest secret. The boy he was keeping in Uitenhage? The native? That is how you manipulated the poor captain from the very beginning, isn't it?"

"My God." Leistner consumed the better part of his brandy. The forgotten cigar rested upon the mantel. Koster circled the loveseat, fingering a volume of Tolkien's *Fellowship of the Ring*. He placed an elbow on the mantel. He jabbed the umbrella at a loose ember, facing Leistner now within an arm's length.

"I believe we understand each other at last," he said. He tossed the reel of tape into the fire.

Leistner sucked air into his lungs. He thrust his chin forward, quickly taking in the room. When his eyes settled momentarily upon the fire irons resting next to the hearthstone, he recognized the opportunity and realized it might be his last. He glanced quickly away, saying, "Oh, the clarity of the situation becomes readily apparent. Yes."

"Good. You see, that's very important to me. A last door closing. The final note to an ill-begotten symphony."

"Ill-begotten you may call it, but I would be leery about announcing its finale." Leistner moved a step closer to the fireplace, calculating. He needed time. "In your jubilation you've evidently forgotten the explosives. In the access shafts beneath the mines?"

"On the contrary. But I never had any intention of sacrificing sixteen thousand good men, Minister, much less several million rand worth of mining facilities. That was your idea, not mine."

"No matter. It's still not over." Leistner inched backward. "Moscow has been well aware of your . . . conflicting interests. Your actions have been monitored with far more enthusiasm than even you could have thought possible. Did you think—?"

"The poker will do you no good, Minister," Koster said, peering down at the fire irons. A swift kick sent the poker, tongs, and shovel sprawling across the floor. Smiling, he raised the umbrella. He touched the edge of the mantel, indicating the forgotten Te-Amo. "Please. I distracted you. Feel free. A good smoke does wonders for the nerves."

The minister glanced at the cigar. He didn't move. Jan Koster drew the umbrella slowly away, but then, with a practiced riposte, thrust the tip against Leistner's neck. The umbrella recoiled like a rifle, silently. A single drop of blood surfaced. Leistner's hand grasped the side of his neck. Horror washed his face.

"The pellet dissolves immediately," Koster announced. "But you know that. A taste of your own medicine."

Leistner tried in vain to protest. The muscles in his neck constricted. Brandy spilled across the hearth. Drops sizzled as they struck hot coals. The snifter tumbled from paralyzed fingers, shattering. The minister lunged toward his assailant, gasping for air as his respiratory system failed, but Koster sidestepped him. Leistner crumbled to the floor.

Koster set the umbrella inside the fireplace. He walked swiftly out the door to the patio. He circled the house and found the fuel storage tank behind the guest house.

After ten minutes of inactivity, Nigel Mansell scrambled to his feet. He retraced his steps back through the forest to a point opposite the south end of the stone wall. He crossed the road.

Here, a perpendicular chain link fence began, running east away from the road. The fence, like the wall, was three meters high, with a similar coil of barbed wire along the top.

Mansell moved along on a soft cushion of pine needles. Ancient spruce again provided cover forward and aft. Across the fence, the grounds were bathed in a soft light. From here, the house stood behind a row of cherry trees and a low hedge of holly berry. The stillness was near-hypnotic; the wind was cold right through to the bone.

And then, forty meters from the road, Mansell caught sight of the body lying inside the fence. He drew the Browning from its harness. He approached the fence in a low crouch, stealing from tree to tree. At the base of the fence lay a pair of heavy bolt cutters. A narrow opening had been ripped vertically in the chain link mesh.

Scanning the open ground leading to the hedge and then to the house, Mansell inched through the gap. The man lay curled in a ball, bound and gagged. Mansell rolled him onto his back. A thick bruise swelled about the temple and ear, but he was still breathing, the shallow breathing of unconsciousness. Beneath him lay a MAC-10 semi-automatic pistol. Next to him, sprawled in a pool of blood, was a huge doberman. A bloodied knife protruded from a gaping wound in the dog's neck.

Jan Koster reentered the house carrying two twenty-liter buckets filled with petrol. Without haste, he soaked the library in gasoline. He took the second can into a family room shrouded in dust covers. Starting in the hallway, he poured gas across the floor, over furniture and drapes, and left a trail leading to a conservatory near the river. He set a lighted match to the trail. Flames galloped through the house to the family room and, in one giant leap, to the library.

Mansell was standing over the second guard, his hand on the man's faint pulse, when he saw flames licking at the windows. Glass shattered. Flames climbed an outside trestle to the second story. He heard an explosion. The roof ignited. Off to his right, he saw a figure scurrying across the yard toward the river. Mansell hesitated. Finally, he raced toward the room off the patio. Flames consumed it. He yanked at the door handle, but fire drove him back. Still, through the open door, he could see an unidentifiable corpse being eaten by fire.

Mansell backed away. Turning, he ran across the yard to the front of the house. Over the conflagratory howl of the blaze, he heard a different sound. The roar of an engine. Briefly, he caught sight of a motorcycle speeding back toward the main road. Mansell glanced back at the uncontrollable fire, and then, deciding, raced back to the opening in the fence.

The fever of waiting and the heat of the tunnel sent waves of delirium through the boy's head. He sucked air into his nostrils and heard the heavy breath of anticipation spreading through the ranks of his comrades down the length of the stone passage. The cool-air generators were no match for the mass of humanity. Comfort lay only in the ticking of the clock inside his head. . . . And then he heard the rumble of the engine overhead. The elevator cables went taut.

He was only nineteen, but Patrick Myeza had considered himself a soldier since the day his mama died of pneumonia two years ago in KwaNdebele. His father spent seven and a half hours on a bus every day traveling between their mud hovel and a factory job in Pretoria that paid R2.35 an hour. Eight kids were too many. The day after his mama died, Patrick crossed the border into Botswana and the jungle training camp that had been his home ever since.

The squeal of the transport elevator as it descended from the Homestake Mining storage shed forty meters above signaled the first joyous moment Patrick could remember since that day.

The elevator stopped with a heavy thud, and the metal screens were swept aside by a man in a light green jumpsuit with a gold Homestake insignia on his miner's hat.

"Move your asses, boys," he shouted. "Move it, move it."

The fever broke. Patrick hoisted the crate of 130-millimeter shells with which he was charged and stepped to the back of the elevator. Bodies and crates pressed in around him. The screens clanged shut. The elevator churned upward. Patrick's beating heart stretched the walls of his chest, and at the moment he felt it would surely burst, the elevator stopped. The cool air of the empty shed touched Patrick's skin, and he knew that Homestake Mining was theirs.

Outside on his hillside pedestal, General Becker watched the second hand on his watch tick past the hour of midnight. He took up his binoculars and stared down at the East Fields compound. He could see the passing minutes working on the once stationary soldiers. In the distance, the Homestake and Highland Vaal plants seemed immune, indifferent. Slip trails of white light illuminated the facilities like patches of day. Blue flames and smoke whipped at the sky. Becker heard the screech of a train whistle.

He brought the binoculars back toward East Fields. It was then he saw the slight figure of a man climbing onto the back of one of the flatcars. He discerned the outline of the man's brown suit, the glint of thick eyeglasses, and knew at once he was looking at Christopher Zuma.

At that moment, Becker felt something that was surely more than relief coursing through his veins. Maybe this time around, he thought, ignoring the harbinger wouldn't be so easy. At last he relinquished the binoculars, satisfied. He turned slowly aside then and slipped back down the mountain to his waiting car.

Nigel Mansell used the military radio in his car to alert the Pilgrim's Rest police constabulary of the fire on Cottonwood Road. He didn't mention the motorcycle. As he sped through town, he could just make out the volunteer fire department's siren.

Mansell judged the distance between himself and the motorcycle to be a full kilometer, maybe two. It was ten kilometers to Sabie, the next town with SAP support. From that juncture, there were four options. East into Kruger National Park—an unlikely choice, Mansell thought. West to Lydenburg and the plains of the highveld; a car might have a chance on the open highway, he realized, and the cycle would be an easy target for roadblocks. That left the two southern routes back to N4; both wound through the mountains, where a motorcycle's maneuverability would be a sizable advantage.

Utilizing the radio again, Mansell contacted the police station in Sabie. It took thirty seconds to arouse a duty officer named Mouton. By the sound of the policeman's voice, he'd been asleep. Brusquely, Mansell explained the situation. "A Security Branch matter," he snapped. He told Mouton to monitor the junctions outside town and to report the motorcycle's direction. "Do nothing else," Mansell ordered. "Do not attempt to pursue."

Suddenly alert, the excited policeman bounded for the door. Three minutes later, he reported back. "He took the second artery toward N4, Inspector. He was nice and legal going through town, but the second he hit R539, he was flying."

R539 via R37, Mansell thought, the route he'd used heading for Pilgrim's Rest. That left two options: the freeway west to Pretoria, and back to Nelspruit. Or a hundred turnoffs in between, he reminded himself. Still, the rider wasn't yet aware that he was being pursued, and that was Mansell's one advantage.

"Is there a faster route back to Nelspruit than the R37 exchange, Sergeant?" he asked.

"If he takes R37, he'll lose three or four minutes," Mouton replied quickly. "The map's deceiving, sir. The quickest route is R539 straight down to the N4 freeway. Nelspruit is twenty-six kilometers due east from there."

Mansell negotiated the turn onto R539 with both hands. The car shuddered, tires protesting. He punched the accelerator and gave Mouton a final instruction. "Contact the nearest district office, Sergeant. Have them spread the word. Roadblock N4 in both directions. Any other artery as well."

"Will do, Inspector. Good luck to you, sir."

The two-lane road wound interminably through hairpin turns and steep grades, gradually releasing the pursuer from the grasp of the mountains. The N4 freeway, by comparison, was wide and straight, and Mansell covered the twenty-six kilometers to Nelspruit in half as many minutes. He saw no evidence of the Highway Police, but, this being the eastern Transvaal, hadn't really expected it.

Nelspruit lay at the base of the Drakensberg foothills, and thus Mansell approached the city from the top of a sweeping gradient. From the peak of this last hill, he could see acres of orange groves and solitary farmhouses that ended abruptly with the dim glow of truck stops and motels at the city limits. The R37 truck route bisected these groves and eventually merged with the freeway a half kilometer outside of town beneath a halo of yellow highway lamps.

Mansell sighted the motorcycle as it shot down the on-ramp onto the highway, pressing but not out of control. Between the military sedan and the cycle were two semis, a pickup truck, and less than a kilometer. Mansell depressed the accelerator. He passed the pickup and then the first semi, a moving van. He fell in behind the other semi as they approached the outskirts of Nelspruit.

At the edge of town, the truck pulled off at the required weigh-in station. Two hundred meters further on, much to Mansell's surprise, the motorcycle slowed down as well. He saw brake lights. The rider steered the cycle onto a frontage road called Airport Drive. He cruised past the Air Africa maintenance center, the Transport Service building, the rent-a-car lot, and the close-in parking garage. He drew up in front of the main terminal. He parked the cycle in a no-parking section in front of South African Airways and dismounted.

He ran inside the terminal shedding a riding jacket and helmet. Mansell parked at the curb behind the motorcycle and set out in pursuit.

At the west end of the terminal he saw the rider jog through an unattended gate marked PRIVATE CARRIERS ONLY. Mansell hurdled the silver turnstile, pushed aside a glass door, and raced down a long staircase to the airfield.

The rider stopped next to a single-winged Cessna. He reached up for the door, opened it, and a narrow ramp dropped down from the side of the plane to the tarmac. He started up the ramp.

Mansell raised his gun. "Police. That's as far as you go," he shouted, gasping for breath. The rider froze. His shoulders sagged. "Let's see your hands. Turn. Slow. Very slow."

Deflated, the rider faced him. Mansell's eyes narrowed; the slender face, the sad eyes, the sandy complexion.

"It's not that I underestimated you, Inspector Mansell," he said.

And the voice, Mansell thought. My God. He heard the voice ringing in his ears. He touched the cassette in his coat pocket. The gun wavered unsteadily.

"Koster," he uttered. "Jan Koster. You."

"Yes," Koster answered. "The end of a race. Someone tires, someone inches ahead. I congratulate you."

"Even a blind donkey can follow the carrots if they're dangled close enough to his nose," answered Mansell coarsely.

"To argue that would be useless," replied Koster.

"Tell that to Merry Gosani. Tell it to Ian Elgin and Anthony Mabasu and Sylvia Mabasu."

"Ian's fate was not a plan of my devising, Inspector. It was a plan which I could not forestall, only use."

Mansell tipped his head forward. Their eyes dueled. "Then it was Leistner? And Terreblanche was his? . . ."

Koster nodded. "Yes. Leistner's plan." He broke away, sighing. "The implant scar, Inspector. The scar on Leistner's right cheek. The screw implant which I imagine must have so perplexed the good dentist in Pampoenpoort?"

"You imagine correctly. He'd never done a screw implant."

"Of course not. It was a European technique," Koster said. "I noticed the implant scar during my first meeting with Leistner, seven years ago in Pretoria. His fatal flaw. The forged dental record seemed a good way to get your attention, Inspector. You see, my brother, my real brother, had been the recipient of a screw implant in the late 1940s, too."

"In the late forties? In Europe? In Russia?"

"Your instincts serve you well, Inspector, though where is not important. However, I think we understand each other," Koster replied. He leaned heavily on the guardrail.

"But you were part of the East Fields scheme from the beginning."

"Yes. No. The plan itself was an unlikely scenario laid in my lap by some fool in Moscow. But I wrote the script. I chose the ending."

"Why?" demanded Mansell. "Why this whole . . . bloody thing?"

Koster shrugged. Then he set his shoulders straight.

"Survival, Inspector. History. Change. A dose of revenge, perhaps, against the madmen who sent me here twenty-three years ago. I was their creation. But their creation went astray." He shrugged again. "Had I tried to abort the situation before it was completed, I would have accomplished nothing. Who would have believed me?"

"Why in the hell didn't you just walk into the prime minister's office and spill the whole bloody mess?"

Koster shook his head. "The prime minister? His addiction to power and his fear of losing it are as warped as Cecil Leistner's were. No, I would have been hunted down and killed, and a new plan would have evolved. No one would have gained, and the losers would still be the losers. Now there are lessons to be learned. History that cannot be ignored. Leistner could never have seen it that way. And his way . . . Well."

It struck Mansell then that Koster knew exactly what was happening at East Fields this very minute. He knew. Had he planned it that way from the beginning?

Koster must have seen the question on his face, and he added, "Zuma and Becker were the essential links, Inspector. Becker being a well-considered gamble. Time and history will be my judge, I suppose."

"Time has a way of spitting out its useless footnotes, Koster, and the deaths of four people will be conveniently tossed into the scrap bucket once someone gets around to writing down this little bit of history."

"A heavy price to pay, I admit." Koster stepped to the end of the ramp, but Mansell didn't have the strength to lift his gun. "Ian Elgin was a fool to think he could manipulate the minister of justice, but it wasn't worth his life. Yet, as I said, I couldn't prevent it, Inspector, so I used it.

"I must admit," Koster added, "that after several trips to Pietermaritzburg, East London, and Port Elizabeth, I grew to know you quite well, Inspector Nigel Mansell. As you can well imagine, that summer you spent exploring caves in Royal Natal stood out in my mind."

A light flickered in Mansell's eyes. His lungs filled with the cool night air and he took a step forward. "A man in a three-piece suit enters a sporting goods store in Port Elizabeth and buys a length of nylon-rayon rope. He makes a point of telling the clerk he intends exploring caves in an area where no such caves exist. You. It was you. A week before Elgin was murdered."

"You'll find the rope in my garage, at the house in Cape Town," Koster answered. "I believe you'll find it still in its original wrap, more than likely in the very bag the sales clerk first put it in. And the typewriter? The antique portable with the mis-set "e," high left? Surely your forensic chief mentioned it?"

"The business card we found on Fredrik Steiner's body," Mansell replied. "The Caves of the Womb."

"Yes, the caves. My personal signature, you might say. I couldn't resist. And it did seem to catch your attention." The memory fixed itself momentarily upon Koster's tired face. "As for the typewriter. It also is in the garage in Cape Town."

A moment of silence was broken when a jetliner with a flying springbok painted on its fin swept into the air behind them, and Koster watched it disappear behind a wall of black clouds.

He glanced back at Mansell, hesitated, and then said, "I tried to save your friend, the detective. I was too late. I'm sorry for that, more so than anything, perhaps. He was a courageous . . ."

There was a shuffling sound at the door of the Cessna. Mansell jerked the Browning up. He spread his feet. A little girl appeared at the landing. Blond, petite, rubbing sleep from her eyes.

"Daddy," she called out. "Can we go yet?"

The gun dropped to Mansell's side.

"This is Hannah. My youngest."

"I'm nine," Hannah announced.

Mansell gazed up at her. Her round face stretched into a wide yawn. A woman appeared at the door next to her, hurriedly drawing the child into her arms. Another girl peeked out from behind the mother, surely Hannah's sister. Mansell slipped the gun back into the shoulder harness beneath his jacket. From the breast pocket he drew out the cassette tape he'd taken from the Clavers' telephone machine—the recording of Merry's death, Koster's own warning.

He tossed the tape to Koster. "The first time you find yourself going to sleep without a few agonizing memories," said the chief inspector, "listen to the first part of that tape."

Then he glanced back at Hannah. He said, "Maybe she'll go back to sleep once you're in the air."

Mansell turned away. From a window inside the terminal, he watched the tiny plane lift off.

By four A.M. the morning of the twenty-third, he was aboard a much larger plane headed south for Port Elizabeth.

At 7:25, Mansell climbed the steps to the Hall of Justice on Chapel Street.

Inside, he flashed his I.D. at the main desk and passed through the metal detector. He felt comfortably buoyant now without the shoulder harness and the gun. He rode the elevator to Security Branch headquarters on the eighth floor. He pushed past the sergeant at arms, tossed his shield on the reception desk, and asked to see Lieutenant Colonel Richard Jones, the head of Security in the Thirty-second District.

When Jones emerged from his office, Mansell presented him with the executive order clearing himself and Delaney of all federal charges.

"Very good," Jones said, taking the order. He raised an eyebrow at the officer behind the desk. "Sergeant?"

"I passed a copy of the order on to Major Wolffe last night, sir, but—"

"That's fine. And?"

"Well, sir. . . ."

"Where is she?" Mansell demanded.

The desk sergeant exchanged a distressed look with the lieutenant colonel, and Mansell had his answer.

He swept aside the swinging gates. He raced past the counter into an open office area cluttered with desks, typewriters, and bent heads. A sign pasted across a metal door at the back of the room read, AUTHORIZED PERSONNEL ONLY. Mansell pushed past the door to the stairwell. He took the steps two at a time to the tenth floor.

The interrogation rooms were located in the north wing. Rushing down the narrow, sterile corridor, Mansell threw open every door. Finally, he heard a low groan coming from the end of the corridor. The official notice on the door read, SECTOR #6. KEEP OUT.

Mansell burst through the door. He saw the hulking torso of Major Hymie Wolffe, a sleeveless T-shirt yellow with sweat, the back of his neck fever-red with exertion, a bamboo stave raised over his head. Delaney was slumped before him. Her arms were extended above her head, lashed with rope hung from the ceiling. Her hair was tangled and matted, her blouse torn. Blood oozed from her nose.

"Wolffe!" The word escaped Mansell's mouth like the cry of a wild animal. He charged forward, grabbing Wolffe by the back of his shirt, propelling him face-first into the concrete wall. He drove his fist into Wolffe's kidney. A second and third blow drove the Security officer to the floor.

"No, Nigel, don't." The words came to him as an echo cutting through a thick fog. Delaney's voice. "Please don't."

Mansell pulled himself away, panting. He grabbed Wolffe by his shirt straps and hoisted him to his feet.

"I should kill you right now, Wolffe."

"Not you, Mansell," Wolffe hissed. His breathing was labored, his eyes touched with pain and hysteria. "You're too civilized."

Mansell saw the bamboo stave lying on the cell floor at Wolffe's feet, and he swept it up. He held the slender stick at eye level, rolling it between his thumb and forefinger.

"Civilized, you say." His voice was hardly more than a whisper. "No, Major, a civilized man would shoot you right where you stand, the demented animal that you are."

The stave went suddenly still in his hand. He moved it slowly toward Wolffe's face, drawing the tip within an inch of his eye. Wolffe pressed himself against the cell wall. A sheen of sweat washed over his chalky skin.

"No, Major. I'm going to take your toys away from you," Mansell said. "I'm going to see to it that you never hold a bamboo stave in your hand again. You ignored an executive order of the prime minister, Wolffe. Are you aware of the penalty for that offense?"

"That order was a lie, Mansell." Wolffe's voice was shrill and broken. "It was a lie."

Mansell's pale eyes hardened. The room was, all at once, very still. Only the sound of Delaney's breathing disturbed it. Mansell pressed the stave closer still. The bamboo touched Wolffe's fluttering eyelid, and he gasped. A moment later, the stave dropped from Mansell's hand. He released his grip from Wolffe's shirt straps, pushing him away. Wolffe slid down the face of the wall to the floor, covering his eyes as Mansell hurried across the cell to Delaney.

"It's over now," he whispered. He freed her hands, dabbed blood from her face, and wrapped his jacket around her shoulders. "It's over now, I promise. Let's go home."

At last, Mansell lifted her into his arms. He kicked open the interrogation-room door. He carried her down the corridor to the stairs. On the eighth floor, they pushed through a line of stunned Security policemen.

They stepped into the elevator, but as the doors were closing around them, Mansell remembered his chief inspector's shield lying on the reception desk. He punched the hold button instinctively. The doors parted. The wallet was there, open on the counter. The gold shield stared back at him. He couldn't leave it, there was no question of that, and yet he hesitated, felt the sudden weariness of the past twenty-four hours wrapping its arms around him.

It would have been easy to blame the encounter with Wolffe, but there was more to it than fatigue and indecision. Mansell knew that the media had already picked up on the successful takeover of the mines. The car radio had given a verbatim account of demands released earlier this morning by Christopher Zuma. Glaring headlines in this morning's *Bulletin* had confirmed the walkout of nearly a million miners nationwide. A sympathy strike by dockers, stevedores, and railroad workers had, according to the page-one account, brought the country to a virtual standstill. Rumor had it that the prime minister would respond to the crisis on national television sometime this afternoon. Yet it wasn't over. Despite his promise to Delaney, it wasn't over. He wondered now if it would ever be.

He heard the sound of shuffling feet, hushed conversation. He saw the others, the Security policemen, their attention turning to the badge. And then, at the very moment when the urge to walk away was at its strongest, he felt Delaney's hand on his face. Their eyes met for a moment. Her face was bruised a ghastly shade of purple, but there was a calmness in her eyes, a warmth to her touch. Why? he wanted to ask her. But he had given up asking her foolish questions. What he saw in her eyes, and what he felt in her touch, was something far more permanent. He stepped out of the elevator then and snatched the wallet from the counter.

When they were outside on the walk, Mansell stopped again. He glanced overhead to the tenth floor. A new pane of glass had replaced the broken one. Bars covered every window now. He looked back at the sidewalk. The concrete below the window had taken on a dull, grayish hue. In the distance, Mansell heard the carillon of bells chiming in the Campanile. To the west, the promise of rain filled the sky.